come back dead

A Scott Elliott Mystery

TERENCE FAHERTY

SIMON & SCHUSTER

SIMON & SCHUSTER
Rockefeller Center
1230 Avenue of the Americas
New York, NY 10020

This book is a work of fiction. Names, characters, places, and incidents
either are products of the author's imagination or are used fictitiously.
Any resemblance to actual events or locales or persons,
living or dead, is entirely coincidental.

SIMON & SCHUSTER and colophon are registered
trademarks of Simon & Schuster Inc.

Designed by Leslie Phillips

Manufactured in the United States of America

1   3   5   7   9   10   8   6   4   2

Library of Congress Cataloging-in-Publication Data
Faherty, Terence.
Come back dead : a Scott Elliott mystery / Terence Faherty.
p.   cm.
I. Title.
PS3556.A342C66   1997
813'.54—dc21   96-36873
                              CIP

ISBN 0-684-83084-1

For Dr. and Mrs. Norman T. Gates

come back dead

chapter

1

A CON WAS in progress. A young man was trying to convince a young woman that he needed dancing lessons. I knew he didn't. Anyone would have known, except this particular teacher. She didn't exactly trust him, but it wasn't over his dancing ability. She figured he was on the make.

She probably figured that often and with good reason. She had the body of a dancer, but not the bony, ethereal kind. A dancer who had grown up on a farm in Kansas was more like it. A dancer who didn't miss meals. And she had big luminous eyes—not innocent, but kind—and lips that had been painted by an artist, maybe the one who specialized in dew drops for Walt Disney. Her hair had been referred to as red, but it looked like a brassy blond, a not entirely unstudied blond. But the hair didn't contradict the impression made by the knowing eyes and the figure, the impression that the woman was as down-to-earth as the guy who delivers your mail.

The young man was another matter entirely. He seemed less substantial than the spiral of smoke rising from my cigarette. Part of the problem was his outfit: morning attire complete with cutaway coat and striped trousers. The feet he was describing as left and left were in shoes that glowed like Dorothy's ruby slippers, their shine protected by spats. But the problem was more than clothes, more even than the fine, slicked-down hair whose high, short part said "toupee" in a refined voice. The guy just wasn't plausible. His ears were too big and his chin and nose too pointy. These elfin features were matched by his thin frame. Though she was no truck driver, the woman he was trying to seduce could have blown him away without drawing a deep breath.

I ground out my cigarette and lit another while I watched the con man's first attempt at dancing. His extreme clumsiness should have tipped her off, but she was too busy protecting her feet to think about it. He ended up sitting on the floor, something you seldom see outside of a roller rink. While still seated, he did something even more unusual. He began to sing.

Now his very implausibility worked for him. It seemed perfectly natural for this wraith in vest and wing collar—seated on the floor, no less—to be singing. Or blowing bubbles out his ears, for that matter. His voice was as thin as the rest of him, reedy in the highest register, but pleasant. Her voice—there was no reason for her not to sing if he was going to—was also light and a touch nasal, but like everything about her except her hair color, it was also believable, a voice you might hear around any parlor piano in America.

After some more playacting on his part, they began to dance in earnest. The con man was transformed, seemingly by the touch of her hand. In the space of a few bars of music, he became graceful, sure. And the confident grace was the missing piece that pulled all his unlikely parts together. He suddenly seemed more real than the studio in which they danced, as real as she was. Or had been. Because she was also transformed, her movements so light and effortless now that the girl-next-door quality fell away like a carnival mask.

Suddenly they were partners in a new con, the illusion that two total strangers could work together like Horowitz's hands, each reading the other's mind, anticipating every novel move. They tapped out a routine that was both complicated and inevitable, the only possible way any two people would dance to this particular music. They carried the con off by making each practiced step seem as natural and spontaneous as the bouncing of her hair.

The studio's centerpiece was a dance floor surrounded by a low railing. At first this railing contained their dancing, though gravity itself barely seemed up to the job. The pair bounced so high with each effortless step that my calves ached in sympathy. But then the railing's inadequacy was revealed. He hoisted her over it and followed, and then did it again just to show how easy it was. At the end of the dance, the pair leapt the railing together, landing with no more force than you'd feel stepping off a curb. They disappeared arm in arm through swinging doors, the transformed man looking back over his shoulder to smile at me lightheartedly.

The whole number had lightened my heart, but the feeling didn't last. After a brief pause, the pair's place in my view was taken by another smiling man, a stout man with wavy hair and a moustache that was barely visible above his fat lips. Behind him was a shiny new automobile fronted by a hand-painted sign that read LOW, LOW PRICES. Before the man could tell me just how low, the picture collapsed into a single bright point of light that lingered in the center of the tube like the last star of a gray morning.

I didn't notice how long the star lingered. My attention was drawn to the woman who had switched off the television set. Ella stood facing me with her hand on the knob. She was wearing a silk nightgown with a lacy bodice. It was similar to the number Rita Hayworth had worn in her famous wartime pinup. Ella could have given Miss Hayworth a run for her money if it hadn't been for a single, prominent imperfection. Her body was in the Hayworth class, but its proportions looked even more dramatic because she was slightly shorter than the actress. In most parts of the country, Ella's hair would have been brown, but here in sunny Southern California, it had just enough golden highlights to pass for blond. Neither her thin lips nor her pale blue eyes were currently set off with makeup, but the eyes at least didn't miss it. They were striking against her tanned face. Her imperfection was nestled between and below those striking eyes: a nose that had once been broken and had ever afterward pointed slightly to her left.

That nose was now pointed at me, and she sighted down it. "Can you do without Fred and Ginger's company for a while, Scotty?"

"In a pinch," I said.

She crossed to the ottoman in front of my chair and sat down, keeping her bare shoulders self-consciously square. "The kids are asleep," she said.

"I hope so," I said, "with you dressed like that."

"Glad you noticed." Ella then did some noticing of her own. She took the burning cigarette from my hand. "I thought you were cutting down."

"You know how we detectives are between cases. It was these or cocaine."

She smiled at one or the other of my little jokes. For me, the funnier one was the idea that I was a detective. I was actually the employee of a security company that ran errands for the Hollywood studios. There had been moments, though.

"I thought you had a new assignment," Ella said. "Didn't you say Paddy had called?"

"Starts tomorrow. I was doing a little research when you came in." I nodded toward the darkened television.

"Uh-huh," Ella said. She thought I did way too much of that kind of research already. She called it living in the past. "Was your subject Astaire or Rogers?"

"RKO."

The initials stood for Radio Keith Orpheum, reflecting the movie studio's complicated parentage: a marriage between a then-new medium, radio, represented by the Radio Corporation of America, and a dying art form, vaudeville. The Keith Orpheum circuit had been the biggest chain of vaudeville theaters in the country, once upon a time. Neither parent had controlled RKO for very long, but the initials had stuck, as had the studio's trademark, a giant radio tower on a slowly turning globe.

Now, in 1955, RKO itself was all but gone. Ella decided I needed to be reminded of that. "There is no such studio," she said. "Not really. If someone's hiring you to find out who killed it, I can give you a clue. His initials are HH."

They belonged to Howard Hughes, RKO's last owner during its days as a going concern. He'd run the studio as his private hobby shop and dating service, making fewer and fewer films each year, and those films increasingly bizarre. When he'd finally sold out, there'd been little left except for some choice real estate and a library of amazing movies like the one I'd just been watching, *Swing Time*, directed by George Stevens in 1936.

Ella reached up, unnecessarily, to smooth her hair. "Did Paddy say what it was about?"

"Not Paddy. You know his style. He'll only tell me what I need to know."

"Just after you need to know it," Ella added, proving that she did in fact know my boss.

To fill Paddy's deliberate void, I'd tuned in *Swing Time* when I'd seen it listed. My motive had really been research, despite Ella's suspicion that I'd been wallowing in nostalgia for the prewar days when I'd been an actor myself. To be specific, I'd been doing background research. Any of RKO's classics would have suited my purpose: *Bringing Up Baby, Stage Door, Top Hat, First Citizen, Gunga Din. King Kong,* even. It was my theory that each studio had its own style, a style that reflected a unique mind-set. Warners, for example, had a brash, East Coast take on the world, the urban immigrant's odd combination of cynicism and sentimentality. MGM had a more typically American outlook that said big was good and bigger was better. RKO's mind-set was modest in comparison. Deliberately modest. Watching Astaire and Rogers, I'd gotten a sense of it again, the idea that the really worthwhile things were simple and stylish and effortlessly competent.

If I'd been the kind of detective who snaps his fingers when he sees a sign for liver pills and announces that the murderer is the local butcher, the kind who makes connections, I could have regained my sense of RKO by gazing at my wife of seven years. Ella was stylish, as the nightgown she was almost wearing attested. And she was competent, a mother of two who had made the transition from studio publicist to freelance screenwriter under her maiden name, Ella Englehart. She wasn't simple, the third item in RKO's formula, but she liked to pretend that she was. She liked to pretend that our whole complicated life together was simple.

"Care to dance?" she asked, lightly stroking my knee. Her touch transformed me as thoroughly as Ginger Rogers had transformed Fred Astaire, but not in the same direction, not toward an almost spiritual gracefulness.

"Who's the code for?" I asked, taking her playful hand and pulling her onto my lap. "Dancing" was the euphemism for "sex" that we used in front of the children.

"I'm not speaking in code," Ella said. "I thought after watching your old pals dance you might prefer it to sex. They seemed to."

"They had the Hays office to worry about."

We kissed, and I thought of the first time we had. I felt our first kiss again, I mean.

"Too bad for them," Ella said.

chapter 2

THE NEXT MORNING I drove to RKO's main studio on Gower Street.
At least the stretch of Gower between the Columbia and Paramount
lots used to be RKO, as Ella would have reminded me if she'd been
along for the ride. It was now the corpse of the studio, laid out in
the California sun for the vultures' benefit. RKO's globe and radio
tower symbol, which was already a landmark when I'd rolled into
Hollywood from Indiana in the late thirties, still perched on the
northwest corner of the property, but the globe's plaster oceans
were overdue for a repainting. My guess was, they'd never get it.

Like many of the studios, RKO was a fortress built to keep out its
own fans, the perimeter of the lot being a series of windowless
buildings and blank, high walls. The fans could have captured the
fortress on this particular day if they hadn't all been home glued to
their television sets. No one challenged me at the gate when I
turned off Gower. Beyond it was a little postage-stamp lawn surrounded by offices, a town square done in miniature. Once, the
little plot of grass had been the best-kept lawn in town. Now it was

brown and dead and needed only a tumbleweed or two to pass for the set of a western.

The absence of foot traffic made it easy to spot my boss, Patrick J. Maguire, who was inspecting the administration building as though he, and not some midwestern rubber company, now owned it. Not that it was ever hard to spot Paddy. He was a big man, not unusually tall but broad, and he always dressed like a plumber who had just won the Irish sweepstakes. In deference to the July temperatures, Paddy's suit was pearl gray, the same color as his familiar homburg, but he'd jazzed things up with a tie whose red-and-white checks and breadth reminded me of a farmhouse tablecloth.

Paddy waved me into an empty parking space, using his cigar as a baton. The corona was still big enough for the job, being unlit. Before I switched off the engine, I pushed in the dashboard lighter. Paddy leaned in the passenger side window expectantly.

"Good man," he said. "Came out this morning without a match to my name." I noted that he had a rosebud pinned to his lapel, the flower looking as indifferent to the heat as the man himself. As the checks in his tie were red, the rose was naturally pink.

"I figured this spaceship of yours would have a lighter," Paddy said. "God knows it has everything except a sense of restraint. The Pope's Sunday duds are plainer."

My car, a DeSoto Fireflite, was still new, and Paddy hadn't gotten his fill of kidding me about it. He was a man who could spot a weakness, and cars were a definite weakness of mine. The whole country had shaken off the gray moderation of the war and its aftermath. I'd followed along to the extent of buying the DeSoto. It had a two-hundred-horsepower V8, leather upholstery in a diamond pattern, and a silly "gullwing" dash, whose beautifully curved metal wouldn't hold a single cup of coffee safely, even when the car was parked. The exterior was equally utilitarian. The front grille looked like a vampire's lower teeth done up in chrome braces. The paint was white and turquoise, the white relegated to the roof and a "sweep-spear" on each side, chrome-trimmed arrows of white run-

ning from the rear whitewalls to just behind the protruding headlights.

"How many times," Paddy began in a put-upon, rhetorical tone,
"have I told you that the best vehicle for security work is something
no one would look at twice?"

"I've lost count," I said, handing him the lighter. My unstated answer was that we did our security work in Hollywood, where
chrome battleships cruised every street. A brown Chevy on black-
walls would have stuck out here like an old maid in a chorus line.
The answer was unstated because I didn't enjoy arguing with Paddy.
Neither of us liked it when he lost.

He got the corona going, filling the car with blue smoke in the
process. I traded the smog for the already hot air of the lot, trying
to appear more relaxed than I felt as I looked the place over. I understood my jumpiness without really thinking it out, remembering
a similar feeling from my time overseas during the fighting. It was
the sensation of being on the enemy's ground. RKO was no longer
a movie studio in any real sense. It belonged to the television sub-
sidiary of a tire company. They'd never make tires here, but they'd
surely get around to making television shows, once all the old
movies in the RKO vaults had been shown to death. I didn't want
to play any part in that transformation. I'd rather have seen the old
studio bulldozed for parking lots.

My beacon in this darkness was Paddy Maguire. I knew he felt
the same way I did about television, which was the way Brook-
lynites felt about the Yankees. Paddy had yet to forgive radio for
killing his first profession, vaudeville. Now radio with pictures attached was threatening to do the same thing to his current meal
ticket, Hollywood. Paddy had sworn that he'd never do business
with the enemy.

It was a blind spot in Paddy's remarkable eye for the main
chance. He'd come to Hollywood shortly before the talkies had
given the town its first big shake-up. He'd been in the right place at
the right time, in other words, but things hadn't clicked for him.

He'd ended up manning the front gate at Paramount, my old studio, where we'd met. But he hadn't stayed in the gatehouse. When he'd heard through his network of old friends that the studios were planning to sever their financial relationship with the local police—a relationship that had saved many a big star's career—Paddy had seen an opportunity for personal advancement. He'd founded the Hollywood Security Agency to provide discreet and often legitimate security services for the studios, major and minor.

After that, Paddy's financial fortunes had paralleled those of Hollywood: up during the war years, when the country had gratefully swallowed whatever the studios had doled out, and gently downward after V-J Day, when the kingdom had begun to unravel. First a government antitrust suit had forced the studios to sell off their theater chains. Then television had reared its ugly head. Through it all, Paddy had remained stubbornly loyal, a fact I was counting on now.

I relaxed completely when my boss turned his attention from his cigar to business and asked, "What can you tell me about Carson Drury?"

"You mean there's someone in this town you don't know?" I asked.

"Geniuses intimidate me," Paddy said. "I used to cross the street whenever I saw Charlie Chaplin coming. I especially don't like boy geniuses. They make me feel dumb and ancient at the same time."

"Drury's no boy anymore," I said. "And his track record says he isn't a genius, either."

"The rise before the fall, please," Paddy said. "I don't like stories that begin at the end."

Paddy didn't need any coaching from me. I guessed that he was testing me, seeing how much background on Drury I needed myself. I went along with the gag. "Drury came to Hollywood the year before I was drafted."

"That would make it '40," Paddy said.

"Right. He'd set New York on its ear with some innovative theatrical productions, including a modern dress *Hamlet* and a revival of *Showboat* that had colored actors in the white roles and vice versa."

"I remember that brouhaha. Drury sang 'Old Man River' himself, as I recall. He was on radio, too, wasn't he?"

"Yes, with a lot of the same actors he used on Broadway. Repertory One, he called the group. He brought them out here when RKO signed him for a two-picture deal. Drury's debut film, *First Citizen,* which he wrote and starred in and directed, was a big success."

"Not with me it wasn't," Paddy said. His broad face, about the same width at the jawline as Pat O'Brien's, took on a sincere reddish cast. "*First Citizen* was D. W. Griffith's life story with the names changed to keep Mr. Drury out of court. Griffith's drunkenness, his affairs, his failure to keep pace with changes in Hollywood—a town he practically founded—were all paraded on the screen. Worse, Drury made Griffith seem like the grand dragon of the Ku Klux Klan just because he used the Klan in *Birth of a Nation.*"

"Some people would say Griffith celebrated the Klan in *Birth of a Nation.*"

Paddy darkened half a shade. "Some people would say Drury kicked Griffith when the old man was down. He was still alive in '41, you know. Still trying to get work from his old assistants who'd risen to run the studios. *First Citizen* didn't help the effort. It didn't make any friends for Drury around this town, either."

"Who's telling this story?" I asked to calm him down.

"You are. And may I say you're killing the morning doing it." He patted the pocket of his vest where his watch used to reside and then extended his left arm to display his new wrist model, a present from Ella. "We're late. You'll have to finish while we walk."

He started off toward the administration building. "What was Drury's second picture?"

"*The Imperial Albertsons,*" I said as I fell into step beside him. "It flopped."

The news cheered Paddy considerably. "Any idea why?"

"No. I was in an army camp when the picture was released. Maybe D. W. Griffith's old friends sabotaged it."

"Funny you should use that word," Paddy said. "What happened next?"

"A series of disappointments and failures and pictures that were announced but never made. Lately, I haven't even heard any announcements."

Paddy held the building's plate glass door open for me, bowing slightly at the waist as he waved me through. "You're about to hear a pip," he said.

chapter

3

ON THE OTHER SIDE of the door was a little kiosk behind which sat an equally little man in a gray uniform. He had thick, round glasses and hair that had been tonsured by Mother Nature. He was swiveled half around in his chair, facing the sound of raucous laughter. The guard turned to us when Paddy asked for Carson Drury.

"Follow your ears till you get to the party," the little man said. "You'll find his highness."

The trail was a short one that ended at cathedral-size doors paneled in blond wood.

"Howard Hughes's own office when he deigned to visit the lot," Paddy said, a little in awe. "Drury's no piker for nerve."

A receptionist's desk sat to our right, but its towering chair was empty. Paddy knocked on the doors loudly enough, I thought, to bother the residents down the block at the Hollywood Cemetery. It wasn't loud enough to interrupt the party, though, so we entered the office uninvited.

In the center of the room, Carson Drury was holding court. The court was small—a woman and two men—but they made up in enthusiasm what they lacked in numbers. The three were seated before Drury—at his feet, it seemed, although their chairs weren't especially low. The impression was created by Drury's famous height. He was six feet seven according to his press agent, but he looked taller because he was extremely thin. He'd actually needed padding back in '41 to play the gaunt D. W. Griffith's fictional counterpart. Drury might have put on a pound or two since, but they didn't show. He still had the figure Tallulah Bankhead had once described as "swizzle stick with mane." The mane was also intact, black and thick and brushed backward from Drury's high forehead. It swept over his ears and ended with a flourish just above his collar. Only symphony orchestra conductors and physicists had the nerve to wear their hair like that. And Hollywood geniuses.

Drury waved us in without interrupting his story. "So the cop pulls us over. Right on Riverside Drive. He parks his motorcycle and marches back to the cabbie's window, pulling his gauntlets off very dramatically. Then he starts tearing into Larry. The cop had a real talent for it, too. None of that 'Where's the fire?' grade of material. I remember that he managed to work Eleanor Roosevelt and Flash Gordon into the same sentence, which I'd hesitate to attempt myself. The only thing Larry, the cabbie, can do is nod back toward me and mumble something about his VIP passenger.

"So the cop comes back and looks in my window. I'm already made up as Lincoln, of course, because I knew there wouldn't be time to change at the theater. Fake beard, nose, mole, black suit, the works. Everything but the stovepipe hat, which was up on the front seat with Larry.

"The cop looks at me and then at poor Alice, who was pulling her dress back into place and straightening her hair. Then the goof looks back at me, and I could see that a fog of disassociation was gathering around him.

"So I say"—Drury reached up with one hand to grasp an imaginary lapel–" 'I beg your pardon, officer, but it's imperative that I reach the theater without delay.' Well, the cop doesn't salute, but he does come to attention. I bang Larry on the shoulder, and he pulls the cab back into traffic.

"Just then, the cop starts running after us, shouting something. I lean out the window in time to hear him yell, 'Don't go to the theater! Don't go to the theater!' "

The two courtiers and the maiden laughed on cue, but the three of them together couldn't drown out Drury. Paddy, who had a healthy laugh himself when he was in the mood, just smiled politely.

When things had calmed down a bit, Drury wiped his eyes and pointed to the carpet at his feet. I noticed then that he was shoeless. That is, he wasn't wearing shoes, but he wasn't exactly without them, either. A dozen pairs were arranged in a semicircle at his feet, toes toward him as though they, too, had been hanging on his every word.

"These will do for starters, Joe," Drury said, turning down the volume on his deep, vaguely English voice a little. "Call me if you get anything new in from Italy." To the second man he said, "Harry, make sure everyone knows that we'll be back in business tomorrow–bright and early."

The two men stepped around Paddy and me on the way to the door. The young woman was following, but Drury stopped her momentarily by saying, "Sue, maybe you can find a cup of coffee for Mr. Maguire and Mr. Elliott."

I was surprised that Drury knew my name, as Paddy tended to limit his supporting players' billing for as long as possible. I looked to my boss for an explanation, but he was busy adding to his coffee order.

"I'd like a little glass of cold water on the side," he said, "if it wouldn't be too much trouble."

Paddy helped himself to Harry's seat, and I took Joe the shoe salesman's. Drury sat on the edge of his desk, his stockinged feet still firmly on the floor, watching as Paddy ground out his corona in a standing ashtray.

Then Drury said, "You didn't care for my Lincoln story?"

"John Barrymore used to tell it better," Paddy said. "He had two women in the cab with him and the cop on horseback."

Drury laughed again, louder and longer than he had at his story. "Sounds like it's lucky for me that Barrymore's dead. Forgive the shoe store," he said to me. "I never have time to shop for things. Or maybe I can't bring myself to waste the time. I found a very civilized way to buy shoes when I was in England during the war; an old, established firm where they measured your feet down to the last bunion and then carved wooden forms to the exact measurements. They had a huge room full of them: the Duke of Windsor's feet, Jack Buchanan's feet, Walter Hagen's feet. After the initial ordeal—my measurements took half a day—all you ever had to do for the rest of your life was write and tell them what you wanted. They whipped the shoes up by hand using your own wooden lasts so you were guaranteed a perfect fit."

He sighed at the memory.

"So what happened?" I asked, nodding at the non-English shoes that had him surrounded. "Did your feet keep growing?"

"No. A German flying bomb flattened the shop late in the war. Hitler couldn't get Churchill, but he managed to take out his cobbler. They rebuilt the place, of course, but I've never gotten back to be remeasured."

He'd been telling the story to me, but when he reached the finish, he looked over at Paddy to gauge his reaction. The half of Paddy's face I could see was skeptical.

"That's the excuse I generally use, anyway," Drury said after a pause. "The truth is, handmade English shoes have been beyond my means these last few years. I made that trip to London back in what I think of now as my salad days, when I was rolling in lettuce. Those days didn't last. So the buzz bomb saved my wooden feet from the embarrassment of being relegated to the basement—or worse, the dust bin."

"You're doing okay at the moment," Paddy observed, glancing around the office.

Drury smiled at his disapproval. "Borrowed splendor, I'm afraid. Ty McNally, the titular head of the studio, told me to help myself to an office. He didn't say it couldn't be the best."

It was surely the biggest—a large room lit by tall windows whose white curtains had horizontal stripes of blue. Compared with the curtains, the brown walls looked especially blank. Drury explained that quality.

"I took down the pictures Mr. Hughes had hanging in here. They were all blowups of actresses with their blouses coming undone. Not to disparage Howard's tastes, but they made the place look like the front office of a brassiere factory.

"And they made Sue here feel self-conscious," he added as the secretary returned carrying three coffee cups and Paddy's glass of water on a silver tray.

She cleared herself of the self-consciousness charge when she bent over to hand me my coffee. In the course of that simple movement, she displayed cleavage that would have earned her a long-term contract if Hughes had still been around. She smiled at Drury, indulgently this time, and closed the double doors behind her.

Drury had already drained his cup. "Is Scott up to speed?" he asked Paddy.

My boss was just tasting his coffee. It was too hot for him, so he added a little water from his glass. "I haven't briefed Mr. Elliott," he said. "I didn't think I could do justice to your . . . scheme."

This time Drury didn't laugh the rudeness away. He looked at Paddy for a while, the skin around his big, dark eyes crinkled as though he were about to smile. He didn't smile, and it occurred to me that the slightly gathered lids were also effective at conveying pain.

I said, "Are you going to be heading up production for this Mc-Nally?"

"No," Drury said. "Not unless a miracle happens. On the subject of RKO's future, the current gossip is correct. The new owners are really only interested in the studio's film library. All nine hundred titles of it, minus one. That one film is the basis of my little project—

or scheme, if you prefer. If the scheme should succeed, who knows? Maybe while I'm saving my own reputation, I can save RKO, too.

"The reputation I'm referring to is my old, circa 1941 model. No one would want to save my current one, which can be summarized as follows: Carson Drury is a man of unlimited talent, almost all of it still unused. After some early successes on Broadway, mostly empty novelties, and one amazing motion picture–probably the stolen work of his partner, his editor, his wardrobe mistress, et cetera–he turned out a steady series of half-realized dreams. No man in Hollywood is so full of ideas or less likely to see one through to the end.

"Anything to add to that, Mr. Maguire?"

"Not a word," Paddy said.

"As negative as my current resume is, that's how positive the 1941 version, the *First Citizen* reputation, was. That Drury was a whirlwind who could star in one Broadway show while producing and directing another and acting in half a dozen radio programs in his spare time. His first movie, his very first one, is considered by many to be one of the greatest ever made."

Paddy reached for his cigar case. Drury retrieved a wooden box from his desktop and held it out to him. "Try one of these Havanas. You'll enjoy the change, I think. I know the rest of us will."

Paddy had already accepted the cigar before Drury delivered his punch line. It was too late to put the cigar back, so he stuck it in the front pocket of his coat.

That little victory put the roses back in Drury's cheeks. He was all smiles again as he asked me, "Do you know what happened to that young genius? What changed my '41 reputation to the current sorry one?"

"Your second picture happened," I said.

"Exactly. *The Imperial Albertsons* happened, the story of a prominent Indiana family that couldn't adjust to the changing world the automobile brought about. Couldn't accept that they weren't going to be royalty anymore because their little kingdom was going away, swallowed up by the single homogeneous nation that new technologies like the automobile made possible."

"Sounds like a great idea," I said.

"It was more than a great idea," Drury said. "It was a great film. That's what haunts me the most. *Albertsons,* my *Albertsons,* wasn't a failure. It was an achieved work of art that became an early casualty of the war."

"How?" I asked.

"We wrapped up the rough editing on *Albertsons* early in 1942. That left the scoring, which I was supervising. Just before we finished that, the State Department called to ask if I'd go to England on a kind of cultural lend-lease to boost morale and make speeches about how committed we were to the war now that the Japanese had dragged us into it. They arranged for me to direct a stage production of *Hamlet* while I was over there, a revival of the modern dress version I'd done in New York in '38. I got the idea to make a documentary film about the production. I had this vision of Hamlet's soliloquy being spoken against the background of the blitz. 'To be or not to be' coming across as 'to oppose fascism or surrender everything.' "

He had the vision again, his eyes focusing on the empty air between Paddy's chair and mine. He came out of it shaking his head. "The *Hamlet* was never produced and the documentary was never made."

"Why not?" Paddy asked.

"Too many shortages. Too much red tape. Too many parties. Too many parties mostly. I'd been working like a madman for years. Like two madmen since I'd hit Hollywood. I needed a break and I took one. In a manner of speaking, I've been on it ever since. While I was drinking my way through the air raids, things were falling apart on the home front.

"Unbeknownst to our hero," he said, patting himself on the chest, "the RKO brass had arranged a preview of *Albertsons* in a little jerkwater town called Yorba Linda. The natives there confirmed the studio's own judgment of the film, which was that it didn't make any sense. All that meant was the studio execs didn't understand it, which was natural enough. No one at RKO had understood *First Citizen* until the East Coast critics explained it to them. The difference was I'd been there to defend *First Citizen*, to protect it. When *The Imperial Albertsons* needed me, I was on the other side of the ocean, drunk, having my feet measured for shoes I'd never buy.

"I'd left my partner from Repertory One in charge of finishing up the film. John Piers Whitehead. Three names for a man who isn't big enough inside to justify an initial. Instead of defending the picture, he conspired with the studio hacks to destroy it. They rewrote the ending completely, the last forty minutes of the film. They brought the cast back in—my loyal company of actors—and reshot it.

"Then they did the unthinkable, the unimaginable: They burned my original ending, print and negative."

chapter

4

A LONG SILENCE followed. Drury was looking around the office, thinking, perhaps, that we were in the very room where the decision to destroy his picture had been made by one of Howard Hughes's less flamboyant predecessors.

"After that," Drury finally said, "the clock struck midnight in a big way. *Albertsons* failed with the critics and the public. That was all my enemies at RKO needed to get me tossed off the lot. I didn't exactly land on my feet, either.

"I'd made a lot of the old timers in Hollywood mad with *First Citizen*," he said, looking pointedly at Paddy. "Those who didn't give a damn about D. W. Griffith's hurt feelings were jealous because the picture was destined to live forever.

"I had offers, but none that ensured my total control over a project. I had to accept deals that gave the studios—Warners briefly, then Universal, then, God help me, Monogram—control of the final cut of my films. That was part of my *Albertsons* legacy: the idea that I could be trusted only so far and no farther, that my brilliance had to be tempered by someone else's discipline. Some committee's discipline, usually.

"It meant that there never really was another Carson Drury picture. Only the butchered remains of a few. Just enough to tilt the scales of judgment against me." He cupped his bony hands and held them like a pair of scales, slowly raising one while he lowered the other. "Enough to convince everyone that *The Imperial Albertsons* was the rule and *First Citizen,* the fluke.

"Well, I'd always been a prodigy. If I was a successful director by twenty-one, it stands to reason I'd be washed up by twenty-five. Damn," he said with his dark grin flashing. "What a second act curtain that would have made on Broadway."

"What's the third act?" I asked.

"Redemption, of course," Drury said. "We have to send the customers home smiling."

He stood up abruptly, circled the desk, and took a seat behind it. "Several weeks ago I read in the *Motion Picture Herald* that Howard Hughes was about to consummate a deal with the American Standard Tire Company of Akron, Ohio."

Paddy, who'd set a personal record for listening while another person talked, finally chimed in. "Everyone in Hollywood read the same piece. It said that the heir apparent of that company, Tyrone McNally, has strung together a little network of television stations that are earning almost as much as his daddy's rubber works. But he needs more entertainment to go with his commercials, so he contacted Hughes a few months back and offered to buy RKO's film library. Hughes made him buy the whole damn studio."

While Paddy was scoring his points, Drury raided the box of Havanas and fired one up. Now he leaned back in his chair, stretching his arms up above his head and leaving them there.

"When I saw that article, I had another one of my visions," he said, staring at his own smoke rings as though they were secret messages. "I called Mr. McNally and offered to take one of his nine hundred new films off his hands."

"First Citizen?" I asked.

"Oh, no." He lowered his arms so he could do his scale routine again. Then he looked down lovingly at the lower hand. *"The Imperial Albertsons.* McNally was happy enough to part with it, a famous box office disaster. He threw in a camera and sound equipment and lights and a lease on a soundstage for peanuts."

I had a vision of my own. "You're going to remake the movie?"

"Not the whole movie. Just the ending, the part Whitehead and his fellow vandals destroyed.

"Think of it! All the actors from *Albertsons* are still alive and well. Joseph Coffin, Ezra Marley, Angeline Van Ness, all the old Repertory One crew. Their characters age over the course of the film, so if anything, they'll need less makeup now than they did in '42."

"Are they willing to do it?"

"They're desperate to do it. They're dying to do it. That gang owes me about a dozen favors apiece. They all started with me in New York. Hell, they only ended up in Hollywood because I brought them here."

"Carried them out on your back, I suppose," Paddy said.

He wasn't going to ambush Drury again, a message the director conveyed with explosive laughter. "Of course on my back. I had to have my arms free for flying, didn't I?"

When he'd laughed himself out, he said, "So I had that debt to call in and another, less pleasant one in reserve."

"The actors owe you because they helped RKO reshoot the picture," I said.

"Yes." He ground out his barely tasted cigar. "They were all under contract to RKO, of course, and obligated to follow orders, but if they'd stood together, they could have saved my film. The irony is that they thought they were doing it for my own good. That sounds naive as hell, but they were kids themselves back then. They know better now, and they're anxious to make amends."

He was leaning across the desk, his long face looking younger, almost boyish under the Huck Finn hair. "Luckily a movie studio is like your grandparents' attic on an epic scale: nothing ever thrown away, some fantastic treasure crammed into every nook. So far we've found the very camera we used to shoot *Albertsons* and sound equipment to match. There are even some of the original costumes in storage, although they may need letting out."

He stretched his arms up again, his hands balled into fists. "After all these years in the wilderness, I'll finally have my vindication. There will finally be a second Carson Drury picture, a masterpiece that will make *First Citizen* seem like nothing more than a step in the right direction."

"While you're counting your chickens," Paddy said, "don't forget to subtract the reason you called us in. The sabotage, I mean."

Drury was in the process of remembering, his smile frozen in place and his outstretched arms slowly sinking into his lap, when Sue opened the door behind me.

"They're waiting for you in the screening room, Mr. Drury," she said.

He sprang from his chair before she'd finished her speech. "Toss me a pair of shoes, Elliott," he said. "Any two as long as one's left and one's right. I forgot that I'd arranged for a team of set designers to see the old version of *Albertsons* this morning. That's turned out to be our biggest challenge: duplicating the old sets."

He came around the desk at a quick march, his untied laces beating time on the tops of his oxfords. "Come on, chaps. We'll work up an appetite for lunch."

Paddy's appetite hadn't needed working up for years. He was already breathing emphatically by the time we rounded the guard's kiosk and traded the air-conditioning for the blazing concrete of the lot. Drury's wind was fine, but he didn't waste any on talking until we were out of earshot of the little guard.

"The sabotage started right after I closed the deal with Mr. Mc-Nally, but in a minor key. First my original shooting script disappeared. Fortunately we found a copy in the studio archives. Then some of our tires were slashed. This was out at RKO's Culver City lot—the old Selznick Studio—where we're actually shooting."

"You're filming already?" I asked.

"Yes. You didn't read that in the *Herald* or the *Reporter,*" Drury said with a satisfied glance at the laboring Mr. Maguire. "That's one of the reasons I picked the Culver City studio: secrecy."

"You were anticipating trouble?"

"No. Just keeping my left up. Part of my damnable reputation is the inability to see a project through to the end. For once I wanted the peace of having to satisfy no one's expectations but my own. I wanted to work without the building suspense that usually accompanies one of my projects. The 'How will Drury screw up this time?' suspense. In its place I got a new kind of pressure courtesy of a faceless, nameless saboteur."

I looked for Paddy to take the podium now that we'd gotten to the actual subject of the meeting, but Drury and I had left him behind. He was standing next to a Civil War–era cannon, surely the veteran of a hundred horse operas, pretending to light the cigar he'd gotten from Drury while he caught his breath. At the moment he was patting his pockets for the matches he'd left at home.

I started back to do the honors, but the long-legged Drury beat me to it. "I think that brings Mr. Elliott up to date," he said as he produced a silver lighter as thin for its length as he was. He held it out like an olive branch.

Paddy twirled the cigar in the proffered flame long enough to have gotten a baseball bat alight. "You told me on the phone that events had taken a nastier turn," he said at last.

"Yes. Two nights ago someone set fire to the editing room where we'd stored the *Albertsons* negative. We would have lost it if it hadn't been for Hank Shepard. He's the publicist on the project. Maybe I should say 'secretist,' since his job so far has been to keep things out of the papers. Hank's a very flexible guy. He's also a brave one. When he spotted the fire, he charged in and saved the film cans. He had to make two trips to get them all."

"Is he okay?" I asked.

"Just singed a little. More to the point, the negative came through the ordeal intact. I'm counting on you gentlemen to keep it that way."

Paddy had found his second wind. "Who besides D. W. Griffith's ghost would give a damn whether you revived your fortunes or not?"

Drury backed away from us as he answered. "I don't know. I honestly don't think I have an enemy in the world—just ex-wives and critics who don't understand me.

"I've got to run now. I've asked Hank to answer any other questions you might have. He's standing guard in Culver City right now. And you're both invited to the Club Satyr tonight. I've rented the place for a little party. Hank's talked me into taking the wraps off the production, and we're going to do it in style. I figure if the studio is blown out from under us, we'll lose the element of surprise anyway. Eight o'clock. Nothing too fancy. Just black tie."

By that time Drury was out of range of our questions. He waved once more and loped off.

"Just black tie," Paddy repeated. "He probably expects us to wait tables."

We started back for the DeSoto, Paddy setting an especially leisurely pace. I said, "You two hit it off famously."

"Did we not," Paddy said. "What a character. Did you catch that accent? Drury picked up more than shoes when he was in London. And him born and raised in Cleveland to my certain knowledge."

Paddy had been born and raised in Baltimore, but there was a wisp of Ireland about his speech—not in his pronunciation but in the way he cast his sentences. At one time I'd thought this was an echo of the immigrants who had raised him. More recently I'd decided that his speech pattern was a souvenir from his days in vaudeville when he'd been a stage Irishman, complete with red wig and greasepaint freckles.

Drury had probably acquired his slight English accent the same way, after one performance of *Hamlet* too many. He and Paddy had a lot in common, genius aside. Both were outgoing personalities used to dominating their little corners of the world. It was a not uncommon quality in Hollywood, and Paddy could dim it down when he needed to accommodate a powerful client. I wondered why he hadn't made that effort for Drury.

"If you don't like the guy, why are we working for him?"

"We're not," Paddy said. "You are. He asked for you by name when he called. Any idea why?"

"No," I said.

"It's just as well. I'll be tied up for the next few days on that little matter we're handling for Joan Crawford. As to why you're working for him, the answer is money. I like to keep a little more coming in than I have going out. The Depression twisted me that way."

"I hope Drury paid us up front," I said. "When he was describing his bad reputation, he left out the part about his checks bouncing."

"That part I already knew," Paddy said. "It may be the secret of the black temper I'm in this morning. I may resent having to take work from Drury in the first place. Time was I would have referred a deadbeat like him to a fifty-dollar-a-day independent down on Hollywood Boulevard. Now I need the business, and I resent needing the business, so I take it out on poor Mr. Drury. Remind me to send him a card at Christmas."

I promised I would.

"While we're on the subject of money," Paddy said, "see if Mr. Shepard can tell you how Drury managed to finance this gamble of his. That may give us a handle on the sabotage. In this town when it isn't ego driving things, it's always money. Call me at home before you head to the Satyr."

"You won't be going," I said, and not as a question. As sociable as Paddy normally was, his wife and business partner, Peggy, was shy. She'd never felt comfortable in glamorous Hollywood, despite her own brief career on the stage. She was growing less comfortable as each year passed. And Paddy was less inclined than he used to be to leave her home alone.

"For once I'm happy enough to please her nibs," Paddy said. "If I had to listen to one more of Drury's stories, I might choke to death on a canapé.

"Don't worry about dropping me; I'll take a cab. Give our love to Ella and the sprouts."

chapter

5

I DROVE TO CULVER CITY by way of a phone booth and a call to Ella. She was free that evening and genuinely excited about Carson Drury's plan to revive *The Imperial Albertsons.*

"That's the best idea I've heard since you proposed," she said.

"We've had two children since then," I reminded her.

"They weren't anybody's idea, chum," Ella reminded me.

As Drury had mentioned, RKO's Culver City studio had once belonged to David O. Selznick. Selznick's later films had opened with a long shot of the lot's centerpiece, an office building disguised as an antebellum southern mansion. It was meant to evoke memories of Selznick's *Gone with the Wind,* a melancholy association, I'd always thought, since the producer had never been able to equal that early triumph.

I wandered Tara's halls for a while without finding Hank Shepard. Finally a young woman in a calico shirt and dungarees took pity on me and directed me to an unassuming building behind the mansion. Tara's garage, I told myself as I knocked on its screen door.

Beyond the door someone was typing as though his life depended on it. He yelled for me to come in without slacking his fire. I followed the sound down a cinder block hallway to a cinder block office lit inadequately by the noon sun bouncing off the street outside and through a louvered window cranked fully open.

When I made my entrance, the typist broke off with a flourish that made me think of Chico Marx's piano routines. He hit the last key with an extended forefinger, the rest of his hand shaped to resemble a gun.

"Bang," he said. "Another press release bites the dust." Then he swiveled in his chair and extended his hand. It was a big hand, but not a hard one. "Hank Shepard," he said. "You must be Scott Elliott. Carson told me to expect you."

Shepard reminded me of friends from my old artillery battery. That is, he reminded me of the way the friends had turned out. He was a well-fed, peaceful-looking citizen who smiled easily and seemed to mean it. He had wavy blond hair worn a trifle high on his forehead, blue eyes that weren't as clear as they probably once had been, and big red ears that drooped a little in the reflected sunlight. One of the ears was wearing a healthy coating of petroleum jelly. Despite the heat, Shepard's white shirt was buttoned at the collar, and his bow tie—white with blue stripes like the curtains in Drury's borrowed office—was knotted tightly. He had rolled his sleeves up, however. I could see that his left forearm was wrapped in greasy gauze.

"Your boss told me you'd been singed," I said. "It looks worse than that."

"It does," Shepard said, holding up his arm so he could admire it. "Luckily this is Hollywood. Nothing is exactly what it appears to be, and nobody's who they seem. What time do you have?"

"Two past twelve."

"Time for my pain medicine. Care to join me?"

He pulled a pint of bourbon from its hiding place behind the typewriter and collected two glasses from a little tray held in place by a big water jug. Shepard's resemblance to my old army buddies was increasing by the minute.

"I wasn't burned," I said.

"Not yet," Shepard said. "But you're working for Carson Drury now, right? So it's only a matter of time." He handed me a generous shot. "Consider this something on account."

I raised my glass. "To heroism," I said.

Shepard held his laugh until he'd downed his drink. "If you're referring to the fire the other night, that was no big deal. Nothing like winning the Silver Star." He looked down at my chest to see if I might be wearing mine.

"Who told you about that?"

"Just some scuttlebutt Carson picked up somewhere. It's true, isn't it?"

"Yes," I said. I pulled out my pack of cigarettes and offered one to Shepard, Ella not being around to frown at me.

She wasn't around, but she wasn't that far away, either. As I lit my Lucky, Shepard said, "And you're married to Pidgin Englehart, aren't you?"

Pidgin was Ella's old nickname from her days as a studio publicist. It was short for pidgin English, an unflattering reference to her early writing style. "More of Drury's scuttlebutt?" I asked.

"Nope, my own. I broke in with Pidgin at Warners right after the war. A great girl, a really great girl."

I thought about working our children into the conversation as a way of wiping the rosy glow of memory off Shepard's face. In the end I just said, "How long have you been working for Drury?"

"Since I quit Warners in '46. It seemed like a good move at the time. Carson was working on *The Gentleman from Macao* back then. Did you see that one?"

"Yes. The closing scene in the house of mirrors is a classic."

Shepard grimaced. "For twelve reels a detective chases this mysterious killer, and all anybody remembers is the shamus looking into the mirrors and seeing the murderer in place of his own reflection. You're supposed to know then that the killer and the detective are the same guy, two personalities in one body. I don't think half of the ticket buyers figured it out or cared by then. That was another picture that got some front-office editing after Carson was asked to clean out his desk."

"I liked it," I said.

"Me, too," Shepard said. "But I'm no judge of celluloid. If I were, I wouldn't still be hanging around, waiting for another heartache."

"You don't give this comeback try much of a chance?"

"Once burned, twice shy, to return to my earlier joke. Let's just say I've lived through more than one of Carson's comebacks. None of the others had the panache of this *Albertsons* stroke, though. I can almost see him bringing this one off. If only . . ."

That dangling *if* brought us around to business. I set my glass on Shepard's desk. "What's the story on this fire?"

"Come on," Shepard said. "I'll show you the scene of the crime."

He led me back out the way I'd come in, briefing me from a little wire-bound notebook as we went.

"A week ago I noticed that Carson's copy of the script was missing. He'd left it on my desk when we quit for the night, and the next morning it was gone."

"Was the place locked?"

"Yep. On account of my typewriter, not Carson's script. But the locks around here are mostly for keeping the doors from blowing open in the wind. The script that disappeared was Carson's old copy from 1942, which we were able to replace, but the stolen script had years of notes and rewrites scribbled in the margins, which we can't replace. That may be a blessing in disguise. Only Carson would spend thirteen years defending his original conception as a work of art while all that time he's rewriting it. He's like that Wordsworth guy."

"What studio's he with?" I asked, kicking an empty soda bottle out of our way.

"Don't give me the tough guy act, Elliott. You know who I'm talking about. Wordsworth the English poet. When he got old, he spent his time rewriting his early poems when he should have been writing new ones. Screwing the early ones up, too, needless to say. Carson has the same tendency, so the notes are no big loss. He's probably scribbled a whole new set by now anyway."

"There was also some vandalism?"

"Two nights later. Carson found that himself. He got back from the dinner break late and saw that the tires on my heap and on Joe Nolan's Chrysler had been slashed. Joe's our cameraman. Carson got a big kick out of that. He has a leisurely dinner, and as a bonus he doesn't have to buy new tires."

"Is security around here that light?"

"It's lighter than a thirty-five-cent lunch. And about as hard to find. It consists of some Keystone Kops that the American Standard Tire Company hired to keep the place from walking away."

"Still, they came through like the cavalry on the night of the fire. It was three days after the tire slashing—night before last, I mean. We'd been working late, talking out Carson's idea of duplicating some of the old sets with matte paintings. Carson broke it up about nine because he had a date with some Mexican starlet. Joe and I killed a bottle, then he left. I was collecting myself for the same effort when I smelled smoke."

I'd been smelling something similar for some time. We rounded the corner of the alleyway and came to another cinder block building. It was one story, like Shepard's garage, but longer, with a series of outside doors like a racetrack stable. The door nearest our corner was gone, replaced by a rectangular black hole. Through it I could see more blackness. The window next to the door had been broken out. Where the white paint on the block wall wasn't blistered, it was discolored by smoke.

"You went in there twice?" I asked.

"Marvelous stuff, whiskey. Of course, I had noble motives, too. Like money. My wagon's hitched to Carson Drury's star, for better or worse. That means it's hitched to *Albertsons*. It's my last chance to turn my years with Carson from a dead loss to a profit. I'll be damned if I'll let some son of a bitch with a Zippo take that chance away."

The alley around us was decorated with half-burned furniture and ruined equipment: the ends of a long table whose middle was missing; the naked frame of a swivel chair, already rusting; a sofa whose charred cushions had been split open. What had once been editing equipment was now a pile of blackened pieces. Only the empty film reels were still recognizable.

"How did the fire start?" I asked.

"Search me. I had the impression that the wire wastebasket under the editing table was the center of the action, but it was only an impression. The fire spread so fast, it seemed to be everywhere at once."

"What did the arson boys say?"

Shepard had left his hat back in his office. He held his little notebook above his eyes to shield them from the sun. "What arson boys?"

"The fire department didn't take an interest in this?"

"We managed to handle it without them." Shepard pointed to a hydrant ten feet away. A reel of hose hung on the building next to it, dirty hose that had been rewound inexpertly. "Like I said, the Keystone Kops earned their money that night. One of them was walking post near enough to hear me yelling for help. By the time I got the last can of film out, there were two of them here, and they'd figured out how the fire hose worked. They had that little room flooded before I'd stopped sizzling."

"They still would have called the fire department."

"Yeah, they would have if I hadn't volunteered to do it for them. I called Ciro's instead and left a message for Carson to get back here quick. He still had the crazy idea we could keep this production a secret. I knew he wouldn't want firemen or policemen or, worse, reporters prowling around."

"How did Drury handle the guards?"

"With one hand tied behind his back. You've never seen Carson's God routine, have you? He drops that radio voice of his into low gear, shakes all the slack out of his spine, and brings his black brows together like a pair of rival bulls. Then he either gives you hell or pumps you full of sweetness and light, depending on which he thinks will get him the most mileage.

"He took the high road and the low road both that night with the guards. First he gave them the impression that he would personally mention their devotion to duty to Tyrone McNally and each and every stockholder of American Standard Tire, and maybe even to President Eisenhower. He then said that the fire had been a careless accident and it would be a shame for anyone to lose his position over a careless accident. A terrible shame. Luckily for them, Carson was in charge. They could count on him to handle the situation with superhuman delicacy. It was a nice little performance. He left those sad sacks feeling like heroes who could be fired for cause at any second. They went away quietly enough, let me tell you."

"Then what did you do?"

"Carson threw the negative in the trunk of his car—it's now in a fireproof vault, by the way—and drove me to the hospital. On the way I convinced him to let me go public with the *Albertsons* reissue."

"But not about the fire."

"No. We can't afford to. It's a shame. I could build a beautiful sympathy campaign out of that." He swept his hand through the hot air to symbolize the huge type he'd need for his headline. " 'Hard luck director's comeback threatened by phantom saboteur.' Something like that might even get Hollywood pulling for Carson for a change. Half of Hollywood anyway. The other half would be convinced that the fire was some publicity stunt we cooked up ourselves."

"What do you mean you can't afford to release the story?"

"I mean it literally. Look, Carson didn't agree to drop all the secrecy business because he owed me for saving the negative. He only gave in because his cash is running out. He needs to find more money now if he wants to get this production finished."

Shepard lowered his notebook visor and squinted upward. "If you're through here, let's find some shade."

I took a look inside the burned-out editing room so I'd be able to tell Paddy I had. Then we walked back toward Shepard's office.

Halfway there, Shepard still hadn't resumed his story, so I said, "Your boss told us that he'd gotten the negative and the equipment he needs for peanuts."

"He did. But this is still Hollywood. The carpenters around here make more than a Corn Belt bank president. So far we've only managed to build one lousy set, a three-story curving staircase that Carson plans to use for exactly one shot."

"Drury said that duplicating the old sets was the biggest challenge."

"What he meant was, paying for them is. We need some backers now. That means publicity—and only positive publicity. No stories about sabotage or vandalism or plain old bad luck."

"So this party tonight was your idea?"

"No. That was Carson staying one step ahead of me as usual. He'd already lined up one potential angel, a buddy of Tyrone Mc-Nally's named Traynor. After Carson agreed to go public with the production, he talked this Traynor into footing the bill for a coming-out party. The hick probably thinks he's going to meet Jane Russell."

Since we'd broached the subject of money, I asked the question Paddy had written on my shirt cuff: "Where did Drury's first bankroll come from, the one that's running out?"

"Eden," Shepard said. "That's Carson's ranch out near Encino. He bought it with his *First Citizen* paycheck, and he's hung onto it somehow ever since. He loves that place. It's a sign of how desperate he is to make good this time that he'd put Eden up as collateral for a loan."

"What bank is holding the paper?"

"Bank? Banks and Carson don't speak to each other. He got the money from the Alora Land Conservancy, a farming cooperative."

"Why would farmers lend money to Drury?"

"They're buying up a lot of land north of Encino to keep it out of the hands of developers. It so happens that a developer named Ralph Lockard has been trying to buy Eden from Carson for years. So Carson went to the Alora people and told them if they wouldn't lend him the money, he'd be forced to sell to Lockard. He convinced them that either way it played out, they'd win. If he pulls this gamble off, Eden is safe. If he doesn't, the conservancy gets it. So the farmers forked over."

We arrived back at Tara's garage. Shepard lounged in the doorway, keeping all the shade for himself. "You haven't asked me yet about Carson's enemies," he said.

"How do you know I'm going to?"

"Carson told me when he phoned."

"He told me he didn't have any enemies."

"That's Carson all over. Never met a man who didn't like him. All the same, he wanted me to be sure to mention John Piers Whitehead."

"His partner?"

"They haven't been partners since *Albertsons* died young—or pen pals or even nodding acquaintances. Whitehead's been here in Culver City, though, sniffing around."

"For what?"

"Redemption, Carson said. I don't know what he meant, exactly, but that's nothing new. He won't even speak to Whitehead. The one time the guy actually knocked on our door, I dealt with him. But he didn't know me and wouldn't tell me his business. I bought him a drink and sent him on his way. He seemed like a harmless enough bird, but I guess you can never tell."

"When was this?"

"The morning before the fire." Shepard took a business card out of his shirt pocket and passed it over. Whitehead's novel-length name was printed on the front of the card in small, raised letters. On the back of the card, a shaky hand had written, "59 Belmont Street."

"Easy enough for you?" Shepard asked.

"Too easy," I said.

"It won't stay that way, pally. Not with Carson in the game. Take my word for it."

chapter

6

I DECIDED THAT MY interview with John Piers Whitehead could wait. An arsonist who left engraved calling cards had a certain fish-in-a-barrel quality that made rushing around seem undignified. My boss thought that money might be behind the attacks, and Paddy's nose for a motive was seldom wrong. So I decided to follow Drury's windfall back to its source. Besides, I hadn't had the DeSoto on a really open road in a week. I topped off the tank and headed north to Alora.

My route took me across the Santa Monica Mountains and back in time. I'd lived in the foothills of those mountains after the war, in a cabin on the estate of an old pal from my Paramount days. So the drive made me nostalgic. I also felt sad because my old benefactress was dead. She'd drunk herself to death in a patient, deliberate way, and the memory of that and the little I'd done to stop it added guilt to my emotional mix.

My friend's problem had been obsolescence. For no particular reason, her comfortable career had ground to a halt in the late thirties, as had Ruth Chatterton's and Ann Harding's careers earlier and any number of others since, including my own. The solution I'd worked out for my obsolescence—punching a clock—hadn't fit her. Her own solution had arrived twice a week in brown parcels too discreet to clink, and that had been that.

South of Encino, I drove through miles of inexpensive houses that looked as if they'd all been shoved off the back of the same flatbed. Each instant neighborhood had a different pretentious name painted on its billboard-size entrance sign, but there was a common denominator. Almost all the signs bore the words LOCKARD DEVELOPMENT CORPORATION.

I'd actually been to Alora once, five or six years earlier. I remembered it as a crossroads town in a dusty corner of the valley. My previous visit could have been the week before for all the place had changed. Its outstanding features were still competing produce markets, one to the north of the town and one to the south, and a Spanish mission–style church nestled, with a few stores and shops, between the bookend markets. In front of the church, an old man was sweeping a broad stone plaza with a narrow broom.

I pulled up as close to the plaza as I could and asked the man for the Alora Land Conservancy. He shrugged and suggested I try the cafe next door. While I had him on the line, I asked how to get to Eden.

"You can never get back there once you've left," the old man said. "That's the whole problem with this life."

He laughed, and I did, too. Not at his joke, but at the pleasure he took in it. He was sun-browned and bent, and his white hair was cut like Moe Howard's. When we had collected ourselves, I thanked him and drove the half block to the cafe. The old man watched me until I opened the front door. It was a slow day in Alora.

The cafe was doing better than the town square. Two of its four tables were occupied, as were three of the six stools at the counter. I made it four. The lone waitress brought me a glass of water and a menu card. I'd only come in for information, but the smell of frying onions altered my priorities. I ordered coffee and a hamburger, and made small talk with my neighbors at the counter.

They were farmers. Growing up in Indiana, I'd learned that there were only two kinds of rain as far as farmers were concerned: not enough and too much. My luncheon companions told me that this year's problem was not enough. I made sympathetic comments and kept my questions general until the waitress came by for my empty plate. Then I asked for the Alora Land Conservancy.

"Follow Highway 27 north," the woman said. "You'll see their place. The office is in an old schoolhouse."

She stood there holding my plate, politely giving me the chance to explain my interest in the conservancy. The farmers on either side of me were equally curious.

"Are you gentlemen members?" I asked them.

"Members of what?" the waitress asked me. I'd heard both men speak, so I knew they could, but in the waitress's presence, they were suddenly mute. She reminded me of Brian Donlevy, sans moustache. That is, she called to mind the foreign legion sergeant Donlevy had played in *Beau Geste*. She had the same ramrod posture and suspicious eyes.

"Members of the cooperative," I said. "The Alora Conservancy."

"That's no cooperative," the waitress said. "Who told you that was a cooperative? Whoever it was was pulling your leg. That's a private company. It's going to be the biggest farm in the valley someday. It may be already."

"Except they're not farming," the man on my left said. "Not above ten percent of their holdings."

"You want them to farm in a drought?" Miss Donlevy asked. "Is that how you build an empire?"

"And they're not extending their leases beyond a year," the man on my right said, as much to divide the waitress's wrath, I thought, as to contribute to the conversation. To me he said, "They leased most of their land back to the farmers who sold it to them. That was part of their sales pitch. But they never give anyone more than a year's renewal."

"If they renew a lease at all," the man on my left said.

The woman let out the breath she'd been waiting to use and drew a deeper one. "So they're going to farm the land themselves, so what? It's what I've been telling you all along. They're putting together the biggest farm in the valley. In the state, maybe. That's the only way to make money farming these days."

"Only they're not farming," the man on my left said.

I broke the cycle by dropping some money on the counter and heading outside. I looked for the old theologian, but he had finished his sweeping and gone off, perhaps to nap. I felt a little like a siesta myself after I'd settled into the DeSoto's front seat, its leather heated to the consistency of putty by the afternoon sun. I drove north instead.

Two miles outside of Alora I spotted the schoolhouse. It was red brick with a metal roof that had recently been painted silver. The building looked so much like a country train station that I glanced around, after I'd parked my car, for the tracks.

The name of the conservancy was painted on the front door in letters that had just begun to fade. The door was unlocked. I pushed it open, setting off a tinny buzzer that buzzed on until I'd closed the door behind me.

I had time to note that the receptionist's desk was unstaffed. Then a man appeared in the doorway behind the desk, pulling on the jacket of a pin-striped suit as he came.

"Oh," he said. "I thought you were my ride."

"Nope," I said.

He looked down at the cluttered desk between us. "I gave my girl the day off." And the month preceding it, to judge by the dust on her desk. It was the same yellow-brown stuff the DeSoto had collected, only thicker. "What can I do for you, Mr. . . ."

He was a young man, and he would look that way for years yet if his hair held out. His boyishness was due to his slight build and to his inability to remain at rest. He didn't appear to be nervous or even especially curious, but he was still in a constant state of motion: buttoning and unbuttoning his jacket, shooting his shirt cuffs, smoothing his glistening black hair, and adjusting the knot in his tie so many times that I felt an urge to garrote him with it.

"My name is Elliott. I'm interested in selling you some land, Mr. . . ."

"Faris. Eric Faris. I'm the land agent for the conservancy. You don't look like a farmer."

Where I hailed from, that was a compliment. I considered returning it; Faris certainly didn't look like a land agent. He looked like the kind of errand boy common around Hollywood, the kind with a college degree in his hip pocket.

Faris checked the dusty window to my right for his ride and then said, "Come in, won't you?"

He led me into his office, which was smaller than the reception area, but cleaner. He opened a window, started to take off his suit coat, stopped, and then started again. He was still working at it when he hit his chair. A calendar hanging on the wall behind Faris's head featured a young redhead in bib overalls cut off at mid-thigh. She'd forgotten to wear anything underneath the overalls, but then, it was July. I decided she was there for the enjoyment of Faris's clients. He looked like the type who preferred his pinups painted in oil.

"What's the Alora Land Conservancy all about?" I asked.

As fidgety as Faris was, he was still paying attention. "You must know that if you want to sell us your land."

"I know you're buying farmland around here for the stated reason of keeping it out of developers' hands. You're willing to lease a farm back to the farmer and even to write a guy a loan. I'd like to hear more about that last option."

"Where is your land?" he asked.

"Doyle Heights," I said.

That didn't register, so I added, "In Los Angeles. It's only half an acre, but the view is terrific. And there's the ambiance. The house next door once belonged to Vilma Banky. Vilma sold the place when talkies came in. She had a Hungarian accent that was thicker than your dust."

"What's the gag?" Faris asked.

"That's what I'd like to know. Is this office really a land conservancy? Some of the locals think it's a front for a factory farm. I think maybe Boeing is planning to build its new bomber out here, and you guys got wind of it."

Faris began the process of putting his coat back on. His jaw was clenched, and the hard line aged his baby face considerably. He unclenched long enough to say, "If you'll excuse me."

"Do you remember a loan you made to Carson Drury?"

"I'm not answering questions about our business transactions or anything else." He shut the window and locked it.

"I'm not here to ask questions. I wanted to pass along a little information. Mr. Drury invested the money you gave him in a motion picture. It's almost certain to make a pile, which means he'll be able to pay you back."

"Delighted to hear it," Faris said.

"There is one little problem, though. Someone tried to burn Mr. Drury's studio down the other night. Maybe so he couldn't make his film. Maybe so he couldn't make his loan payments."

Faris actually stopped yanking at his wardrobe for a restful second or two. "What has that to do with us?"

"I just thought you'd like to know. Forewarned is forearmed, after all. If there's one more accident, the police will be around to see you. When they ask you what goes on here, you'll have to tell them."

I wasn't altogether disappointed when a car horn sounded outside, shattering the mood of the moment. I'd strung Faris along about as far as I could on the little I knew.

He saw me to the door. Out front, his ride was seated behind the wheel of a jeep. He was a Mexican wearing a straw hat turned up in front. The hat was the color of the jeep and my car and everything else the dust could reach. The man under the hat was big enough to make the war surplus Willys look like a kiddie car. He joined Faris on the schoolhouse steps, from which they watched me drive off.

I drove north, away from Alora, to a slight rise in the road from which the silver roof of the land office was just visible. I parked there and smoked a Lucky and waited. I hadn't finished the cigarette before I saw a little cloud of dust rise from in front of the building, signaling the jeep's departure. It headed south, and I followed it, debating with myself over which would be easier to force, the office's window or the door.

I never found out. When I neared the little building, I saw the Mexican sitting on the front steps. Across his big knees he balanced a baseball bat. That was gilding the lily, in my opinion.

I waved to him as I drove past.

chapter

7

"THE SEVEN YEAR ITCH," Ella whispered. The whisper was appropriate as she was standing toe to toe with me, tying my tie. I'd once tied a mean bow tie all by myself, but the knack had faded when I'd married, along with several other practical talents—the ability to find the tie, for example.

"Marilyn Monroe," I whispered back.

"I'm not referring to the movie *The Seven Year Itch*," Ella said, not whispering now and then some. "I'm talking about the phenomenon, the tendency of an American husband's mind to wander when he reaches his seventh wedding anniversary. Our seventh is coming up."

"I knew what you meant," I said. "When my mind wanders, it wanders to Marilyn Monroe."

It was bad timing on my part, as Ella had just gotten to the climactic tightening of the finished bow. She took me in half a collar size and then turned away. She was currently wearing a full-length slip cut down to the small of her back. The material glowed like old ivory in the makeup lights of her dressing table.

The slip was a little wrinkled where it fell across her hips. I smoothed it for her and quoted Dick Powell: "I only have eyes for you."

"I'm not afraid your eyes are wandering," Ella said. "I'm worried about a vacant look they've had lately. I'm wondering where you are these days."

It was the second time I'd heard that complaint since I'd returned from scenic Alora. I had decided that it was too late in the day to be strong-arming John Piers Whitehead or anyone else. So I'd driven home to Doyle Heights to wash the valley dust off my car in the driveway shaded by Vilma Banky's hydrangeas. My five-year-old son and three-year-old daughter had helped me, but they hadn't cost me more than an extra thirty minutes.

I'd had plenty of time afterward to mix myself a drink before placing my call to Paddy. Between sips of gin and vermouth, I'd told him what I'd learned from Shepard and found in Alora.

"It would be interesting to know who really owns the land conservancy," I'd said as I'd wrapped things up. "Are you still in solid with that government clerk in Sacramento?"

"Detectives in the movies do that kind of spadework themselves," Paddy had replied.

"They don't have my active social life."

"Or your modest attention span. I swear, Scotty, I don't know what's gotten into you lately. You haven't been this moony since the war."

I had no way of knowing that Ella would shortly take up the same theme in a different key, or I would have been even more surprised by Paddy's rebuke. As it was, I'd been spurred to stick my neck out a little.

"See if your contact at the statehouse can come up with a connection to Ralph Lockard. He's the developer I told you about."

"The one who wants to carve up Drury's estate?"

"I guess it is a long shot. Drury would have to be an idiot to borrow money from the front men of the guy who's after his land."

"I'm liking this angle more and more," Paddy had said. "Don't wear out my girlfriend dancing."

Paddy's girlfriend was applying her eye shadow, so I wandered out to the hi-fi, which happened to be next to the built-in cabinets that served as our bar. It was a Spanish bar, the cabinets' dark wood deeply carved, reflecting the style of the house: 1920s hacienda. Ella did a little more redecorating every time she sold a script, but the house would never be the kind of low-maintenance, low-character box the Lockard Development Corporation was stamping out in the valley.

That didn't bother me. I mixed a pair of Gibsons and started a record playing, "Everything but You." I made the selection randomly, but it had resonance for Ella.

She sipped the drink I handed her and said, "There was music recorded after 1949, wasn't there?"

There was, even new music by Duke Ellington, the composer of the song that was currently playing, but the new stuff wasn't the same. Ellington had fallen into a malaise since the new decade had started, dropping old side men, changing record labels, maybe—I was secretly afraid—losing his way. The phenomenon wasn't one I liked to think about.

"I may have a copy of 'Doggie in the Window' around here someplace," I said.

"Good-bye seventh anniversary," Ella replied.

■ ■ ■

Ella—dressed in a deep coral gown—and I arrived at the Club Satyr a little late. That is, we were only a little late as far as Drury's party was concerned. We were a decade late for the Satyr. Back in the early forties, it had been one of the town's hottest night spots. After the war it had struggled on as a place where you could always get a table when the other clubs were full. Now you could rent the whole building on short notice for ready money.

The building in question was a long, low one set into the side of a wooded hill. The entryway was a little tunnel with an arched roof and blank walls broken only by a hatcheck window. The girl who smiled out at us from the window had been in grade school when they'd laid the hallway's carpet. I caught my toe on a half-parted seam of the stuff and swore softly.

For some reason the old club was hitting me square in the mood that Ella and Paddy had both noted, which I'd dubbed "Mood Indigo" as a nod to Ellington. Being the strong, silent type, I'd thought the mood was my little secret, and it bothered me that everyone but the kid who mowed our lawn had spotted it.

Ella, who'd brightened considerably at the sight of the old nightclub, had a secret of her own. She said something I couldn't hear above the growing jumble of voices and music. She tried again as we arrived at the threshold of the main room: "We've been here before."

"Probably a dozen times," I shouted back.

"No. I mean, we've been through this night before. Think about it and get back to me later."

Just finding her later was going to be a challenge. The old nightclub was jammed with people, some in the black tie and evening gowns Drury had specified, others in more casual, colorful attire. Their host didn't seem the least bit put out by the variety. He'd followed his own instructions and worn a black tie, but it was big and limp and made him look like a prosperous poet. He was towering over the crowd near the center of the room, his leonine head just brushing the bank of cigarette smoke trapped by the textured plaster of the ceiling.

"They still turn out for Carson Drury," Ella said.

And free liquor, I thought, but it wasn't worth shouting. I was scanning the room for the quietest corner when Drury caught my eye and signaled me to fight my way through to him. I waded into the crowd, Ella following close behind me with one hand on my collar, steering me gently. I didn't mind the backseat driving because my concentration was lagging a little. Ella's thumb was playing with the hair on my neck, and her body pressed gently against my back every time I paused to avoid a full glass or a lit cigarette.

Beyond Drury was a little stage whose proscenium arch was a miniature imitation of the acoustical shell of the Hollywood Bowl. I'd noted on an earlier visit to the club that the arch was a phony, a skillful painting done on the flat back wall by some set designer who dabbled in trompe l'oeil. In front of this special effect, a little combo was doing its best to sound like an orchestra. As we struggled forward, they struck up the theme from an old Cary Grant movie, *Mr. Lucky.* The song was called "Something to Remember You By," and it gave me the answer to Ella's riddle about having lived this night before.

I couldn't turn to face her in the press of people, so I twisted my head around and said, "You're thinking of the evening we met."

Ella rewarded me with a pat on the head, while I thought back to that first meeting. It had taken place at a party promoting a movie in progress, but that's where the similarity to the current evening ended. I remembered a bigger band and a smaller crowd and a hotel ballroom the size of a polo field. But I knew there had to be some common ground. Now that Ella had prodded my memory, I was feeling the déjà vu in spades.

I turned my head again and shouted, "What's the connection?"

Ella pressed hard against me this time so she could speak the answer in my ear: "You're the connection, Scotty. I haven't seen you so lost since that first night."

chapter

8

DRURY WAS IN THE MIDDLE of another story, his meal ticket voice easily reducing the hundred or so other speakers in the old nightclub to the category of background noise. He was reminiscing about the night he'd offered to fight Errol Flynn outside the Satyr, back during the club's heyday and his own. Drury had reached the story's payoff—Flynn marching out the front door, rolling up his sleeves, while Drury ran out the back—when Ella and I arrived in his presence. The little combo on the bandstand wrapped up their tribute to Cary Grant at that same moment, allowing Drury to greet us at his normal but still generous volume.

"You're hiding something from me, Scotty," he said, speaking so seriously that I almost looked down at my empty hands. "Out with it."

Before I could start searching my pockets, Drury took Ella's hand from my shoulder and guided her around in front of me. "I've been hoping to meet you, Mrs. Elliott. Or do you prefer Miss Englehart?"

"Call me Ella," she said, leaving Drury's question hanging in the smoky air.

"I admired your screenplay for *Private Hopes*," he said. "In the hands of a gifted director, it would have won you the Academy Award."

Drury's gifted hands were still holding Ella's. He backed up his compliment with enough detail to convince me that he'd actually seen Ella's movie, and I wondered if she was the reason Drury had asked for me when he'd called Hollywood Security. While I considered the pros and cons of feeling jealous, Drury's previous audience—an actress who specialized in low-budget swashbucklers, her current husband, and a singing cowboy who now owned a string of hamburger stands—drifted away.

One faithful listener hung on, a moustached guy with a serious tan whose glass was half-empty and whose bleary blue eyes were half-full. His handshake was firm enough, though, and his diction exact if a touch provincial.

"Gilbert Traynor," he said when I'd introduced myself. I recognized the name from my talk with Hank Shepard. Traynor was Drury's latest gull, the guy who was paying for the room and the band and the drink I'd yet to find. I thought about asking him whether he'd met Jane Russell yet, but kidding a drunk wasn't my idea of a fun evening. Instead, I asked after his connection to Drury, McNally the rubber company heir.

Traynor's sleek head did a cross between a shake and a bob. "Not here tonight. Wish he were. Ty and I were fraternity brothers at Purdue."

The name of the Indiana school and the familiar, hard-edged quality of Traynor's speech allowed me to place him geographically. Tyrone McNally and his tire company were from Ohio, which is where I'd mentally slotted Traynor during my talk with Shepard. But the publicist had said only that Traynor was from the Midwest. Now I belatedly made the connection to the Traynor Automobile Company of Traynorville, Indiana, a little, one-industry town an hour north of Indianapolis.

"Your family built the Traynor Phaeton Six," I said. "It was a beauty."

Traynor's eyes became a little less glassy. "Yes, it was. All we make nowadays are parts for other people's cars. More money in that and less risk. Not the same as having your name across the front of a finished car, though."

Hank Shepard shouldered his way through the Carson Drury fan club members to my left. He took Traynor's half-empty glass and handed him a full one. "There you go," he said. He banged me on the shoulder. "What do you think? Is this great or is this great? What can I get for you?"

I looked around for Ella, but she and Drury had been squeezed out of earshot. "I'll take a Gibson," I said.

"A Gibson," Shepard repeated, his pug nose lifted high for effect. "And you're the guy who tried to tell me he'd never heard of Wordsworth. Be right back."

Traynor was looking down at the drink in his hand with a slightly puzzled expression, as though the glass had refilled itself.

"Can I get rid of that for you?" I asked.

"No. It's all right. I'll nurse it. How do you happen to remember the Phaeton Six?"

I told him I'd grown up in Indiana, where I'd often heard Traynor mentioned in the same breath with Cord and Duesenberg. He shook my hand all over again.

"It's great to meet another Hoosier out here. Just between you and me, I've been feeling a little like a bumpkin tonight. I'm almost anxious to get back to Traynorville where I can actually snub people."

I smiled at his joke, but it was easy enough to picture Traynor playing lord of the manor at some Traynorville barbershop or the local equivalent of the Club Satyr. He was handsome by small-town America standards, at least in profile. Full on, his head looked a trifle narrow, and his regular, delicate features seemed pinched together. It wasn't a major defect, but it meant that, by Hollywood standards, he was the next nearest thing to invisible.

My highly visible wife squeezed in beside me, and I did the introductions. Traynor waited politely until she had extended her hand, then he pumped it so hard that Ella had to adjust the straps of her gown when he'd finished.

"I was just telling your husband that I've spent my life dreaming of escaping from Traynorville, Indiana, and tonight I'm missing the place. Doesn't say too much for the depth of my soul, does it?"

That sounded like Ella's department, so I let her field the question while I looked over the crowd for firebugs. Most of the people I recognized were inhabitants of the permanent understory of the Hollywood forest, the writer-agent-designer–size plants that got along so well in the shade of the big trees. The trees themselves were noticeably absent. Aside from Joseph Coffin, there were only one or two genuine stars, and those were older, slightly out-of-date ones. In fact, the age of the crowd in general made the gathering feel more like a reunion than a coming-out party.

The auld lang syne flavor was reinforced by the photographs that decorated the walls of the club, blowups of publicity stills from the original filming of *The Imperial Albertsons* in 1942. The costumes that the actors wore in the photos were all turn-of-the-century, but they weren't what made the pictures seem like period pieces. It was the photography itself, the otherworldly clarity of it, a style that had been losing ground to grainy realism since the fifties came in. The subjects of the photos were also out of step with the new reality. They weren't real human beings or even meant to pass for real human beings. They were Hollywood stars from the age when the title had really meant something.

I was reminiscing so hard that I didn't notice Hank Shepard return until he handed me a Gibson that filled a highball glass.

"The large economy size," he said. "It'll save me a trip or two to the bar. Suddenly, I'd rather be dancing—if you and Pidgin don't mind, that is."

"Ella," I said, but the combo had come back to life, and Shepard didn't hear me. I watched him pantomime his invitation to Ella. She seemed to remember him, but none too fondly, which pleased me.

Still, she acquiesced. They headed for the dance floor together, Ella leading the way.

I looked around for Drury, thinking that I might pass the time by quizzing him on Eden and the gamble he'd taken with it. Before I could find the director, Gilbert Traynor and his bottomless glass found me. He took me by the arm and led me away from the packed center of the room, to a corner near the unused end of the bandstand. The peewee orchestra was directing its efforts toward the crowd we'd left behind, so here, on the group's flank, it was almost peaceful.

Traynor was feeling as nostalgic as I was, but over a different lost time. "Funny you should mention the Phaeton Six tonight," he said, his hand on my shoulder. "I'd just been thinking about the old days when the family built automobiles instead of rearview mirrors. Carson got me thinking back. He told me about this movie of his over lunch." He gestured toward the photos on the wall behind me. "*The Imperial* something."

"*Albertsons*," I said.

"Thanks," Traynor said. "Carson had no idea—couldn't have had any idea—what that story meant to me. It was my family's story. The Traynors could have been the heroes of his movie, the inventors who changed the world with their automobile and put the goddamn Albertsons in their place."

I'd gotten to know Drury too well over the course of the day to believe that he was unaware of the parallels between his movie and the sentimental Traynor's family history. I should have warned the sap—one Hoosier to another—to keep his checkbook buttoned up, but that would have been taking bread out of Paddy's mouth as well as Drury's.

"What do you do for the company?" I asked.

"I'm the president, which is another way of saying I don't do much. That's the real problem with the Traynor family. The pioneers and the inventors are dead. The only ones left are the figureheads. The hood ornaments, I should say."

Traynor kept talking, but I stopped listening. Over his shoulder I could see the dance floor and on it Ella and Shepard. Ella had just moved the publicist's right hand upward from the small of her back where it had strayed. The big hand strayed even farther down when she released it. Ella was trying to push herself clear of Shepard as I handed my drink to Traynor. I reached them just as the grinning Shepard blocked Ella's openhanded left cross by grabbing her wrist. I grabbed his in turn and squeezed it until he let Ella go.

"Excuse us," I said to her as I twisted Shepard's arm around behind his back. All I heard of her reply was my name.

Shepard was facing the double doors of the kitchen, conveniently enough. I shoved him forward, and we passed harmlessly through the intervening dancers as though Hermes Pan himself had choreographed our exit. Shepard stretched out his free arm to push open the swinging doors, almost decking a Chinese waiter with a tray of little sandwiches. The waiter smiled broadly as we passed him.

When the doors swung shut, I could hear Shepard addressing me. "Will you listen to me, Elliott? Let go of my goddamn arm and listen to me."

I looked around for the exit that Drury had used on the night he'd snookered Errol Flynn, but I couldn't find it. Meanwhile, the kitchen staff—more Chinese—were taking a lively interest in us. I spotted another swinging door and pushed Shepard through it. We ended up in a walk-in pantry lined with shelves of cans and boxes. It was only five feet wide and ten feet deep, but that was big enough for my purposes.

I gave Shepard a shove toward the far end of the closet and released his arm. He twisted around to face me, still talking a blue streak.

"Get out of my way, Elliott. I'm warning you. You lay another hand on me, and you'll hear some things you'd rather not know."

"Like what, for example?"

Shepard looked smug and said nothing.

"Things about my wife?"

The smug look became a sneer.

"Like she slept with a few soldiers she felt sorry for during the war?" I asked. "Like she fell to pieces inside when her brother was killed in France? That she was so deadened by it that after the war she'd wander home with any man who came along, even a heel like you?"

Shepard had paled steadily as I'd squandered his bargaining chips. I stepped forward, nice guy that I was, to catch him if he fainted. He took advantage of my good nature and threw a right, telegraphing his plan with a nervous glance at my idle left hand. With that kind of notice, I could have blocked the punch in my sleep. Awake I did even better, hitting Shepard square on the chin and driving him into the loaded shelves behind him.

In a movie the shelves would have collapsed, showering the publicist's blond head with noisy odds and ends and maybe even a bag of flour as a topper. I had to make do with Shepard collapsing in his own little heap, the collar of his tuxedo jacket up around his droopy ears.

Ella was waiting for me outside the kitchen doors. She didn't look the least bit concerned for my safety, I was flattered to see. No one else took any notice of my return or Shepard's absence. Certainly the musicians didn't. They were laying into "Stardust" like they held the copyright.

"Let's dance," I said.

"I promised the next one to your friend from Indiana," Ella said. "But now that he's seen the way you cut in, he'll probably give up his turn."

"That'll save you from hearing about Traynorville," I said, taking her in my arms.

"Hearing more about Traynorville, you mean," Ella said.

We began to move to the music, but not in our old, easy way.

"I can handle guys like Hank Shepard," Ella said. She'd meant her delivery to be matter-of-fact, I thought, but it came out sounding tired.

"Just like I can tie a bow tie," I said. "Only being an old married guy, I don't have to."

We struggled on, trying to find the walnut shell under which the band had hidden the beat. When Ella spoke again, she returned to the subject of Traynorville.

"Quaint little custom you Hoosiers have, naming towns after yourselves. So nice for the post office. There's an Elliottville, I presume. Or is it Elliott Town?"

"Elliottopolis," I said. "We had to change it, though. Pronouncing it gave people the hiccups."

"Seeing it in print would cure them," Ella said. Then she put her head on my shoulder.

chapter

9

ELLA AND I LEFT the party early, soon after Hank Shepard emerged blinking from the kitchen. The next morning we slept in as long as the kids let us. I hung around the house after that, playing catch in the front yard and listening for the phone. I was expecting a call from Paddy announcing that we'd been fired because I'd pasted Drury's right-hand man. I wasn't sure how Paddy would take it, but my guess was he wouldn't be pleased. He would have preferred my pasting Drury.

The call hadn't come by ten o'clock, so I drove downtown to 59 Belmont Street, armed with my winning smile and a hip flask. Shepard had mentioned buying John Piers Whitehead a drink before he'd sent him packing. From what I'd seen of Shepard, the drink might have been his own idea. Then again, it might have been Whitehead's price for cooperating. So I decided to have a second payment handy.

Belmont Street was not included on chamber of commerce tours of Los Angeles, to judge by its weedy lawns, quilted pavement, and the veteran sedans and coupés squeezed against its curbs. The residents were spaced out better than their cars. Whitehead's block had only small apartment buildings and private homes, although several of the bigger houses had been divided into flats.

Fifty-nine Belmont had never been a private home. The white stucco building with the red tile roof contained four apartments, two up and two down, the upper ones serviced by a balcony that spanned the front of the building and a staircase that ran from the balcony to the front walk.

I couldn't find a directory, so I checked each apartment in turn. Whitehead lived on the southern side of the second floor. He'd lived there for some time, too. The little paper nameplate in the slot on his mailbox had acquired a sepia tone.

The man who answered the door could have used some sun himself. His wool vest and tie were inappropriate for July in Southern California, but they looked—and smelled—like Whitehead had worn them through a decade of Julys. His head was small and well along on its way to hairless. What hair he had left was combed forward like an antique Roman's. He had the features of a Roman senator—his nose high-arched and his chin square—but his skin was blotchy, and his eyes had a yellow cast. I was prepared for Whitehead to be older than Drury—everybody seemed to be—but not this much older. I guessed him to be in his late fifties, which meant he'd been pushing forty when he and the teenage Drury had set Broadway on fire.

"What do you want?" he asked.

"I represent Carson Drury," I said. "I'd like to talk with you." As I said it, I realized that I was up against the same problem Hank Shepard had faced when he'd dealt with Whitehead. Drury's old partner hadn't confided in Shepard because he hadn't known him. Whitehead didn't know me, either, or so I thought. I had one of my Hollywood Security business cards out, but I didn't need it.

"You're Scott Elliott," he said, shaking my hand. "You were in *Rhythm on the River* with Mary Martin and Bing Crosby and Basil Rathbone."

"That picture was made fifteen years ago. How do you happen to remember it?"

I'd said something wrong. Whitehead's smile faded away. "I remember things," he said.

"May I come in?"

Whitehead half-turned toward the dark room behind him and then shook his head. "I was just going out. For breakfast," he added.

"I can always use a second breakfast. I'll buy if you'll let me tag along. It isn't every day somebody recognizes me."

I was trying to point out that we had something in common: membership in the Has-Beens of America Society. That link or my offer to buy won the point for me. Whitehead kept me waiting while he found the jacket that matched his vest. Then he led me east on Belmont to Olympic Boulevard.

"It's just a short walk," he said. "I never drive."

As we passed the DeSoto, I considered tossing my flask through its open window. Now that I'd actually met Whitehead, I was even less comfortable with the idea of liquoring him up. He wouldn't have thanked me for the gesture. When we reached the corner, he gazed at a bar called Maxie's as though it was the girl he'd left behind.

Across the boulevard from the bar was an old-fashioned, railroad-style dining car. "There we go," I said. "Just what we need."

I took Whitehead by his patched elbow and led him across the four lanes of homicidal traffic. The diner's lunchtime crowd hadn't arrived yet, assuming the place had a lunchtime crowd. I found us a booth with plenty of privacy and ordered coffee and bacon and eggs from a waitress who didn't know she was dealing with two celebrities. Whitehead seconded my choices without much enthusiasm. After the coffee arrived, I offered him a cigarette. He held it very delicately, between his thumb and forefinger, but he drew on it like a man siphoning gasoline.

"What exactly are you after from Drury?" I asked.

His yellowed eyes avoided mine like twin butterflies dodging the same net. "Oscar Levant was in that movie, too," he said. He moved his tongue around in his mouth, inspecting his teeth. *"Rhythm on the River."*

"I remember," I said.

"Not as well as I do," Whitehead said, his voice so dry it brought dusty Alora to mind.

"How could that be?"

He shrugged and cleared his throat.

"Have some coffee," I said.

"Don't have a taste for it, thank you."

"Let me sweeten it for you." I unscrewed the top of the flask before removing it from the pocket of my suit coat. There wasn't much room in Whitehead's mug. Just enough for one healthy shot of rye.

He didn't ask why I wasn't joining him. He was beyond that kind of pleasantry. He took the mug from me and made room for another shot. I poured it and put the flask back in my pocket. I didn't bother replacing the cap.

"What are you doing for Carson?" Whitehead asked, his feathery voice gaining strength with each word. "Are you in production now? You can't be acting for him; he's using the original *Albertsons* cast."

"You answer one for me first," I said. "How is it you knew about Drury's latest project? It was supposed to be a secret."

"Kay Lamantia told me." Whitehead was holding his mug beneath his Roman nose, inhaling its fragrance. "Kay was our costume designer on *First Citizen* and *Imperial Albertsons.* Carson tried to hire her for the reshoot, but she wouldn't come out of retirement. She was nice enough to call me for a chat."

He took another killer drag on his cigarette and waited for me to live up to my end of our bargain.

"The company I work for was hired by Drury," I said. "We're in the security business. I haven't been an actor since the war. There are various schools of thought on why my career ended. One is that the studios lost interest in me. Another says that I lost interest in acting. I like to think I just aged out of my character, like Mickey Rooney."

Whitehead actually looked as though he wanted to console me, which didn't brighten my day. "You asked me how I happened to recall that movie of yours," he said. "It's a funny thing. I don't remember the movie I saw last week as well as I do *Rhythm on the River*.

"We went to its premiere shortly after we arrived in Hollywood— Carson and Alice, the socialite Carson was married to at the time, and I. He was already having an affair with that German actress, but poor Alice didn't know it. She and Carson were like two children at that premiere. So excited to meet Mr. Levant, I remember. I remember everything about that night: what Alice wore, where we sat, who snubbed us and who was nice, where we ate afterward. The entire golden time between that premiere and our own is sealed in my memory forever. They were the happiest days of my life."

"The happiness ended with the *Albertsons* premiere?"

"No, with the premiere of *First Citizen*." He looked down at the last swallow in his mug and decided to hoard it. "We had to release the picture in New York, you know. Hollywood was up in arms over our treatment of D. W. Griffith. But the change of venue worked to our advantage. New York still loved Carson, so the first night was a triumph. Poor Alice was gone by then, but then so was the German actress. Carson had moved on to that opera singer person. I remember feeling sorry for Alice that night in New York, which was vanity on my part. I was next on Carson's hit list."

The waitress brought our food, cutting off Whitehead's performance. I thought I'd have to prime his pump again, but after he'd pushed his plate away untouched, he helped himself to another Lucky from the pack I'd left on the table and continued his story.

"Carson's always been an artist who dictated his work. Brilliant? Yes. Inspired? Yes. But utterly dependent on other people to bring his ideas to life. On Broadway I was the expert he needed. In 1938, when he found me, I was heading up a little theater group for Roosevelt's

Works Progress Administration, producing, directing, raising the curtain, collecting the tickets. One day Carson showed up on my doorstep with notes for a radical new *Hamlet* under his arm. He'd just gotten back from Europe, where he'd been touring with a circus.

"That's what my life was like from then on, a circus. Before I knew it, I was producing a *Hamlet* directed by and starring Carson Drury in a barn of a theater called the Empire Palace. It was the kind of theater you book ice shows into, not Shakespeare, but Carson filled it night after night. The play would have run for a year if its star hadn't gotten bored.

"After that it was one project after another. More of them failed than succeeded, but that didn't matter. Carson always used a new idea to eclipse an old failure. Together we formed Repertory One, with Carson as the brilliant innovator and me as the one who changed the light bulbs."

Whitehead pushed his empty mug across to me. I signaled the waitress, and she brought her coffeepot over.

"Just half a cup, please," Whitehead told her.

She noted his full plate, sniffed at his breath or maybe just at him, shrugged, and went away.

I filled the empty part of his cup. He nodded in acknowledgment and drank, this time in a slow, thoughtful way.

"I got my first hint of trouble when we moved into radio. I was out of my depth at first, and Carson knew it. I was even more lost at RKO."

"Why did he even bring you out here?"

"He was a little frightened of the move, I think. He wanted familiar faces around him. But he felt at home soon enough. Carson has a natural genius for gauging the potential of a medium—and exploiting it. It wasn't long before he'd surrounded himself with the best soundmen, cameramen, special effects artists. He began dictating to them directly, shutting me out.

"It was worse after the *First Citizen* premiere. Everyone in town was calling Carson a genius, even the people who hated him. He barely involved me in *The Imperial Albertsons*. He would have shut me out completely if he hadn't hated dealing with the studio executives. He used me as a buffer, so he could pretend the front office didn't exist. He regretted that later. As did I."

"Let's talk about that," I said. "What happened after the *Albertsons* preview in Yorba Linda?"

Whitehead drained his mug and pushed it across to me. We'd reached the point of diminishing returns as far as his drinking was concerned. He was slurring his words, and his cheery bonhomie was starting to turn belligerent. Worse than that, I knew my little flask was nearing empty.

"First the answer," I said, "then the drink."

"To hell with you, sir," Whitehead said. "They sell the stuff across the street."

"Sell it is right. I'm giving it away."

"The devil you are," Whitehead said. In the end, though, he came across.

"The preview was a disaster. There was talk of shelving the picture completely, of scrapping it entirely. Think of what that would have done to Carson's reputation."

"And yours," I said.

"And mine. So I negotiated a way out for us. I agreed to make the changes the studio required. Our film editor was a talented young man who wanted to direct. Under my supervision he reshot Carson's dark ending, substituting a positive, uplifting one."

"A happy ending," I said to sum up.

"We calmed the studio's fears and got through a second preview. We saved the picture. I saved the picture."

"Whose idea was it to burn Drury's footage?"

Whitehead's eyes took evasive action again. He pushed his empty mug forward an inch. "I don't know. Someone in the front office."

We'd returned to my first question. I poured out what was left of the rye. "Why are you still interested in *Albertsons*?"

Whitehead was muttering again. "Is that so strange? It was my film, too."

To a greater extent than I'd been told. That suggested another possibility. "It won't be your film if Drury pulls this off. He'll do to your ending what somebody did to his. Does that bother you? Would you try to keep that from happening?"

"Why would I want to? That ending brought me nothing but misery. My friends at RKO didn't keep me on a week after Carson was fired. They used me and discarded me. I curse the day I agreed to change *Albertsons.* I'd burn my ending myself if I could."

"Three nights ago somebody tried to do just that. Only this somebody tried to burn the whole negative, Drury's work and yours."

Whitehead spilled what was left in his mug onto the rubber tabletop. We watched it run to a low spot under the napkin holder. Then he whispered, "You said *tried.* Is the film safe?"

"For the moment. It's my job to keep it safe."

Whitehead was closing up shop. He started to work his way out of the booth, a slow inch at a time. "Tell Carson I'll call on him."

"Why? What is it you want?"

A little of Whitehead's belly fire flared back to life. "Haven't you been listening to me? It was my film, too. All of it. My future, too. If there's any future left in *Albertsons,* part of it is mine."

AFTER WHITEHEAD stumbled out, I felt like taking a shower or a poke at someone. Hank Shepard again preferably. But Shepard wasn't around and no volunteers stepped forward, so I used the diner's phone booth to call Hollywood Security.

Peggy Maguire answered the phone. I was used to her voice brightening at the sound of mine, but the reaction still gave me a lift. After I'd married, Peggy had stopped asking whether I'd eaten and reminding me to wear my hat in the sun. But I knew she still wanted to ask and remind. She and Paddy had no kids of their own, and she'd had to make do with her wayward employees.

When I asked for her husband, she said, "He's off holding Joan Crawford's hand."

"What's that pay an hour?"

"My guess is, he's paying her."

I asked if the boss had left me any messages about the Alora Land Conservancy. It would have been fast work if Paddy had traced the company's ownership, so I wasn't surprised when Peggy said, "Alora who?"

I rang off after promising, for old times' sake, to eat a good lunch. First, though, I'd have to work off my second breakfast. Paddy had kidded me about detectives in the movies doing their own spade-work, but I knew from my own movie going that they often skipped the research and bluffed out a hunch. I decided to give that approach a try.

I got the address of the Lockard Development Corporation from the remains of the diner's phone book. On my way across Olympic Boulevard, I thought about checking in at Maxie's, the bar at the corner of Belmont, to see if Whitehead had stopped by for a nightcap. I decided I didn't want to know.

The Lockard office was in Burbank, in a modest building surrounded by sample homes. Each show home had a name that had probably taken more time to work up than its floor plan. On my way to the office I passed the El Dorado, the Exeter, and the Petite Maison, dodging a different salesman at each house, bright young men with too many vitamins in their systems, like the Alora land agent, Eric Faris.

The interior of the office building was air-conditioned and deeply carpeted. I asked the receptionist, an ash blond with the posture of a gymnast, for Lockard.

"Sorry," she said in the breathy kind of voice that was popular that year. "He's not in the office. Too nice a day for that." She was older than the salesboys out on the lot, but not too old. My age, in fact.

"Is he out on a building site?"

"Too nice a day for that, too," she said. "Only the peons are stuck at work on a day like today. Is that your Fireflite parked out front?"

I said it was.

"Nice." She ran the safe end of a gold ballpoint around the crisp edge of her lipstick. "Is it as fast as it looks?"

"No," I said. On the off chance we weren't talking about my car anymore, I added, "Not these days."

"Too bad," she said.

The phone on her desk rang. She answered it without taking her eyes off me. She was still playing with the golden pen, now tapping a desk calendar with it. She told the party on the other end of the line, "Let me check." Then she swiveled her chair around to consult a ledger on the credenza behind her.

I stepped up to consult the open calendar. The spot she'd been tapping with her pen was a one-word entry for two o'clock. The word was Riviera.

She swiveled around again as I reached the office door. I touched my hat brim, and she winked at me.

Riviera Country Club was west of the city, just off the Coast Highway in Pacific Palisades. I'd filled a vacancy in a foursome there once for Olivia De Havilland on a sunny Sunday afternoon and come away dreaming of my own membership. I must have dreamt about it pretty damn intensely. That one round had been played during Roosevelt's second term, but the clubhouse still looked familiar to me. It rose up from the rim of Santa Monica Canyon like a Spanish monastery standing guard over its vineyards—these vineyards being tight, wooded fairways and half-acre greens.

I asked the kid drafted to park my car if Ralph Lockard was on the premises. He directed me to a basement grill. There, feeling out of place in both my street clothes and my income bracket, I asked again for the developer. The bartender directed me back outside, to the practice putting green.

"Look for the Big Ten lineman," he said.

My plan was to throw Lockard off balance by showing up unexpectedly and hitting him with his secret tie to the Alora Land Conservancy. If he didn't look blank or faint dead away, I'd keep him off balance with one tough question after another until I knew everything about him but his hat size.

The plan broke down shortly after I cast my shadow across the line of the developer's putt. He looked up at me without coming out of his crouched stance.

"You're Elliott, I presume," he said.

He was certainly big enough to have played lineman, maybe without pads. His broad nose was as concave as Whitehead's was convex, and his eyebrows were thickened by scar tissue. His eyes had a faraway look. I decided that it was a trick of their slate gray color. There was nothing faraway about the examination he was giving me.

"I've been expecting you," he said, "but not here. How did you track me down?"

"The caddy master's on our payroll."

He stood up and pushed his white cap backward on his head. The resemblance to Ben Hogan didn't end with his hat. He was dressed in a white polo shirt and black trousers. A gentleman golfer, down to the little leather kilts on his shoes.

"Whose payroll would that be?" he asked.

I gave him the business card I'd had ready for Whitehead and asked, "Your man Faris told you I'd be calling?"

"Let's get this over with. Faris is my employee, and the Alora Land Conservancy is my company. You knew that already."

"Actually, I was playing a hunch."

Lockard shrugged. "You would have found out soon enough. It's all a matter of public record. All legal and aboveboard."

"No misrepresentation?"

"No."

"Not even in the line you're handing the farmers about saving their land from developers?"

"I am saving it from developers. Other developers. Look, we give the farmers a minimum number of years the land will be protected. That minimum will be met, believe me."

"Then the farms get the Lockard touch."

Another shrug. "It'd happen sooner without the conservancy. And the farmers wouldn't do any better financially. We're paying top dollar, and they know it."

"How about the ones who wouldn't have sold to a developer at any price?"

"You're getting too hypothetical for me. I deal in facts and figures. Let me lay a few out for you. In 1944, only one hundred and seventy thousand people lived in the San Fernando Valley. By 1960, five years from now, there'll be a million people out there. I'm selling homes as fast as I can build them, but I'm only one of the guys doing it. If I still want to be in business in '60 when the last schmo moves in, I've got to line up the land now."

He paused to greet a couple of gray-haired gentlemen who looked as if they were playing hookey from the top floor of the same bank. Then he stepped closer to me so he could continue his lecture in a quieter voice.

"The Alora Conservancy isn't a scam to cheat the bean growers. It's an end around the other developers, the chumps who think the western end of the valley is still sitting there for the taking."

"Where does Drury's ranch fit in?"

"Have you ever seen it?"

"No."

"It's the best land left in the valley—rolling pasture, some woodland, good water. It'll be the best thing I ever do. No tract homes there, believe me. They'll be little estates, no two alike, with a lake as the centerpiece and a private golf course. I may retire there myself."

"Assuming you get the land. Or is that an assumption?"

Lockard tugged his cap back down and resumed his stance over his last three practice balls. "I don't scare as easily as Faris. In fact, I don't scare. We had nothing to do with any fire, if there really was a fire. Anyone who runs around saying we did is going to find himself in court. That goes for Drury and any shady characters working for him."

Before I could express my hurt feelings over the shady crack, another golfer joined us. Judging by his straw hat and its natty Hawaiian ribbon, he modeled his swing after Sam Snead. "Ready, Ralph?" he asked. "We're on deck."

"Be right there," Lockard said.

"Imagine how I felt," he said to me when Snead had gone. "I've wanted Eden since I struck out on my own in '49. Drury wouldn't even haggle with me. Then he turns around and drops the ranch in my lap."

"It hasn't dropped yet."

"It will. And without me shaking the tree. I may only be a social-climbing carpenter, but I have a lot of contacts in the movie business. I know Drury's history as well as he knows it himself. Better, if he believes half the bullshit he spreads around. He needs my help to fail like the Dodgers need help to blow a World Series."

"Checked the paper lately?" I asked. "Brooklyn is pretty hot this year."

Lockard stroked the first of his three balls into the back of the cup. "It's July, buddy," he said. He rammed the second putt home, but it still dropped. "For the Dodgers, I mean." The last ball hung for a second on the lip and then fell. "For Drury, it's late September."

chapter

11

I DIDN'T HANG AROUND to watch Lockard tee off. He was surely willing himself a long, straight drive, and I didn't want to see it come to pass. I reclaimed the DeSoto and drove east to Beverly Hills where the originals of the little estates Lockard dreamt of building resided. My appetite hadn't returned—if anything, it had wandered farther away—so I had to lie about lunch when I called Peggy to tell her where I'd be. On the same stop I bought a fresh pack of cigarettes, Old Golds instead of my usual Lucky Strikes. They were my ticket of admission for the visit I intended to make, not unlike the whiskey I'd used earlier with John Piers Whitehead.

I'd been thinking of stopping by to see Torrance Beaumont ever since Ella's bout of déjà vu at the Club Satyr. The party she'd been remembering that night, the party at which we'd met, had promoted a Tory Beaumont picture that had ended up unfinished. It never would be finished now, not with Beaumont starring. The actor was terminally ill with cancer.

I'd been visiting Beaumont every couple of weeks or so for a year, as part of a rotation of his old friends and drinking buddies. During that year I'd watched him struggle back from eight hours on an operating table and then begin a long, steady slide. For one reason or another I hadn't been by the estate on Summit Drive for a month, and I felt bad about that. But I wasn't going now because my conscience bothered me. I was going because everything bothered me.

The wrought-iron gates on Summit were open, so I drove through them and parked on the curving drive, pausing to admire the Technicolor landscaping that Beaumont had paid for but probably couldn't describe: the hibiscus, the oleander, the fuchsia. Then again, maybe Beaumont could name every gaudy plant and do it in Latin. Maybe he'd started them from seeds in his own little greenhouse. If he had, he'd never admit it.

Beaumont liked the tough guy image that Hollywood had given him, the most enduring of the several identities he'd assumed in the course of a long acting career. I'd always thought of him as a well-educated, sensitive man who wore his gangster persona for the same reasons he liked a beat-up old suit: because it was comfortable, because it helped him fit in. Since his illness, I'd come to see that I'd sold him short. Toughness was more than a pose for Beaumont.

His house was a Tudor revival whose previous owner had been a successful plastic surgeon. Beaumont called the place Nose Job Manor and liked to tell people that he got it as a settlement when his face lift didn't take.

The heavy front door was answered by the English butler. Everyone called him Moody, but I was never sure whether that was his name or a brief description. After he'd greeted me, Moody managed to ask where the hell I'd been keeping myself without actually putting the question into words. Not trimming his eyebrows gave him certain advantages in the emoting department. He took me through the quiet, cool interior of the house. At the glass doors that overlooked the pool, he stopped long enough to ask if I required cigarettes. I tapped my pocket, and he led the way out.

The big, kidney-shaped pool was backed by a bathing pavilion that looked like a Chinese pagoda. Either the pavilion's architect hadn't noticed the pile of Tudor on the other side of the pool, or else he'd wanted to make some personal statement on the East-meets-West debate. As we crossed the lawn, I noted two fresh wheel tracks in the grass and looked around for the wheelchair Moody had used to take his employer out to the water. It was hidden away somewhere safe. The chair Beaumont now occupied was wheelless and straight-backed, and it had arms flat and broad enough to hold a glass.

The man in the chair was wearing an old yachting cap, an older windbreaker, and gray suit pants that had been pressed sometime in the last twenty minutes. He sat with his feet and knees together, the knees leaning a little to one side. The glass on the arm of his chair was empty.

As Beaumont and I shook hands, Moody brought a chair around for me, placing it upwind of his boss.

"What brings you here, soldier?" Beaumont asked. "I thought you'd forgotten my address. The usual Gibson for Mr. Elliott, Moody, and another scotch for me. Better make it a pitcher of Gibsons. He looks like he's seen a ghost."

That was a joke at Beaumont's own expense. He'd spotted how shocked I was at the change in him. Luckily, my reaction amused him. Or maybe my attempt to hide it did.

"And you wanted to be an actor," he said. "Take off that goddamn tie and relax."

I loosened my tie, dug out the Old Golds, and lit one, blowing the smoke in Beaumont's direction. He drank it in with half-closed eyes.

"How are you doing?" I asked.

"Swell. This has been a good day. If I could just put some damn weight on, I'd turn the corner."

He'd been on the wrong side of that corner for months. Never what you'd call a heavyweight, he now had a quality in common with the very old: the ability to inhabit his clothes without really wearing them, without filling them out or giving them shape.

Without bringing them to life. The only things alive about Beaumont were his dark eyes. The eyes had grown huge in his dried-apple head, as though they were the center of the cancer that was eating him, and not his lungs.

"What have you been up to?" he asked.

"Today I got an alcoholic drunk so he'd spill the story of his life. After that I tried to threaten a gorilla with social pretensions over at Riviera."

Beaumont repeated the name a little dreamily as the next wave of my smoke passed over him. "Riviera. I was there for the last round of the '48 Open, sitting on the clubhouse verandah, drinking rusty nails."

"Who won?"

"As I recall, it was the rusty nails. Who won today?"

"The gorilla. He called me a shady character."

"Your job didn't end up being about rescuing fair maidens from dragons or helping little old ladies across the street, did it, soldier?"

"No," I said.

Moody returned, carrying a little tray with legs. It held Beaumont's drink and a sweating shaker of Gibsons. Moody poured one into a stemmed glass and added a single onion, transferring it from a bowl of next of kin using tiny silver tongs.

"To old times," Beaumont said. He took a sip of his drink and then set it down carefully. I did my bit with the Old Gold again.

"Is it your job that's bothering you?" Beaumont asked when the last of the smoke had moved east.

"What makes you think anything's bothering me?"

"You're not the usual cheery visitor I've been getting lately. Seems like everyone who stops by to see me is so pumped full of sunshine they make Ed Wynn look like a wooden Indian. You're a refreshing change of pace."

"Thanks." I ground the cigarette out in the ashtray the thoughtful Moody had provided.

"Light up another," Beaumont said. "They don't bother me."

"Why the hell don't you just smoke one yourself?"

"The doc says no. As long as I'm doing good, I'm going to let him call the shots."

I wondered who was pumping who full of sunshine now. I took a drink and lit another cigarette.

"Is it your job in general that's getting to you," Beaumont asked, "or just working for Carson Drury?"

"How did you know I was working for him?"

My reaction brought out Beaumont's old, wolfish grin. "I recommended you. Drury came by to see me. Smoked the same lousy cigar the whole time, the bum. He'd heard about the fracas we got into in '47. Wanted to know all about it. All about you."

That solved the mystery of Drury asking for me by name. "It's not him," I said. "In fact, I kind of like the guy. He's one of the few people I've met lately who thinks that Hollywood has a future."

My host chuckled. "The bad news being that Drury hasn't been right about anything since he started shaving."

"You think he's wrong about Hollywood?"

"Dunno. I know that what you mean when you say Hollywood—namely, the town you left behind when you went off to play Sergeant York—that town is dying. A fellow with time on his hands could ride around on a white charger trying to save it, but he'd just be wasting his energy. Nobody can stop things from changing, usually for the worse. 'Things fall apart,' as Yeats said." He hastened to add, "He was a poet, I think, or a bartender.

"The only thing certain is, when the studio system finally croaks, something else will come along to take its place. Whether it'll be a Renaissance or the Dark Ages is anybody's guess."

We drank in silence for a while to give Beaumont a chance to catch his breath. Then I asked him if he remembered a guy named Vincent Mediate.

"I remember the gun he waved in my face," Beaumont said.

"I've been thinking of him on and off today."

"Because of Drury?" There was a similarity. Mediate had been a boy wonder in his own right, although he'd never enjoyed Drury's level of success.

"No," I said, "because of something Mediate told me once. He said the ex-serviceman's dream of a wife and a little house in the sticks was going to seem like a trap someday. Funny how he could spot my end coming but couldn't see his own."

"That's the way it usually works," Beaumont said. "So you're feeling trapped?"

"Not exactly. I'm feeling like a guy who spends his days rolling drunks. I meant to do more than that. I think I did do more than that, once."

Beaumont drew himself up in his chair, the effort making us both wince. "You're a prize sap, Elliott. You always have been. You told me once that every man's life should fade to black after he'd done his one heroic thing. It was crap then and it's crap now. If that's all there was to heroism, who couldn't win a medal? It's living through the empty days that takes sand. And carrying your weight and a little extra."

He left off there, pale and out of breath. Before he built up steam again, Moody rejoined us. "Telephone for Mr. Elliott," he said.

I stood up. "I should be going anyway," I said.

"Yeah," Beaumont said. "You should. Go home and tell your wife she married a cream puff. And take those damn things with you."

I picked up the pack of Old Golds I'd carelessly left on the silver tray. When Moody and I reached the house, I handed him the cigarettes for his reserve supply.

"What's the latest word?" I asked.

"No hope," he said.

He led me to the phone and then went back outside.

I said, "Elliott," into the mouthpiece when I'd gotten my fill of the quiet.

"Scotty, this is Peg. Get out to the RKO lot in Culver City as fast as you can. Paddy's on his way there now. There's been some kind of accident. Carson Drury's been hurt."

chapter
12

I WAS THE LAST to arrive at RKO Culver City. I learned at the antebellum front office that an ambulance had already called for Carson Drury and carried him away. I found Paddy Maguire at the scene of the accident, the soundstage where the *Albertsons* had been shooting. He was patting the hand of Drury's beautiful secretary, Sue, and doing it in a genuinely disinterested way. She appeared close to shock, and Paddy looked a little stunned himself. His homburg was pushed well back on his head, exposing the tuft of gray hair he liked to tug when he was puzzled. He'd already worked the tuft into something resembling a startled paint brush.

Behind them was the set Hank Shepard had described to me: a three-story staircase spiraling up into the rafters of the stage. It was built of dark, heavy wood and backed, on each landing, by stained-glass windows. It had to be a small piece of the Albertsons' mansion, after their fall from grace. Some of the windows had broken panes, and the stairway carpet was in tatters. If that wasn't giveaway enough, the whole set was covered by the dust of ages.

When he spotted me, Paddy passed Sue to a willing set hand and crossed the stage to meet me. His greeting was milder than the one I'd been imagining. "This is a damned odd business, Scotty."

"Sorry I wasn't here," I said.

"So am I, but not because I think you could have spotted this coming. If you'd been here, though, you could tell me what happened, and that would be a blessing. There had to have been a dozen witnesses on the set, no one of whom saw anything useful.

"What's certain is the camera crane tipped over. Drury was on the camera platform, alone, trying to work out the shot he wanted. The cameraman, Joe Nolan, should have been along for the ride, but he was working on some problem with the lighting. There was just the crane operator, a guy named Smith, who was seated on the controls down on the chassis.

"Smith raised Drury and the camera up and started to swing it to the right, away from the stairway set, for the start of the shot. The crane tipped over and landed in the empty center of the stage. No one ended up underneath it, thank God, or we'd be dealing with a death."

"What happened to Smith?"

"He stayed at the controls as long as he could and then stepped off. Being down on the base of the thing, he was never in any danger."

We walked across to where the crane lay on its side. It looked so much like a fallen animal that I had to fight the temptation to pat its battered side.

"How's Drury?" I asked.

"From what I'm told, he was conscious when they carried him out and dictating orders to everyone in sight. I guess he was thrown clear just before the crash. The camera wasn't so lucky."

A man was examining the remains of the camera, a short man with broad shoulders and heavy forearms that were dark with hair. "Joe Nolan," he said as he shook my hand.

"It's a total loss," he said to Paddy. "Just like I guessed."

"How about your other guess?"

"I was right there, too. This was no accident. Part of the crane's counterweight has been removed." He led us to the base of the crane where racks of metal plates had been fitted to balance the weight of the camera.

"This is an old crane," Nolan said. "Weights have been added over the years to accommodate a bigger platform and different cameras. There's a whole rack of weights missing that was here yesterday. I know. Jack Smith and I tested this rig just before quitting time."

I could see sweat on his scalp through his thin, black hair. "My chair ended up under the camera," he said. "If I'd gone up with Carson today, you'd be burying the camera and me in the same hole."

"I've heard that this camera was the original one from *Albertsons*," I said.

"And *First Citizen*," Nolan said. "It was already a veteran in '41. But you couldn't beat it for the kind of shots Carson loves, those mile-deep shots where the middle ground and the background are as important as the foreground. I don't know how we're going to replace it."

I turned to Paddy. "The camera may have been the real target. Not Drury or anyone else. Without that camera, he may not be able to match his new footage to his old film."

"The target was never just the camera, buddy," Nolan said. "Nobody sends a camera up on a crane by itself. Whoever did this was counting on hurting someone or didn't give a damn whether he did or not. We should be talking to the cops right now."

"We'll let Mr. Drury make that call, if he's able," Paddy said. "My associate and I are on our way over to see how he's doing."

I waited until we were in the DeSoto and Paddy had completed his cigar-lighting ceremony before I seconded Nolan. "It's time for the police."

"Past time for them," Paddy said, "which is one of the things that makes calling them in so awkward. Another is that we don't have the first idea what's really going on. I don't mind helping the police now and again, as you know, but they're damned unpleasant people to have along when you're feeling your way through a mine field. Heavy-footed, if you get my meaning."

As usual he ignored the dashboard ashtray and held his cigar arm outside the car, as though helping me signal for a right. This time he actually was.

"Turn east at the next corner and stay on Slauson. According to Drury's secretary, he was taken to a ritzy private hospital in Huntington Park. On our way there you can tell me what you've accomplished. You can skip the part about pasting Mr. Shepard. Drury filled me in on that this morning."

"Sorry to get you involved," I said.

"Don't give it another thought. If this Shepard had slighted Ella in front of me, he'd be sharing Drury's hospital room right now."

I told Paddy of my breakfast with Whitehead and the long shot that had come in for me at Riviera.

"That's more like it," Paddy said. "What's had me flummoxed from the start is the idea that anyone gives a damn whether Drury makes his comeback or no. That and the odd way this business has escalated. A script stolen, tires slashed. That's nuisance stuff. Then there's a fire that could easily have burned down an entire studio. Talk about upping the ante. Now we have an arranged accident that has double homicide written all over it. What happened to turn our vandal into an arsonist and would-be murderer?"

"Maybe we're dealing with two threats," I said. "That penny-ante stuff could have been John Piers Whitehead's way of getting attention. But I can't see him destroying the negative or hurting anyone."

"And I can't see two saboteurs working the same side of the street. It's too big a coincidence. We'll concentrate on this Lockard fellow. He can explain to us later why he started with half measures. Maybe he was testing the water, seeing how much security the lot really had."

"Maybe," I said.

"Lockard's surely the answer to my first puzzler: Who on earth would take Drury and his movie so seriously? It sounds like Mr. Lockard has more invested in Drury's ranch than money. And he just may be the type to use strong-arm tactics."

"But he doesn't know anything about the movies," I said. "He wouldn't know how important that camera was to Drury's plans."

"Forget the blooming camera. The target was Drury. The camera was an innocent bystander. I can't wait to tell the quiz kid that he borrowed money from the guy who'd most like to see his precious movie floating belly up. Don't spare the horses."

Drury's ritzy hospital was called the Petry Clinic. It occupied an old mansion that must have been too heavy to truck east when downtown Los Angeles engulfed the neighborhood in the twenties. The place was built of roughly finished red sandstone and had an octagonal tower that ended in toy battlements. There was a lighted window at the top of the tower, standing out like a beacon against the evening sky.

"God appears to be in," Paddy said as we climbed the front walk, Paddy climbing in a flat-footed, deliberate way.

"Joan Crawford wear you out?" I asked.

"That'll be the day."

While I asked a nurse at the reception desk for Drury, Paddy collared a doctor. Dr. Petry himself, it turned out. He had Paddy's waistline, but not his height. His skin was so flat and perfect that I suspected powder.

"You'll be relieved to hear that Carson is in no danger," he told Paddy as I joined them. He paused to let us express our relief and then hurried to fill the dead air. "He fractured his left fibula just below the knee. I'm preparing to set it now."

Paddy seemed more interested in the interior decorating than Drury's fibula. The crystal chandelier that graced the entryway fascinated him in particular. "Aren't broken bones a trifle beneath your notice here?" he asked.

"Our specialty is a certain class of patient," Dr. Petry said, "not a class of injury or illness."

"What class of patient would that be?" I asked.

"They're gentlemen and ladies who require a high level of personal attention. And an even higher level of discretion."

"Sounds as if we're laboring in the same vineyard, Doctor," Paddy said. "That being the case, would you extend us a professional courtesy? I'd appreciate a word with our client while you're mixing your plaster."

The doctor bowed ever so slightly and showed us to Drury's room. It wasn't, as Paddy had guessed, in the tower. It was on the first floor, overlooking a stone verandah and a formal garden lit by floodlights.

Carson Drury was sitting up in bed. Even so, his uninjured leg, stretched out in front of him, came close to touching the ironwork of the footboard. The broken leg was suspended above the mattress, being tugged back into alignment by weights and pulleys.

Hank Shepard was there, as I'd expected, standing at the head of Drury's bed. I hadn't expected the other visitor, Gilbert Traynor. He was standing by the windows, admiring the floodlit landscaping. The lighting made the ornamental trees and plants look like a garden at the bottom of the ocean.

" 'Enter old Polonius, with his man,' " Drury said. There was a bruise on his forehead—already purple—and he was pale, but he could still project from the diaphragm. "If you've come to offer me a refund, I'll take it." He sounded serious enough, but he ended the crack with a friendly laugh.

Paddy didn't join in. "You might want to hear our report first."

"You've found out who did this?" Shepard asked. He looked from Paddy to me, remembered our parting exchange at the Club Satyr, and looked away, embarrassed.

"We've a candidate in mind," Paddy said.

Drury turned his head in Traynor's direction, and Shepard, Paddy, and I followed his gaze. Traynor, who was dressed for an-

other evening on the town, reached up to finger his black bow tie—
a floppy tie, I noted, like the one Drury had worn the evening before.

"You've not met Mr. Maguire, have you, Gilbert?" Drury asked.

Traynor crossed the room to shake Paddy's hand. Afterward, he
kept crossing, sidestepping in the general direction of the door.

"Guess I'll be going, Carson," he said. "Just came by to see how
you were doing and to repeat my offer. I think under the circum-
stances you should really consider it. Not right this minute, I mean,
but when you're feeling better. In the meantime, I'll just toddle off.
Unless, of course," he said to Paddy from the doorway, "I'm your
man."

"We'd have shot you long since," Paddy said affably. "Enjoy your
evening."

"Now we can speak freely," Drury said. "Give me the bad news,
Maguire."

"The accident was deliberately staged. Someone removed a por-
tion of the crane's counterweight. In the wee small hours, most
likely. I checked with the guards. Even if they kept to their
schedule, they wouldn't have stopped by that soundstage more than
a couple of times between midnight and dawn."

"How about my camera?"

"It was pronounced dead at the scene."

Drury nodded. "You said you had a suspect in mind. Do you also
have a name?"

"Ralph Lockard."

"The developer?" Shepard asked.

"And Mr. Drury's secret benefactor. Lockard owns the Alora
Land Conservancy, as my associate here discovered. Lockard set it
up to put some farmland on ice, but his scheme produced an un-
foreseen bonus. He was offered a choice parcel of ground called
Eden as collateral for a loan, a parcel he's been lusting after since
Truman beat Dewey. He figures to get it, too, when the borrower
defaults. My guess is he's been trying to improve his chances."

Not having lines in that part of the scene, I'd spent my time watching Drury's reaction and Shepard's. Like Paddy, I'd expected the Lockard revelation to give Drury yet another knock on the head, perhaps the one that finished him. It hadn't happened. After some initial unease, Drury had actually begun to smile. Hank Shepard wasn't bearing up so well. He was staring at Drury as though nothing in their long association had prepared him for this latest foul-up.

Drury must have felt the daggers. Without taking his eyes off Paddy, he said, "Relax, Hank. Everything's under control."

"You knew all along, didn't you?" Shepard said.

"It wasn't all that hard to work out. Was it, Scotty?" He winked at me. "Ralph Lockard. His very name gives him away. Sounds just like the villain in a melodrama, the evil banker about to foreclose on the widow's mortgage. I guess that makes me the widow."

Paddy had been upstaged again, and he knew it. "You figured the Alora scam out and borrowed the money anyway?"

"Of course. I needed to raise as much money as I could. A committee of bankers wouldn't have given me a nickel more than Eden is worth. In fact, they would have insisted on giving me a nickel or two less. Mr. Lockard was much more generous. Most people are willing to be generous if you can convince them they're cheating you."

"He won't begrudge you the extra he paid," I said, "as long as he ends up with Eden."

"Then we'll just have to see that he doesn't end up with it—the four of us, working together. Maguire, you can keep an eye on the evil Ralph Lockard. Meanwhile, Scotty, you and Hank and I will slip clean away."

"Away where?" Paddy asked.

"Indiana. Traynorville, to be exact. Last night I happened to tell Gilbert Traynor about a little idea I'd had in the bath. As you gentlemen know, we've been having trouble with sets and locations. That's a delicate way of saying we're likely to go broke trying to duplicate what the RKO set department whipped up for us in 1942. It occurred to me that we could move the production to Indiana–where *Albertsons* happens to be set–to some little town that time forgot. We'd have all the sets and locations we need then and have them for the asking. Gilbert liked the idea. You might even say he loved it. He told me he'd contribute to the production financially if we'd make the move. That was the offer he repeated just now."

"What's in it for him?" Shepard asked.

"He's starstruck and homesick in about equal parts. This way he gets to have the best of both worlds. He can go back to Indiana with a trainload of walking, talking Hollywood celebrities. He'll be the Hoosier Frank Buck."

Shepard wasn't jumping on any bandwagons. "*The Imperial Albertsons* was shot in a studio and on a back lot. You'll never match the old footage if you go out on location."

"I had the same reservation, Hank. But we've no choice now. Our camera's gone. We can waste our time hunting around for a replacement, or we can make a virtue of a necessity. We'll save the old footage of the Albertsons' glory days and reshoot their whole decline and fall. Think of what we'll gain: a sharp visual break that will make the first half of the film seem like a long dream sequence. It will be followed by a shock of harsh reality that will give the audience a taste of what the Albertsons are feeling as they awake from their dream. The critics will eat it up, Hank. They'll absolutely eat it up. When I get the Academy Award for best director, I may thank Ralph Lockard from the podium."

He patted the pockets of his dressing gown. "I seem to have lost my cigar case in all the confusion. Can I try one of yours, Maguire? It'll get me in the mood. They're rolled in Indiana, aren't they? Or is it Kentucky?"

Paddy handed one over and lit a kitchen match with his thumbnail. As his concession speech, he said, "West Virginia. Wheeling, West Virginia."

chapter

13

"THE KIDS AND I can stay with your father in Indianapolis. We wouldn't be in any conceivable danger."

It was Ella's third trip around that rhetorical barn, and she was no longer treating her argument very seriously. So I gave her an unserious reply: "You're underestimating my father."

"I've only met the man once, Scotty. It would be hard for me to recognize him, never mind estimate him."

I said, "Touché," in the hope of moving to a new subject. I didn't want my parting conversation with Ella to be about my father, especially since we were naked just then and enjoying a rare evening of unselfconscious intimacy. The children were spending the night with their ersatz grandparents, the Maguires.

The ploy worked for the moment at least. "How many shirts should I pack?" Ella asked.

"How many do I own?"

"Right. You should be taking a trunk, not a bag. You don't even know how long you'll be gone."

"Drury's calling this a scouting expedition. He won't commit the crew and the cast until he's sure of his ground. If I can, I'll sneak back before the actual filming starts."

"If it ever does start," Ella said. "You could spend the rest of your life driving Carson Drury around while he trades in his last brilliant idea for a new one."

"That's Hank Shepard's job, not mine."

I regretted mentioning Shepard as soon as his name was out of my mouth. Ella sat up, drawing a sheet around her raised knees. I sat up, too, thought about a cigarette, but decided it wasn't worth spoiling what remained of our earlier, happy mood. There was still a chance that we'd merely interrupted our lovemaking and not called it a night. A chance that Drury and Shepard and Indiana were all still part of another world.

By way of sustaining the note, I scratched Ella's back lightly, working my way downward from her shoulders. She waited until I'd reached my standard finish, a trip up her spine from the small of her back. Then she bent her head forward until her almost-blond hair hung down toward the sheet that covered her toes. "You missed my neck," she said.

As I corrected the oversight, I told her that I'd stopped by to see Torrance Beaumont. Ella said, "Poor Tory," with so much feeling that I figured she didn't need updating on his chances. I did pass along his message, though.

"He told me to tell you you'd married a cream puff."

"If he'd seen you at work just now, he'd have had to eat his words."

"Thanks, coach," I said.

"What did you do to get under his skin?"

I'd told him I was feeling trapped by my life. That line would have played even less well now, so I said, "I wasn't smoking fast enough for him, I guess."

"That reminds me. I got you a going-away present."

She tossed off the sheet and left the bed and then the room. It was a warm night, but the place felt cool without her.

She came back carrying a wooden box. "I didn't have time to wrap it."

"You didn't have time to buy it," I said. "You didn't know I was going away until tonight."

"So you're getting your Christmas present early. Open it."

The box didn't contain my Christmas present. It held the latest gambit in Ella's campaign to come between me and my Lucky Strikes. The complete inventory was one briar pipe with a straight stem, a leather pouch of tobacco, a shock of pipe cleaners, and something that looked like a cross between a tenpenny nail and a paring knife.

"That's a combination tamper and reamer," Ella said.

"Of course it is. But what am I supposed to be? Are you trying to turn me into a banker?"

"I'm trying to keep you from ending up like Tory Beaumont. You have two children. It would be nice if they got to know you. I happen to think you're worth knowing."

She was close enough to kiss, so I kissed her. I had big plans for that kiss, but they didn't work out. Ella broke it off and said, "It would also be nice if the kids got to know their grandfather."

"They're doing fine with Paddy. Tonight he's teaching them to play blackjack—or how to use a blackjack. I forget which."

"Why don't you want us along, Scotty? Is it because of your father?"

"No. He's why I don't want to go myself. Drury's why I don't want you three along. Drury and the black cloud that's following him around. The next time he falls off something, he could land on one of you."

Ella wouldn't let me change the subject a second time. "Why don't you and your father get along?"

"He's never forgiven me for not becoming a doctor, like he is."

"Your father's a lawyer, not a doctor."

"He's not? What am I thinking of?"

"A movie, you goofball. *The Thin Man Goes Home.*" She threw a pipe cleaner at me. "And before you laugh yourself sick over your little joke, let me remind you that William Powell takes Myrna Loy home with him in that picture."

"Where she ends up knee-deep in dead bodies. I'd never do that to Myrna's knees—or yours, either."

"What came between you and your father, Scotty?"

"Hollywood did."

"Are you sure it wasn't me?"

Shepard came to mind again. Specifically, the satisfying picture of him slamming into a wall of can goods. "Indiana's quite a ways away," I said. "How bad do you think your reputation was?"

"Not was, Scotty. Is. Some things don't change. Maybe nothing does."

"That would suit me fine," I said, thinking of Beaumont's opposing philosophy, the idea that the world was a rug that unraveled behind you as you walked.

Ella interpreted my comment personally and kissed me for it. It was my lucky break and I ran with it, so to speak.

■ ■ ■

Not all that many hours later I was standing beneath the Olympic-size clock in the waiting room of the Union Station, getting my final pep talk from Paddy Maguire.

"Need anything?" he asked, looking first at the drugstore and then at the newsstand.

"A mental examination. Or one for you. Why are we going along with this stunt?"

Paddy tapped the breast pocket of his suit, causing the cigar ash on his lapel to avalanche silently. "Because of a very generous payment in advance for two weeks of your time."

"Are you sure it isn't because Drury has you down two sets to none in your battle of wits, and this is your only hope of a rematch?"

"I'd settle for the last word," Paddy said. "I might get it, too, if I can tie up Mr. Lockard or whoever's behind this business while you three are off screen-testing the wheat."

"The corn, you mean," I said.

"All right, the corn. I must say, Scotty, I expected you to be in a better mood today—after the romantic evening I arranged for you."

"Ella will be sending you a nice note."

"Only one?"

"As I was saying: Doesn't this Indiana trip seem awfully quick to you? The guy falls off a crane one afternoon, and the next day he lands on the Super Chief."

"Only the best for Drury," Paddy said, deliberately missing my point. "He could have saved Gilbert Traynor some money by taking the plain old Chief."

"Nobody in Hollywood takes the Chief anymore except agents and kept women."

Paddy's ear for a pirated movie line was almost as good as my own. "Would that be from *Union Station?*"

"No," I said, "*The Hucksters,* Clark Gable and Deborah Kerr, 1947."

"A good year, that."

"What's with this Dr. Petry?"

"I just spoke with him. He came by to tuck Drury into his compartment. You'll have your hands full just getting the wonderboy about. Petry says it will be weeks until Drury is even up to using crutches."

"So why is he letting Drury go? You'd think Petry would want to keep him under observation for a day or two at least."

"Society quacks like Petry follow orders; they don't give them. Mostly the orders involve prescriptions the patients shouldn't have. They were the bane of this town before the war. High-class pill pushers, half of them, and I'm not talking about Bayer aspirin. I shut one or two of the rotten ones down myself, when I first hung out my shingle. This Petry must be clean, though, or smarter than he looks, to still be in business.

"As for Drury's timing, that suits me down to the ground. I want him off somewhere safe and remote. If our saboteur follows his pattern, getting a little bolder each time he strikes, his next move could be very serious."

"What's more serious than attempted murder?"

"Murder, of course. And I don't mean murder by way of the hocus-pocus somebody pulled on that camera crane. Mr. Joe Nolan's fears to the contrary notwithstanding, that isn't how you actually go about killing a fellow. You put a gun to his head and wish him a nice trip.

"And speaking of guns, you have yours, I assume."

"It's in my case, which is on the train by now, I hope."

"What's this bulge, then?" Paddy reached into the inside pocket of my suit coat and extracted my new pipe.

"A present from Ella."

He stuck it into my mouth and stepped backward to get the full effect. "Very becoming. The Arrow Shirt people should be paying you a retainer."

I started to say that I'd take a return trip ticket, but the man on the public address system cut me off. He announced the last call for the Super Chief, eastbound for Chicago.

chapter

14

THE SUPER CHIEF MADE the trip to Chicago in forty hours or so, as advertised. Drury could have given me the exact time if I'd thought to ask him. He was remarkably well informed for a man who never left his compartment and who sat with his back to the passing scenery. He asked me if I'd seen the Grand Canyon when I checked on him once and, later, whether I knew that we'd averaged eighty-two miles an hour between Garden City and Lamar. Maybe he'd made the trip so often he had the rails memorized.

Shepard kept Drury company most of the time. The two played game after game of chess using a beautiful little traveling set whose pieces had tiny pegs on their bases that corresponded to holes in the squares. I never saw more than a few moves of any one game, there being no room in the compartment for me to sit down. From what I did see, though, Shepard was more than holding his own. He played a rapid, aggressive game, leaning over the little board like an arm wrestler. Drury leaned well back; his propped-up leg would permit no other arrangement, but it seemed to me to be his natural stance. He played slowly, examining both the board and Shepard as he worked out his moves.

For the most part I kept myself company, reading or haunting the club car where I worked at breaking in my pipe. The project brought Ella to mind, but then, almost everything did. It got so bad that I left the train during the twelve-minute stop in Flagstaff and sent her a telegram: "Start packing. I'll call when coast is clear."

The girl who took it down for me smiled to herself, perhaps imagining some complicated, interstate tryst between this Mrs. Elliott and the stranger before her with the gurgling pipe. I let her imagine.

Our train had a two-story, domed observation car, called a "Pleasure Dome Lounge Car" by the railroad, apparently with a straight face. Hank Shepard found me sitting beneath the pleasure dome late on the second night of our trip.

"Having trouble?" he asked, pointing to my pipe. It was sitting in an ashtray, surrounded by the dead remains of a pack of matches.

"Can't keep it lit," I said.

"It's like sex, I'm told. The less you think about it, the better you do."

We both regretted the analogy as soon as it was spoken, Shepard more than I.

"Try one of these," he said, shaking a cigarette out of his pack. "They stay lit all by themselves."

I accepted the cigarette gratefully, which relaxed Shepard. He lit one for himself and settled back in his chair. "I want to apologize for the other evening," he said. "I've been wanting to since I sobered up the next morning, but too much started happening. Thanks for letting me off with a poke on the chin."

He ran his hand back and forth beneath his pug nose a few times. It was the kind of manly expression of emotion Wallace Beery had done so well.

"You'd been drinking," I said to give him an out.

"I drink all the time," Shepard said. "It doesn't usually make me a heel. That night, though, I was high on more than booze. I had the feeling that things were finally coming together for Drury and me, that we'd finally found our way out of the fun house."

He looked up through the glass ceiling of the dome. I looked up, too, amazed again at how many stars you could see when you got away from the lights and smog of Los Angeles.

"I felt like I owned the place that night," Shepard said, a little in awe. "Like I was in command of things for once." He looked down from the sky, and his voice lost its hushed quality. "Sort of like the flea deciding he owns the dog.

"Anyway, I wanted to say I'm sorry. One lesson I learned in the infantry is that you have to get along with the guys in your squad. They're the ones watching your back, after all."

"We felt the same way in the field artillery."

"Then you know that the last thing you want is for the guy next to you to develop an ambivalent attitude toward your health and well-being. I'm afraid your attitude toward me has sunk way below ambivalent."

"You figure we're heading into a battle zone?"

"I haven't a clue where we're heading," he said, looking upward again. "And I have the feeling I wouldn't like it if I did know."

"I'll watch your back," I said.

Shepard stuck out his big, soft hand. "Thanks, pally."

■ ■ ■

We traveled by day coach from Chicago to Traynorville, sitting in facing seats with Drury's plastered leg acting as our fourth. Drury was disguised almost as effectively as his leg. He wore Shepard's hat, my dark glasses, and his own two-day growth of beard. Not that you could see any of that. His first line of defense was a *Chicago Tribune,* unfolded to its full size.

Meanwhile, Shepard and I relaxed in our anonymity, meeting people's eyes and, in my case, even saying hello.

"You don't know all these people, do you?" Shepard asked as our car filled up at South Bend.

"Hoosiers still say hello," I said. "They don't have to know you."

"Probably leave their chicken coops unlocked at night, too," Shepard said, amazed. He leaned past Drury to peer out the window. "It's flat, too. Flatter than the beers of yesterday."

"Hank's that rare thing," Drury said, lowering his paper to half-mast. "The native of California. Only the northern half of Indiana is really flat, Hank. All its irregularities were pushed down into southern Indiana by a glacier about a million years ago."

Shepard looked to me for confirmation. "Before my time," I said.

Thanks to his radio work, Drury's voice was easily as famous as his face. His brief geology lecture had attracted the attention of several of our near neighbors in the coach. Drury noticed this and buried himself in his paper again.

It was Shepard's turn to chuckle. "Carson's that unrare thing," he said to me unsoftly. "The celebrity who's afraid of his fans."

Fortunately for Drury, our fellow passengers were as polite as they were friendly. No one bothered the great man during the ride to Traynorville, a ride that felt slow and bumpy after the Super Chief. They didn't even make a fuss at the Traynorville station, where the process of unloading the director turned into a small circus. Drury's wheelchair had traveled in the baggage car, and it was waiting on the platform when we finally got him down the narrow stairs of the day coach.

"I have it on good authority," Drury said as he settled himself, "that this is the very chair Lionel Barrymore used in *Young Dr. Kildare*."

The chair was old enough to have been Barrymore's, or Dr. Gillespie's. It was a huge wooden model with wheels like an antique bicycle's. They were arranged like a high-wheeler's, too, with the big ones in front and the little ones behind.

Drury noted my inspection. "I don't trust the modern practice of putting the little wheels up front. Has to be inherently unstable. The big wheels should always lead the way."

"He's stating his personal philosophy," Shepard joked, but absently. He'd spotted Gilbert Traynor at the far end of the platform, and he was waving to him. "I didn't expect Andy Hardy to come after us himself."

I had, but I'd been wrong about something else. Traynor had seemed ill at ease in Hollywood, unsure of himself and his ground. I'd expected him to be changed for the better by his return to his natural habitat, relaxed and confident if not downright arrogant. But it hadn't happened.

None of the platform workers knuckled their foreheads to Traynor as he crossed to us or even seemed to notice him. I might not have myself without Shepard's help. Traynor had been dapper if slight in his tuxedo, but now, in a too-flashy sports coat and baggy trousers, he just looked undersized—an undersized man on the far side of young who wasn't particularly happy to see us. He had the look of a guy who had awakened after a hard night's drinking and found a stranger in his bed. Three strangers, in fact.

If Drury was put out by the absence of a brass band, he didn't let it show. He wrung Traynor's hand, shaking a little life into him in the process.

"Welcome to Culver City east," Traynor said, smiling thinly. "I've arranged for you to stay at our farm, Riverbend. You'll have plenty of privacy, and there's a room in the barn that would be perfect for your editing."

"What's there to edit?" I asked.

"*The Imperial Albertsons*," Drury said. "Gilbert was nice enough to fly the negative out while we three provided a diversion by taking the train. Did I forget to mention that part of the plan?"

He'd forgotten to mention it to Paddy, too, or I'd never have been sent alone to guard two targets, the film and its director. Shepard tossed me a suitcase. "Get used to the feeling, pally," he said.

Traynor had brought along an appropriate vehicle, a wooden-sided station wagon. It wasn't a new one, but it was impeccably maintained. On each varnished door, a familiar symbol was painted: the blue winged T of the Traynor Automobile Company.

On our way to the farm—Drury seated sideways on the backseat and Traynor, Shepard, and I jammed into the front—our host gave us the nickel tour. A nickel's worth was all there was to Traynorville. It was a county seat, but a small one, its business district not much larger than the courthouse square. The square was something of a community attic, as it was decorated with the castoffs of several wars. I spotted a World War I artillery piece, a French Seventy-five. Shepard was more interested in the exhibit on the next corner, a V1 flying bomb mounted on a concrete pedestal.

"Don't get many English tourists here, I see," he said.

Beyond the square, the residential neighborhoods turned modest in a hurry. Traynor pointed out exceptions to this rule, Victorian survivors he thought might interest Drury. One of the old mansions did. Drury had Traynor drive by it several times.

"That belonged to my great-uncle," Traynor said, "my mother's uncle. I'm sure the current owners would welcome the chance to be involved with your film."

The old house was currently a funeral parlor. Shepard noted its sign between discreet sips from his flask. "If things turn sour," he whispered to me, "they can bury the damn negative."

Out loud he asked, "Where's this factory of yours, Gilbert?"

"It's on the west side of town, west of the rail yard. We have to head east to get to Riverbend."

Instead of explaining our hurry, he launched into a description of the farm. He ended it by saying, "It's the original Traynor homestead, settled by my great-grandfather in 1852."

"What did he build?" Shepard asked.

"Nothing but his own life. The Traynors weren't manufacturers then. My grandfather got that started. He founded a coach works. Later, with my father's help, he turned it into an automobile company. Grandfather kept the old homestead, though. I think he honestly believed there'd be some call for a Traynor museum someday. Something along the lines of what Henry Ford did in Dearborn.

Grandfather hated Ford, but he would have loved to have had his success. Anyway, we've held on to the shrine and kept it up. But nobody actually lives there. Nobody except Clark, the caretaker.

"I should tell you about Clark before you see him—meet him, I should say. He's a disabled veteran, not that he's really very disabled. He can outwork most of the able-bodied men we employ at the works. But he does have a stiff leg and an arm he can't raise above his shoulder. He was busted up pretty badly in Europe. Blown up and sewn back together again. And he was disfigured. That's really what I've been trying to say. That's the worst part for Clark. The doctors weren't able to give him back much of his face.

"He ended up in a VA hospital down in Indianapolis. We advertised for a caretaker after the war, and he applied. I was feeling sentimental about veterans at the time because of a loss my family had suffered, so I insisted we take Clark on. It's worked out about as well as it could have, I guess. We needed the help, and he needed a place to be away from people."

"What will Mr. Clark think of us?" Drury asked.

"He won't bother you. He has his own cabin back on the wooded part of the property. You probably won't see much of him, unless something goes wrong at the main house."

"Count on us becoming old friends in no time," Shepard said.

chapter

15

CLARK WAS WAITING for us at Riverbend. The property's name was painted on an elegant colonial sign at the end of a long gravel drive. The farmhouse at the other end of the drive wasn't elegant or colonial. It was a simple white-frame model whose front porch was as wide and almost as deep as the building behind it. I'd seen hundreds of farmhouses like it growing up, but none that had glowed like this one. The windows had certainly been washed that morning, and the white paint around them shone just as brightly in the afternoon sun.

The property was framed by fields of corn that ran all the way to the road, giving the front yard the look of a green alley. There wasn't a dandelion visible in that gently rising lawn or a dead branch in the giant tulip poplars that stood on either side of the porch. Beyond the rightmost tree and across a gravel courtyard was the main outbuilding, a barn. It was a dark, unweathered red with white trim, and its highest gable bore the date 1852. Traynor had said it himself: The place was a museum without customers.

The museum's custodian stood on the front porch, dressed in an undershirt and holding a saw that gleamed like a naked sword. To protect himself from the sun, Clark wore a ball cap with a long bill. It hadn't kept his face from burning to about the same shade of red as the barn. At first glance his face seemed less disfigured than worn away. Traynor parked the wagon about twenty yards from the porch. From that distance I could just make out that Clark had a flat, featureless nose, no cheekbones to speak of, no eyebrows, and only a faint, uneven trace of lips, tightly drawn.

Clark stood in place while Shepard and I got Drury's chair down from the roof of the wagon and loaded him into it. The caretaker didn't offer to help, but he didn't hide himself, either. I decided that he and Traynor together—or coincidentally—had hit upon the least painful way for the three of us to make Clark's acquaintance: an extended period of stealing glances at him from a distance.

The saw in Clark's hand and a toolbox at his feet were explained by a recent addition to the front porch steps. It was a ramp for Drury's wheelchair, a long ramp with a very gradual incline. When Drury saw it, he thrust himself forward across the gravel, making a wide turn that brought him to the end of the ramp. With no more running start than that, he was able to ascend unaided to the porch.

"Perfect," he said when he'd gotten there. "Absolutely first rate." He extended his hand to the retreating Clark and held it out until Clark returned to take it. "Thanks for the ramp and for taking us in."

Clark said nothing that I could hear. He didn't have much time to reply before Drury wheeled his chair around and took off down the ramp. Shepard and I moved instinctively to head him off at the bottom, but he stopped in a shower of gravel without our help.

"Works going down, too," Drury said. He craned his head around to address the caretaker, but Clark had disappeared inside the house.

Traynor was still standing by the station wagon. "I'll help you with your bags," he said from there. "Then I'll let you settle in. The wagon's for your use while you're here."

Drury wheeled himself back to the car. "Gilbert, if I start

thanking you, I won't know where to stop. So I won't start. But I hope you know how I feel."

We could all tell how Gilbert felt: uneasy. "I've a favor to ask," he said. "My family would like to meet you. We're having a little dinner tonight at our place, Traynor House. Nothing very formal. Just my mother and my sister-in-law. You're all invited." His voice trailed off on, "If you're not too tired."

"Can't think of a nicer way to spend our first evening in Indiana," Drury said.

I could have come up with a short list. Traynor, too, from the look of him. He glanced at Shepard and me almost pleadingly, and we chorused in with Drury. Traynor gave us directions and then took off in a low-slung Studebaker President Speedster. The coupé was sleek in outline and garish in color, a lime green over lemon yellow.

Shepard watched him go. "There's a guy who fits right in around here, I don't think."

"No," Drury said. "Poor Gilbert is definitely out of step."

I ad-libbed a line: "Is it just me, or did he seem less than thrilled about having us over tonight?"

"He's uncomfortable, Scotty, that's all. This whole town is a suit that Gilbert has outgrown. With our help, he's going to cast it off."

"And come out as what?" Shepard asked. "A butterfly?"

"A free man," Drury, the model free man, replied. "In the meantime, it won't kill us to spend some time with his family. In fact, it could help us. Out in Hollywood, Gilbert confided to me that beyond a certain point, his ability to invest in the picture will be dependent on the goodwill of his mother. He's the president of the Traynor Company, but she's still firmly seated on most of the Traynor money. So we have to make a good impression on the old lady, and Gilbert's nervous about it."

"Him and me both," Shepard said.

▪ ▪ ▪

We met the first requirement of a good impression by arriving on time. I drove the wagon through the front gate of Traynor House at five minutes to eight. There was no actual gate, just two slightly tapered brick pylons that might have supported one. All they were currently supporting was a pair of globe-shaped copper light fixtures, weathered green. The pylons were inset with ceramic tile in a geometric pattern. Drury had me stop the wagon so he could examine the tile.

"You're the Hoosier, Scotty. What does that design mean?"

"Money, straight ahead."

The house was an imposing pile of the same tan brick as the pylons. It had a green tile roof and sprawling one-floor wings on each end of the main structure. During the short trip up the crescent drive to the front steps, Drury gave us a pocket lecture on the influence of Frank Lloyd Wright.

"Not a Wright house, obviously, but you can see the Prairie School touches. Many of the mediocrities who criticized Wright eventually adopted his ideas. That's frequently how a genius does his most lasting work: not through his own creations, but in unofficial collaboration with his enemies."

I waited for some wry response from Shepard on the autobiographical quality of Drury's observation, but none came. The publicist had been quiet since we'd settled in at Riverbend—Drury in a first-floor sitting room converted to a bedroom and Shepard and I upstairs. Now he was positively grim. I checked Drury's expression in the rearview mirror. He was perfectly composed, but eager, too. I'd seen the combination before on long-lost soundstages. It was the contained excitement of a well-prepared actor anxious to get on with his scene.

The front door was answered by a maid more formally dressed, in shiny black and starched white, than the three of us. She let us in as far as a paneled foyer. Directly before us, an extra-wide staircase rose to a landing and then split off in two different directions. Like Drury's unlucky movie set, the landing was backed by a stained-glass window. This one was representational, a rolling green landscape across which an antique car was traveling. A Traynor Phaeton Six.

"Wonderful," Drury said, by which I guessed he meant awful.

To our left was a large, brightly lit room. Gilbert Traynor was standing in its doorway, waiting for his cue. When Drury spotted him there, he crossed to us. "Thanks for coming," he said. "Mother will be down in a minute. You'll want a drink first. And you can meet Linda."

He led us into a powder blue room decorated like a standard living room but big enough to handle a dance. In front of a limestone fireplace stood a conventional grouping of sofa and chairs so dwarfed by the room's proportions that they looked like a showroom display. A woman sat alone on the sofa. Oddly, she didn't seem at all dwarfed by the room, or intimidated by the procession bearing down on her. She was wearing a dark red cocktail dress that came within an inch or so of being off the shoulder. Her dark lipstick matched the dress, as did the stones in her golden jewelry: necklace, earrings, and bracelet.

She was holding an unlit cigarette. Perhaps she'd been holding it for hours. Shepard was pushing Drury's chair and Gilbert had his hands in his pockets, so I found my lighter and circled the low, gilt table, adding to my list of observations as I went. Her slightly slanted eyes were a mossy brown, her small nose was upturned, and her dark brown hair was pulled back, loosely on top and tightly on the sides, and gathered in a roll at the back of her long, slender neck.

Everything pretty much tallied until she thanked me for the light. Her voice was down-home Hoosier without a single rounded edge. If my rusty ear could be trusted, she was from that part of the state where Drury's glacier had deposited all the hills.

I was surprised enough by that to miss my chance to introduce myself. Gilbert did the honors, billing me somewhere below Drury's wheelchair. Linda Traynor wasn't put off by the slight. She seemed genuinely impressed by Drury, and she gave Shepard a friendly smile. But her dark eyes kept stealing back to me. And I hadn't even remembered to bring my pipe.

"I've made some martinis," Gilbert said. "Can I interest anyone?"

"Put an onion in Elliott's," Shepard said. "He only drinks Gibsons."

"Why," Linda asked, "does substituting an onion on a toothpick for an olive on a toothpick give a glass of gin and vermouth a whole new name?"

She asked the question of me, but Drury fielded it: "It's a tribute to Charles Dana Gibson, the famous illustrator. Years ago he ordered a martini at The Players Club in New York. The bartender was out of olives, so he snuck a pearl onion into Gibson's glass. The innovation should have been named for the bartender—old Charley Connolly—but Gibson got the credit. Not that it matters. The olive fanciers have kept the Gibson a footnote."

"Does that make you a believer in lost causes, Mr. Elliott?" Linda asked.

"Just a believer in onions," I said.

By that time Gilbert had handed round the cocktails. He turned toward an oil painting that hung over the fireplace, a portrait of a very young army lieutenant, and raised his glass to it.

Linda said, "We really should toast our guests tonight, Gilbert. Gilbert and I have a little tradition. We always toast his brother, my late husband, Mark."

That was the family loss Gilbert had mentioned back at the farm. He'd tried to make it sound like a minor loss then. Now he looked as if he'd just gotten the bad news.

"Let us join you," Drury said, raising his own glass. "To Lieutenant Traynor."

"To Mark," Gilbert said.

Shepard was standing close enough to the portrait to identify the ribbons on the uniform. "He won the Silver Star, too, Elliott."

"Posthumously," Linda said. "His mother insisted on its being added to the painting."

"It was only right," a voice behind us said. The voice belonged to a small, thin woman in black who was standing in the doorway of the room. "Mark paid for that medal very dearly."

"HELL OF AN ENTRANCE," Shepard whispered as the woman slowly crossed the ballroom and joined us by the dead fireplace.

She had Gilbert's delicate features and narrow head, made to look even narrower in her case by stiff gray hair teased outward and by folds of skin that allowed the lower part of her face to drain directly into the high neckline of her black dress. But she had none of her son's hazy amiability. At the moment he didn't have much left of that himself. He repeated the introductions in a monotone, ending with, "Gentlemen, this is my mother, Marvella Traynor."

I thought Drury might say "wonderful" again when he heard the woman's first name, but he was on his best behavior. Sitting in his chair, he was at just the right height to look Mrs. Traynor square in the eye. They stared at each other for the time it took me to finish my drink.

Then she said, "I saw you in 1943 at a bond rally at the armory in Indianapolis. You performed a scene from Shakespeare, a dialogue between Othello and Iago. You played both parts and convinced me I was listening to two separate men."

"Thank you," Drury said. "It was an idea that fascinated me at the time: the possibility that conflicting personalities might be sides of a single person. I ended up using it in a little picture called *The Gentleman from Macao*. Perhaps you saw it."

"No," Mrs. Traynor said flatly. "I seldom go to those. I'll never forget that bond rally, though. You followed the Andrews Sisters on the program. They were exceedingly loud, but the crowd seemed not to mind. In fact, many of the young people stood up and danced in their places. I remember feeling sorry for you when you came onstage all by yourself with the crowd still unsettled. But by the time you'd finished, the place was as quiet as an empty church. I'll never forget that."

I wondered if Drury had. That Indianapolis rally had surely been one stop in an endless succession of stops. Drury had probably topped the Andrews Sisters every time he'd grabbed the microphone. Or maybe he hadn't. Maybe that evening in Indy had been a shining moment, a small success he'd misfiled among all his failures.

He straightened himself in his chair and said thank-you again, sounding this time as though he really meant it.

"I'm anxious to hear more of your plans for my son, Mr. Drury. Perhaps we can speak of them at dinner. It's ready now, Gilbert, I believe."

Dinner was served in an elegant, oval room that impressed even Drury. He presided over the meal, telling stories about the '43 bond drive that Mrs. Traynor had brought back to life for him. She sat at the head of the table and watched him. As she watched, she chewed each mouthful of her meal forty or fifty times. I never actually caught her swallowing. She might not have had any reason to.

Drury made two mistakes during his performance. One came after he'd segued from his wartime reminiscences to his plans for reviving *The Imperial Albertsons*. He hadn't gotten past his sketch of the movie's basic premise—that the coming of the automobile had blasted a moribund society—before Mrs. Traynor gave her molars a rest and broke in.

"You called the Albertsons social dinosaurs, Mr. Drury. Just what did you mean by that?"

"Please call me Carson, Mrs. Traynor," Drury said, his accent as English as it got. "I meant that the dinosaurs expected, if the creatures thought at all, that their warm, comfortable world would last forever. In the same way the Albertsons expected their almost feudal life of ease and privilege to last forever."

"If the creatures thought at all," Mrs. Traynor added coldly.

Drury was so taken aback by her sudden hostility that I was able to hit on its explanation first. "Your son showed us around town today, Mrs. Traynor," I said. "We saw the mansion your uncle once owned. It must have been quite a place in its day. It reminded me of the Morris-Butler House in Indianapolis."

"You've been to Indiana before?"

"He was born and raised in Indianapolis, Mother," Gilbert said. He said it in a condescending way, as though she'd missed a sign pinned to my back.

She didn't take offense. "I have many fond memories of my uncle's house, Mr. Elliott. We always spent Christmas day there. My mother's family were the Pallisers, once the most prominent family in this county."

The local branch of the Albertsons, in other words. Drury had gotten that message loud and clear. "Then you know the tragic implications of our story firsthand, Mrs. Traynor," he said, "the basic truth that you have to adapt to survive."

"I must admit that you adapt very well, Mr. Drury," she said. She capped the line with a tiny bite of dressing. Before she began to puree it, I thought I saw a faint trace of a triumphant smile.

Drury's second slip occurred after Mrs. Traynor had come down with a headache and retired. Linda Traynor, who'd been content to sit back and listen during dinner, asked Drury if he'd worked out the cost of finishing the picture. Drury blew her some smoke about the numbers being someone else's worry, that they always managed to work themselves out and that he preferred to concentrate on the creative aspects of the film. The speech sounded canned, and his delivery of it was halfhearted. He frequently looked away from his audience and toward Mrs. Traynor's empty chair, as though her headache had somehow taken him off the clock. It hadn't.

Linda interrupted him when he mentioned his muse for the third time. "You won't mind my speaking frankly, I hope," she said, her voice trading its drawl for a steely terseness. "We'll get along a lot better that way. When Gilbert first wired that you might be coming out, I had our lawyers make some inquiries. We learned that your last three pictures didn't recover their basic production costs. I believe you call it the negative cost in your business."

"Yes," Drury said, "we do."

"That caused us some concern. Gilbert's interest in this project is such that we may be willing to lower our normal requirements for a return on our investment. But naturally we'll need to have a clear idea of our potential risk."

"Naturally," Drury said, adapting yet again to the changing situation. "If you can give me a few days to scout locations and revise my shooting schedule to reflect what I find, I think I'll be able to give you some solid numbers."

Linda thanked him and went off to check on her mother-in-law.

Shepard gave her a ten count before piping up. "So, Carson, what do you say we bring the maid back in. Maybe you can go oh for three."

Drury laughed himself out of wind. "Let's leave the poor maid alone. The way my luck is running, I'll probably remind her of an ex-husband. God, I could do with a drink. Do you have any crusty old port in the basement, Gilbert?"

"Yes, I think so. Come help me with the glasses, Scotty."

I trailed him to the living room's discreet corner bar. An even more discreet push button was set in a brass plate on the bar's side. Gilbert held the button in for a moment. Then he poured brandy into two balloon glasses and handed me one. Before I could ask what had happened to Plan A, the formal maid rustled in.

"Greta, please take a bottle of port and a box of cigars to Mr. Drury and Mr. Shepard. Tell them we'll be in directly."

He'd somehow talked and emptied his snifter at the same time. He collected the brandy bottle and led me toward his brother's shrine. "Sit down, Scotty. I'll feel better about facing Carson after he's had a drink and I've had several."

"He dropped the ball in there, not you."

"Carson may not see it that way, once he's had a chance to reflect."

Gilbert played with a gold tassel on the arm of the sofa, giving me a chance to reflect. "You didn't tell Drury that your sister-in-law is involved in the Traynor Company's financial decisions?"

"Linda makes the Traynor Company's financial decisions. I told Carson that I'm president of the company, and that's true as far as it goes. But the head of our board of directors is L. D. Traynor. That's Linda."

He watched me closely while he caught up on his drinking. "I didn't expect the chairwoman-of-the-board angle to throw you, Scotty. Your wife has a successful career of her own."

"L. D. Traynor's sex doesn't throw me, but I am surprised to hear that an in-law is running the family company."

Gilbert shrugged. "That's just an example of 'talent will out.' " He filled his glass again, checked mine, and set the bottle down on the gilt table. "Linda has a genius for business. Nobody knew that until after Mark was killed, not even Mark himself. He only knew that he loved Linda and that loving her infuriated our mother. That's something of a hobby with us Traynor boys."

"Why would Linda infuriate your mother?"

"Because Linda's family lacked little things like social position and money and indoor plumbing. Mark met her when he was stationed down at Camp Atterbury in southern Indiana. Met her, married her, and went off to be killed.

"It's a shame Mother didn't take to her daughter-in-law. Linda's own mother died in an accident when Linda was very young. Mark told me the story, which was an ugly one. Linda watched her mother step in front of a truck during a shopping trip to town. It would have been natural for Linda to reach out to her mother-in-law as a substitute, but Mother wasn't interested. It was fortunate for Linda that Dad wasn't as fussy socially."

Gilbert filled his glass again, this time without a glance at mine. "My father had his first heart attack a few months after Mark died, probably because Mark had died. That left Mother in a fix. I was away at school and destined for the army myself—too late to see any action, incidentally. Mother knew nothing about business, the Pallisers being above trade, but there was Linda. She'd been helping Father since Mark shipped out. They got along well, Dad and Linda. They had a lot in common."

The memory made the mild Gilbert mildly jealous. "Like what?" I asked.

"Just a practical, do-your-job-and-shut-up way of looking at the world. Quiet competence, Mother calls it. The kind of thing they can't teach you in years of college, as I was to learn. Dad was the first to recognize Linda's potential. He had an eye for potential. During his illness, Linda became his deputy at the plant. By the time he had his second attack, she was practically running the place. A natural genius, as I said."

"It must have been tough on your mother, having to depend on a woman she didn't like."

"It was, but Mother had no choice. Linda was essential to her plan for the future. Rather, she was essential to Mother's plan that there be no future. You see, my mother's life stopped the day the telegram came about Mark. That's a cliché, I know, but everything about her has become a cliché: the endless black dresses, the room preserved just as Mark left it. Just like in a movie."

Gilbert leaned toward me. The brandy in his glass and in his face picked up the golden glow of the table. "I was struck by that quality of our lives when I was out in movie land. I'd gone out there to get away from this house for a while, but somehow I hadn't gotten away. I finally realized it was because I'd been living in a movie for years. A movie without an ending."

He stopped speaking and focused on something over my left shoulder: Linda Traynor.

"You're neglecting your guests, Gilbert."

"Sorry, Linda. I had to hear about Scotty's Silver Star. I got caught up in the story."

He hurried off to rejoin Drury. Linda didn't, so I hung around, too. On our walk in to dinner, I had noted that Linda was tall with wide shoulders that made her look slender and almost boyish. Now, standing next to her, I tossed out the boyish part.

"Were you two really talking about the war, Mr. Elliott?"

I didn't answer right away. I'd never lied to a board of directors before.

"It's all right," she said. "I'm fond of Gilbert. I know he has to have his little plots and schemes."

"Doesn't sound like a very endearing quality."

"You have to understand his motivation."

I'd have to guess it, too, because she wasn't about to fill me in. She sat down in Gilbert's vacated seat on the sofa, the full skirt of her dark red dress arranging itself artistically across the cushions. She collected a cigarette from a box next to his forgotten brandy bottle and pushed the box across to me. I took a cigarette—a Turkish blend Fatima—as I resumed my seat, figuring it would have been the least of Ella's worries if she'd been around to worry. The Fatima was the least of my worries.

"Gilbert calls you Scotty. May I?"

"Yes," I said.

"How did you come to win the Silver Star, Scotty?"

"I got it for not being killed."

"Just the opposite of my husband's method."

The remark was tossed off and even a little brutal, but that was the way some people dealt with the war. "He must have died doing something important," I said.

"No. Mark just died, a mile or two into Germany. The medal was his mother's idea, something she used the family's influence to get. She said earlier that he paid for it dearly. Actually, she paid for it by buying mountains of war bonds."

"At the armory in Indianapolis?"

"That would be a coincidence to make your skin crawl, wouldn't it? No, she didn't buy that particular block in Indy. Mark was still alive when Mr. Drury and his muse floated through in 1943." She repeated "muse" and shook her head.

"Drury's not as phony as he comes across," I said.

"He has a fancy line of bullshit, though, doesn't he?" She said it to shock me and succeeded. "Not a very endearing quality."

"You have to understand his motivation," I said.

Linda smiled. "Sophisticated people say 'touché' at moments like this. In Indiana we sometimes say 'to hell with you.' "

"I seem to remember that."

"Are you Mr. Drury's advocate?"

I wasn't sure how much Gilbert had told her about our California troubles, so I held back. "I'm the guy who drives his station wagon. All I'm looking for is job security."

"It's not all it's cracked up to be," Linda said.

"SO I TALKED MY GUARDIANS in beautiful Cleveland into sending me to Europe alone. This was when I was scarcely old enough to have a driver's license. They were thinking of something along the lines of the old grand tour, maybe because that's the way I sold it to them. Take the left that's coming up, Scotty."

"Huntington's straight ahead," I said. It was the end of our first week of location scouting, and Drury had yet to find a town to double for Indianapolis in the twenties. Hank Shepard and I were taking turns driving the great man from one prospect to another while he rehearsed bits of his autobiography. At least that's what Drury did when I was on duty.

"Nevertheless, we'll turn," he said. "You never get anywhere in this world taking the direct route. I rather like that line. Remember to quote it twenty years from now when you're interviewed about the time you spent wandering Indiana with Carson Drury."

He said it in the self-mocking tone he adopted when Shepard wasn't around to provide sarcastic asides. The director and publicist's relationship had turned out to be more complicated than I'd guessed back in Hollywood. I was often reminded of an ancient Roman custom I'd read about in school, or maybe seen in a Cecil B. DeMille epic, the practice of having a slave ride in a conqueror's chariot during a triumphal parade to whisper in the hero's ear: "You're not the big shot you think you are." When he was around, Shepard provided that service for Drury. When Shepard wasn't around, Drury did the whispering himself. In either case the service struck me as unnecessary. Drury was years past his most recent parade.

"Where was I?" he asked after I'd dutifully made the turn onto the more interesting, less recently paved road.

"On the grand tour."

"No, that was only the dodge. I promised my keepers I'd see museums and opera houses, but instead I visited brothels and music halls. My tour was twice as broadening as the one I was supposed to be making, but it was also twice as expensive. I was broke by the time I reached Paris. Stone-broke for the first time in my life."

The memory stopped him cold, which was easy enough to understand. His first experience with empty pockets was an important milestone for Drury, on the order of the first time Esther Williams had gotten wet. It was my chance to turn the radio on and find a ball game, but for once I was caught up in Drury's story.

"So what happened?"

"Oh. Well, I fell back on an honorable American tradition and joined the circus. The Banfi Family Circus, to be precise. It was as old and flea-bitten a troupe as you're imagining right now, but noble for all that. Noble *because* of that. The circus had the same kind of redeeming aura that turns the open sewers of Venice into a tourist attraction, an aura that's part decay and part romance. I often thought of that circus during the war years, wondering whether it was surviving Hitler. It consoled me to think that, as the circus had already survived Napoleon and the Kaiser, it could surely outlast a paperhanger.

"You had to be a Banfi to perform in the circus; it was some kind of union rule. So I became Carlo Banfi, juggler, tumbler, and first assistant to a knife thrower named Guido. He was training me to be a knife thrower, too, old Guido was, until I ran afoul of young Maria, his daughter.

"Stop the car, Scotty! Pull over and stop!"

There was no room to pull over. The road, which had turned to gravel, was barely wide enough to keep the ditch lilies on either side from depositing their pollen on the wagon's paint. So I stopped in the middle.

"What's the matter?"

"That tree, do you see it? The sycamore in the cornfield."

"What about it?"

"I've seen several like that, not all sycamores, but trees left growing in the middle of fields of corn. Big, beautiful trees without any competitors to ruin their shapes. Why are they there? Were they left when the field was cleared? Have they grown up since? Why would a farmer let a tree grow up like that? It costs him ground he could plant, and the shade surely stunts part of his crop."

"There's more to life than corn," I said. "Maybe the farmer likes to look at the tree."

"Could that be it?" Drury asked, every bit as convinced as he would have been if I'd told him the sycamore had sprung up overnight. "There may be more to you Hoosiers than meets the eye."

We started off again. This time Drury resumed his story without a prompt. "Maria had a libido that made mine look middle-aged. And she worked for free. It was an altogether idyllic situation, which meant it couldn't last. Sure enough, we were discovered one balmy night in the circus hay wagon by none other than Guido himself. He wasn't carrying his cutlery, or I wouldn't be talking with you now, but I did have to resign my membership in the Family Banfi on short notice. I hotfooted it to the nearest American embassy and wired home for a boat ticket.

"Six months later I was playing Hamlet on Broadway. Two years after that I was in Hollywood. Since then I've been knifed in the back many times, but never, thank God, by Guido."

I fell into thinking about Drury's most recent knifing. He did, too, or else he read my mind.

"What do you suppose Gilbert Traynor is really up to, Scotty? Was my original guess correct? Is he just rebelling against the old apron strings a little belatedly? Are we the equivalent of the Banfi Family Circus in his journey toward manhood? Or are we a curveball Gilbert is throwing his sister-in-law, the chairwoman of his company?"

"I don't know. Gilbert may not know himself."

"Those are the most dangerous kind of people, the ones who don't know why they do what they do. Unfortunately, they're also the most common kind."

It was another quote for my future interview, but I didn't write it down. "Are you thinking he won't come across with the money?"

"I'm not sure," Drury said. "Gilbert doesn't seem to have any particular regard for money. It's a means to an end for him, not a thing in itself. That's the way I feel about the stuff. I've turned down any number of acting jobs over the years, which is to say, I've turned down a great deal of money. It would have been wiser by far to have taken the money, but I've never enjoyed acting in another man's film. I've never enjoyed jumping through someone else's hoops. I'm not enjoying it now."

■ ■ ■

Huntington was yet another bust. As a consolation we got back to Riverbend relatively early in the day. Hank Shepard was asleep on the front porch, his stockinged feet propped on its railing. He didn't stir during the noisy process of unloading Drury's chair and the noisier process of unloading Drury. But when the rubber wheels of the wheelchair reached the worn wood of the porch, he opened his eyes.

"Damn, it's hot. Who'd have thought it'd be so hot so far north?"

"Scott and I have already discussed how broadening travel is, Hank. Maybe if you drank lemonade instead of beer, you'd feel peppier."

Next to Shepard's chair was a galvanized steel tub in which floated the smooth, clear remains of a block of ice. Shepard looked at the tub and then at the empty bottles arranged around it.

"Those aren't all mine. Clark did his share." He mopped his face with the handkerchief Drury offered and then hung the linen square from his shirt pocket to dry. "We had quite a chat. I put in a good word for you, Elliott, but Clark wasn't having any. I can't figure out how you got on his—no pun intended—bad side."

Neither could I, but I was definitely there. The disfigured veteran had taken to Drury from the first and eventually to Shepard, but Clark and I had started slowly and then backed up.

The situation tickled Shepard. "Maybe it's those ex–movie star looks of yours, Elliott. Maybe Clark was a looker himself in the good old days."

"How about the phone, Hank? Were there any calls?"

"Yeah, Carson, I forgot. Louie B. Mayer called. He wants to have you over for cocktails. Turns out he owns a farm near goddamn Fort Wayne. Or was it Muncie? Who the hell is going to call us here? Who even knows where here is?"

"That's fine with me," Drury said. "We may have left our friends behind, but we've also left our troubles behind."

Shepard wasn't listening. "The phone did ring once. It was for you, Elliott. Your grandmother called from Indianapolis. She said she was expecting you for Sunday dinner."

"She did?"

"Yeah," Shepard said. "She's frying a chicken and making the dessert you like, the banana pudding with the little vanilla cookies in it. I told her you'd grown. She should fry two chickens. You can bring us back the leftovers."

"That's a good idea, Scotty. Take the wagon and drive down there Sunday. You've earned a break."

"How about the rest of us Indians?" Shepard asked. "It's Friday night. What do you say we try out that guest membership Gilbert got us at the Toonerville Country Club? I'm ready for a big weekend."

HOME BACK TEAM

chapter

18

I'D GOTTEN THE DAY'S only phone call, and I also received the evening's first visitor. I'd passed on Shepard's expedition to the Traynorville Country Club. I didn't want to hear all the Indiana jokes the place was bound to inspire, so I told Drury I wanted to call California and waved good-bye as the almost-sober Shepard drove him away.

In fact, I did plan to call Ella. I wanted to thank her for arranging my little dinner party on Sunday. I'd worked it out this way. She had somehow guessed or just known that I hadn't called my father, that I was waiting for the ideal moment to do it, a moment that had passed years before. To speed matters along, Ella had called my grandmother and spilled the news that I was in Indiana.

My desire to thank my wife was only one of my reasons for hanging around the farm. I was also hoping that Clark would stop by, looking for another chat. So I set myself up in a front porch rocking chair with my neglected pipe and worked on the wording of my opening line to Ella.

Clark never showed. Instead, just as the sun was beginning to set, a car came up the long drive. It was another Studebaker President Speedster, a solid black one this time. The coupé stopped at the foot of the front porch steps.

It took me a moment to connect the car's driver with the lady in crimson and gold I'd met at the Traynor manse. This evening Linda Traynor was wearing a simple white blouse and an A-line khaki skirt. Her long hair was also at ease. It had a reddish tint in the last of the natural light. Linda gave me a chance to take all that in by pausing next to the car to take in the sunset. It had turned out to be a beauty. Towering thunderheads had built up in the west. They'd been a dazzling white when I'd sat down, but now those canyons were a blue-gray foreground for the bloody afterglow.

"Thank God for sunsets and thunderstorms," Linda said. "Without them, Indiana would be a frightening place to live."

"Thunderstorms always made it more frightening for me," I said.

"When they're on top of you, yes," Linda said from the safe distance of the drive. "I don't like them then myself. But my office windows face the west. Sometimes I can see a really big storm when it isn't much closer than Illinois. I sit and watch it coming at me, filling the sky, making the plant and Traynorville look like one of the matchbox towns Annie and I used to build in the yard back home.

"A person needs the sense that there are bigger things out there. Bigger powers. Bigger concerns. If you live near the mountains or the sea, that lesson is always staring you in the face. It doesn't stare you in the face around here. Our horizon is the nearest row of trees. Nothing very awe inspiring about that. Nothing to contradict a sense of your own importance. So I say thank God for sunsets and storms."

Delivered in her rural twang, the last line came out sounding like a call for an amen. I didn't add one, not feeling in an amen mood. According to Linda's theory, Los Angeles, stuck between the ocean and the mountains, should have been a little basin of mental health and well-ordered priorities. That hadn't been my experience.

It was my turn to speak, though, so I asked, "Who was this Annie you used to build towns with? Your sister?"

"No," Linda said. "I never had a sister or a brother. Or even a close friend. Our farm was pretty isolated, so I made up a friend and named her Annie, after my mother."

The admission made her sad. To distract her I said, "I didn't know Studebaker made a black Speedster. I thought they were all two-tone."

"The production ones are. I asked for a black one. My widow's weeds, I guess."

"Does everyone in your family drive a Studebaker?"

"Everyone in my family drives a tractor," Linda said. "The Traynor family favors Studebakers because the Traynor Automobile Company provides a lot of their parts."

"Gilbert told me about that. He said he'd rather build cars than parts."

"He'd rather dream about building them."

"At the moment I hope he's dreaming of making a movie."

"I think he's dreaming even bigger than that," Linda said. Instead of elaborating, she returned to the topic of business. "It was my idea to develop strong ties to Studebaker. Seemed like a wise move at the time, safe and secure. Now Studebaker is losing money, and my board is scared."

"I hope we're not adding to your worries," I said.

"Maybe your visit will help take them off my mind." She ascended Drury's ramp, walking splay-footed in her flat shoes, like a girl. "Don't get up, Scotty. You look too comfortable. All you need is a knife and a piece of wood and you could whittle."

"All I need is a knife," I said, holding up my cold briar pipe.

"Don't carve up that pretty thing. It suits you."

"That's what my wife thinks." I said it thoughtlessly, but it came out sounding very calculated.

Linda stopped in her tracks a few feet from my chair and then leaned back against the porch railing. "Is Mr. Drury available?"

"No. He and Mr. Shepard are having dinner at the country club."

"With my brother-in-law?"

"Not unless they ran into him by accident."

She nodded. "We've kept him pretty busy this week at the plant. It's his punishment for taking a vacation. So you're here by yourself?"

It was a chance to mention my call to Ella, but I didn't want to hide behind her twice in the same conversation. "Clark's around someplace."

"I wouldn't count on that. It's Friday night. Clark likes to have a drink or two on Fridays, usually at a little bar on the square named Augie's. Our locals may not be the most sensitive people in the world, but they clear a space for Clark. The ones who aren't sensitive know better than to tangle with him."

"How well do you know Clark?"

"Nobody knows him well."

We listened as the evening sounds of the farm slowly gave way to the night sounds, Linda leaning back and looking off to the west and me rocking and not whittling. I'd forgotten to switch on the porch light, and my guest slowly grew less distinct than her trim, white blouse. Just before she disappeared completely, I asked, "Can I take a message for Drury?"

"You might ask him if he knows an Eric Faris."

I stood up. "I know Faris. He works for a Los Angeles land developer named Ralph Lockard."

That checked for Linda. "Mr. Faris is here in Traynorville. He came by to see me today."

"Why?"

"To sniff around, I think. And to make trouble for you boys. He said that his employer wanted to tell us, as a courtesy, what a risky proposition *The Imperial Albertsons* is. Mr. Lockard must be afraid that Mr. Drury might look like a gilt-edged bond to us simple country folk."

"Did Faris explain Lockard's interest?"

"Suppose you do."

When I didn't jump at the chance, she said, "I asked Mr. Faris about you, Scotty. About your relationship to Mr. Drury. He called you a Hollywood operative. That sounds romantic."

"It's not," I said. "I work for a firm called the Hollywood Security Agency."

"As an investigator?"

"As a hand holder, usually."

"I didn't think you were one of Mr. Drury's yes-men. Mr. Faris didn't tell me why Mr. Drury had hired you."

"Lately it's been to push his chair around." To keep her from pressing me for the truth, I answered her earlier question about Lockard's interest in *Albertsons*. I told her about Eden and the Alora Conservancy. Against the background of the black, humid Indiana night, the San Fernando Valley seemed remote and unlikely.

"Poor Mr. Drury," she said when I'd finished. "Nobody seems to care about his movie–not even the people who are giving him money."

"How about telling me Gilbert's angle?"

"I'll have to figure it out first. And I'll have to get to know you better."

As a step in that direction, she leaned forward and kissed me. I saw the kiss coming from a long way off, like Linda's hypothetical thunderstorms, but I still managed to be standing there when it landed. I kept standing there as Linda descended to her car, her footsteps sounding lightly on the hollow stairs and then on the gravel.

"I also wanted to tell Mr. Drury something about my mother-in-law," Linda said from the darkness. She opened the coupé's door, and its dome light lit the scene. "Marvella has to be in control."

"So does Drury."

"That could be interesting." The dome light went out, and the engine came to life. Given the absence of mountains in Indiana, I was able to watch the car's taillights for quite some time.

When they finally disappeared, I entered the house, kicked a few things, and switched on a lamp. An old, dial-less telephone shared the table with the lamp, looking like Alexander Graham Bell's personal contribution to the Traynor collection. I spoke first with a local operator, who sounded impressed, and then with a long-distance specialist, who sounded bored, even after I'd given her a Los Angeles number.

While I waited, I sat down on a rickety settee with intricately carved woodwork. The carver had had a lot of walnut to work with but nothing particular to say. The result was a jumble of busy geometric patterns, like the tooling on Gene Autry's saddle. The whole room was a jumble. Across from my settee was a glass-fronted bookcase holding a collection of arrowheads and a desiccated hornet's nest. To the left of the case was a tall secretary, and to the right was a miniature pump organ. Framing the organ was a pair of spindly, ladder-backed chairs in search of a dining room table. Two large, oval portraits decorated the wall above the organ. They were early photographs, so early that the sitters hadn't learned yet from Hollywood that you should smile like a maniac when your picture is taken.

Ella came on the line, sounding farther away than California. Farther away than China. "Scotty?"

"How'd you guess?"

"I was hoping it would be you. I thought it might be."

"Did you recognize my ring?"

"In a way. I had a feeling. It ran from the small of my back to the nape of my neck."

While I pictured that familiar route and listened to her talk, my plan for grilling Ella over my family reunion slipped clean out of my mind. She told me that the kids had been mildly violent but not outright antisocial at a neighborhood birthday party and that she'd gotten a nibble on a screenplay she was finishing up. She said it all at shorthand speed, mindful of the cost of the call. With the last of her breath she said, "Your turn."

"I miss you."

"Is that the whole speech?"

"This may be a party line."

"Thanks for the warning. Paddy called today to see how you were doing. He wanted to know if we'd heard from you."

And why he hadn't. "Tell him he let one of Ralph Lockard's men slip through his fingers. He's out here with us, a guy named Eric Faris."

"A goon?"

"A college kid, but Paddy should still know about it. And tell him the *Albertsons* negative is with us, too. Drury had Gilbert Traynor sneak it out."

"If you called to put my mind at ease, you're doing a lousy job."

"I called to hear your voice." It was almost my signature line—I'd been using it since our early days together.

Ella recognized the wrap-up. "Be careful, Hoosier."

"I haven't been a Hoosier for a long time."

"That's true out here, but you may turn into someone else entirely in Indiana. Keep checking the mirror."

"I will," I said.

chapter

19

IT OCCURRED TO ME as I hung up the phone that I hadn't told Ella about Linda Traynor or her parting kiss, making me an accessory after the fact. The slip hadn't been entirely accidental, either. I wasn't afraid that Ella would be jealous; a woman who could recognize my ring knew me better than that. There was a chance she'd play jealous, though, as one more justification for her own trip to Indiana.

My resolve not to have my family in the same state with Carson Drury, which had weakened on my trip east, was feeling its oats again. The whole Indiana setup—Gilbert Traynor's coy absence, our isolation on the farm, Marvella Traynor's hostility, and now Eric Faris's sudden arrival—was making me jumpy. So was the dark night outside, which sounded as alive with invisible life as any jungle. I felt as much an outsider in that jungle as Hank Shepard did, which bothered me. I decided that Indiana and I needed a little quiet reacquainting.

I walked out through the back of the house, past Drury's room and through the kitchen. I stepped out boldly enough through the screen door, but then I caught the door before its old iron spring could slam it behind me. I shut it soundlessly and stepped out across the dry, clipped grass, making a show of looking for stars. There weren't any. The western thunderheads had snuck up after dark and surrounded me. I could hear them rumbling overhead, but it was a peaceful rumbling, like the sound of a sleeping cat.

The backyard was much smaller than the front and more functional. As my eyes adjusted to the darkness, I could see the little outbuildings and coops that marked the edge of the lawn. Unlike the traditional red barn, these buildings were white, as white and empty as the house usually was. I knew from daylight inspections that beyond the sheds was a field, tilled but not planted, and beyond the field a clump of woods that held Clark's cabin. I wasn't feeling that adventurous, so I headed for the barn, whose white trim floated in the darkness like a child's chalk drawing.

At the barn's side door I found more of Clark's handiwork: the side rails for another ramp. When finished, it would allow Drury to ascend unaided to the editing room that Clark and Shepard were setting up inside. The ramp was a low-priority project because Drury had shown little interest in getting inside the barn, aided or unaided. His dithering bothered Shepard, who had paid for special delivery of the editing equipment from Chicago, but it pleased me. The delay meant that the precious *Albertsons* negative was still safely tucked away in one of the Traynor Company's vaults.

I opened the barn's door and stepped up onto the raised floor, fingering the air ahead of me like a blind man as I searched for the dangling light chain. I found it with the end of my nose. The fixture that came on when I yanked the chain was brand new, and it would have been more than adequate for an operating room. I counted the pieces of equipment and furniture like a good night watchman, checked the metal cabinet installed in one corner to make sure Drury hadn't slipped the negative onto the farm when I wasn't looking, and switched off the light.

I was blind again outside, so blind that I couldn't be sure I saw what I thought I saw: a figure near the corner of the house. The figure seemed to melt away as I strained to make it out. I started to run. I had my night vision back by the time I reached the corner of the house, but it didn't buy me anything. There was nothing between the side of the house and the wire fence that marked the edge of the yard except for a bed of peonies, the plants bent over almost double by their blooms.

I circled the house twice without seeing anything but great places for a prowler to hide. Then I went back inside and sat in the parlor—well away from the lamp I'd left burning—to wait for the return of the country club set.

It was nearly midnight when I heard the station wagon on the gravel drive. Not long afterward I could hear Drury himself. From what I could make out, he'd had another brainstorm at dinner. He was talking about filming the new, improved second half of *Albertsons* in color.

"That's a great idea," Shepard said while the last note sounded by the wagon's brakes was still scaring the crickets. "I love it. I've loved it ever since I saw it done in *The Wizard of Oz* in '39. Maybe you can say they stole your idea."

"It wouldn't be the first time someone stole an idea of mine before I had it," Drury replied good-naturedly. "Why not color? Think of the impact going from black and white to color will have. The audience will know the Albertsons have arrived in a new world."

"Why not CinemaScope or goddamn Vista Vision? Maybe their new world is wider, too. You know why not. Because we don't have the money. We're in a hole right now, and every new idea you get digs it a little deeper. I don't want to hear another one. And I'm not just talking about tonight. I'm talking about the rest of my life. No more."

I felt the same way about it. I didn't want to referee another round of Drury and Shepard's long bout. I could wait until morning to tell them that Eric Faris had shown up and that I was seeing ghosts. I left Shepard to struggle with Drury's wheelchair alone and went up to my room.

I thought I'd have to wait until the house settled down before I could sleep, but I dropped off right away. I was deep into a dream about a twister chasing Judy Garland across a black-and-white prairie when Hank Shepard woke me.

"Roll out, pally," he said. "We've got company."

I tried to raise my arm to read the luminous dial on my watch, but that was the arm Shepard had grabbed to wake me and he hadn't finished grabbing it. I didn't think it could be dawn yet, but my room was almost that bright. I could make out Shepard's face. It was gray and glistening with sweat. I wanted to ask him if he'd seen my ghost, but I couldn't form the words in time.

"Hurry up," he said, releasing my arm. "Carson's down there alone." He turned in the doorway. "Bring that cannon of yours."

I climbed into my pants and pulled my gun—an army surplus forty-five—from the bottom of my suitcase, shaking its holster onto the floor as I padded out into the hallway. Across the hall was the front of the house and Shepard's room. It was the source of the false dawn; that is, Shepard's twin windows were the source. His room was lit faintly from outside by a flickering light coming from the front yard. I didn't cross to the windows, but I did check my watch on my way down the stairs. It was two-thirty.

The front parlor was also lit from outside, but not faintly. Two pairs of headlights were pointed into the room, converging on the doorway where I stood. The lights were almost blinding, but they weren't the first thing I saw in the yard. Between the crossed headlights and eclipsing them was a burning cross.

"Some old friends of mine have come to call," Drury said. "Come and see." He'd wheeled himself right up to one of the front windows. To make himself an even better target, I thought.

I was doing a fair job of that myself. I stuck the automatic into my belt at the small of my back and stepped up beside him. There were figures moving about in the dazzling light—hooded figures in white robes, holding torches.

I had a flashback as vivid as the scene before me, a memory of a Klan march I'd seen in Indianapolis as a boy. There had been hundreds of robed figures that night, carrying torches of their own and scaring the life out of me. I hadn't been that scared again until the day I stepped onto Utah Beach. But that rally was thirty years in the past. The figures outside the farmhouse made no more sense now than a squad of Nazi infantry would have.

"I guess I really should say they're old friends of D. W. Griffith's," Drury said. "They've never been that fond of me. In fact, after the *First Citizen* premiere, I had a very lively correspondence with them. It was a one-sided correspondence because their letters were always anonymous."

He was talking big, but he had the sense to do it in a low voice. I stepped back toward the antique phone without turning away from the lights.

"Don't bother, Scotty. I've already tried it. The line's quite dead."

"Where's Shepard?"

"Here," he said. "I was checking the back of the house. There's no sign of anyone back there. Could be a trap, or it could be a way out." He pointed toward the back door with a gun, a thirty-eight Police Special.

"Put that gun somewhere where they can't see it," I said.

"To hell with that. I want them to see it."

"Do as he says, Hank. They can see us better than we can see them. You could have a rifle trained on you right now."

Shepard stuck the revolver under his shirt while Drury talked on in his comforting whisper. "That's always been the secret of the Klan's power. They can see you, but you can't see them. They know who you are, but you don't know who they are. You don't know which of your smiling neighbors might be underneath the hood."

"Where the hell is Clark?" Shepard asked.

"That's what I'm saying, Hank. For all we know he's right outside. Or if we're lucky, he's gone for the marines."

"Three of them are coming forward," I said.

Two of the three carried torches. They were escorts for the third man, who walked between and a little in front of them. Each torch-bearer had a round insignia on the left breast of his robe. The figure in the middle had two insignia on his chest, and his robe was gathered at his waist with a crimson cord. He was the one who spoke when the trio reached the edge of the gravel drive.

"Carson Drury, defamer of the Ku Klux Klan, we know you're in there. Come out and hear your sentence. Come out now, or we'll burn you out."

"The Great Oz has spoken," Drury said almost to himself.

His calm voice stopped me from reaching for my gun. I glanced over at him. He was running his long fingers through his uncombed mane, calming it, too.

He caught my eye and smiled, his teeth glinting in the headlights. "How many torches do you see, Scotty?"

I counted the ones held up by the figures around the cross and others out in the darkness that were just flickering points of light. "Twelve."

"What the hell difference does that make?" Shepard demanded.

"Just figuring the odds, Hank. If I were shooting this scene, I'd use torches scattered here and there myself. I'd have to. I couldn't afford to fill the yard with extras."

"This isn't a goddamn movie."

"Everything's a movie nowadays, Hank. That's what I think. That's the world Hollywood has given us. And a man can write himself as big a part as he can handle."

He backed his chair away from the window, almost knocking Shepard down. Then he wheeled himself toward the front door. "If you'd be so kind, Scotty."

Shepard grabbed at the chair. "Are you crazy?"

"I'm just scared, Hank. And mad."

I had my hand on the doorknob. It felt cool and peaceful behind the door, out of the glare of the lights. Drury was also in the door's shadow, but his eyes were still bright. He nodded to me.

I pulled the door open. Drury battered the screen door out of his way and bumped over the sill before Shepard or I could cover him. He wheeled himself forward until his extended cast hit the porch railing. I stepped up on Drury's left, smelling kerosene and thinking again how much the eye holes in the loose white masks looked like the sockets of a skull.

Drury pushed his cast off the chair. It hit the porch floor with a thump that shook the windows of the house. Then he stood up, swayed once, and caught the railing with both hands.

"I'm Carson Drury," he said. He projected the words effortlessly, filling the night with them, making the head Klansman, when he spoke again, sound like the village soprano.

"Carson Drury, defamer of the Ku Klux Klan, you are not welcome here. You will leave this place by sundown tomorrow or suffer our wrath. Your evil work has not been forgot. It will never be forgot. For the Bible says, 'God will bring every work into judgment, with every secret thing, whether it be good, or whether it be evil.' "

"I think of that verse from time to time myself," Drury said. "But I prefer these:

He that dwelleth in the secret place of the most High shall abide under the shadow of the Almighty.

I will say of the Lord, He is my refuge and my fortress: my God; in him I will trust.

Surely he shall deliver thee from the snare of the fowler, and from the noisome pestilence.

He shall cover thee with his feathers, and under his wing shalt thou trust: his truth shall be thy shield and buckler.

Drury had started in an easy voice, almost crooning the psalm. Now, as he released his grip on the rail and raised himself to his full height, his voice doubled its force:

Thou shalt not be afraid for *the terror by night;* nor for the arrow that flieth by day.

Nor for *the pestilence that walketh in darkness;* nor for the destruction that wasteth at noonday.

A thousand will fall at thy side, and ten thousand at thy right hand; but it shall not come nigh thee.

He broke off there, leaving a silence that the flaring and crackling of the cross couldn't fill. Nothing happened for a year or so. Then, from the far corners of the yard, torches began to move toward us. I shifted my weight to the balls of my feet.

The first man to reach the cross threw his burning torch at its base, and the others followed suit. Then a car door opened. That was a cue for the three Klansmen at the edge of the drive. First the torchbearers and then, almost reluctantly, the man with the crimson cord fell back into the darkness. A motor came to life and then another. The two pairs of headlights moved back in tandem toward the far end of the lawn. Then they turned for the gravel drive and disappeared into the night.

"Where's my chair gotten to?" Drury asked. He'd grabbed the rail again, but he was still tottering.

I maneuvered the chair behind him, and he collapsed into it, laughing wildly. "Was ever rabble in this humor wooed? Was ever rabble in this humor won? If I hadn't gotten a little light-headed toward the end, I could have worked them till they were singing spirituals!

"Remind you of the war, Scotty?"

"This was over quicker."

Drury laughed again, less nervously. "I hope you're right."

chapter

20

THE NEXT DAY WE HAD a council of war. That is, we had one eventually. At first light I drove the wagon to the nearest farm and used the phone there to call the local law. It arrived at Riverbend in the form of the county sheriff himself, Sheriff Frank Gustin. He was a big man with a round, downy face and rosy cheeks. While he listened to Drury's account of our night, Gustin stood with his straw hat planted squarely on his head and his hands on his gun belt. He didn't make a comment, ask a question, or even blink very often. The sheriff's immobility had Shepard rolling his bloodshot eyes. Even Drury, who could sell a story to a lamppost, seemed to lose heart.

When he finished listening, Gustin went out to look at the charred pole that was all that was left of the Klan's cross. I joined him there.

"So what do we do?" I asked.

"Damned if I know, Mr. Elliott." He gave me a long-toothed smile and took off his hat. His blond hair was cut so short that it had a pink cast from the skin underneath. It gave off a rasping sound when he scratched his head. "I didn't want to sound ignorant in front of Mr. Drury–not someone I've listened to on the radio a hundred times. But the truth is, I'm flat stumped. It's a relief to say it out loud.

"I mean to say, the Klan, for God's sake. You gentlemen wouldn't know, being from California. You probably think we midwesterners keep eye holes cut in our sheets so we'll be able to wear them on short notice. But the Klan is dead and buried around here."

"I grew up in Indianapolis," I said. "I remember the Klan."

"Remember it from the twenties, right? So do I. They came close to running this county back then, from what I've been told. They would have run it if it hadn't been for the Traynors."

"They fought the Klan?"

"The old man did. Mark and Gilbert's father. From what I hear, he went toe to toe with them pointy heads. See, he was hiring a lot of immigrants for his factory at the time, a lot of them Catholic. The Klan didn't like it, but old man Traynor never backed down."

"Do you think one of the motives for this cross burning could have been revenge against the Traynor family?"

"I'm telling you, the Klan is history. There's nobody left to take revenge for anything, not for what the Traynors did in the twenties or for some movie Mr. Drury made whenever."

"Nineteen forty-one," I said.

"That's another thing," Gustin said, scratching away again at the five o'clock shadow on the top of his head. "Even if the Klan were meeting once a week around here like the Rotary, why would they still be mad about something that happened in '41? It's like a ghost story where somebody rises up from the grave fretting over something no living soul can even remember."

Gustin reached out to poke the blackened post. It didn't disappear. "I'd hate to think this was a slap at the Traynors. They're good people. The folks in this county owe them a lot. Me, especially. I'm an appointee, you know, and the Traynors did the appointing. Sheriff Pyle, my predecessor, had a heart attack last year. He could have told you all about the Klan if he were still with us."

More to the point, he could have told Gustin what to do next. Luckily, there were other people around to provide the service. Two of them arrived just then in a low, black car.

Linda Traynor got out of the driver's seat of the coupé before the dust had settled behind it. She was wearing another crisp white blouse, this one with short cuffed sleeves. There was a wisp of orange scarf tied around her neck. It matched her uncuffed, Saturday-morning slacks. Her brother-in-law also looked as if he'd been caught on his way to the golf course—or maybe the polo field if he'd gotten around to building himself one. Gilbert shook my hand but didn't meet my eye.

"Sorry I haven't been out to see you," he said. "Hope you've had everything you've needed."

"And then some," I said.

"We tried calling, Scotty," Linda said, "but your phone is out of order."

Gustin, who had been standing at attention, finally thought of something practical to do. "I'll radio for a repairman."

"Already taken care of, Frank," Linda said. "Why didn't you call us, Scotty?"

"Carson didn't want to bother you," I said, being careful not to say "frighten you off" by mistake.

"He should have known we'd hear," Gilbert said. "Everyone in Traynorville knew about it within an hour of your call to the sheriff."

"A fair number of people knew about it before that," I said.

Linda led the parade in to see Drury. She headed up the little conference that followed, too. This time, Gustin sat down, with his hat off. We all sat, the six of us, in a circle of chairs while Drury told his story again. Given a more appreciative audience, Drury put a little more into it. I was surprised to hear, for example, that I'd stared down the mob with flinty eyes. Gilbert and Linda both glanced at me on that line. I couldn't call up flinty on short notice, so I just smiled modestly. Neither Traynor smiled back.

"I'd like to apologize to you three on behalf of the town," Gilbert said.

"We owe them more than an apology, Gilbert. We owe them action."

Gilbert looked as stuck for an inspiration as Gustin had been. Then he said, "There is that Faris person."

"Who?" Drury asked.

It was my dropped ball, so I picked it up. "Eric Faris, Ralph Lockard's man from Alora. He's here in Indiana. Mrs. Traynor stopped by last night to tell you that. I forgot about it in all the excitement."

"Think you could find Mr. Faris for us, Frank?" Gilbert asked. "Maybe bring him here for a visit?"

"If he's still in Traynorville, we'll find him." Gustin went out to his car to make the call.

Linda didn't stop him, but when he'd gone, she said, "No stranger from California could arrange a cross burning in Traynorville."

"It has always amazed me what money can arrange," Drury said. It was a casual comment, but it killed the conversation. We all sat watching one another until Gustin came back in.

"He's likely to be staying in the hotel in town or the motel out on 32," the sheriff said. "It won't take long to check."

"You should be staying at the hotel, Mr. Drury, or at our home," Linda said. "You shouldn't spend another night out here."

"I can't let myself be scared off by some thugs in bed linen, either," Drury said. "I have my reputation to think of. Anyway, I'm safe enough here with Hank and Scotty and Clark."

"Clark made himself plenty scarce last night," Shepard said. "I wonder if he knew what was going to happen."

"Something may have happened to him," Gustin said. "I'd better go back and check."

I was curious about Clark's absence, too, so I volunteered to go along for the walk. Linda made it a threesome. "I could use the exercise," she said.

This time Gustin led the way. It was an easy route to follow. Clark's solitary comings and goings had worn a smooth path from the collection of outbuildings, along the edge of the fallow field, and into the woods.

Gustin pulled away from us as we neared the field. Linda had lost the take-charge air she'd arrived with, or she'd set it aside. Even her purposeful walk had changed, becoming so hesitant that she actually stumbled once on the featureless path.

I caught her arm. "If seeing Clark bothers you, maybe you should go back."

"It's not that. I wanted a chance to talk with you about last night. Alone. Now I don't know how to start."

"Drury didn't leave anything out of his report except maybe the bit about how scared we were."

"That's not the part of last night I mean, and you know it. Don't make this harder on me than it has to be."

Gustin had stopped to examine the ground at the point where the field met the woods, and we caught up to him there, cutting our private conversation short.

"Deer tracks," Gustin said as we came up behind him. "I do a little hunting," he explained to me. "I wonder if Clark does. This would be a great spot."

"Clark doesn't like guns," Linda said.

Clark's home was a hundred yards or so into the woods. The cabin, which stood up off the ground on fieldstone pilings, was built of hewn timbers notched together at the corners and chinked with cement. The wooden shingles of the roof were green in spots, and the door and the window frames were unpainted, their wood as gray with weathering as the timbers. The only decorative thing about the building was its chimney. In place of the flat, sharp-edged stones that held up the cabin, the chimney's mason had used rounded stones from the bed of a creek or a river, probably the river that had given the farm its name. I couldn't see any water or hear any, so I asked Gustin where it was kept.

"The west fork of the White River is just through those trees behind the cabin. Isn't that right, Mrs. Traynor?"

"Yes. We'll wait here while you knock, Sheriff."

Gustin hitched up his holster and stepped forward. The cabin door opened before he reached it. Clark came out as far as the top step. I'd seen him several times over the course of the week, and I'd almost gotten used to his face—or his lack of a face. But I was shocked all over again by the sight of him in the cabin doorway. It took me a second to realize that it was the first time I'd seen him without his ball cap. The cap had hidden a scar that ran across his forehead, a jagged dividing line between the pale, ordinary skin of his scalp and the red, raw remains of his face.

Clark missed the cap, too. He raised one hand to cover the scar, pretending to shield his eyes from sunlight that was barely penetrating the canopy of trees. "What do you want?" he asked.

The question hung there for a moment, allowing me to think, not for the first time, that the voice didn't match the man. It was too soft, too genteel. It seemed especially out of place against the background of the rustic cabin.

Then Gustin said, "We wanted to see if you were all right. There was some trouble at the farm last night."

"What trouble?"

"May we come in?" Linda asked.

"You're welcome and you," Clark said, looking from Linda to Gustin, "but not him."

"Mr. Elliott is a guest of our family," Linda said.

"He's not my guest," Clark said.

Linda stepped closer to me. "If he's not welcome here, I'm not staying, either."

"Suit yourself."

The insubordination so moved Gustin that I thought he might pull his gun. He collected himself with an effort. "If you two would like to start back," he said, "I'll be along directly."

Linda nodded and led me away. It was an opportunity to resume our interrupted talk, but she was too shaken to take advantage of it. She did take advantage of my arm, though. She slipped her own arm under mine after another misstep, and left it there.

When we were clear of the woods, she said, "I apologize for Clark. He can be difficult. And unreliable. I meant what I said earlier. You three should come and stay with us at Traynor House."

"Put Drury under the same roof as your mother-in-law? That wouldn't make your life any easier."

A little of her hard edge came back. "What do you know about my life?"

I knew what Gilbert had told me, that Marvella had seized on her son's widow as a way of keeping the Traynor Company alive. But I didn't mention that. Gilbert was in enough hot water with his boss. I said, "The warning you passed on last night about Marvella–about her having to be in control–that's based on your own experience, isn't it? It can't make life very easy for you."

"It makes it impossible," Linda said. She slid her arm out from under mine. "I forgot you were an investigator. Or is this a sample of your hand holding?"

"I'm also a good listener. If you ever want to talk about it, give me a call."

She didn't have a chance to turn the offer down. Gustin came up behind us then at a quick march. If he'd seen the local gentry walking arm in arm with the rabble, he kept it to himself.

"Clark was drunk last night, ma'am. That's all there was to that. He got back from Augie's around midnight and fell asleep or plain passed out. Didn't hear any of the commotion. I can check in town to verify the timing."

"Don't bother," Linda said. And then, less curtly, "Thank you, Sheriff."

She had reason to thank him again when we reached the house. Eric Faris was already there, in the custody of a beanpole deputy. The baby-faced land agent was even more fidgety than he'd been in Alora. Of course, he now had something worthwhile to fidget about. He straightened, smoothed, and scratched away, presenting quite a contrast to Gustin, the deerstalker, who could do stock-still as well as any tree stump.

Their confrontation took place in the parlor with the rest of the cast looking on. It was a short confrontation, as it consisted of Gustin asking Faris where he'd been at two that morning and Faris stammering, "In bed."

Before Gustin could ask about witnesses, Linda Traynor stepped in. "That should do for the moment, Sheriff. Mr. Faris, we know why you've come to Traynorville: to make trouble for Mr. Drury. We asked you here this morning to tell you that while Mr. Drury is staying in Indiana, he is under the protection of the Traynor family. You'll find that means something around here."

Faris had found that out already.

"I'd also like you to pass a message along to your employer in California. Please tell him that the Traynor Company is prepared to offer Mr. Drury whatever financial backing he needs to finish his picture."

That was news to everyone in the room, including, it seemed to me, Gilbert. The way he looked at Linda reminded me of how Drury studied Shepard during their chess games when the publicist made an unexpected move.

Linda was all moves now. Her energy was back, and she fairly glowed with it. "Sheriff, please arrange to have deputies posted here tonight. You can coordinate it with my brother-in-law. He'll be staying here, too."

That was surprise number two for Gilbert, but he recovered faster this time. He said, "I'd like to be here if those hooligans come back," with conviction, meeting his sister-in-law's gaze and holding it. "Ask Mother to send some things over."

"I will," she said. "Mr. Faris, I'll drop you at your hotel on the way—or the train station, if you'd prefer."

chapter

21

THE KLAN DIDN'T SHOW UP on Saturday night, maybe because they didn't like crowds. Gilbert Traynor stuck by us and even seemed to enjoy himself once he'd had enough to drink. The suitcase Hank Shepard retrieved for him from Traynor House contained, along with a week's supply of clothes, two bottles of very good scotch. Two bottles of liquor should have been at least a week's supply, but it turned out not to be.

Drury and Gilbert killed the first soldier as the long afternoon turned into a longer evening. Our resident genius was in a celebratory mood. He composed telegrams to half of Hollywood, which Shepard dutifully wrote down and then tossed into a stack in the corner. Gilbert started out less jolly than his guest, but he warmed to Drury's planning and dreaming as he drank.

Between bottles we, the condemned, had our dinner, a lavish five-course affair sent over by the Traynor chef. It was one of Shepard's inspirations.

"I did a little organizing while I was over at the mansion," he told me when the food arrived. He was in a jovial mood, too, though for once he wasn't drinking. "It would have been a wasted opportunity if Carson had sent you after Gilbert's suitcase, Elliott–Eagle Scout that you are."

It was a harmless enough remark, but he leaned into it as though he was expecting the jibe to earn him another poke on the chin. He'd been quiet since the Klan's visit, maybe because he'd just held up under it. So I figured he was taking his embarrassment out on me.

Halfway through the second bottle, Drury was wheeled off to bed. Gilbert and Shepard had the first shift of guard duty, which is to say, Shepard had it. By that time Gilbert was only a threat to Klansmen who got close enough to breathe on. I'd been waiting all day for a chance to talk to him alone. The chance came at the start of his watch when Shepard asked me to sit with Gilbert while he walked to the end of the drive to check on Gustin's men.

I knew as soon as I sat down opposite Gilbert that interrogating him was a waste of my sleeping time. He'd acquired that Cheshire cat look drunks sometimes have, the drunks who figure the booze has made their brain cells swell up. He was sprawled on the old walnut settee, his thin frame making so little impression on its rounded, rock-hard cushions that I expected him to roll off at any moment.

"You're not enjoying this party, are you, Scotty?" he asked when he'd grinned himself out.

"Whose party is it?"

Gilbert waved vaguely in the direction of Drury's unsent telegrams. "Carson's, I guess. Or maybe Linda's."

"Or maybe yours," I said. "What's really going on here?"

"You don't know, do you? And it bothers you that you don't know."

"Yes," I said. "When you tell me, I'll sleep a lot better."

"Me? I don't know what's going on." He waved his empty hands at me like a magician reassuring a mark. "Something's going to happen, but I don't know what it will be."

"Or much care," I said.

"No, I don't. That's one difference between us. You don't like not knowing the schedule of events, but I love it. What I hate is always knowing what's going to happen. Not knowing's more fun."

"It's a shame you missed the war," I said. "You would have enjoyed it."

That was the wrong remark to make because it sent Gilbert off on a tangent. "I often wonder how I would have done if I'd seen some fighting. My mother doesn't wonder. She knows I wouldn't have done as well as Mark. I never did as well as Mark. That's one of the worst things about his being dead. I can never top him now. He'll always be that much ahead of me."

My guess was that Mark would have traded his permanent lead for his brother's long life, but it would have been rude to point that out. I sat watching Gilbert's eyes glaze over until Shepard came back from his reconnaissance. The publicist was gray in the face again.

"Trouble?" I asked.

"Heart trouble," Shepard said. "I just bumped into Lon Chaney, Jr., out there. Clark, I mean. He scared the crap out of me, looming out of the dark like he'd just popped up from the ground. That guy's quieter than an Indian."

"What's he doing?"

"Keeping a watch of his own, with a length of pipe for a nightstick." Shepard shuddered. "Go on to bed. There's no chance of my dozing off now."

Clark was still patrolling when I relieved Shepard around three. I learned that from Sheriff Gustin, who had come by to share my watch. Gilbert Traynor was snoring away on the parlor settee, so Gustin and I set up camp in the kitchen.

I made us a pot of coffee. While it was bubbling away, I asked the sheriff about the Traynors' caretaker.

Gustin looked at the screen door and the black yard beyond as he answered. "Don't know him very well," he said, echoing Linda

Traynor. "He mostly keeps to himself, just like you'd expect him to, poor guy. Every now and then some drunk looks at him the wrong way and ends up bloodied. Clark's a mean fighter, bad arm and all. But that doesn't happen very often. Most everybody around here tolerates him, and he tolerates most everybody.

"You're the exception to that rule," Gustin said, looking back from the screen door to me. "I've never known him to turn away a person like he did you. And in front of Mrs. Traynor, too. What did you do to rate that?"

"I don't know. We started out okay. Then he'd suddenly had enough of me."

"Excuse me for prying, but were you in the service?"

"Yes," I said. "The army."

"Overseas?"

"Yes."

"That's stranger still. As prickly as Clark is, he'll usually cut a veteran a break. He only gives me the time of day because he knows I carried a rifle around Italy."

"I was in the artillery."

"Oh," Gustin said. "Does Clark know that?"

"He might." He might have heard it from Hank Shepard, the man who was so tickled by Clark's dislike of me.

"That's it, sure as you live. Clark was wounded by artillery fire. U.S. artillery fire. One of our batteries got its signals crossed and kicked the hell out of Clark's unit. Killed a bunch of his friends and blasted Clark into little pieces."

"Where did it happen?"

"In the Hurtgen Forest, I think."

"I missed that slaughterhouse."

"I don't imagine that makes much difference to Clark. You're artillery, and that's that."

I nodded. That did seem to be that.

■ ■ ■

At first light, when it was obvious that nothing was going to happen, Gustin left and I turned in again. When I awoke for the second time that day, it was to the sound of Drury calling my name–yelling my name, actually.

I found him in his bed, his lap and legs covered with sheets of discarded newspaper. He held an undiscarded sheet in clenched hands.

"That back stabber is here. He's followed me. Am I never to be rid of that spineless excuse for a man?"

Shepard was standing in a corner, looking unmoved. "Whitehead," he said.

I reached for the newspaper, and Drury reluctantly handed it over. It was the state edition of an Indianapolis paper, the *Star Republic*. Whitehead's elaborate name jumped out at me from a two-paragraph story at the bottom of the page. The headline was HOLLYWOOD PRODUCER VISITS.

Beneath the headline was the announcement that John Piers Whitehead, "distinguished Broadway director and Hollywood producer," had arrived in Indianapolis to direct a production of *Knickerbocker Holiday* for a local college's summer theater. The story's second paragraph was a quote from a college professor named Walter Carlisle, who gushed about how lucky he and his school, Butler University, were. His enthusiasm left me wondering if he and Whitehead had ever met.

I glanced over my shoulder toward the parlor. "Does Gilbert know about this?"

"No," Shepard said. "The Traynor dogsbody who brought the Sunday papers took what was left of Gilbert home."

"Forget Gilbert!" Drury thundered. "We have to take action. This is the most transparent ploy I've ever seen, hiring himself out to direct some summer musical. He's just trying to get close enough to sabotage me again." He held his hand out for the paper, and when I'd given it back, he crushed it into a ball.

The same man who had taken the Ku Klux Klan in his stride was

in a genuine rage. That or the odd way in which Drury's Hollywood
enemies were reassembling themselves around us had me seeing
spots. I shook my sleepy head, but the picture didn't get any
clearer.

From his neutral corner, Shepard said, "I've been trying to tell
Carson not to get himself worked up until we know the score. I told
him you could check it out during your visit to Indianapolis."

"What visit would that be?" I asked.

"Have you forgotten your grandmother's dinner invitation?"
Shepard asked back.

I hadn't forgotten it. I'd decided that the Klan threat had can-
celed all bets. "I can't leave after what's happened."

"Yes, you can," Drury said, shaking the balled-up paper at me.
"You have to put the fear of God into that wretched person. You
have to scare him off."

"You'd better wire Paddy for a replacement," I said. "Leg
breaking is a separate department."

"Carson didn't mean it that way," Shepard said. "Just talk to the
guy, that's all we're asking. Then go visit the folks. Stay over if you
want to. We'll be okay without you for one night. Leave that how-
itzer of yours where I can find it and have a good time. Bring me
back a drumstick."

chapter

22

SO, WHILE TRAYNORVILLE waited for whatever was going to happen to happen, I went visiting in Indianapolis. I took Highway 32 west to Noblesville and west from there to the highway's intersection with 31, where I turned south. About an hour into my drive, I passed through the belt of little communities that separated Indy from the serious farmland. Those towns were bigger than I remembered, almost sprawling into one another and the city without a break. Indianapolis itself looked like the blueprint for the decade: clean, quiet, and prosperous. Fat, dumb, and happy, Shepard would have called it. Every block had people dressed up for church and enough gaudy, new sedans and coupés on patrol to make me feel homesick for my DeSoto.

I didn't drive very far into Indy. Butler University was on the city's north side in a section of upscale homes and wooded streets. The school was upscale itself, with stone buildings done up in a streamlined Gothic style that said middle of America, middle of the century, middle of the road. It wasn't a university really, not if you went by acreage. Just a nice little college appended to the largest basketball facility in the state, the Butler Field House. The university's teams played there, of course, but more important to the average Hoosier, the field house was the place where the finals of the state high school basketball tournament were held. That made it more than a sports facility. It was the local Lourdes, a redbrick cathedral whose altar was a stretch of varnished hardwood with a font at either end.

I found myself in the shadow of this shrine after I'd determined that no one was home at Butler's theater department on this hot, still Sunday afternoon. I'd asked around for the school's summer theater; it was next to the field house, an open-air theater nestled in a natural bowl in the trees.

I inquired at the box office for Whitehead and, when that drew a blank stare from the kid behind the window, for Professor Walter Carlisle, the man quoted in the *Star Republic* article. Carlisle was on hand, supervising the construction of risers on the theater's wooden stage. The sound of hammering covered my descent on a gravel path past row after snaking row of green folding chairs. Even so, the man who turned out to be Carlisle spotted me before I'd made it to the end of the aisle. He climbed down from the stage and came up the path to meet me.

I'd left my suit coat and hat in the station wagon, rolled up my sleeves, and loosened my tie. Carlisle still made me look like a member of a wedding party. He wore an almost white undershirt, fatigue pants cut off at the knees, and army boots that made my feet feel so nostalgic, they ached. Carlisle might have earned his boots the hard way, although he looked a little too old to be a veteran. He was forty-five by my guess, but fit, his walk and his build both athletic. His sunburned face was dominated by a jutting, ball-shaped chin, but that impression might have been due to the way he stuck the chin out toward me, like he was spoiling for a fight.

"Help you?" he asked when we came together a few rows shy of the orchestra pit.

I determined that he was the professor I was looking for. Then I asked after John Piers Whitehead. "I read in the paper that he was in town."

"And you are?"

I thought about omitting my connection to Drury and trying to pass myself off as an old Hollywood friend of Whitehead's. Carlisle was more likely to reveal the producer's current whereabouts to a friend than a draftee leg breaker. But I didn't try it. The professor was still sticking his chin out at me, looking as though he knew exactly who I was and why I was there. And I had a second reason for showing my hand: I didn't like my chances of scaring off Whitehead, a man with nothing to lose. Telling Carlisle the whole story might accomplish the same thing. Once he realized that Whitehead was using him and his theater as part of a vendetta against Drury, the professor might yank Whitehead's meal ticket and send him packing.

Unless, of course, Carlisle already knew all about Whitehead's schemes and didn't give a damn, which turned out to be the case. He listened calmly while I identified myself and told him why I was in Indiana. But when I started to describe the sabotage attempts against *The Imperial Albertsons,* Carlisle began to shift his weight from boot to boot. By the time I reached the accident with the camera crane, he'd had enough.

"Anyone who thinks that John Piers Whitehead could hurt another human being never met the man," Carlisle said, a single pulsing vein splitting his high forehead. "I've known him for twenty years, and a more sensitive human being never drew breath."

"You knew Whitehead in New York?"

"Yes. He gave me my first job at the height of the Depression when I was fresh out of college. Not just a job, either. He gave me a love of theater and a mission to protect it. His little government project was doing just that. We thought of ourselves as the Irish monks of a new dark age, keeping the candle of learning, of theater, alight."

"Then Carson Drury switched you over to electricity."

"Carson Drury," Carlisle repeated, using the tone most people reserved for Hitler or Joseph McCarthy. "That charlatan. He co-opted our project, turning it into his own private stock company, Repertory One."

"And giving you the heave-ho?"

"No. He never fired me or anyone else. He left that kind of unpleasantness to John. Drury simply deserted us, dozens of theater people desperate for the work. He ran off to Hollywood with a few of the chosen and left the rest of us to starve. Luckily, I had a friend in John Whitehead. His letter of recommendation got me my first teaching position. I've followed the jobs ever since, ending up here."

We both looked around at the little theater in the hollow. It was a long way from New York.

"Let's talk about how Whitehead landed here," I said.

"Why would I discuss that with you?"

"You might be as curious as I am about what he's up to."

"There's nothing mysterious about that. He and I have kept in touch. He wired me last week to let me know that he was going to be in Indiana. He asked me to arrange some temporary employment, lectures or teaching. I got the idea of asking him to direct the last production of our season. I was scheduled to do it myself, but I decided I'd earned a break."

"Some break. You've hired a guy who can't direct his own feet."

Carlisle unbent a little. "All John needs is a little rest."

"In a sanitarium. You didn't know about his drinking, did you?"

"No. Our correspondence dropped off during the past few years. I wasn't aware that he'd fallen on such hard times."

"But when he wired you out of the blue for a job, you found him one."

The chin came up again. "I owed him that and more."

"When did he tell you that Carson Drury was here in Indiana?"

"Not until after he arrived. He came off the plane from California drunk. I couldn't believe the change in him. He told me then about Drury's plan to refilm *The Imperial Albertsons.* John's life is somehow tangled up with that film. He sees this as his last chance. I won't be the one to take that chance away. I won't hand him over to Drury or to you, so don't even ask me where he is."

That left me without another question, so I made an observation. "If you were really Whitehead's friend, you'd get him as far away from Carson Drury as you could."

Carlisle surprised me by nodding in agreement. "Drury is really the addiction for John, not alcohol. Or maybe the movie business is. If only he'd gone back to New York ten years ago. He's still respected there—or he was, for a long time after Hollywood had forgotten him. I've often wondered why he stayed out there where he wasn't wanted."

I'd worked out an answer to that very question during my drive down from Traynorville. I was expecting my father to ask why I'd stayed on in a town that didn't want me. I tested my answer out on Carlisle. "Some people have only one genuine love affair in them."

chapter

23

I HAD SOME TIME before my next appointment. I used it to visit Crown Hill Cemetery, which was only a mile or so from Butler. Crown Hill contained the highest ground in the city, the actual peak being the site of James Whitcomb Riley's grave. The Hoosier poet wasn't the cemetery's only celebrity. The place also housed John Dillinger, the Hoosier gangster.

I'd come to Crown Hill to visit my mother's grave. I needed the help of the resident caretaker to find it, and it embarrassed me to ask him. It needn't have. The caretaker had no way of knowing that I was June Elliott's son and that I hadn't been by to visit her since the day of her funeral, five years before. And if he had known, he wouldn't have cared. He probably guided a different neglectful son or daughter every day of the week.

After the Crown Hill stop, I drove around the city for a time, ending up on Meridian Street, the most important north-south street in Indianapolis. With the east-west Washington Street, it formed a gigantic cross on which the city was laid out. But Washington had never been very fashionable. Nor, for that matter, had south Meridian. North Meridian was the address to have, so that was where my father had to live. He couldn't afford a mansion like Traynor House, duplicates of which lined Meridian north of Thirty-eighth Street. So he'd settled for an apartment building a little to the south of Thirty-eighth, the Woodruff Building. It was a Greek temple inflated to six stories, the kind of temple the Greeks would have built if Archimedes had gotten around to inventing the elevator.

Farmers ate their Sunday dinners early, so my father ate his fashionably late. I got to Meridian Street about four, and I still had time to pace the sidewalk and smoke a Lucky from the pack I'd bought after leaving the cemetery. That purchase was my revenge against Ella for organizing this little dinner party. A couple of cocktails would have been better preparation, but there was no place to buy one in Indianapolis on a Sunday. So I finished my cigarette, passed another one to the Woodruff's doorman, and took the building's tiny elevator to the fifth floor, thinking how like my dad it was to have missed the penthouse by a single stop. How like the Elliotts in general.

I knew my grandmother would answer the door, and she did. Outside of Hollywood, where a star might change hair colors as often as husbands, it was common for people to pick a certain style at a certain point in their lives and stick with it until the finish. My grandmother had made her final selections around 1935. They included hair in tight curls worn short and steel-rimmed spectacles that somehow looked frilly against her soft, jowly face. The way that face lit up when the door opened reminded me of another homecoming a decade earlier.

"Tommy," she said, using the name my parents had given me and Hollywood had taken away. She said it softly, just as she had the day I'd stopped by on my way to California after the war, so as not to ruin the surprise for the rest of the family.

There was no family left to surprise except my father, which meant I wasn't surprising anyone. He was sitting in an overstuffed chair next to the radio cabinet in the formal, little living room, lying in wait for me. My grandmother had seemed unchanged to me, perhaps because I'd always thought of her as ancient. I'd never thought of my father that way. I was shocked to see how he had aged, how dull his eyes were, how little color was left in his hair and the skin of his face.

He'd always reminded me of Walter Huston. Not the crazy prospector of *The Treasure of Sierra Madre* Huston. Not the character actor but the leading man. The Walter Huston of *Dodsworth,* a tall, dignified midwesterner with a long, thin face, a squared-off nose, and eyes that were narrow without being shifty. Now my father only reminded me that Walter Huston was dead.

He shook my hand without getting up from his chair.

"How are you?" I asked. It was as close as I could come to asking if he was ill.

"Fine" was as close as he could come to telling me.

We got through dinner on the strength of my grandmother's cooking and her storytelling. When she finally ran out of family stories, I considered telling a few of my own about the California branch of the Elliotts. Instead I told a story about a favorite actor of my grandmother's, Ronald Colman. I'd met Colman some years earlier in a professional capacity. I related the outlines of that case to give my grandmother a chance to catch her breath and to give my father an idea of how I spent my days. My better days. She listened wide-eyed. He rubbed the edge of his knife with his thumb and said nothing.

After the banana pudding dessert, I helped my grandmother clear away the dishes. When I came back into the dining room, my father was gone. I spotted him slipping into a room down the hall, his study, a place that had always been off-limits to me. So much for that, I thought, but my grandmother thought differently. She was waving me on with both hands like a third-base coach who knows that the catcher has forgotten his glasses. I rounded the dining room and headed for the study.

My father was seated behind his desk, cleaning his pipe; that is, he was going through the motions of cleaning it, working a furry bit of wire around and around in the stem, reenacting a ritual I'd surely watched from my cradle. It really was a ritual this time and not a practical exercise. The pipe cleaner came out as white as it had gone in.

I could have asked him for some tobacco from the glass jar on his desk if I'd remembered to bring my pipe. I lit a Lucky instead and took a long, self-conscious drag.

"I suppose you're drinking now, too," my father said.

"When I don't need a clear head for shooting craps."

He acknowledged the joke by grunting. "I suppose the war did that to you."

"Turning twenty-one did that to me, which happened some years back."

"Don't remind me. I hate to think of the time that's gone."

And the people, I thought. "Your grandchildren are doing fine, by the way. And your daughter-in-law." That didn't even rate a grunt. "They wanted to come out to see you, but I thought it might be dangerous."

"Did you think I'd bite them?"

"I meant the job I'm doing is dangerous." I gave him a rundown of the attacks on Drury's movie, ending with our visit from the Klan.

That got his full attention. He left off packing his pipe with tobacco, the step I'd actually wanted to see.

"The Klan?" he repeated. In his incredulity he sounded like an older, better educated Sheriff Gustin. "You saw Klansmen?"

"And a burning cross. It brought back the night they marched here in Indianapolis. I thought they were coming for you that night."

"I was too small an annoyance to merit that kind of attention. I'm proud to have been an annoyance to them, though, proud to have had a small part in ridding the state of them." He went back to packing his pipe before adding, "For a time at least."

"You believe they're still around?"

"As long as hate is around, the Klan will be. I won't live to see a world without hate. But it is surprising to hear of Klansmen showing themselves again. Something's not right about that. You should look into it."

"I will," I said.

We'd made some real progress. Somehow, my run-in with the Klan had validated me in a way no amount of Hollywood name-dropping could ever do. The smart play would have been to quit while I was ahead. I bet on another roll.

"I went by Crown Hill Cemetery on my way here."

My father set his pipe down unlit. "I'm sure your mother would have appreciated the effort. Think of how much more it would have meant to her if you'd made it during the years it took her to die."

It was a lead-in for the question I'd been dreading all day, a variation on the one Carlisle had asked of Whitehead. Why had I stayed on in Hollywood, a failure, when I could have come home to help her? My father stopped short of asking the question, but I answered it anyway.

"She knew how important that dream was to me."

"Yes," my father said. "I never understood it, but she did. It's a shame the dream didn't work out for either one of you."

■ ■ ■

That exchange really ended my visit, but I sat out the evening in the formal living room for my grandmother's sake. It was after ten when I started for Traynorville with Shepard's leftover chicken for company. I drove more slowly going back on the lonely, underlit roads. It was nearly midnight when I arrived at the end of River-bend's gravel drive.

I knew right away that something was wrong. There were no sheriff's deputies at the spot where the drive met the road. The farmhouse was dark. I thought in the time it took me to reach the house that the farm was deserted, that Drury and Shepard had packed up and moved to Traynor House—or all the way back to Hollywood.

I smelled smoke as soon as I climbed out of the wagon. It was wood smoke, and it was coming from the barn. I ran across the gravel courtyard, my footfalls sounding like rifle fire in the stillness of the night. When I reached the grass near the building, I heard a softer sound: the crackling and popping of kindling. It led me to the back of the barn. There, someone had made a pile of sticks and dry grass and set it alight. The flames were licking away at the barn's tinder siding.

I kicked the pile apart and threw handfuls of dirt on the barn wood where it had begun to char. Then I backed toward the house, scanning the darkness and reaching for the gun I wasn't wearing.

I hadn't gotten very far before I noticed that the light was on in the little tack room I'd checked on Friday night. I decided to check the room again.

Clark hadn't had time to finish the ramp for Drury's wheelchair. He'd been too busy wandering around looking for Klansmen to flatten with his lead pipe. I stepped over one of the rails and then stopped to listen. The door to the room was slightly ajar, throwing a thin shaft of light across the yard. There was no sound to go with the light, but there was another smell. Spent powder.

I pushed the door open and saw a man lying on his back on the raised floor near the room's far wall. It was Hank Shepard. I noted that his eyes were open and his arms were limp at his sides. I didn't bother saying his name. Shepard wouldn't have answered me. He had a bright red stain on the front of his white shirt. It was centered above his heart.

24

IT WAS ANOTHER BAD connection, worse than the one I'd had the night I'd called Ella. This time, though, I was calling Paddy Maguire, a man who had learned to speak on the telephone back when it was commonly believed that the lines were hollow and the system ran on lung power.

"Hank Shepard murdered? Mary, Mother of God. What about Drury?"

"Napping in his wheelchair when it happened. He'd had dinner with Eric Faris, Ralph Lockard's man. Set it up on the sly and sent me off to see Whitehead in Indianapolis so I wouldn't know about it."

"John Piers Whitehead's in Indiana, too?"

"We're expecting Garbo at any moment." I could only guess how the joke came across in California. In Indiana, it sounded as flat as the beers of yesterday, to use Shepard's phrase. It was Monday afternoon, and I was pretty flat myself. I hadn't spent much time sitting down in the hours since I'd found Shepard. I certainly hadn't shaved or changed my shirt.

"What did Drury want from Faris?"

"I haven't gotten that out of him yet. He's pretty shaken. Faris picked Drury up about seven and took him to a roadhouse halfway to Indy. They left Shepard at the farm to keep an eye on the place. Drury had chased off the sheriff's men we'd had on guard, probably to keep them from telling the Traynors about Faris coming by."

"What sheriff's men?" Paddy asked, sounding no farther away now than Kansas City.

"There was some trouble a couple of nights ago. It's a long story. I'll write you a letter."

"And forget to mail it probably," Paddy said.

"Faris drove Drury back around eleven. Shepard was gone. Drury figured he was visiting the caretaker on the far end of the property. He fell asleep waiting for Shepard to come back. He may have heard a shot a little while after that. He didn't wake up enough to be sure."

"What *are* we sure about?"

"I found Shepard's body in the tack room of the Traynor barn at twelve-fifteen. He'd been shot at close range with a good-size round. A forty-five, probably. The muzzle flash scorched his shirt. The bullet went through him and ended up in the wall of the barn. The sheriff's people have it."

"Is this Sheriff Whosits up to a murder investigation?"

"It's Sheriff Gustin, and no, he's not. But Gustin's smart enough to know he's in over his head. He's already called in help from the state police and a crime lab down in Indy. Gustin has the Traynors' political clout behind him, so he's getting everything yesterday."

"How about you, Scotty? Do you have this Gustin's ear? Are you on the inside of the investigation?"

"I'm calling you from the sheriff's office right now." I didn't tell Paddy that I was there for questioning, that I was so much on the inside of the case that I'd actually made the list of suspects, that I should have been calling a lawyer on the phone Gustin had provided instead of making long-distance calls collect.

"Good man," Paddy said. "You know my methods. Apply them. Use this Gustin character's inexperience to your advantage. Tell him you've seen more murders than newsreels. Encourage him to lean on you."

The beanpole deputy who had escorted Faris to Riverbend after the cross burning arrived at my borrowed desk. He wasn't smiling.

"I think Gustin's ready to start leaning on me right now," I said. "Call Ella before the afternoon papers come out. The story will have broken by then. Tell her I'm okay. I'll call her later."

The sheriff's office was in the county courthouse in the center of the Traynorville town square. It was an old brick and limestone building, dating from the pre-automobile time that Drury so despised. It had the same blackened woodwork as Riverbend, stone floors that should have been cool but weren't, and high ceilings with lazy fans. The fans were my age, probably, but they looked glaringly modern against the tiles of pressed tin that covered the ceilings.

The deputy escorted me to a room that was even hotter than the rest of the courthouse. Paper shades had been pulled down to cover windows as tall as a man; yellowed, rain-spotted shades that cut off the light and the air without blocking the heat. Gustin sat behind the centerpiece desk, looking even pinker than usual. He'd rolled up his sleeves and undone his tie. So had the state police lieutenant from Indianapolis, whom I'd met at the farm, and a civilian I hadn't met. I figured him to be the county prosecutor's man, and that was the way Gustin introduced him. Gustin didn't introduce the male stenographer or the woman seated in the corner behind the stenographer. That last introduction would have been silly, given how chummy Linda Traynor and I had become. She looked perfectly cool in her tan suit, her expression especially so. The only surprising thing about her presence was that she wasn't installed behind Gustin's desk.

The sheriff said, "You'll be happy to know that your gun is in Indianapolis right now."

"My gun that hasn't been fired in weeks?"

"Your gun that hasn't been fired since the last time it was cleaned," the state cop, whose name was Zimmerman, said.

Gustin ignored the interruption. "The murder bullet is also at the laboratory. We should hear something soon. We've been promised top priority for the ballistic tests."

"Thanks for going to so much trouble to clear me," I said.

"You're a professional, Elliott," Zimmerman said. "You know we have to check every lead." He was a leather-faced citizen, wire thin and as seasoned as the courthouse woodwork. With him around, even Paddy would have had a hard time landing the job of wise, old counselor.

"You've spoken with Drury," I said, "so you know I was hired to protect Shepard, not shoot him." Specifically to watch his back, I reminded myself for the sixtieth time.

"We learned more than that from Mr. Drury," Gustin said. "He told us you'd had a run-in with Shepard back in Hollywood. That was confirmed by Gilbert Traynor. Mr. Traynor saw Shepard get fresh with your wife and saw you drag Shepard off. According to Mr. Drury, you assaulted the guy."

"I tagged him on the jaw. That's what you do to a drunk who gets fresh with your wife. You don't murder him."

Gustin shifted in his chair, which for him was quite an attack of nerves. He started to glance over toward the corner where the invisible Linda Traynor sat, but caught himself. "Shepard did more than get fresh with your wife. He'd had a prior relationship with her. He told Mr. Drury that he'd thrown that and other things in your face."

I'd have to apologize to Ella for dismissing her concerns too casually. They *had* heard about her reputation in Indiana, courtesy of Carson Drury. It would have been nice to have returned the favor and implicated Drury somehow. Nice but impossible. Shepard's killer had stood close enough to him in the murder room to touch his shirt with the muzzle of the gun. That left Drury out because the wheelchair ramp for the tack room was still unfinished. I had to look elsewhere for a substitute fall guy.

"Where does the Klan fit into this?" I asked.

"I told you Saturday," Gustin said. "There's no Ku Klux Klan left in this county."

"Sorry. I meant the Fuller Brush men who torched the cross on our lawn on Friday night. They threatened to burn us out, remember? I found Shepard in a barn that was ten minutes away from being a bonfire."

"A barn being set afire doesn't necessarily point to your visitors from the other night," Gustin said. "We've had barn burnings in this county before, God knows. There was a spate of them during the war, from what I've heard. Besides, anybody might have thought to burn that barn to destroy evidence."

Anybody, including me. I dodged in another direction. "How about a tie-in to a Hollywood fire? Or did Drury forget to mention the sabotage against his picture? That cast on his leg is a souvenir of the last attempt. He could easily have been killed in that accident. Now someone has been killed—the guy who went into a burning building back in Culver City to save the movie's negative. He ends up shot in a burning barn in Indiana where the negative was going to be edited. Maybe the murderer thought it was already there. Maybe Shepard surprised him."

"He left his revolver in his room," Gustin said. "The night I came by to sit with you, Mr. Shepard never let that gun get out of reach."

"Besides," Zimmerman said, "nobody around here cares about a motion picture negative. Your saboteur would have to be an outsider. And our other visitors from California are accounted for. Faris spent the evening with Drury. After he got Drury back to the farm, he left. Drury watched him drive off and noted the time. So did the night clerk who saw Faris arrive at his hotel. We've clocked the drive, and the times check out. Faris stayed up for a while, talking to the clerk. She had him in sight until well after the time you say you found the body.

"The other fellow, John P. Whitehead, was in Indianapolis. He's staying at the home of a friend, a Professor Carlisle. The prof says Whitehead was there all night Sunday."

"Even so," Gustin said, "we're bringing Mr. Whitehead up here for questioning." He made another of his aborted glances toward Linda. It told me that Whitehead was scheduled for the Traynor treatment. He was going to be warned off as Faris had been. I wished Linda luck with that.

"I was in Indianapolis myself," I said, "as I seem to remember telling you."

"I've spoken to your father," Gustin said. "He told me you left his apartment at ten. If you got to the farm a little after midnight, you didn't make very good time."

I didn't bother explaining it. No excuses about the roads being bad or me being down or the station wagon being a plow horse would have bought me anything. Gustin and company were right: I could easily have shaved twenty minutes off the drive. That would have given me enough time to shoot a squad of Shepards.

"You've gotten a time of death?"

"Not even an official cause of death," Gustin said. "Our coroner, Dr. Cortese, is still at it over to O'Connor's."

"The funeral home?"

"And morgue, when we need one. Doc Cortese is very methodical and very cautious. When he does get around to giving us a time of death, it'll be as vague as a horoscope. Seeing how warm it was last night, I'm guessing he'll say that the murder could have happened anytime between eleven and the minute before you phoned it in."

I noted that Gustin had been too polite to say "the minute after you phoned it in." The whole interrogation had been polite. With no more to go on than Gustin had, the L.A. cops would have been sweating me good, just to keep their joints limber. The Traynorville murder squad was going through the motions, following its leads, as Zimmerman had said, but not pressing. Either the Elliott charm was working its way past my wilted linen, or someone was looking out for me. This time I was the one who almost looked at Linda Traynor.

I decided to test my pull. "Is that all you have to ask me, or is there something else about my wife you'd like to drag up?"

Gustin darkened a shade. "We expect the results of the ballistic tests today. If you keep us informed of your movements, we'll be able to return your gun."

Or club me with it if the slugs matched. "I'm not going anywhere," I said, "except maybe to bed."

I stood up. Nobody batted an eye, so I went out the way I'd come in. Linda Traynor followed me into the outer office.

"I'm sorry about all that, Scotty," she said.

"Thanks for keeping me out of a cell."

"I had to. I need to talk with you. Could we have dinner tonight?"

"How about lunch tomorrow? I may be awake by then."

"Come by the plant. Anyone in town can point you to it."

She didn't have a chance to set a time. John Piers Whitehead was led in just then by a bored-looking state trooper. Whitehead had cleaned himself up since we'd had breakfast together back in Hollywood. His shirt was white and crisp, and his plaid suit was fresh from some tailor's needle. We'd traded wardrobes, I thought wryly. That might have been why Whitehead didn't say hello. He looked past me to Linda as though he'd never seen me before. Then he was ushered into Gustin's presence.

Linda joined the procession. Over her shoulder she said, "Please don't stand me up."

chapter

25

THERE WAS A RUCKUS going on downstairs. I could hear it from the second-floor hallway outside Gustin's office. The hallway led to a balcony from which I could see the large main room of the first floor. The rotunda, they probably called it. The third of this area nearest the front doors was filled with reporters and photographers. They were all talking at once, as people in their line of work tend to do, firing questions and demands at the courthouse guards who were holding them in check with the aid of fat red ropes strung between brass stanchions, the same setup they use in movie houses to organize the popcorn line. I gathered, as I descended from the balcony on a sweeping marble staircase, that the reporters wanted to talk with Carson Drury.

At the bottom of the stairs I met my friend the skinny deputy. He wasn't surprised to see me walking around loose, which told me he was a man in the know. I asked him where Drury was hiding.

"Out back," the deputy said without taking his eyes off the reporters. "They're trying to sneak him out of the building. Follow the signs for dog licenses."

I did, winding my way past offices that became progressively less grand. I found Drury near a back door, but not too near it. He was being looked after by Gilbert Traynor and an older gent in a chauffeur's uniform. I took a liking to the chauffeur right away. He was the only one of the three who didn't grimace at the sight of me.

"Scotty," Drury said. "Sorry we didn't wait for you. We didn't know how long you'd be."

"But you were guessing twenty years to life."

Gilbert actually cringed. "It was our duty not to hold back evidence," he said. "We didn't have a choice."

He meant that he hadn't had a choice once Drury had let the Ella-and-Shepard cat out of the bag, which was true. I asked, "Where are you off to?"

Gilbert turned to the chauffeur. "Would you see if there's any sign of the ambulance, John?"

"It's an old ploy I used in New York in my radio days," Drury said to cover the chauffeur's exit. "I found out it wasn't illegal to use an ambulance for something other than a medical emergency, so I hired one to get me between the studios when scheduling was tight. The city has since passed a law against it."

"The spoilsports," I said.

Drury was looking about the way I felt. His trademark hair was stringy and dull, and his chin was blue. There were matching circles around his big, soulful eyes. Gilbert, on the other hand, was as natty as ever. "Keep up appearances" was probably the Traynor motto. But he was spending a lot of time smoothing his perfectly trimmed moustache.

"Carson can't go back to the farm," he said. "The reporters have already come in from as far away as Chicago. So I've had the top floor of the Roberts Hotel cleared. We can protect Carson there—from the reporters."

"Good idea," I said. There was one possibility I hadn't discussed with Gustin and Zimmerman. Shepard might have been killed by mistake or because he had stumbled on someone intent on murdering Drury. That meant my post was at Drury's side, but I had no intention of staying there. So Gilbert's plan to lock Drury away suited me fine.

"I've arranged to have Carson's things brought over from the farm," Gilbert added. "I'll have yours fetched, too."

"Don't bother. If it's all right with you, I'll stay where I am."

"You're not resigning, are you?" Drury asked.

"Not yet. I am dropping the driving and chair pushing and light hauling. I'm going to do what I was hired to do and figure out what's really going on. I can't get that done if I'm holed up in the presidential suite."

"But you'll report to me," Drury said.

"Right now I'm doing my reporting to Sheriff Gustin. It's a condition of my parole. Besides, it's my duty not to hold back evidence."

That echo made Gilbert cringe all over again. "I'll check on John," he said and left us.

Drury got in the first lie. "I really didn't mean to make trouble for you, Scotty. I've been in a daze since you woke me with the news about Hank. You don't know what his death has done to me. It's more than the shock of losing a friend. I feel as though I've lost a part of myself. I may have been looking around for someone to blame, I don't know. I remembered how you'd struck Hank, and I resented you for it. But that was just a product of my confusion. I could never believe you'd kill him. As for dragging your wife into this, I can only apologize for that, deeply and sincerely."

"I'd prefer to discuss it when you're out of the wheelchair. In the meantime, you can make things up to me by staying put at the hotel."

"Do you think I was the real target last night?" Drury asked with something like his old élan. The idea clearly appealed to him. Some people would take any spotlight, even one attached to a gun.

To deflate him I said, "Probably not. You were a sitting duck, before and after Shepard caught it. I think the real target was the *Al-*

bertsons negative. Anyone who'd cased the farm and knew what editing equipment looks like could have counted on that negative showing up in the tack room sooner or later. That person could have been checking the barn every night—at least the nights the sheriff's men weren't there."

Drury looked past me. "Where's that ambulance?"

"Why did you give the deputies the night off? It was because you were meeting Faris last night, wasn't it?"

"Of course. Do we have to speak of that now?"

"Yes. Once you're boarded up inside the hotel, you may forget to give me the password. What were you after from Faris?"

"Money," Drury said through bared teeth. "Money. Money. Money. All I've ever wanted to do with my life is create beauty. And I've spent most of my time begging money from men who wouldn't know beauty if they woke up in bed with it."

"Why would you need more of Ralph Lockard's money? Linda Traynor's promised you the moon."

"A very apt image, I'm afraid. Haven't you caught on yet to the dynamic of the Traynor family? You've spent as much time with them as any of us. More time than any of us with Linda. Poor Hank was jealous of that."

"What dynamic are we talking about?"

Drury brought his elegant hands together, the tips of their tapering fingers touching. "The individual members of the Traynor family are in tension, in opposition, like the stones of an arch. The opposing forces are held in place by a keystone, but they're pressing the stone, too, threatening to crush it. Linda Traynor is that keystone. She's holding the family together, standing between Gilbert and his mother. She's taken the place of her dead husband in the family as well as the business, but her situation is far from secure, which means that my financing is far from secure. If Linda should decide to give up the fight or if she throws the dynamic out of balance by siding with Gilbert and ends up ousted from her job, her promises to me won't mean much.

"That was the background for my dinner with Eric Faris. I wanted to reopen negotiations with Lockard while I appeared to be in a position of strength. If he thinks he isn't going to get Eden, he might be interested in a percentage of the profits from *Albertsons* in exchange for an infusion of cash."

"Lockard's not interested in any movie profits."

"But he might have been interested in increasing the mortgage on Eden to an amount that no one—not even the Traynors—would consider paying off."

Drury shook his head. "It doesn't matter. None of my scheming matters now. Not with poor Hank gone."

He gazed off into the middle distance while I wondered if he was being sincere for once or just improvising another scene. I hadn't made up my mind before Gilbert opened the courthouse door to announce the arrival of the ambulance.

I hung around long enough to see Drury off. Then I snuck away myself in the station wagon Gilbert had generously left at my disposal. I drove to the O'Connor Funeral Home and morgue, thinking about how Shepard had once joked that O'Connor's might end up burying the *Albertsons* negative. Now Shepard was somewhere in the old Victorian pile himself, being explored by the deliberate Dr. Cortese.

Paddy had told me to use his methods. One that came to mind was his talent for obtaining official police information before the police had it themselves. I decided to chat up Dr. Cortese.

The front door of O'Connor's was locked, which seemed odd on a business day during business hours. I rang the bell until it couldn't hold my attention any longer. Then I took a walk around.

The place had more doors than a fun house: French doors painted shut on the front porch, doors under a porte cochere where the gentry had once been handed into their broughams—now probably the place where caskets were handed into their hearses—padlocked doors for coal delivery, and three different back doors. Two of this trio served the kitchen, and one, at the bottom of a short flight of steps, led to the basement. That was the door I chose, because its lock was a model I'd teethed on at the Maguire School of Charm and the Dance.

Once inside I didn't tiptoe. It wasn't a place where I felt comfortable tiptoeing. I'd let myself into a dimly lit storage room stacked with caskets. From there I went down a corridor of white-painted brick, saying hello every few steps and ducking my head under caged light bulbs whose switch never came to hand.

There was a light at the end of the corridor, spilling out from a side room. I found Hank Shepard in the room, alone, beneath a sheet on a long metal table that had a conspicuous lip around its edge. At least I assumed it was Shepard. I never got around to looking under the sheet.

Someone else started calling hello, someone in the house above me. A door opened somewhere, and the lights in my corridor came on. I could see a stairway at the far end and the feet and legs of a man, the feet wearing socks and no more. When the rest of him appeared, it was wearing a white lab coat and glasses that reflected the light of the naked bulbs, hiding the eyes behind them. He stood stooped over, and the hair he wore parted down the middle was shot through with gray.

"Dr. Cortese?" I asked.

He didn't make any jokes about how glad he was to see me instead of his patient wandering around. He was too filled with anger for jokes; his little, white fists vibrated with it.

"I'll have you arrested. As God is my witness, I'll have you locked up. I gave you fair warning to stay away and to keep your cameras out of my place." He looked me over for a Brownie.

I held up my empty hands. "I'm not a reporter," I said. "And I just came from the sheriff. He's not arresting me today."

"Who are you?"

"My name is Elliott." I was going to tell him that I was a friend of Shepard's, and maybe even the Traynors' for good measure. I didn't have to.

"You're one of the fellows from out at Riverbend," the man said.

He straightened up slightly as the anger drained out of him. "You're the one who found our guest there."

"That's right. Are you Dr. Cortese?"

"No. The doc's gone. I'm O'Connor. I own this place."

I apologized for letting myself in. "I rang the bell, but no one answered."

"I heard you ringing. I thought you were a reporter. They've worn out that bell today. Did you come to see your friend? I haven't cleaned him up yet. He won't clean up, much. Not after the examination the doc gave him."

"What did Dr. Cortese find?"

"Nothing the rest of us didn't already know. Your friend died of a single gunshot wound. A contact wound, the doc called it."

"Time of death between sunset and sunrise?"

O'Connor smiled. He had a gold tooth that somehow inspired confidence. "Sounds like you know our coroner. Eleven to midnight is what he said."

Just as Gustin had guessed. I'd wasted my time coming to O'Connor's. The owner looked as if he'd waste the rest of my day if I let him. He was scratching at his chin and considering me.

"Heard you had trouble out at the farm the other night," he finally said.

"Did you?"

"Heard there was an old-time cross burning out there."

"Did you happen to hear who did the burning?"

"Names, you mean? Wouldn't be anybody I know. There's no Klan around Traynorville. There was once. But there hasn't been for thirty years."

"That's what people keep telling me."

O'Connor scratched some more. "I have something here you might be interested in."

"My widow will make my funeral arrangements," I said.

That got a chuckle out of him. "I'm not selling, I'm showing. Excuse me."

He squeezed past me and headed toward the storage room where

I'd come in. Before he got there, he took a left. Another overhead light came on. The light was still swinging on its cord when I reached the doorway. I could see trunks and packing cases in the moving light. O'Connor was in a far corner, pulling at a canvas tarp.

"Found this in the basement when I bought the place," he said. He had the tarp off by then. It had covered two figures, each between three and four feet tall. They were dressed in the regalia of the Ku Klux Klan and mounted one behind the other on a four-wheeled cart.

"That's a man in front and a woman in back, though it's hard to tell with them robes. The women didn't wear masks with their pointy hats is how you tell. Their robes were shorter, too. That's one part of the Klan platform I could agree with."

The male mannequin was dressed exactly as the speaker at the cross burning had been: a round emblem on each breast and a red cord around his waist.

"What is that thing?" I asked.

"It's a parade float, a little one. Left over from one of the parades the Klan held back in the twenties. Like I said, I found it down here when I bought the place."

"This house once belonged to the Palliser family, didn't it?"

My local knowledge impressed O'Connor. "There's a name you never hear anymore. Yep, the Pallisers built this house."

"Were there any owners between the Pallisers and you?"

"Nope." I could see his eyes now. They were congratulating me. "I bought it from old man Palliser's estate."

O'Connor threw the tarp back over the float, hitting the light and sending it swinging again.

"Why do you keep that thing?"

He chuckled again. "You should know why, after what you went through the other night. This float doesn't belong to me. Not my property at all. If the rightful owners should show up looking for it, I sure don't want to disappoint them."

chapter

26

A SENTRY WAS ON DUTY in front of the pylons that flanked the Traynor House drive. His navy blue uniform didn't belong to a sheriff's deputy or a state trooper, so I figured him for a private guard. He was leaning against a navy blue sedan, reading a newspaper. Reading about Hank Shepard, ten to one.

I slowed the wagon and tried to think of a story that would win me an audience with Marvella Traynor. I was too sleepy to work one out, but it didn't matter. The guard hardly glanced at me before waving me through the pylons. As I passed his sedan, I spotted a logo on its front door: the Traynor Company's winged T. My wagon had the same decoration, which had led to the guard's mistake and, probably, to his eventual firing. Well, things were tough all over.

The mansion's front door was answered by a familiar face: Greta, the rustling maid from the Traynors' dinner party. Like Whitehead at the courthouse, Greta seemed to have forgotten me.

"I'm working my way through college selling magazine subscriptions," I said to fill the rustling void. "Is the lady of the house in?"

"Mrs. Traynor is indisposed."

"There's one disease poor people were spared," I said, but the sociology was wasted on Greta. "Please tell her that Scott Elliott is here. I have a question to ask her regarding her late uncle's hobbies. Please add that I'm up to my knees in newspaper reporters."

Greta checked my knees, nodded, and shut the door. She shot home the bolt for luck.

The bolt was withdrawn again before I'd finished a Lucky. Greta led me back to the oval dining room where Drury had laid an egg on our first night in Indiana. There were French doors on one end of the oval. Greta opened one for me and sent me out into the world on my own.

The doors led to a stone terrace. It was also oval shaped, but one end was squared off by the side of the house. The rounded end was edged with a low stone railing. Small statues were spaced out along the railing's cap. I studied the statue behind Marvella Traynor as I walked toward her across the hot flags. It was a female dancer, dressed in a toga and frozen in an awkward pirouette. I glanced at the other statues to confirm that they were all dancers, each caught in a different pose. Beyond their static chorus line was a backdrop of hazy blue sky.

Marvella was reclining on a chaise lounge on the leftmost edge of the terrace. To the left of her chair were stairs that descended to a formal garden. Beyond and below the garden, the White River wound its way toward Traynorville. Marvella sat with her back to the scenery in the shade of a big striped umbrella that rose from the center of a glass-topped table. Tea for one had been set on the table near Marvella's elbow. She didn't have to worry about the tea getting cold on her today, I thought.

Her attire was as out of step with the heat as her choice of drink. She was wearing a long housecoat in a Chinese print of red and black with a high collar and a skirt that fanned out across the bottom of the lounge chair. Her head was supported by pillows, and she held a black handkerchief to one temple. From something—the handkerchief or the woman or the garden below us—came the scent of jasmine.

I was scented without jasmine, so I kept my distance. "I'm sorry to have come by when you're not feeling well," I said.

"How dare you be polite to me after you've blackmailed your way into my house," Marvella said. " 'Come by,' indeed. You've intruded. You and Mr. Drury have done nothing but intrude—into my community, into my family, and into my privacy."

If I accomplished nothing else, I'd brought her color back. "You forgot to list Mr. Shepard," I said. "He's the one who was found dead this morning."

"You're correct," Marvella snapped. "I have forgotten Mr. Shepard. Very shortly I will have forgotten you. Now, what did you have to say regarding my uncle?"

The gloves had come off in a hurry, but I was ready to play it that way. "He was a member of the Ku Klux Klan. Given his position in this county, he was probably *the* member."

"It was not unusual for men of position to belong to that organization during the troubled times between the wars. They were men who recognized the threat to our country posed by the unwashed of Europe. You're too young to remember those days."

"I remember the nights. And the men in the robes."

"It may interest you to know, then, that some of those men have achieved high office in this state. Those men will answer a telephone call from me."

"Will they also answer a call to arms?"

I'd noted before that Marvella's eyes were small, like Gilbert's. They had an intensity, though, that Gilbert's lacked. It was a fire no big doe eyes could ever handle.

"I beg your pardon?" she said.

"I'm asking if the men who burned the cross at Riverbend were supreme court justices and state senators."

"You have the gall to accuse me of organizing that?"

"Do you have the gall to deny it?"

"Most emphatically." The hand holding the black handkerchief came down on the arm of her chair with a sharp crack. "And I'd advise you not to repeat that accusation in front of reporters. The world may be falling apart, but in this corner of it, the Traynor name still means something."

"Your daughter-in-law is fond of saying that."

"My daughter-in-law," Marvella sneered back, "will never be a Traynor in anything *but* name."

"That's true of you, too, isn't it? You're really a Palliser, after all. You're part of the old regime. How did you wind up married to the man whose factory was attracting those unwashed Europeans to your little kingdom?"

Marvella stuck out what chin she had and said nothing.

"I've heard that your late husband fought the Klan. That must have made for some lively dinner conversations."

"Is everyone in Hollywood as romantic as you and Carson Drury, Mr. Elliott? I used to think that you movie people saw through your own fables, that you only stamped them out to please a maudlin public. Mr. Drury seems genuinely to believe that this century has been some long morality play, with the little people triumphing over the mean, old, rich people in the end." She laughed at that idea with a ridiculous, twittery, Billie Burke laugh.

"The Pallisers did lose," I said.

"Did we? Am I about to be thrown off your estate? The Pallisers of this world don't lose, Mr. Elliott. We survive, that's the basic lie of Mr. Drury's silly movie. He really believes that his Albertsons would sit around waiting for progress to ruin them and then throw themselves under its wheels so he could have a symbolic ending for his tale.

"We don't fade away, we fight back. We die fighting if need be, like my son."

"Your son died fighting the kind of men who burned the cross at Riverbend, Mrs. Traynor." I had it all tied together in a neat

package. But it so happened that my debating partner had a uni-
fying vision of her own.

She sat up and stretched her head to the limit of her withered
neck. "My son died because his country was drawn into a European
war. It wasn't enough that they came here in their millions to
threaten our way of life. We had to sacrifice the cream of our manhood to save them from themselves. Had Mark survived, he would
have taken his place in this community. He would have resisted the
forces that threaten it."

He would have been out burning crosses himself, in other words.
I couldn't believe that. "Your son was a Traynor, not a Palliser. No
Palliser would have married Linda."

Marvella fell back onto her pillows as though I'd slapped her.
"No Palliser would have stayed married to her," she said, her voice
a moan with teeth. "She was a phase Mark would have passed
through if he'd been spared. She was a token of his token rebellion,
a symbol of the idealism of the war years. He would have rid himself of her soon enough."

She had me there. A lot of wartime marriages had ended just that
way—not because the combatants and the noncombatants had lost their
idealism but because they'd lost the only thing they'd ever really had in
common: a cause, an enemy. Mark and Linda might have struggled on
with Marvella as a replacement enemy. She might have been the one
Mark outgrew. But I couldn't bring myself to hit the old woman there.

"He can never be rid of her now," she was saying. She made it
sound like the worst part of his being dead.

Then, in a stronger voice, she addressed the heated air behind
me. "There you are, finally."

I turned in time to see a man step from a small door close to the
center of the house. It was the navy blue guard whose job I'd jeop-
ardized. He lost all my sympathy by fingering his nightstick as he
crossed to us.

"May I have the sports section if you're finished with it?" I asked
when he arrived.

"Remove this man from the estate," Marvella said.

The guard left off fingering his nightstick and started fingering his gun. He jerked his head toward the house.

I tarried long enough to bid good-bye to my hostess. "Don't forget me yet," I said.

chapter

27

I WAS DEAD ON MY FEET when I got back to my own palatial estate, Riverbend. I had my own security guard, too, a lone sheriff's deputy, back on duty after a fatal night off. At least the Traynors' arrowhead collection and stuffed birds would be safe now from souvenir hunters. The deputy saved me a phone call to my probation officer, Frank Gustin. I watched in my rearview mirror as he radioed in his report: Suspect has returned to the scene of the crime. Over and out.

I cleaned myself up and changed my clothes, intending to hike down to Clark's cabin to discuss the night of the murder. Clark had told Gustin that he hadn't heard or seen a thing on Sunday night. He'd stayed sober, just in case the Klan returned, but he hadn't left his cabin. It wasn't much of a story, but I wanted to hear him tell it again.

I made the mistake of sitting down first—just for a moment—in one of the front-porch rocking chairs. When I woke up, it was dark, and headlights were coming at me down the drive–Sheriff Gustin's headlights, as it turned out.

Gustin climbed the porch steps gingerly, like a man who had ridden in on horseback from Illinois at least. I wasn't the only one in Traynorville who had missed a night's sleep.

"Sorry to wake you up," Gustin said. "Anybody who can sleep in this heat in a hickory rocking chair must need his rest."

"Pull one up," I said.

"I daren't. I'm on my way home right now. Be lucky if I make it. I just stopped by to give you this like I promised. If you're fool enough to stay here by yourself tonight, you may need it." He held out a flat, triangular paper parcel. My gun.

"I take it the bullets didn't match."

"You wouldn't believe how much they didn't match." Gustin didn't explain that odd remark, but he looked as though he wanted to.

"Flat stumped again?" I asked, to remind him of the morning after the cross burning when I'd been his sounding board.

"Not again. Still." He shuffled his size twelve boots. "I heard you were out at Traynor House this afternoon. What were you after?"

"Mrs. Traynor didn't mention that when she phoned in her complaint?"

"No."

"And it would have been impolite for you to ask."

"Go easy on me, Elliott. I'm not one of your movie big shots. I'm just a hick sheriff trying to feed a family year in and year out on less money than your Mr. Drury paid for his last car."

"Sorry," I said. I found my cigarettes and shook one out for him. In the light of my match, he looked as if he'd aged ten years since Saturday. His eyes were closing by themselves, and what I'd previously taken for down on his fat cheeks was now plain old stubble.

"I went to Traynor House," I said, "because I learned that Marvella Traynor's uncle may have had ties to the Klan. How is it you didn't know about that family skeleton?"

"I did know about it. At least, I think I did." He pushed his straw hat back. "I mean, if anyone had asked me, I could have told them.

But I didn't make the connection myself. Why would I have? Old man Palliser died twenty years ago."

I could hear him scratching his head in the darkness. "Wait a minute. You aren't saying that Mrs. Traynor sent those spooks over here to scare you off, are you? Marvella Traynor, the woman who makes up the annual shortfall in the hospital fund out of her own pocket?"

"And passes out turkeys at Christmas time, probably," I said. I swatted at a mosquito too slowly to worry it. "Best put that thought out of your mind, Sheriff. You've got kids to feed."

We sat and smoked and didn't talk. Gustin might have been thinking about his family and how complicated his life had become. I was thinking about Linda Traynor, the last person to share a quiet evening on the porch with me, and how complicated her life had to be.

Linda was more than an unloved daughter-in-law. She was, as Marvella had put it, the symbol of her late husband's rebellion against his family. It wasn't an uncommon role for a newlywed to play, but Linda had been stuck in it for a decade and more, waiting for a man who was dead to return and resolve the situation.

Gustin ground out his smoke. Then, good ex-soldier that he was, he policed the area, pulling his cigarette stub apart, scattering the tobacco and tearing the paper into little bits. As he tore, he said, "We're never going to find the gun that fired the murder bullet."

"Why not?"

"Because the bullet we pulled out of the wall had no markings on it. They tie a bullet to a certain gun because the rifling inside the gun's barrel scores the bullet. You probably know more about that than I do."

"I'm familiar with the theory. Was the bullet too misshapen for the marks to be read?"

"Nope. It was in good shape. At the range it was fired, it passed through Shepard like he wasn't there. Then it found itself a nice, worm-eaten old beam to stop in. There were just no marks to read."

"Every modern gun leaves those marks."

"Then this bullet was fired by a blowgun. And don't say that blowguns don't leave scorch marks. I know they don't. I'd be searching every house in town for a smoothbore musket, but the lab boys say the bullet is modern. It's a standard, forty-five-caliber ACP round."

"That doesn't make sense."

I could just make out Gustin's picket fence grin. "Flat stumped, huh? Welcome to the club."

"Thanks."

"I did have an idea I wanted to run by you. You've heard of zip guns, I suppose."

"Yes. They're homemade handguns that use a few inches of pipe for a barrel."

"Unrifled pipe. I've never seen one, but I've read about them. Teenage gangs back east are using them. Maybe the gangs out your way, too."

"So you think a visitor from L.A. might have snuck one out in his shaving kit? Why? Real guns aren't hard for grownups to buy in Los Angeles. They're even easier to buy in Indiana. Besides, I've never heard of a forty-five-caliber zip gun. They're usually twenty-twos. Even with that light a load, they're as dangerous to the shooter as they are to the target."

"If you've got a better idea—" Gustin broke off talking and drew his gun. It was the fastest move I'd ever seen him make. "I thought I saw somebody out by the barn. You go around the far side of the house, and I'll go straight at him. Don't shoot at anything in a uniform."

I had the paper wrapper off the automatic before I turned the near corner of the house. As I reached the far corner, I saw a running figure. He was crossing the backyard from my right to my left, going away from the barn and toward the wire fence that bordered the lawn.

I broke into a flat run, crossing the lawn at an angle to cut off the runner at the spot where he'd hit the fence. There was more moon out than there'd been on the night I'd chased a specter around the farmhouse. I could see that tonight's ghost was wearing a suit and a felt hat and that he was carrying something cradled in his arms. That burden gave me an advantage in speed. Even so, I didn't think I'd reach the fence first. But I'd get there in time to grab him as he climbed it.

Only he didn't bother climbing. He ran through the fence at full speed as though it weren't there. His secret was a gap in the fencing between two posts, set a man's width apart. On the other side of the gap was a solid wall of green corn, prematurely tall.

I stopped to listen. The sound of the man thrashing at the corn led me to a path that ran along the fence in the direction of the road. I started gaining again as soon as I was on the path, running with my gun arm out to keep the razor-edged corn leaves out of my eyes. I could feel my last cigarette as a finger poking me square in the chest.

I caught the guy twenty yards later, taking him down in midstride with my left arm around his knees. The fall knocked away the last of my wind. I clapped my gun to his head, misjudging the distance enough to get a grunt out of him.

"Damn," he gasped. "You trying to bust my ear?"

"Shut up," I managed to say. I could hear the cavalry coming up behind us. It actually sounded like cavalry; the sheriff's gun belt was jangling and creaking like harness.

"Got him?" Gustin asked between breaths.

"Got him."

"Damn," the man said.

One of the items of equipment on Gustin's belt was a flashlight. He switched it on as I rolled our guest over.

The light revealed a round, pale face, not recently shaved, and rabbity eyes behind horn-rimmed glasses that had somehow survived our fall.

"Casey Atherley," Gustin said in the injured tone of a fisherman who has landed a tire. "Photographer on the *Traynorville Beacon*."

"I think I broke a rib," Atherley said.

Gustin prodded the prone photographer's rib cage with the toe of his boot. "Feel that?" he asked, though Atherley had already yelped.

"What are you doing out here?" Gustin asked.

"Trying to take a picture of the murder room."

"With what?" This time the boot stopped just short of Atherley's ribs. He writhed anyway.

"My camera. I dropped it when I fell."

I found the camera in the weeds a few yards down the path. It was a newspaper photographer's standard issue, a boxy Rapid 60. It made a sound like pennies in a tin bank when I picked it up.

"I thought you had orders to stay away from here," Gustin said.

"That was before the murders. The Traynors can't kill this story now. There's no reason why the *Beacon* should miss out on it. I'd like to stand up."

"That might be dangerous," Gustin said. "We haven't determined the extent of your injuries yet." His boot caressed Atherley's side.

My own ribs were starting to ache. I was seeing a part of Gustin I wouldn't have guessed existed. But for Linda's intercession, I might have gotten to know it very well.

I still had her share of the family clout behind me, so I said, "Let him up."

Gustin stepped back, and I helped the photographer to his feet.

"How did you get past my man?" Gustin asked.

"This is a farm, for Christ's sake, not an island. Anyone with eyes and a sense of direction can find a way in. I found a pull-off on the side of the road out of sight of the drive and the house. I parked there and poked around and found this path."

"Show us," Gustin said.

Atherley led us out of the field, walking slowly, with one hand to his sore ribs. I thought our run had taken us most of the way to the road, but we'd actually covered less than half the distance. We came out of the field at a point where the road descended to cross a creek on a one-lane bridge. Atherley's ancient sedan was parked on the shoulder next to the bridge, out of sight, as he had said, of Gustin's man at the entrance to Riverbend.

"Keep an eye on him," Gustin said to me. "I'm going to walk up a ways and signal my deputy. Then Casey and I will take a ride into town."

When Gustin had jangled off, Atherley sank down onto the fender of the sedan. I'd tucked my automatic away in my belt. That left my right hand free for swinging the damaged camera back and forth. Atherley's eyes never left it.

"I might be able to help you," I said, "if you come clean with me."

"Come clean? I thought only people in the movies said that."

There was more left in him than I'd thought. "I'm feeling like somebody in the movies tonight. Tell me about the last time you were out here."

"You mean the eighth grade field trip when we heard all about how wonderful the Traynor family was?"

"I mean Friday night when you saw me coming out of the tack room of the barn and ran."

"I was under strict orders to stay away from this place. It would have been more than my job is worth for me to have poked around out here."

"And yet here you are, up to your neck and sinking fast."

"Okay, wise guy. It was me you saw on Friday. I was looking for a lead on what Carson Drury was up to in Traynorville."

"Are you sure you hadn't been tipped about the cross burning?"

"No. I wouldn't have run off if I'd known that was going to happen. A photo of that would have been my ticket out of this burg."

"So you came back Saturday night to photograph the farm house burning down."

"No. Okay, yes. I tried to. I got as far as the gap in the fence and spotted that faceless guy, Clark, prowling around, swinging a pipe." His eyes went back to the swinging camera. "That guy gives me the creeps. I snuck back out the way I'd come."

"How about Sunday night?"

"I was home all night. I can prove it."

"You'll have to. What brought you back here tonight?"

"No one's gotten a picture of the murder room. I figured this was my big chance and I was going to take it, Clark or no Clark. But before I could get inside the barn, the Traynors' pet sheriff blundered in."

I held up the camera and checked the big bowl of the flashgun. "No bulb."

"Must have fallen out when I dropped it."

"Huh. The film in here is unexposed?"

"Right."

"So I can check for damage and not ruin anything?" I started to fiddle with the camera's switches and buttons.

"Stop that," Atherley hissed. "All right. I took a picture. If you keep fooling around, you'll screw up the plate."

I tossed him the camera. "What plate?"

He unloaded it faster than I could tie my shoe. I held my hand out for the film, and he passed it over.

"Got a spare?"

"Of course."

"Reload it. Gustin's going to expect to see film."

Atherley was such a pro, he could load the camera and talk at the same time. "What's your angle, buddy?"

"I want to know who burned that cross and why. Get me some names, and you can have the film back."

"This murder won't be news forever."

"Then work fast."

chapter

28

I PASSED ON MY planned walk to Clark's cabin. I was lucky to make it back to the farmhouse parlor. After stashing Atherley's film in the glass bookcase, I settled into the least uncomfortable chair with my back to a corner and my gun within reach. At dawn I pried myself from the chair and went upstairs to bed. I got up again around eight, dressed, and drove into town to a drugstore on the corner opposite the Roberts Hotel.

The drugstore had a lunch counter, which, a little after nine, was still doubling as a breakfast counter. At a tiny griddle squeezed between a soda fountain and the town's original refrigerator, a man in an apron and a white overseas cap was frying eggs. The cook found me more interesting than the eggs he dropped onto the hot, brown steel at my request. He kept looking from them to me over his rounded shoulder. I figured he saw a lot of eggs, so I didn't let the attention go to my head.

When he brought the victims over, he said, "You one of the reporters? 'Cause I didn't see you with that crowd yesterday."

"Maybe I just got in," I said.

"You're up early, too," the man said. "The reporters were drinking till all hours in the hotel bar, from what I hear. Don't expect to see any of them till noon. Sure as you're born, I'll be stuck frying eggs and toasting bread until two at least."

"Could be a story in that," I said, but he didn't believe me.

After I'd eaten, I sat drinking coffee and reading real reporters' stories about the murder. The only out-of-town papers in so far were the state editions of the Indianapolis dailies, the *Star Republic* and the *Times*. You could tell which political party got the Traynors' financial support from the way the Indy papers played the story. The *Star Republic* gave the few facts everybody already knew without mentioning the Traynor family or speculating very hard about Carson Drury's business in Indiana. The *Times,* which was the Democratic paper, managed to mention the Traynors while speculating. It reported a rumor that Drury was in town to do research for a film on the Traynor family. That guess was truer than any of us could have imagined back in safe, quiet Hollywood.

Neither paper mentioned the results of the ballistics tests, but the *Times,* at least, knew that the tests had been ordered. It identified the owner of the suspect gun as "Thomas S. Elliott of Los Angeles," without listing any of my film credits. Fame was fleeting after all.

At ten I crossed the street to the hotel and asked at the front desk for Drury. I asked quietly, but the question still caused several of the dozing fedoras in the Roberts' two-story lobby to tilt backward. Not all the reporters had drunk the night away. The clerk made a phone call on my behalf and then nodded to a man stationed near one of the elevators. That man relayed the message to the elevator operator and then nodded to me as I entered the car. I nodded to the operator to keep the string going, thinking as I did it that Gilbert Traynor must have been handing out sawbucks the way Paddy passed out cigars.

Gilbert had mentioned clearing the top floor of the hotel for Drury, but I'd passed it off as a figure of speech. That it hadn't been was conveyed to me by the elevator operator, a strawberry blond trainee who held the door open when we arrived and said, "Seventh floor, ladies hose, novelties, and movie stars. Watch your step."

"Watch yours, kid," I said, but it didn't lessen his smile by so much as a tooth.

The kid's warning came back to me when the door to Drury's suite opened to my knock. I found myself face-to-face with John Piers Whitehead. Seeing Hank Shepard would have been a little less of a shock. Whitehead had been transformed again. To the new clothes I'd noted yesterday he'd added a new face. That is, he wore an expression that transformed his patrician features: a look of perfect peace and happiness.

"My dear Elliott," he said, taking me by the hand. "Sorry we didn't have a chance to speak yesterday. Wasn't the moment to speak, I'm sure you'll agree. Carson has made time to see you now, so you and I will have to save our visiting until later."

He led me into the suite while I wondered in a dazed sort of way how Drury went about making time. With a magic wand, probably. There didn't seem to be any end to his talents.

Whitehead's remark turned out to have a much simpler explanation. The sitting room of the suite was being cleared of a small crowd as we entered. Still present were two stenographers, a barber, a manicurist, and a valet who made his exit carrying an armload of Drury's suits.

The man himself had traded in his wheelchair for a plush Queen Anne number with a matching hassock for his cast. The cast looked as though it had been freshly painted, but it might have been picking up a reflection of Drury's own glow. His long hair was carefully combed for once, and his lounging pajamas and dressing gown were hot from a presser.

"Scotto," he said while the extras were still milling about, collecting their props. "How are you?"

I didn't feel up to answering him. He smiled even more and said, "As you can see, I've availed myself of the hotel's marvelous staff. I haven't had this kind of attention since I arrived at RKO back in '40."

The second stenographer smiled her good-bye, and we were

three, Whitehead hovering by the door. Drury was still waiting for me to speak. When I didn't, he turned his radiance on Whitehead. "Scotty and I will need a few minutes, John."

"Of course," Whitehead said without losing his own beatific smile.

Drury tried waiting me out again, but his nerves weren't as starched as his loungewear. "Damn it, Scotty, say something. Give me one of those deadpan lines you like to use when you're pretending to be a hard case. I'll write one for you. How about, 'Doesn't the hotel have a masseur?' Or 'Wanting to look your best for the funeral?' Or you could stretch your character a little and paraphrase Milton: 'Carson Drury would rather rule in Indiana than serve in Hollywood.' "

The last line was Hank Shepard's kind of material. Drury and I had that insight at the same second. I watched him sag under the weight of it.

Before he caved in completely, I asked, "What is all this?"

"A play, Scotty. A farce I'm improvising to get me through today. All those hirelings you chased out of here were intended to take the place of one man, my friend Hank Shepard."

"Including John Piers Whitehead?"

"Most especially John. Why not?"

"Because you're supposed to hate Whitehead's guts. He's Judas, remember? The man who ruined your career. Or has anything you've told me been on the level?"

Drury had spent enough time in a wheelchair to react instinctively when he wanted to move. He reached for the wheels and came up with two handfuls of air. I was left to guess whether he'd have run me down or run away.

"Seems I'm staying put," he said, his anger sliding into sheepishness so smoothly that I wanted to shake him by his silk lapels. "And I suppose I owe you an explanation. After you hear it, you'll owe me an apology."

"After I hear it," I said.

"John came by to see me last night. Called up from the front desk as though there'd never been a falling out between us. As though we were back in New York in the old days and he'd stopped by to discuss our next project."

"And you let him up?"

"Yes. I was pretty low last night, Scotty. Low and lonely. Hank gone. You off somewhere." He looked up to see how guilty I felt over that and let it drop. "I remembered Hank urging me to talk to John, to reconcile with him. I thought I owed it to Hank to try.

"I was shocked to see how John had aged, and flattered to realize how much my small gesture meant to him. I understood for the first time that his misjudgments at RKO had hurt him more than they'd hurt me, in part because I'd been too self-obsessed to forgive him."

"Luckily for Whitehead you've grown out of that."

Drury's professionally shaved cheeks flushed a little. "Luckily for John I haven't. I still need people around me to affirm my vision through their dedication, as Hank did, and to take me down a peg from time to time when I threaten to become bigger than the vision. Hank did that, too."

"Whitehead's a lush. He's past providing witty byplay."

"I'm aware of John's condition. It's what brought my whole inspiration into focus. I saw that any scheme for redeeming myself and my reputation was doomed to fail if it didn't include John. We were cast into the wilderness together. We have to come out together. We have to be together to recreate our brief time of success."

We stared at each other for a while, Drury fidgety and expectant. I was remembering what Drury had called the morning: a play, a farce. That explained his impatience. He was anxious for his reviews.

"What are you thinking?" he finally asked.

"That your dialogue is better than your story."

Drury pulled the open neck of his pajamas closed against a draft. "Did you stay at the farm last night as you planned?"

"Yes."

"Why did you do that?"

"What do you mean?"

"Why did you take that risk? Why did you wait alone in the dark for the killer to come back and try again? Don't say it was your job. It was no part of your job. And it wasn't out of fondness for Hank. You didn't even like him. His weakness was womanizing, and you couldn't forgive him for that. So why did you hold your vigil?"

"I promised him I'd watch his back. I let him down."

"In other words, you did it because you felt you owed Hank and you wanted to make good your debt. There's no rational way to repay a dead man, so you did something irrational. I'm trying to resolve the same dilemma."

There was a delicate little nothing of a table within reach of Drury's throne. It was just big enough to hold a box of his cigars. He helped himself to one while I worked out what he'd tried to tell me.

"You can't save Hank Shepard," I said, "so you're saving Whitehead instead."

"It's a way of repaying a small part of my debt to Hank."

I wondered if we'd finally arrived at the truth. I was tempted to say no sale, to see if Drury would produce yet another, more ingenious explanation, but I'd run out of time. There was a sound on the other side of the sitting room door like a dead branch tapping at a windowpane at midnight. It was Whitehead's knock.

"Your eleven o'clock appointment has arrived early, Carson," he said. "Should I ask him to wait?"

"No, John. Send him in. I've learned the folly of keeping secrets from Mr. Elliott."

Eric Faris entered, looking so much like a man being chased that I checked the doorway behind him for a pursuer. No one else came through it, not even the obsequious Whitehead.

"Eric," Drury said in his familiar way. "What's the matter? Has the IRS caught up with Mr. Lockard?"

"I've come to ask for your help, Mr. Drury." Faris glanced at me to indicate that he'd take my help, too, and the maid's, if one was handy. He had the same cornered look I'd seen in Casey Atherley the night before when Gustin had been towering over him. It turned out that the same man was towering over Faris, in a manner of speaking.

"You know Sheriff Gustin," Faris said to Drury. "You could talk to him for me. He's asked me to stay in Indiana for the time being. I'd rather not stay. I mean, I can't stay. I haven't slept since I heard of the murder—or eaten. I never should have agreed to come out here in the first place. Mr. Lockard insisted that I look after your loan personally, but I'm not the man for the job. I'm an accountant by training, not a . . ."

He left us wondering what he wasn't. An enforcer? A spy? An agent provocateur?

"A field man?" Drury suggested helpfully. Faris's panic had brought back his high spirits. "What would Mr. Lockard say if you were to desert your post?"

"I intend to resign as soon as I can get back to Los Angeles. If you would just speak to the sheriff."

"I'm afraid you're overestimating my influence with Sheriff Gustin," Drury said. "I doubt I could get myself or Mr. Elliott or Mr. Whitehead out of Indiana right now. A chair for our guest, Scotty."

I managed to get one under Faris before he collapsed. Drury was close to collapsing himself, into laughter.

"You're not the first man to lament a bargain he struck with the devil," he said. "The only thing I can offer you is some advice that's helped me over the years: Sit back and enjoy the ride."

chapter

29

WHEN I LEFT THE SUITE, Drury was still consoling Faris and mocking him by turns. Neither project held much interest for me. I was hoping instead to get Whitehead's version of the Great Reconciliation of 1955, but the beneficiary of it had hidden himself away. I didn't feel up to searching the entire seventh floor for him, so I rode the elevator down and crossed the street to the drugstore where I'd had breakfast. I stopped in there long enough to place a collect call to Los Angeles.

It took the operator a while to get the call through, which gave me time to think about my sudden urge to talk to Ella. It was going on four days since I'd spoken to her, during which time I'd had plenty of telephones around and no desire to use one. I decided that my change of heart was due to Sigmund Drury's recent psycho-analysis. I had run an unnecessary, irrational risk by staying alone at the farm, and I owed my wife an apology for that. Then there was the little matter of my upcoming luncheon engagement with Linda Traynor. The call was my last chance to walk into that an honest man.

I could tell from Ella's hello and the way she answered my questions about the kids that my extended silence had bothered her. She asked if I'd caught Shepard's murderer yet and then laughed at herself ruefully.

"Listen to me," she said. "I sound like I'm asking whether you caught your limit of trout or had a good time playing poker with the boys. Like I'm jealous of all the fun you're having. Sorry about that."

"I'm the one who should be apologizing," I said.

"For what? Sending your love through Paddy Maguire?"

I'd forgotten that particular offense. "Among other things."

"Let's hear the latest transgression."

"I'm having lunch with Gilbert Traynor's sister-in-law. She's a war widow, and she's in some kind of jam."

"What does she look like?" Ella asked. She was suddenly as merry as Drury had been when Faris had come in groveling.

"A backwoods Gene Tierney. She kissed me the other night when I wasn't looking."

"Where would that have been? And don't say down by the garden gate. Are we talking about lips, cheek, or the top of your curly head?"

She was almost laughing at me now. I felt a lot better myself. "I'll call again soon."

"Take care of yourself, Scotty. At lunch especially. I don't know about the Hoosier Elliott, but the Hollywood version has always been a sucker for a lady in distress."

■ ■ ■

Gilbert had given me vague directions to the Traynor plant on our first day in Indiana. I drove west out of town, past the rail yard. From there I was able to follow my nose. I'd recognized the aroma of good old Indiana coal burning by the ton, coal that had so much sulfur in it you could smell its soft, yellow smoke for miles.

The actual plant reminded me of one of the middle-of-the-pack Hollywood studios—Paramount, maybe, or Universal. It had a fancy front gate like Paramount's, this one done up in wrought-iron scroll-work and crowned with the inevitable winged T. The gate also had the inevitable guard. He wore the same navy blue uniform as the guy who'd escorted me from Traynor House, but today's model was friendlier—especially after I'd told him about my appointment with Linda Traynor.

He directed me to a modest but modern office building whose windows were continuous bands of glass encircling each floor. Once again I ended up on the top floor, this time in a waiting room that made Drury's borrowed office back at RKO seem Spartan.

For company I had the Traynor portrait gallery. There were life-size portraits of Gilbert's grandfather, a heavyset gentleman with a Snub Pollard moustache; Gilbert's father, painted so late in his life that the artist had captured traces of his failing heart; and Gilbert's brother, Mark. He was in civilian attire and looked older than he did in the service portrait that hung in Traynor House, which didn't make sense. I considered the possibility that the painter came back every year to add a gray hair or two or a wrinkle, anything to keep up the illusion that Mark was still alive and running things. I wouldn't have put that past Marvella.

"You're standing in my favorite spot." It was Linda, in a tailored navy suit and very quiet shoes. The suit's jacket had a white collar and three-quarter-length sleeves that ended in white cuffs.

"I didn't mean to startle you," she said. "And I'm sorry for keeping you waiting. I forgot that I was meeting with the board this morning."

"You make it sound pretty routine."

She shrugged with her eyebrows. "It is nowadays. Not so many years ago, the prospect scared me to death. I'd stand where you're standing now, trying to figure out what Mark would do about some problem if he were here. The answer always came to me sooner or later. Feel like a drive?"

We took Linda's Studebaker Speedster, which I drove. The coupé had a small-block V8 that didn't have as many horses as the one in my Fireflite. But those horses were hauling a smaller, lighter car. It certainly felt like a rocket after the milk wagon I'd been driving around Indiana. When I looked down at the black-on-white instrument panel, we were doing seventy. We were out in the country by then, on 236, the state road Linda had told me to take.

I started to rein the coupé in, but Linda said, "Have fun. It's strange, but none of our family cars has ever been stopped for speeding."

That wry comment was the last thing she said except for "left" and "right" until we arrived in a little place called Middletown. When we reached its half-block business district, Linda said, "Park anywhere."

She'd thrown off her suit jacket back at the Traynor parking lot, revealing a sleeveless white blouse. Now she unpinned her auburn hair and shook it out until it lay across her wide shoulders, the hair almost red in the noonday sun.

She led me down the street to a place called the Old Post Tavern. "Nobody knows who I am in here. Do you think you can go an hour without saying the word Traynor?"

"I've gone years without saying it."

Until we'd arrived in Middletown, I'd been hoping for some country club or at least a secluded restaurant with a bartender who knew his way around a Gibson. The Old Post was neither of those. The front door was propped open to let the heat circulate, and it was guarded by a sleeping yellow dog. Linda scratched its ear before stepping over it. I just stepped. Beyond the dog was a long bar, dimly lit but well manned. I took one look at the bartender's straw hat and mentally changed my drink order to cold beer. Several of the customers greeted Linda, calling her "little lady" and "darling."

Beyond the bar was a section of tables, most of them occupied. We found an empty one in a corner. Three of the table's four legs were the same length.

Linda had brightened up enough to grin at me as we sat down. "Were you expecting the Stork Club?"

"No," I lied.

"I like this place. I feel at home here. And they make a good ten-derloin sandwich. Order it deluxe if you want tomato and lettuce."

"I know what deluxe means. I'm a Hoosier, too, remember?"

"You're a city boy," Linda said. "Like Mark. You should have seen him down at Camp Atterbury learning to be a soldier. I'd never imagined a grown man could be so lost out of doors. And him going off to war. I think I fell in love with him because he was so lost and because he stood for a world I'd only seen in a movie or two, a world where men didn't all farm and hunt and spit for no reason. Mark offered me a way out of the simple, little world I knew. I was thrilled to leave it behind. I'd be even more thrilled now if I could get it back."

She fell into a brown study until the waitress came to take our order. Over lunch Linda asked me questions about the army, short questions that required long answers. I played along until we'd turned down the peach cobbler and the waitress had taken away our plates.

Then I said, "What did you want to talk to me about?"

"I need your advice. I should just go to Sheriff Gustin and get it over with, but I thought I'd ask you first. It's about the murder."

"What about it?"

"I'd arranged to meet Hank Shepard the night he died."

"Why?"

"Why do you think? He was a man, and I hadn't been with a man in one hell of a long time. Don't get any more genteel on me, Scotty. I couldn't stand it. Shepard came by Traynor House on Saturday afternoon to pick up Gilbert's suitcase. I offered him a drink while he waited. Just a drink. I didn't know his reputation then, but I found out what he was like soon enough. Before I knew what was happening, we were going at it pretty seriously.

"It wasn't like the other night with you, Scotty. I wasn't the aggressor, and Shepard wasn't a gentleman. Or maybe I did lead him on without realizing it. Maybe I'm looking for another man to step in and change my life for me. That would be sad and pathetic, wouldn't it?"

"What happened?"

"Nothing, really. Not when Marvella could have walked in at any moment. He asked me to come by the farm on Sunday night. He said you'd be away in Indianapolis, so I agreed."

That explained a lot: Shepard's chipper mood on Saturday afternoon, his crack about how sending me after Gilbert's bag would have been a wasted opportunity, his eagerness for me to make the drive to Indy on Sunday.

But it didn't explain everything. "Shepard couldn't have known that Drury was going to send the sheriff's men away. Weren't you afraid they'd see you?"

Linda echoed the photo hound, Casey Atherley. "Anyone who wasn't born in a city could find a quiet way on and off that farm. I wasn't worried about them or about Drury, stuck in that wheelchair of his."

She fell silent again. I said, "So?"

"So nothing. I didn't go. I lost my nerve. And I couldn't be disloyal to Mark."

Glad as I was that she hadn't gone, I couldn't understand her reasoning. "You speak of your husband as though he's still alive."

"Living with Marvella, it's easy for me to think of Mark that way. I have to make an effort sometimes to remember he's dead. On the night I promised to see Shepard, I felt like one of those wives who played around while their husbands were overseas. God help any woman in Traynorville who did that. We had two or three, and we shunned them worse than any lepers, shunned them until they moved away. Somebody did even more than that."

"Like what?"

"Do you remember Sheriff Gustin telling you yesterday about barn burnings during the war? They were connected to the cheating wives. I never knew who was behind the burnings—they happened just after word had come about Mark, and I was in shock—but the farms involved belonged to men who were known to be taking advantage of other men's war service. The men had their barns taken away, and the women had everything taken away.

"Last Sunday night I felt like one of those poor souls myself. I still feel that way."

"You didn't go."

"No. But Hank Shepard died. I can't help feeling that he died because I'd promised to meet him, because I wanted to meet him so badly."

It wasn't an idea that required a rebuttal. I waited for it to fall apart on its own.

"I know," Linda said. "It doesn't make sense. It's just my guilt getting to me. Maybe I'll feel better after I talk to Frank Gustin. I've wanted to talk to him, but I've been afraid of its getting back to Gilbert and Marvella. When I heard yesterday that your wife had had her own run-in with Shepard, I thought I'd talk to you first. I thought you'd understand."

That made sense in an oddball way. She couldn't confess to Mark, so she'd picked another wounded husband as a stand-in. I didn't mind. And I didn't see what good Linda's story would do Gustin. It explained why Shepard had remained alone at the farm, but not who had taken advantage of the opportunity.

"Why don't you wait and see if telling me helps," I said. "Maybe you've gotten it out of your system already."

chapter

30

A MESSAGE WAS WAITING for me at the main gate of the Traynor plant when Linda and I got back from Middletown. She was wearing her suit jacket again, and her hair was pinned up tighter than Eric Faris's nerves. The Traynor guard touched the brim of his hat to her before addressing me.

"The sheriff wants you down at the courthouse. Something important."

Linda climbed out of the coupé. "Use this car for a change," she said. "It's more your style."

The important something Gustin had to see me about turned out to be a visitor from Indianapolis, my father. My father the lawyer, to be precise. He was sitting in the sheriff's waiting room, ramrod straight and dressed for a day in court, right down to his old brief-case and his favorite prop, a pair of gold pince-nez glasses that were currently parked in the breast pocket of his three-piece suit. I remembered the glasses from my time in the visitors gallery as a boy when he would adjust and readjust them on his nose while he marshaled his thoughts or wave them in front of a witness like a hypnotist's watch.

"Tom," he said when I stepped up to him, "you've had us worried."

By "us" he had to be referring to himself and my grandmother. The only other person in the waiting area, Gustin's maiden-aunt receptionist, was indifference itself.

I asked her to thank the sheriff for tracking me down and led my lawyer out into the slightly cooler hallway. "Did you think I'd been arrested?" I asked as the door closed behind us.

"I didn't know what to think. First the sheriff called to check your whereabouts on Sunday. Then the *Times* made it sound as though you were a suspect in the murder investigation. It said your gun was being tested."

I held open my coat to display the forty-five. "It passed."

At the sight of the gun, my father's normally narrow eyes grew wide, as though I'd revealed a tattoo or other, less artistic needle marks. I felt an impulse to apologize to him for the way I'd turned out, for rejecting his plans for me as too small and then ending up smaller by far. The impulse passed.

"Let's find a quiet place to talk," I said. "There are benches out on the square."

I'd covered up the gun again, but my father was still looking at it. He roused himself. "Is it too early for a drink?" he asked.

It was my turn to stretch my eyelids. "Not where I've been living," I said.

I happened to know of a place nearby, Augie's, the bar on the square where Clark drank his Friday nights away. I expected a twin of the Old Post Tavern, but Augie's surprised me, pleasantly. It had pine paneling indirectly lit, an oval bar surrounded by booths, and almost no business on this Tuesday afternoon. The bartender–Augie himself–had even heard of Gibsons.

I watched him mix one while my father selected a booth. "I think I know a customer of yours," I said for no particular reason.

"That so?" Augie said. He had long sideburns like the ones some of the men from my old battery had worn, the kids from Tennessee.

"His name is Clark. I'm told he's a regular on Friday nights."

"Maybe on Monday nights, too, from now on," Augie said. "He was in here last night, drinking to get drunk like he always does. I thought we were in for trouble from the look he had. I don't mean his expression. He don't have but one expression. Don't have enough face left for two. You have to tell his mood from his color. The darker he gets, the closer I keep my old keg tapper." He reached under the bar and pulled out a short wooden club with holes drilled in its head, the holes crudely filled with lead. "He was plenty dark last night, but nothing happened."

"Was he here last Friday night?"

"Yep. Stayed till closing, too, which he hasn't done for years. When I locked up, he was out on the square, pissing on that old French gun. He likes to do that. Don't know why."

I thought I did, but I kept my guess to myself. I paid Augie and carried the drinks over to our booth. My father took the smallest possible sip of his rye and water and then opened the briefcase that shared his side of the booth. I thought he might produce some evidence he'd brought along to prove my innocence—my report cards or my honorable discharge—but the only things that came out of the case were his pipe and a pouch of tobacco.

"I've been trying to learn to smoke one of those," I said.

"Really? How is it going?"

"I don't seem to have the knack."

"Like most bad habits, it doesn't come naturally," he said. "You'll get the hang of it in time. You're packing the bowl too tightly, more than likely. Half as much as it will hold is about right. Loosely arranged. Leaves room for the smoke."

As he demonstrated, I asked, "How did you come up from the city?"

"By the Interurban," he said, naming the system of glorified trolleys that connected Indianapolis with neighboring towns. "I can catch the five o'clock car home, as you don't need my help."

He was already slipping back into the person I'd visited on

Sunday, the old man sitting by his radio. It was enough to make me wish I'd been arrested.

"I'm not making much progress," I said. "I wouldn't mind talking the case over with someone."

"I'd be pleased to listen."

During my visit to his apartment, I'd told him about the sabotage attempts in Hollywood and the Klan visit to the Traynor farm. So I launched into the murder without preamble, starting with the moment when I'd found the body and the twelve hours afterward during which I'd told my story over and over to different policemen. I described Faris's alibi and Whitehead's and my lack thereof. I explained Gustin's interest in me by admitting that Shepard had gotten fresh with Ella at Drury's party. My honesty had its limits, though. I didn't say that Ella had known Shepard earlier. I also omitted, for practice, Linda Traynor's unkept appointment with Shepard.

Through all that, my father smoked and said nothing. I slipped out of sequence, telling him first about the strange results of the ballistics test and Gustin's guess that the murder bullet had been fired by a homemade gun and then about the Pallisers' connection to the Klan. I'd saved that for last, thinking it would be the part that interested him the most. I was wrong. I noticed that his eyes weren't focusing on me, and his pipe was smoking itself.

I stopped short of my big scene with Marvella Traynor and said, "What's wrong?"

"That bullet. Something about that bullet." He set his pipe down on the table, leaning it against his forgotten drink. "I was counsel to Indiana's production board during the war."

"I remember," I said.

He pulled his glasses from the pocket of his jacket and began tapping the table with them. "I remember a project—a top secret project—a handgun for the OSS. The code name for the gun was the Flare Projector, but even back then people were calling it the Liberator. It even had a nickname, the Woolworth gun, because it was so inexpensive to make. The frame was stamped steel, and the barrel–this is what brought it to mind–the barrel was unrifled."

"What did the OSS want with a gun like that?"

"They intended to drop them from planes behind enemy lines for use by resistance forces. They did drop them, over a million of them, in Europe and the Philippines. I would have forgotten all about that gun except that I ran across one after the war. Rather, a friend of mine did, a friend from the production board. He saw one in a gun shop in Indianapolis. Evidently some of our boys brought them back as souvenirs."

"Gustin and Clark are veterans," I said, thinking out loud. "Hank Shepard was himself. But then, half the men in Indiana are."

"Let me finish, son, and maybe you won't have to search from house to house for this gun. One job of the production board was assigning projects to various factories around the state. As you know, certain industries went over to war production completely, like the automobile industry. The bigger plants built tanks and planes, and the little ones picked up piecework and special projects like this gun."

"The Traynor plant."

"That's what I'm trying to tell you. If my memory isn't failing me, the works right here in Traynorville made that gun. It was supposed to be a secret project, as I said, but a lot of the people around here must remember it. I'm surprised that sheriff of yours doesn't."

"He's not my sheriff," I said. "He belongs to the Traynors."

chapter

31

GILBERT TRAYNOR was seated in his office at the Traynor Automobile Company, looking smaller than life, as he almost always did. This time the culprit was his desk. Being Gilbert's, it was naturally out of step with the rest of the company's furnishings, which might have been listed under the heading "Overinflated Leather" in some supplier's catalogue. The desk, on the other hand, was out of a world's fair exhibit on the office of tomorrow: an elliptical slab of exotic wood, supported by three legs, one of them a sweeping, inverted fin.

As I waited for our meeting to begin, I had a second thought on the subject, deciding that Gilbert was being dwarfed by his tie. Not a bad trick, either, because the tie was an exceedingly narrow bit of striped silk. He'd loosened it, perhaps when he'd heard the five o'-clock whistle blow, which made the tie look as if it had been knotted for a larger man.

"What's the emergency, Elliott?" he asked mildly but warily.

There was no emergency, at least no new one. I'd implied that there was at the plant's main gate when my initial call to Gilbert's office hadn't gotten me inside. I'd winded myself and the Studebaker racing to the Interurban stop with my father and then to the plant to catch Gilbert before he escaped into his mother's fortress, Traynor House. When I'd been told by Gilbert's secretary through Gilbert's front-gate guard to make an appointment, I'd realized that the plant was Gilbert's own fortress. So I'd tried to give the impression that the murderer was snapping at my heels, or vice versa.

The ruse had worked, but we'd both had time to think about it while I'd taken the elevator up to the bridal suite. Gilbert had gotten suspicious. I'd gotten angry.

"Why am I using the tradesman's entrance with you?" I asked. "I thought we were on the same side."

"I have a business relationship with the man you work for," Gilbert said, no longer mild, but under control. "Not with you. When Mr. Drury finishes with your services, I won't even have that distant connection. I'll expect you to vacate the farm and return the company car."

It was the morning after in a big way for Gilbert and me. He'd been friendly enough at the courthouse on the prior afternoon—penitent, even, over his role in bringing my fight with Shepard to Gustin's attention. I asked myself what had happened since to change things.

"Your mother mentioned my stopping by for tea, I take it."

"How dare you be flip about threatening my mother?" Gilbert demanded, sounding so much like Marvella that, angry as I was, I felt sorry for him. "How could you abuse our hospitality like that?"

"As I recall, your mother did most of the threatening. And since when is burning crosses on people's lawns called hospitality?"

There didn't seem to be much of anything in Gilbert, not even fight. He sank a little in his jet-pilot chair and started to pull at his moustache.

"Why didn't you tell us your uncle had been bucking for grand dragon of the Klan?"

"Would you tell anyone that? What good would it have done to dig that up? My uncle has been dead for twenty years. He wasn't under one of the hoods you saw. Neither was I."

I had been considering the latter possibility, thinking back on Drury's insight into the Klan, the idea that the frightening thing about it was its facelessness. Drury had also guessed that Gilbert was using us and *Albertsons* to rebel against his family–more specifically, against his mother. But when the chance had come for Gilbert to rebel in a big way, he'd ignored it.

"If you'd reminded Gustin about the Pallisers," I said, "you might have given him the real motive for the cross burning. It wasn't revenge against Drury for *First Citizen*. It was an attempt to scare him out of Indiana so that he couldn't separate you from your money."

Gilbert thought it over. "There's no way we'll ever know that for sure. Frank Gustin isn't going to give my mother the third degree."

"I know. He has a wife and kids to feed."

"So do you," Gilbert said, suddenly as sentimental as Paddy on Saint Patrick's Day. "You should be thinking about getting back to see them. They're missing you a lot more than anyone will ever miss Hank Shepard."

Spoken in Gilbert's wistful tone, the reference to my family and the possibility of never seeing them again didn't come across as a threat or even a veiled threat. But it was surely a warning.

"Are you ready to tell me what goes on in Traynorville?" I asked.

"I told you before, I don't know myself." It was clear that not knowing no longer excited him. He told me why next. "Hank Shepard would still be alive if I had guessed what was going to happen. Right now I'd just like to go home. Carson is coming to dinner, and I should be there when he arrives. If you'd get to the point of this meeting, I'd appreciate it."

"Tell me about the Liberator."

"It was a bomber, I think," he said, wary now in spades.

"I mean the pistol."

"I know what you mean. Who told you about that?"

A man who was overdressed for the Interurban car he was riding, a man who had shaken my hand good-bye, but hadn't told me he loved me or that he forgave me for deserting my dying mother. It was a good thing I had seen enough movies to read all that into the handshake.

"An old friend," I said. "He told me the Liberator was a forty-five-caliber handgun made right here by the Traynor Company during the war. It fires a standard round through an unrifled barrel, which means it will blow a hole through a guy at close range and leave behind a bullet with no scoring."

"No what?"

"No marks made by the rifling inside a normal barrel. Any bullet fired through a normal gun has them. That's why I'm a free man. My gun scores a bullet. The gun that killed Shepard doesn't."

I hadn't expected that to be news to Gilbert, but it was. Somehow he hadn't gotten today's briefing from Gustin. He wouldn't have gotten one if he was busy pretending that none of this was happening. He'd be hiding in his office, reluctant to see even me. He'd be back to defending the family he'd previously wanted no part of. I'd misjudged the entire interview, I realized, right down to handing him the one piece of information I should have held back.

I watched him figuring and refiguring over the course of a long minute. Then, without taking his close-set eyes from the point in space where they were focused, he reached out with his right hand and pulled open a drawer concealed behind the shark's fin leg of his desk. He rummaged in the drawer, still gazing into space. Then his hand came out holding a gun.

It came out so slowly that I had plenty of time to get my own gun out and ready to fire. That drew Gilbert back to earth. "This isn't loaded," he said.

"Mine is," I said. "Put yours down on the desktop and push it across to me."

He looked as though he'd rather throw it at me, but he did as I said. "I used that as a paperweight for years. We have one in the company trophy case, but there were extras, so I appropriated one. It reminded me that the company had done some important work during the war."

I put my Colt away and examined the Liberator. It was small and light, so light that I might have mistaken it for a toy gun if I'd just happened across it. As my father had said, the frame was formed by two pieces of stamped metal, joined along the gun's vertical axis and spot-welded together. These halves were clamped around the short barrel. The barrel received some additional support from the trigger guard, a broad, flat band of steel that curved up from the metal grip to encircle the tube at a point very close to its smooth bore. At the opposite end, the barrel had been reinforced by an extra sleeve of pipe crudely welded into place. The whole assembly was painted olive drab.

"How do you load it?"

"I don't know. I was still in school when that was made."

I'd figured it out by then. The hammer was made of pot metal and shaped like the plug at the end of an electric cord. The hammer pivoted out of the way, and the rear sight slid upward to expose the breech. Nothing was in the chamber now, not even the faintest whiff of spent powder.

"I told you it hasn't been fired," Gilbert said.

The best proof of that was the fact that the gun was still in one piece. It was hard to imagine a Liberator having a long service life. I found a sliding panel on the bottom of the grip. It opened to reveal a compartment as empty as the chamber but bigger.

"What went in here? Spare rounds?"

"Nylon stockings, probably," Gilbert said, "for bartering with the natives. I promise you, that gun hasn't been out of this plant."

"Let's check the one in your trophy case," I said.

"Fine. It's on the way to my car."

I pocketed the Liberator. Gilbert thought about that, but didn't say anything. He climbed into the padded shoulders of a sports coat and led me to the elevator. We rode down without chatting.

I hadn't noticed a trophy case on my way into the office building. It wasn't a problem with my eyesight, either. Gilbert double-timed us out of the modern office block and across a brick plaza to an older, lower structure identified simply as "Building 1." Inside were half a dozen Traynor automobiles, including a midnight blue Phaeton Six. Gilbert ran his hand over its gleaming fender without breaking stride.

At the center of the car collection sat the trophy case. It contained the whole history of the company: silver loving cups and jugs from races that early Traynor cars had won, framed newspaper articles and ads for later models, and chrome-plated examples of the pistons and rods and other odds and ends the company had fallen into making when it had stopped building cars.

In a place of honor at the center of the case was something I hadn't expected to see: a tiny, silken banner with a gold star embroidered on it.

"Mark's, of course," Gilbert said, following my gaze. "From the front window of Traynor House. The ladies of the plant made it for my mother after he was killed."

I remembered the little banners from the war years. Almost all the houses had had one, or so it had seemed. A star for every son or daughter in the service. A gold star for every son or daughter who wasn't coming back.

"Your mother gave that up?"

"There's your damn gun," Gilbert said in reply.

The Liberator was affixed to a wooden plaque. The brass plate beneath the pistol read: OSS LIBERATOR, 1,000,214 PRODUCED, 1943.

"Do you want to dust the plaque for fingerprints?" Gilbert asked.

I had him open the case so I could see how securely the pistol was fastened to the board. I decided it would come apart before it would come off.

"Satisfied?"

"I will be when you tell me about the other examples."

"What other examples?"

"You said back in your office that you took one of the Liberators because there was one in the trophy case and extras. How many extras? Just answer me. Don't work out the chances of lying to me first, or I'm going to the cops—the real cops, not Gustin."

"There were two extras, mine and another."

"Where's number two? Traynor House?"

"You don't want to know where."

"Why not?"

He rammed the glass door of the case closed, rattling the whole display. "Because it makes you a suspect again."

"It was at the farmhouse? I never saw it."

"You'll have to convince the police of that, not me."

It was an easy bluff to call. "The police are going to be busy asking why you never mentioned this gun."

"I never even thought of it. The world is full of guns. I didn't know about any marks on any bullets. I didn't even know the Liberator wouldn't make them. I had no reason to connect that relic with the murder."

He'd let his voice get out of control. He heard it bouncing around the museum and shrank a little more. "If the reporters get hold of this, they'll storm the house. You have to help me keep this quiet, Scotty."

Hank Shepard's murder was doing wonders for broken relationships. First Drury and Whitehead had mended their fences. Then my father and I had. Now Gilbert was holding an olive branch out to his business associate's hired man. Waving it in my face, in fact.

"What are we going to do, Scotty?"

"Go home and enjoy your dinner," I said. "I'm going to take your farmhouse apart."

chapter

32

THE TRAYNOR FARMHOUSE had already been taken apart, figuratively speaking, by Gustin's troops the day after the murder. I didn't think they'd have missed a clue as obvious as a gun, not even a gun that looked like a toy. Then again, after they'd found my automatic, which hadn't been hidden at all, they might have lost interest. So I decided a search was worth my time. I had a second, better reason for putting in the effort: I couldn't think of another move.

I stopped at the end of Riverbend's drive when the deputy on duty waved me down.

"Sheriff's looking for you, son," he said. He was the oldest deputy I'd seen so far. Gustin was having to call in the reserves to man his investigation and keep the Traynors happy.

"If you heard that before three o'clock," I said, "it's old news."

"Just checking," the deputy said.

"Any visitors?"

"Just that Clark guy. Saw him on the farmhouse porch. I didn't drive down to ask him his business. I figure his business is no business of mine."

I hadn't the deputy's sensitivity regarding other people's privacy. It would have held me back professionally. Unfortunately, Clark was no longer on the farmhouse porch when I climbed out of the black coupé. He wasn't in the house, either. But someone had been. There were subtle signs.

The visitor had anticipated my plan to take the farmhouse parlor apart, but he had done it literally. The old settee and the spindly chairs were on their sides, and the hooked rug was in a heap in the corner where someone had thrown it. The secretary had been opened and its drawers turned out. Every shelf of the glass-fronted bookcase had been emptied. Its collections—the arrowheads and butterflies and horseshoes—were scattered around the room. The old hornet's nest had been ripped in half lengthwise.

The object of the search hadn't been Casey Atherley's film. I found the plate among the broken butterflies and pocketed it. I didn't find the Liberator. I checked the halves of the hornet's nest for a cavity big enough to have held a gun. There wasn't one, but I did note that the hands that had dug their fingers into the nest were bigger than mine. Clue number one. Clue number two was the pump organ. It now sat at a forty-five-degree angle to its wall. I tried pushing it back into place and found that it was a job to shift it at all. My two clues pointed in the same direction as the tip I'd gotten from the old deputy: to Clark.

I checked the rest of the farmhouse. None of the other rooms had been disturbed. Nor had the tack room of the barn, with one notable exception: The rails for the wheelchair ramp that Clark had never gotten around to finishing had been kicked to splinters. It was enough to make a guy circumspect if he were inclined that way.

I left my suit jacket and hat hanging on the back door of the house. It was too hot to wear them hiking. And without the jacket, only a blind man could miss the big gun I was wearing. For safe-keeping, I took Gilbert's Liberator along, tucked in my belt at the small of my back.

I followed the packed-dirt path back to Clark's woods, watching a red-tailed hawk circling overhead, and whistling as I went. The tune had popped up out of nowhere, but its name hadn't tagged along. Then it came to me. It was the title song from *Rhythm on the River,* the epic that had made such an impression on John Piers Whitehead. I switched over to "Everything but You."

I stopped whistling altogether when I reached the last of the cleared land. Clark's woods had been nothing more than a stretch of nondescript hardwood on my previous visit when I'd had Linda Traynor and Gustin along for company. Now I noticed every tree, reciting their names—sycamore, shagbark hickory, green ash, maple—as I scanned them. The pride of the collection was a pair of old oaks that straddled the path, their crowns forming a single canopy of green so dark it looked black in places. As I passed between the oaks, I heard the sounds of wood being split. The alternating splintering and thudding relaxed me. It placed Clark up ahead, not behind the next tree or the last one I'd passed.

He was still at it when I reached the clearing that held his cabin, working one-handed with an ax that looked like a Boy Scout hatchet in his good hand, his right. He was working bare-chested, which let me confirm what I already knew: He was built like Max Baer in his prime. The exception was his left arm, which, while far from withered away, was less substantial than the rest of him. Gilbert had told me that Clark had an arm he couldn't lift above his shoulder. Even from across the clearing I could see the outward mark of the damage: a deep triangular scar on the back of his left shoulder, bloodred with his exertions.

His face, when he finally noticed me at the edge of his clearing and swung around, was also dark red, a bad sign according to Augie. But he was no authority. He'd been wrong, for example, when he'd said that Clark had only one expression. With his eyes squeezed down to slits, Clark conveyed hatred very well.

"How'd you know?" Clark asked. He spoke conversationally, but his words carried easily across the hot stillness.

"How did I know what?" I replied as innocently as I could. I thought he was asking how I'd tied him to the destruction of the farmhouse. I wanted him to mention it first.

"How'd you know that this wood splitting isn't getting the job done for me?"

He wasn't wearing his red cap, so I got the full benefit of his disfigurement: the normal scalp and bit of forehead and the red rawness below, still looking after all these years like the skin had just been ripped away by the blast of a shell. The only thing that damped down the effect at all was the distance I'd left between us— a safe thirty yards.

"What job would that be?" I asked, genuinely lost now.

"The job of wringing out my bad temper. I thought if I split a cord or two it would go away, but it hasn't. There's no resistance to this stuff. The ax goes through it like it wasn't there. I don't want splitting. I want smashing."

I'd been Paddy's straight man too long. I couldn't keep myself from asking, "Where do I come in?"

"I figured you were volunteering to go a few rounds with me. Shepard told me you'd boxed a little in the service."

"Shepard talked too much."

"Yeah, he did. My face brings that out in some people. Either they can't think of a word, or they can't shut up. So what do you say?"

"Nothing. I'm the kind who can't think of a word."

Clark brought the ax down on the stump he was using as a chopping block, burying the head without putting much effort into it. He started across the clearing to me.

"It's a funny thing," I said. "I go months in Los Angeles without drawing my gun. In Traynorville I have to do it twice in one day."

"If you pull that gun out," Clark said, "I'll make you use it."

"That'll teach me a lesson." I said it in my best offhand, tough-guy delivery. Torrance Beaumont couldn't have done it better. It was a tone of voice that meant business in any corner of the country, but it didn't impress Clark. He kept limping toward me, slow but steady.

When I was down to my last fifteen yards, I said, "What were you looking for up at the house?"

"You can guess what it was," Clark said, "since you're guessing I was up there looking."

"Okay." I reached behind my back for Gilbert's paperweight. "I'm guessing it was this."

Clark stopped in his tracks at the sight of the Liberator, and I breathed again. "How did you find that?"

"I backtracked from Hank Shepard's body."

"I didn't kill Shepard."

"Everybody tells me that. It's amazing he's actually dead."

Clark took another step. I raised the empty gun. He laughed at it. "You're holding a smooth barrel three inches long. You couldn't hit me from there once in twenty tries. And you've only got one try."

"So I'll wait."

He stopped again. A fox squirrel climbed down on a hickory branch to my right and began to scold me. It knew better than to scold Clark. The caretaker was staring at the gun in my hand. As I watched, he licked at his ragged excuse for lips.

"I've heard you don't like guns," I said. "How is it you know so much about this one?"

"I've spent a lot of time studying it," Clark said. "I have a lot of time, and it was around. In the farmhouse."

"In the bookcase?"

"In the secretary. Wrapped in an oiled rag. It's been there since I hired on."

"Tell me more."

"It's called the Liberator and sometimes the Woolworth gun. It was dropped behind enemy lines with a round in the chamber and ten spares in the grip. The grip also held a little instruction sheet with pictures instead of words. It showed that the only way to kill a person with the gun was to clamp it to the side of the target's head."

"Or poke him in the chest," I said. "It doesn't say Woolworth on it anywhere—or Liberator, for that matter. Where'd you pick up all those details?"

"Around town. The locals made the damn thing. I've heard talk. At Augie's, mostly."

"Last Monday night?"

"No, years ago. Nobody's mentioned that gun recently. Nobody's connected it with the murder."

They would, I thought, once word got out about the ballistics test. After that, the Traynors would be prisoners in their own little kingdom.

Then I remembered what had brought me to the cabin. "You tore the house apart looking for this thing. You knew it was the murder gun. How did you make the connection if you didn't do the shooting?"

"I admit I looked for the gun, but it wasn't because of the murder."

"Why then?"

"I missed it. Woolworth gun isn't the only nickname that pistol had. It was called the suicide gun, too, because using one was practically a suicide mission. To kill a Nazi soldier or a Japanese sentry, a resistance fighter had to get close enough to shake his hand. Not the kind of job you'd expect to walk away from."

That was as much as he'd tell me, but it was enough. "You miss having the gun around because it gave you an out."

"That's right. It was for my personal liberation, for when I couldn't stomach another moment of my life."

The confession should have been the cue for yet another reconciliation. I was willing, but not Clark.

"Give me that gun," he said. "You can unload it first if it makes you nervous. I won't beat the teeth out of your head if you do it right now."

"Sorry," I said. "This isn't your gun. I picked this one up at the Traynor plant an hour ago."

Clark's color had faded during our heart-to-heart. Now he darkened dangerously. "Where's mine?"

"Only the murderer knows that. You can help me find him."

"How?"

"Tell me about the night of the cross burning."

"It was a Friday. I was at Augie's as usual. I got drunk. I came home. I passed out."

"You stayed at Augie's until closing. You haven't been doing that lately. You wanted to stay away from the farm as long as you could and come back as drunk as you could. You knew something was going to happen."

"What if I did?"

"Tell me who tipped you off."

"You don't want to fool with those guys, Hollywood. I'm Santa Claus compared to them."

"I'll take my chances."

Clark shrugged with his good shoulder. "You've got it coming."

chapter

33

BUSINESS HAD PICKED UP at Augie's. A half-dozen men were spaced out around the bar, and two of the booths held couples. From a back room came the clack of pool balls. It was the last of the after-work crowd, I decided, lingering over their aperitifs.

I sat down at the bar and listened to the Gale Storm record playing on the jukebox until the man behind the bar noticed me. He was my friend with the Civil War sideburns, Augie himself. He broke off a conversation on the evils of fluoridated water and strolled over.

"Didn't expect to see you back in here," he said.

"Why not?"

"You didn't finish your drink this afternoon. From what I could tell, your friend didn't even start his."

"We had to see a man about a train."

"Make you another?"

"No, thanks." I didn't have a prayer of blending into the crowd holding a cocktail glass. "Draw me a beer."

When he brought it back, I said, "You can do me a favor."

"Is that right?" Augie asked. The question was a Hoosier standard, a way of keeping a conversation going without committing oneself.

"I'm looking for a man named Nast. He's a foreman at the Traynor plant."

"I know Nast."

"I'm told he's in here most evenings. Is he here tonight? I'd like to talk with him."

"You said you wanted a favor. A favor would be warning you when Nast is coming so you could go the other way. He's nobody you'd want to know."

"Is that right?" I asked, to practice my blending in.

Augie didn't think much of my technique. "That's damn right," he said. "He's been a pain in this town's butt since his dishonorable discharge from the Marines. Took a sailor's eye out in a bar fight. After that he turned mean."

"How's he stayed clear of the law?"

"Friends in high places."

The county had only one place that high. "He doesn't sound like the Traynors' type."

"Let's say they like him better than they like the United Auto Workers. Nast hired on at the Traynor plant during some big strike after the war. Started as a scab and worked his way down. There's always some dirty job needs doing in a factory that big. Nast is what you might call the foreman of the dirty job detail."

"A dirty job is just what I wanted to see Mr. Nast about."

"You still want to see him?" Augie asked, speaking a little louder, as though he suspected that my hearing was bad.

"More than ever," I said.

"Try the poolroom then. Wait a minute." He took away my glass of beer and handed me a bottle of the same brand. "Nast used a broken bottle on that sailor. You might want to have your own along to even things up."

I overtipped him and followed the sound of men laughing. It led me to a back room that duplicated the proportions of the pool table it held exactly. There was just enough room around the table—an old one with ivory inlays and woven leather pockets—for the players and their cues. Four men stood around the table, three in a group to my left and one across the table from my doorway. The loner was the only one holding a stick. He was using it to tell a story.

"Skeets was drunk," the man said. "That's all there was to it. He'd done everything to prove it except hit the floor with his chin. He should have gone home, but he wanted to play pool in the fanciest hall in Noblesville. You know the place—never a stray piece of lint on one of their tables. No sir. And each table lit by a big old fixture with a glass shade that some beer company gave 'em."

The three-man audience made various noises to show that they knew the fancy Noblesville pool hall. I didn't, but no one had taken any notice of me yet. Certainly not the speaker, a thin hatchet-face with a squint that was distributed unevenly between his dark eyes. I identified him from Clark's description as the man I'd come to see. Clark's information was verified by the storyteller himself. That is to say, I recognized Nast's reedy voice. He was the leader of the cross burners, the man who had pronounced Carson Drury's doom.

"The trouble started when old Skeets tried to make a shot behind his back," Nast said. He acted it out, bending forward and placing his left hand on the felt of the table to form a bridge for the cue. His right hand was behind his back, but the cue it held was aimed at the ceiling. "He was too drunk to know where his stick was pointing, which was up. So he's poking away with it and looking down at his left hand, sort of amazed, you know, that there's no cue down there when he knows he came in with one.

"Meanwhile, the cue is banging the glass shade above the table." He demonstrated on the green shade that hung over Augie's table. From the look of the battered paper cone, it had heard the story before. "Whack, whack, whack. Skeets keeps banging that shade, all the time looking down at the table with a 'What the hell?' on his face.

"Across the room, the pantywaist they've got running the place starts yelling." Nast made the half step climb to a falsetto. " 'Take it away. Take that stick away from him. Take it away.' "

I was expecting a bigger finish, but that was all I got. The other listeners, who probably knew the story better than Nast, signaled the curtain by laughing wildly. Nast was pleased, until he finally got around to acknowledging me.

"Don't strike you as funny?" he asked.

"Guess you had to be there," I said.

"Who the hell are you?"

I drank some beer. "Don't you recognize me?"

"No."

"I must look different by torch light."

That got a snicker out of the other three. Nast quashed it with a glance. "I don't know what you're talking about," he said.

"If you have a minute, I'll explain it." I backed out of the doorway and sat down in the first booth I came to. Nast joined me after a moment, carrying his own beer bottle, an empty one.

"Buy you another?" I asked. "Or do you just keep that around for self-defense?"

Nast smiled. He had a complexion as ingrained with dirt as a mechanic's fingertips and hair as black as Drury's, thick and heavy with tonic—Wildroot, by the smell. "Somebody's been talking about me."

"That's definitely the problem," I said.

He raised his empty without looking away from me. Augie brought him another. I noticed that the bar owner was carrying his weighted club in his hip pocket.

When I reached for my wallet, Nast shook his head. "I run a tab. Whether I pay it or not is Augie's lookout. You said something about a problem."

"Word's getting around about the cross burning at Riverbend. When it gets to the right ear, you'll be in trouble. For starters, you're going to lose your job."

"You're pissing in the wind, trying to scare me," Nast said. "I'm not going to lose an hour's pay."

"Don't count too much on the Traynors backing you. I don't think you have the right one in your corner. And none of them is going to want any part of a murder charge."

"Murder?" Nast asked, mixing curiosity with offended dignity.

"You ought to get somebody to read you a newspaper now and then. We had a guy killed at Riverbend the other night. It was two nights after you told us to leave town or else."

"I still don't know what you're talking about."

"I'm talking about you murdering a guy or being set up by someone to take the blame for the murder. My guess is somebody's setting you up, you and your merry men."

"Guess and be damned," Nast said. "You can't prove anything."

"That's where your men come in. There are too many of them. When they figure out that they're accessories in a murder, one of them will come forward to tell what he knows. After that, they'll be lining up to sing. This is an electric chair state."

Nast took a drink, jerking the bottle up and down again so quickly that the beer foamed over and ran down his hand. He dried it on his shirt. "What's your price?"

"I want the guy who shot Hank Shepard. If it wasn't you, you'd better start talking. For starters, you can tell me who set up the cross burning and why."

"I can't afford to be seen jawing with you," Nast said, glancing nervously around the bar.

I glanced, too, collecting a few hard looks for my trouble. Even the jukebox had turned against me. Hank Williams was crooning "Your Cheating Heart," a song that brought Ella and Linda Traynor to mind simultaneously.

I blocked out both of them. "It's me or the police," I said. "Me *and* the police if I don't like your answers."

"I'll talk to you," Nast whispered, "but not here. Meet me in the rail yard west of town in half an hour."

"The rail yard next to the Traynor works? Doesn't sound like a neutral site."

"You go there first and check it out if you don't trust me. It's a big open space with an old switching tower. I'll meet you by the tower."

"All right," I said.

"I'll yell something at you now, and you get up and leave, okay? I'll say, 'Go to hell,' and you leave and I'll follow."

"Half an hour."

NAST WAS A CONVINCING actor, at least when he was playing a heavy. He cursed me out of the place, to the visible gratification of the other customers. My friend Augie shook his head like a man who had backed the wrong horse.

I was tempted to cross the square to Gustin's office and arrange for some company, but I didn't want to be the last one to arrive at the rail yard. And I didn't want the trail to end at Nast. The loyal sheriff might be content to hang everything on him and call it an evening. I wanted more than a fall guy.

I'd driven past the yard on my way to the Traynor plant, but I hadn't taken much notice of it. There wasn't that much to notice, as it turned out, just a big open space next to the rail line with parallel sets of track connected by switches. Nast had picked a place where he'd have an easy time spotting a trap. I hoped I would, too. I could see only two potential trouble spots: the two-story switching tower at the center of the yard, where Nast and I were to meet, and a string of three boxcars parked back in one corner.

The sun had set while I'd interviewed Nast. It was going on full dark as I scouted the yard. I'd hidden the useless Liberator under the front seat of the coupé and moved my Colt to the pocket of my jacket, where I could keep my hand around it. I made the trek over to the parked boxcars, slipping and sliding on the clinkers that paved the place as I walked. The boxcars were closed up tight and sealed. I checked the switching tower next. It was a wooden structure, its siding protected by soot and little else. The tower was dark, and its single door was locked. Across the street, the factory was lit up like a ball diamond awaiting a night game. I could see the guard's shack at the main gate a hundred yards down the road. I could even see the guard himself. He'd hear a shot from there, asleep or no. And I'd hear anyone sneaking up behind me. The clinkers made a sound like glass being ground with every footstep.

I decided that I had nothing to fear except a rifleman lurking in the weeds at the edge of the yard. And an operative who worried about an invisible rifleman was no use to anyone. All the same, I kept close to the tower as I waited and shielded the burning end of my Lucky.

Nast showed up twenty minutes later. He parked his truck on the shoulder of the road, next to the rail line. I could just make him out as he crossed to the tower, scanning left and right as he came on. I did some scanning myself, watching the rest of the yard for any sign that Nast hadn't come alone. I didn't see so much as a cat.

When Nast neared the tower, he called out, "Hey! You there?"

I waited until he turned away from me before I stepped out, my gun drawn. "Don't move," I said.

I patted him down and then stepped back toward the tower. "All right. Let's talk about the Klan."

"There ain't no Klan around here," Nast said. "I'd be the first one to sign up if there was. Those robes we had on the other night were hand-me-downs. They had so much moth ball in them I'm surprised you didn't smell it from the house."

"Where did you get them?"

"A lady's attic. What do you say we talk on the other side of the tower, away from the road."

"I like it here. What lady are we talking about?"

"You know the one—the lady who wants to keep her son away from you flimflammers."

A train sounded its whistle at a crossing not far away. "Marvella Traynor?"

"Mrs. Traynor to you," Nast said, showing his canines.

"What did Mrs. Traynor tell you to do?"

" 'Put the fear of God in them' was what she said. She had it all laid out. She even wrote down my speech for me herself on a little card."

"Happen to have it on you?"

"Don't you wish. I used it to light the cross."

The train whistle sounded again, much nearer. "That'll be the through freight on its way to Indianapolis," Nast said. "You'll begin to feel the ground shake directly."

I already could. "Why didn't you come back to the farm Saturday night and finish the job?"

"That was never part of the deal. It was one night only—scare you and get out. Fifty dollars a man and liquor. If it had been up to me, I would have burned you out on Friday night instead of standing there getting preached to by that Drury. I wanted to ram his big speech back down his throat so bad it hurt."

"Why didn't you?"

"Mrs. Traynor doesn't like violence." He was having to work at projecting the words, the sound of the approaching train having grown steadily. I could see its headlight flickering on the farthest pair of rails. "She thinks you can scare a person into damn near anything. Scare 'em or wear 'em down. She's wrong. It doesn't work on everybody."

He kept on talking, but I couldn't hear him anymore. I couldn't hear anything but the freight train. The sound seemed to be everywhere in the yard, rising up through the ground beneath me, bouncing off the tower behind me. Cutting me off, I suddenly realized, flanking me.

I swung around in time to catch the first blow on my forehead. It wasn't hard enough to knock me out, but it made me a spectator for what happened next. My arms were grabbed, and I was hauled to my feet. Then I was dragged across the yard by two men. I measured our progress by the iron rails that struck out at my feet and ankles. I tried shouting, but the passing train was so loud I couldn't hear myself.

When we reached the parked boxcars, my escort steered me between two of them and dropped me onto the tracks. I was shoved and kicked beneath the locked couplers while I breathed in a dust that was half coal and half rust with old oil thrown in for body. Then I was seized by men waiting on the other side. They pulled me through, yanked me up onto my feet again, and banged me against the side of the car.

All the exercise had helped to clear my head. I struggled with the men holding my arms, but I couldn't shake them. They had plenty of help on hand if they needed it—three at least, besides Nast. He was standing in front of me, admiring my gun and lecturing. The sound of the passing train was muted by the wall of cars. I could hear Nast clearly. Overhear him, as he wasn't addressing me.

" 'Go check it out,' I said, 'if you don't trust me.' So off he goes. I got Zack here on the phone before the bar door closed behind him. 'Get your ass out of that factory and across the street,' I said. 'Lock yourself in that switching shed and lie low. I'll have him there when the Indy freight comes through. You step out then and whack him. Whack, whack, whack.' "

This time his audience laughed genuinely. I had to admit it was better than the Noblesville pool hall story.

"You wide awake?" Nast asked me. "I'd hate for you not to feel what's coming."

"Do it and get it over with," the man holding my right arm said. "That train's going to be out of here and gone."

"To hell with the train," Nast said. "It's done its job. Gag the son of the bitch if you're worried about the noise."

"You're just getting in deeper, Nast," I said while I still had a chance to speak.

"That's me," Nast said. "Never in but in all the way." He handed my automatic to the man beside him. "Hold that, Zack, but don't get too fond of it."

Zack stuck the gun in his belt.

"I told you scaring doesn't work with some people," Nast said to me. "You gotta get right down to convincing. You gotta beat it into 'em. Beat 'em and beat 'em until they'll never again lift their heads or look a man in the eye or answer back. Till all they'll want to do with the rest of their lives is sit quiet and mind their own business."

"What was that?" the man on my right asked.

"What's nothing," Nast said and hit me in the stomach. I doubled over in spite of the best efforts of the pair holding my arms.

"Lift him up, goddamn you," Nast said. "How'd you expect—"

He stopped speaking and left the ground. I had a glimpse of his wild expression and the bottoms of his boots, and then he was gone. His place was taken by a bigger man in a red cap: Clark. He held one of the onlookers by the shirt with his left hand and hit another across the throat with the edge of his right. Next to him I could see the man Nast had called Zack struggling to pull my gun from his belt. Before I could call out, Zack was struck down from behind.

The editing became choppy after that. I saw Clark tackle a man without letting go of the one he held by the shirt. Then my left arm was free. I pivoted toward the man who still held my right, taking hold of his ear and ramming his head against the side of the car. I had to repeat the message several times before it got through. He released my arm, and we grappled until our legs became tangled. We went down on the roadbed, me on the bottom. Before I could roll him off me, he went limp. I shoved him aside and sat up, still gasping from the only blow Nast had landed.

The battle had moved on. I could hear scuffling off by the edge of the field. Near the boxcars, all was peaceful. Only one man was on his feet. He stood before me, breathing as hard as I was and swinging something like a sawed-off ball bat in his hand.

"Still charging in where angels fear to tread," he said between breaths.

It was Paddy Maguire. I knew it before he struck the kitchen match and held it to his cigar, the cigar he'd had in his teeth through the whole action, I was sure.

"What are you doing here?" I asked.

"Saving you from a beating, of course," Paddy said. "And not for the first time, though I've never had to travel by airplane and train before to get the job done." He helped me to my feet and handed me my gun. "Ever think of tying that to your wrist?"

"How did you track me down?"

"That was Mr. Clark's doing. Where is he, anyway?" The sounds of distant fighting had stopped, but there was no sign of Clark.

"I'd better go see," I said.

"I'll go," Paddy said. "You rest yourself."

We were still playing Alphonse and Gaston over it when Clark loomed out of the darkness. He was carrying a man under his arm. He dropped him on top of a moaning figure at Paddy's feet.

"Nast got away," he said. "My fault."

"We'd better let Gustin know," I said.

Clark nodded. "I'll call him from the guard shack at the factory."

I started to say thanks, but Clark was already limping off. I thanked Paddy instead and asked him again how they'd found me.

"I just missed you at the farm," Paddy said. He was fanning himself with his hat. It wasn't his usual homburg. Even in the dark I recognized the gray straw number that Paddy wore to the racetracks back in Los Angeles. It was his idea of an Indiana disguise, I realized. He'd be in bib overalls next—pin-striped ones, probably.

"Fortunately," Paddy was saying, "I happened across Mr. Clark before I'd sent my cab away." He looked off in the direction Clark had taken and dropped into his stage whisper. "Cost me a year's growth seeing him for the first time unprepared. You leave more out of your reports than you put in."

"Sorry," I said.

"Clark told me where you'd gone and what was likely to happen to you. He was feeling guilty over it, poor man, so he agreed to help. We went together to interview the owner of Augie's."

"I notice he lent you his keg tapper," I said, pointing to the club Paddy had tucked away in his jacket pocket.

"You might say that. Then again, you might say that Clark confiscated it after Augie tried to hit him over the head with it."

"Why would he do that?"

"Maybe because Augie is Nast's brother-in-law. He knew all the details of Nast's plans for dealing with you. Shared them with us, too, after a bit of Clark's persuading. Augie will be pouring drinks with his feet for a while, I'm afraid."

Nast's men were coming around, one by one. Paddy nudged them into a line, using the keg tapper as a prod.

"Sorry to have cut things so close," he said. "I should have been out here yesterday. I started packing as soon as I heard about Shepard's murder, the investigation of which, I'm sure you'll agree, deserves the best brains in the firm. However, there were one or two loose ends to tie up before I could get away."

"Such as kissing Joan Crawford good-bye?"

"Such as dropping by to see Ralph Lockard. I thought a general discussion of the murder might panic him into an indiscretion. Wishful thinking on my part. But that's enough of me reporting to you. Now you report to me."

I described my day, laying on the details for once. As I finished, we spotted a flashlight bobbing around in the yard. It belonged to a Traynor guard.

"The sheriff's men are on the way," he said after Paddy had whistled him over.

"Where's Clark?" I asked.

"He took off after he passed on his message. I don't know why."

"He's like that Lone Ranger fellow," Paddy said. "Doesn't hang about when his job is finished."

The guard looked around the dark yard and shivered. "Anytime Clark wants to start wearing a mask," he said, "it'll be okay by me."

chapter

35

AN HOUR LATER we were seated in Gustin's office sipping bourbon—
the sheriff, Paddy, and I. Gustin had earned his drink. He'd spent
most of the time since we'd arrived on his doorstep interrogating
Nast's men, using the same hardball approach he'd tried on Casey
Atherley the evening before. This time I hadn't interfered, which
may have explained why I needed a drink. Or it may have been
because all Gustin's squeezing had gotten us nothing. None of our
guests—five local toughs, each at home in a courthouse cell—knew
who had hired Nast to burn the cross at Riverbend. They only
knew that Nast had hired them. So they couldn't confirm my story
that the mastermind had been Marvella Traynor. They gave the
sheriff the names of the other flunkies involved, and that was it.

It was the sheriff's bottle, but Paddy was doing the pouring out.
Like any good bartender, he was also serving as a mediator, taking
a reasonable line between Gustin's refusal to bother the Traynors
and my insistence that we bust their door down. I'd seen Paddy
work the same scam many times, but it still bothered me. I was way
past playacting myself.

"While we're sitting here," I said, "Nast is getting away."

"I've put out a bulletin for my men and notified the state police," Gustin said. "We're watching his house and Augie's. We'll get him."

"He wouldn't go home," I said in what seemed like the hundredth take of the same scene. "He'd go to Traynor House. He'd go there to get orders or traveling money or both."

"We don't have anything but Nast's word—the word of a lying, trouble-making son of a bitch—to tie the Traynors in with him and his cross burning," Gustin said. He was repeating himself, too, and tired of doing it. "We don't have anything at all to tie them in to the murder."

"We have that." I pointed to the gun on Gustin's desk, Gilbert's copy of the Liberator. "That ties the Traynors in and tight."

"I'm grateful to you for bringing me this. Fifty to one, it's the murder weapon, or its brother is, I mean, the gun from Riverbend. But just because the Traynors made the thing doesn't mean one of them used it. Anyone who's been in that farmhouse could have found the gun. It's a better tie to Clark or Mr. Drury or you."

I understood the threat folded into that casual observation. So did my boss. "More to the point," Paddy said, "our friend Nast could easily have gotten his hands on that gun. We know he's been to the farm. And he worked at the Traynor plant. He surely heard all about the Liberator."

"How is it you didn't know all about that gun, Sheriff?" I asked.

Gustin emptied his glass. " 'Cause I was in the service when it was made, same as you. If any of them were dropped in Italy, they didn't land near me. I never laid eyes on one until you handed this over."

Take it or leave it, he was saying. Believe me or go to hell.

Paddy poured another round. "Let's not lose sight of Mr. Nast," he said, addressing Gustin. "You think he might be trying to make trouble for the Traynors, might even be a threat to them. My operative here thinks he might be working for one of them. It sounds to me as though, either way, Nast's trail points to Traynor House."

Paddy had taken the right line as usual. I could see that in the sheriff's uncharacteristically mobile features. He sat staring into the gap between Paddy and me with his lips moving silently, like a grade-schooler lost in his times tables. He was obviously torn between protecting the Traynors from me and protecting them from Nast. The struggle I saw in his face made me feel better about Gustin. He had to sincerely believe that Marvella Traynor was innocent in order to buy any part of Paddy's suggestion that Nast was a threat to her.

Before the sheriff could decide which way to jump, his telephone rang. He answered it, his poker face slipping back into place automatically.

"Gustin." He sat for a while listening. Then he said, "Right away" and hung up.

"Seems we're going to Traynor House after all, gentlemen. Mr. Drury's lost another assistant, name of Whitehead."

Paddy swore. "Shot?"

"Vanished," Gustin said.

■ ■ ■

Paddy and I slipped through the gateless pylons of Traynor House with the front bumper of our borrowed Studebaker almost touching the rear bumper of Gustin's official car. Linda's Speedster might have gotten us past the guards—doubled since my last visit—all by itself if it hadn't been for Paddy blowing our disguise. He rubbernecked out his open window and waved at the armed sentries like the grand marshal of a parade.

Greta opened the front door as we climbed the steps. She led us into the dance-hall living room, where Linda, Gilbert, and Drury were waiting.

Gustin introduced Paddy to Linda and Gilbert, not knowing that the two men had met briefly in California. Nothing in Gilbert's vague response tipped the sheriff to his mistake. The wariness I'd noticed in Gilbert earlier was still present, but it had taken on an out-of-focus quality because he'd been drinking.

The last time I saw Drury, he'd been enthroned in his hotel suite, playing the life of the party. He wasn't playing anything now, but sitting as he was, a little way from the light with his head bent and his eyes dark hollows, he reminded me of one of his famous Broadway roles, Abraham Lincoln.

Linda just looked tired. The dark green of her dress seemed to have drained the color from her skin, allowing the blue veins in her temples to stand out clearly. Her eyes were as sunken as Drury's. I remembered his image of Linda as a keystone, under constant pressure from opposing forces. She looked as if she'd taken all the squeezing she could bear.

The sight of me didn't help her. "Scotty, what happened to you?"

I had tried to dust the rail yard off my suit, but traces lingered. I couldn't do anything about the egg on my forehead, not even hide it. We hadn't been able to find my hat. Nast was wearing it, probably.

"I'd like your mother-in-law to hear that story," I said. "Where is she?"

"Resting," Gilbert said. "She hasn't been down this evening. She dined in her room. She knows nothing about Mr. Whitehead's disappearance."

He was changing the subject, but that was fine by Gustin. "Suppose you tell us about it," he said.

Gilbert collected himself with the aid of a quick pass at his brandy snifter. "We four had dinner, Carson and Mr. Whitehead and Linda and I. Afterward, Linda went up to check on my mother. I came in here to find us some port."

He looked up at me on that line. The look told me that Gilbert had used the excuse of going out for port as a way of getting a few minutes alone with his bar, just as he had on the night I'd dined at Traynor House. Tonight's dinner hadn't gone well, either, for some reason.

"I left Carson and Mr. Whitehead in the dining room," Gilbert continued. "When I came back, Mr. Whitehead was gone. Carson was concerned, so I went out and looked around. I couldn't find a trace of Mr. Whitehead. I'm sure he just took a walk. I don't know why we're bothering you with this, Sheriff."

"We're bothering him, Gilbert," Drury said in a voice that went from a whisper to the size of the room in a heartbeat, "because I insisted that we bother him. Because I don't intend to sit by while another member of my company is murdered just to save your family embarrassment."

"Take it easy," Gustin said. "Tell me what happened after Mr. Traynor left the dining room."

"Nothing happened," Drury said. "John and I sat there for a time. Then he stepped out for a breath of air. He wasn't feeling well."

Gilbert snickered into his balloon glass.

"How did he leave?" Gustin asked. "What door did he use?"

"He went out through the French doors at the end of the dining room," Drury said. "I heard him go through them. I didn't see him. My back was to the doors." He slapped the arms of his wheelchair to explain why he hadn't turned to watch Whitehead's exit.

Linda said, "Those doors lead onto the terrace on the bluff that overlooks the river. There are steps from it down onto the grounds."

"What time was this?" Paddy asked.

"Around nine," Drury said.

"After dark, then," Paddy said. "Not the best time for a tour of the gardens."

"He wouldn't have seen much in any case," Gilbert said to his drink.

"Why not?" Gustin asked.

"Because he'd had too much wine," Drury said. "That was my mistake. I should have insisted that there be no wine at the table. John has a problem with alcohol, Sheriff. I knew of it, but I'd never actually seen him in that condition. I underestimated its hold over him. He'd been sober since coming to see me yesterday."

"So what we have here," Gustin said, "is an alcoholic who fell off the wagon and wandered away." It was as close as he could come to saying that his beloved Traynors had bothered him over nothing.

"What we have here," Drury fired back, "is a sick man who is missing at night in a town that sheds its skin at night. I'm sure you've noticed that, Scotty. You will, too, Maguire, if you don't catch a bullet first. Traynorville, this sweet, little, bucolic place, changes at sunset. Crosses are burned. People are killed or they just vanish. If a total stranger were driven out into that darkness, I'd raise hell until I knew he was safe. I won't do less for an old friend."

"I haven't heard anything about anyone driving Whitehead out," Gustin said.

In reply, Drury glared at the culprit. Not Gilbert–Linda.

She looked at each of us in turn without raising her head from the back of her chair. "I had to pass on some bad news at dinner. I had to tell Mr. Drury that I was withdrawing my offer of financial support for his film.

"It's our board of directors," she said with a second glance at me. "I met with them this morning. They were very concerned about the negative publicity generated by the murder. It isn't just a case of not involving the company's funds. The board feels that any further investment by the Traynor family could be damaging as well."

"I've already told you," Drury said, "that I refuse to discuss any business matters until John is found."

"You brought it up," Gilbert snapped. "Linda's only explaining why Whitehead started drinking. It's true," he said to Gustin. "Whitehead was fine up until that point. Wouldn't touch a drink. But after Linda gave us the board's decision, he started in. He was drunk from the first glass of wine. I've never seen anything like it."

"However he got drunk," Gustin said, "he got drunk. He's probably out there now, sleeping it off. I don't see any cause for alarm unless you think he might be a threat to himself."

"There's another possibility," I said. "If Nast came straight here from the rail yard, he would have arrived about nine o'clock. Whitehead could have blundered into him."

"Nast?" Gilbert and Drury asked in chorus.

I answered Gilbert. "One of your top employees."

"I know who he is. How does he figure in any of this?"

"Nast led the Klan raid at Riverbend. The raid was a sham, as I told you in your office this afternoon. And it was thrown together for the reason I gave you then. Your mother didn't want Carson Drury to get his hands on any Traynor money. The raid didn't get that job done, but it looks as though Hank Shepard's murder has."

Gilbert turned to Gustin. It was almost a family reflex in times of stress. "Did Nast really say that my mother was involved in the cross burning?"

"Mr. Elliott claims that he did. Nast and some of his men jumped him over at the rail yard earlier this evening."

"If it hadn't been for Mr. Maguire here and Clark, I'd still be there," I said. "I'd be the one whose disappearance is no cause for alarm."

"You think Nast may have come here?" Linda asked, alert now and all business.

"We don't know where he is," Gustin said. "He got away from Clark at the rail yard."

Drury literally pushed himself into the center of the conversation, ramming the gilt coffee table with his chair in the process. "If this Nast killed Hank as a way of ruining me, he could easily try again with John."

"Wait one damn minute!" Gilbert shouted. "You're trying to implicate my mother in a murder!"

He and Drury started yelling at each other. The actor's golden larynx gave him the edge, but I could still make out Gilbert demanding that Drury leave his house. Paddy and Gustin stepped in at that point. The sheriff gently sat Gilbert back down on the sofa, while Paddy wheeled Drury into my neutral corner.

Through all of it, Linda remained in her chair. If her board of directors ever got this worked up, she surely sat it out with the same quiet dignity.

"It's clear we have to act, Sheriff," she finally said. "We have to make certain as a first step that John Whitehead is safe."

"Yes, ma'am," Gustin said.

"Please see about organizing a search. Use any of the Traynor Company resources you need. I'll arrange for you to interview my mother-in-law tomorrow morning—or tonight, if you insist."

"But not them," Gilbert rasped, gesturing at Drury, Paddy, and me. "They leave this house right now."

"I think that would be best," Linda said. Looking me in the eye, she added, "It would be the best thing for everyone."

chapter

36

WE HAD A TIME getting Drury and his chair into Linda's coupé, but we finally managed it. Drury was squeezed in sideways on the backseat, and his chair propped the trunk lid open. I would as soon have had Drury in the trunk. I wasn't buying his concern over Whitehead's safety. Paddy shared my suspicions, but they seemed to improve his opinion of Drury.

When we were on the open road, Paddy said, "All that Sarah Bernhardting around back there was just playing for time, wasn't it?"

"It started out that way," Drury said. "Watch the bumps, Scotty, please. I'm halfway through the roof back here already."

"It was a smooth stall," Paddy said. "I've not worked a better one myself."

I let the car accelerate another five miles an hour.

"I had to try something," Drury said. "I had to have time to think. Linda didn't give me a chance to discuss things with her or even to beg. She's like another person when it comes to business. 'You're through. Sorry. Good-bye.'"

"Poor John's breakdown gave me an out. I didn't plan that, Scotty, so if you're trying to break my neck as a punishment for it, you can slow this car down right now. I didn't even turn a blind eye to John's drinking. I tried to stop him, but I couldn't."

"Whose idea was it for him to wander out of there?" I asked.

The question took my mind off my driving. We hit a hole in the road at speed, and Drury grunted.

"It was his idea, damn it. It happened just the way I told Gustin. One minute John was sitting there in a daze. Then he was out of his chair and making for the door. I thought he was going outside to be sick. I'm going to be sick myself if you don't slow this car down."

Paddy tapped my arm. "Rein the beast in, Scotty. You're making the scenery blurry."

Paddy wasn't watching any scenery. He'd shifted in his seat so he could watch Drury. "You say your play started as a stall. What changed it?"

"You did, coming in with your story about Scotty being attacked. Unlike the sheriff, I believe what Scotty said about Marvella Traynor's guiding hand. It confirmed my own assessment of the cross burning."

"You knew that was all an act?" I asked, slowing the car involuntarily.

"Of course I did. Really, Scotty, you disappoint me. I'm used to people assuming I'm smarter than I am. You seem to think it's the reverse. Everything about that night said theater. You'll remember that the so-called Klansmen didn't even surround the house. They were giving us plenty of running room if we wanted to make a break for it. The last thing they wanted was a real confrontation.

"And do you really believe I shamed that crowd into skulking away? I have to admit I believed it myself at the moment it happened—I was that drunk on adrenaline. Later, when I'd had time to reflect, I realized that they would have left whether I'd opened my mouth or not. They had to leave for the same reason any actors leave any stage: They'd run out of script."

"Why didn't you share some of this with Gustin?" I asked.

Paddy, the worker of angles, told me. "He thought the knowledge gave him an edge in his dealings with the Traynors."

"I didn't foresee that things would get out of hand," Drury said.

"What was your excuse for keeping quiet after the murder?" I asked. "Things were out of hand but good by then."

"I couldn't see any connection between Marvella's desire to keep her son safe from me and Hank's death. From the start I've thought that was a false trail. The two events have to have sprung from two very different minds. The murder was an act of cold brutality, while the cross burning was set up to minimize the chance for violence."

Because Marvella hated violence, I thought, according to Nast.

"You seemed to see a connection between the cross burning and the murder just now," Paddy said. "That's what got us the bum's rush from Master Gilbert."

"I've never been so thoroughly misunderstood," Drury said. "Gilbert thought I was implicating his mother in the murder when I've felt all along that she couldn't be involved. My mistake was forgetting that she had to be working through an agent, a henchman. To think of me forgetting that, a man who's had to work through other people—set designers, lighting technicians, cameramen—all his life. I also forgot the basic truth of working through others: Nothing comes out exactly the way you intend. It's entirely possible—probable—that she lost control of this Nast, that he took matters into his own hands and the murder was the result."

It fit with what I knew of Nast and his impatience with Marvella's tactics. I'd paid dearly for that insight into the situation. Drury, the wheelchair-bound detective, had achieved it without getting his fingernails dirty. It was too late to get back at him for it by driving badly. We were only a block from the hotel.

"Adding Nast to the equation changes everything," Drury said. "None of us is safe while he's loose. I insist that you fellows stay in my suite tonight, for your own safety."

I saw Paddy's ample chest rise and fall in a silent laugh. "Thanks for thinking of us," he said.

Drury explained how he and Whitehead had snuck out of the hotel past the reporters, and we reversed the process, wheeling him in through the loading dock and taking him to the second floor on a freight elevator that smelled like last week's eggs. I took the stairs down to the lobby and then ascended again on Drury's private elevator to pick up the director and Paddy.

After we'd looked for Nast under every seat cushion and mattress in Drury's suite, our host relaxed a bit. "You fellows order dinner if the kitchen's still open, and a bottle of anything you want."

Paddy checked his waistband for slack. "There's a thought," he said. "But I have to see about having my bag sent over first. I left it at the train station."

I volunteered to go after it. "I have to collect some things from the farm."

"Not now," Drury said, losing his composure in a rush. "Not at night, Scotty. I wasn't kidding when I said it wasn't safe to be out in this town after dark. Promise me you won't go near that farm until tomorrow morning."

"Okay," I said, "the train station and back."

Paddy followed me as far as the front door of the suite. "The train station and back," he repeated. "No side trips to Traynor House."

"Marvella's safe from me, for tonight at least," I said.

"I wasn't thinking of that worthy," Paddy said. "I had her daughter-in-law, Linda, in mind."

"Come again?"

"I saw the way you two were looking at each other. Most especially, I saw the way she was looking at you. You didn't by any chance forget to tell her that you're a married man, did you?"

He wasn't joking, so I didn't. "No," I said.

"Good. Then there's no need to cushion her for the coming blow. It's coming by train, by the way."

"What is?"

"Who, you mean. And the answer is Ella. She was packing for her train when I took off with the dawn patrol this morning. She's tucked in her berth right now, I hope."

Ella must have been packing when I'd called her that morning. She'd kept quiet about her plans—and about Paddy's—paying me back for my own silence or just avoiding an argument.

"Are the kids with her?"

"No. They're staying with Peggy. Ella would have flown out with me, but she wanted to give us a chance to wrap things up."

"Some chance. How long do we have?"

"Let's see. We've still a tiny bit of Tuesday left. Ella will be in on Thursday's milk train. Call it a day and change."

"All the time in the world," I said.

Paddy gave me a parting pat on the back. "You've always done your best work under pressure."

■ ■ ■

I was still daydreaming of Ella, tucked away in her berth, as I crossed the hotel lobby. As a result, I didn't notice Casey Atherley until his stout form was blocking my path. He'd cleaned up nicely, but his right ear was still red and swollen from its contact with my automatic.

"I thought I saw you down here just now," Atherley said, "but you nipped into that off-limits elevator before I could catch you."

While he talked, I checked the pocket of my suit jacket where I'd stashed his film when I'd found it in the litter of the farmhouse parlor. Remarkably, given the waltzing I'd done in the rail yard, the film was still there.

"We have to talk," the photographer said.

"If you're here to tell me who burned the cross at Riverbend, you're a little late."

"Yeah, I heard. I'm selling something else now. Let's go into the bar."

The bar turned out to be crowded with reporters, so Atherley led me into a little sitting room nearby, the room where hotel guests composed their postcards.

Sitting down felt way too good. "What do you have?"

"Information intended for Sheriff Gustin," Atherley said, "only the sheriff hasn't gotten it yet because he's out beating the bushes for some guy who's lost. My courthouse contact passed this tidbit on to me. Interested?"

By way of answering him, I produced the film plate and tapped my knee with it. The eyes behind the horn-rims bounced in rhythm.

"The tip was about another of you California guys. Eric Faris was the name. He's supposed to be staying close to Traynorville on orders from Gustin."

"I know that part."

"Well, Faris was picked up tonight by the Indianapolis police at the airport down there. He had a ticket for a westbound flight, but he was drunk, and they wouldn't let him board. He started a row, and the police hauled him in. He's in their drunk tank now. Some bright boy made the connection to our murder and called the sheriff for orders. Gustin will probably have Faris shipped back up in the morning. In the meantime, though, an enterprising fellow could have a chat with him."

"How does this enterprising fellow get in to see him?"

"A pal of mine on the *Indianapolis Times* is owed a favor by an Indy cop. I'll set it up for you."

I handed the film over. "Seems as though you're paying double for this."

Atherley didn't see it that way. "I haven't forgotten who pulled Gustin off me last night."

I stopped at the front desk long enough to arrange for Paddy's bag to be brought over by cab and to write a note to go upstairs with the bag when it arrived.

Then I headed out into the darkness that Carson Drury feared so much.

chapter

37

THE FRIEND OF Casey Atherley's friend did more than get me in to see Eric Faris. He also made me the gift of a private room for the interview. It was a small, dirty room whose single table had more cigarette burns in its top than I had teeth, but I didn't complain. I lit a cigarette of my own to kill the smell of urine coming from the room's dark corners. Then I waited.

Faris was delivered a few minutes later. He came in squinting and shielding his eyes as though the dim overhead light was a Los Alamos sunrise. He was in the no-man's-land between drunk and hungover, and he wasn't happy about it. I wasn't thrilled to be up and around myself, so he got no sympathy from me.

I'd kidded myself the previous day about having traded wardrobes with John Piers Whitehead, but Faris seemed to have genuinely done it. He'd lost his suit jacket. From the slept-in look of the rest of his outfit, I guessed that he'd been using the coat as bedding and left it behind in his cell. His tie was missing, but his collar button was still fastened. He'd undone his cuffs instead, without

rolling up his sleeves. That gave them the flowing look of a cler-
gyman's vestments. This sacramental effect was undercut by the tail
of his shirt, by one small corner of the tail that stuck out through the
open fly of his trousers.

Of the bright, young eager beaver I'd met in Alora, there wasn't
a trace. I remembered Shepard joking about how unsettled and un-
settling life around Drury was. That wasn't the half of it, I thought,
as I watched Faris teaching himself to sit in a chair. Time spent with
Drury wasn't just eventful, it was hazardous.

"They told me my lawyer was in here," Faris said. "You're not a
lawyer."

"I've been going to school nights. Cigarette?"

Faris declined. "Not good for you," he said. A man after Ella's
heart.

"Neither is skipping out on a murder investigation."

"Hanging around was worse," Faris said. "My nerves couldn't
take it."

"I know. You couldn't eat, you couldn't sleep. Did you get per-
mission from Ralph Lockard to skip out?"

"No. I tried to explain it to him. He ordered me to stay put."

"Explain it to me," I said. "I want to know why you're so frightened. You didn't arrange for the cross burning. We've proven that.
You have an alibi for the night of the murder. What's scaring you?"

"Why should I tell you anything?"

"Why not? You quit your job when you bought that plane ticket.
We're not on opposing sides anymore. And I may be able to help
you tomorrow when you go up against Gustin. I could put in a good
word with Linda Traynor."

"Her," Faris said and shook his tousled head.

"What's that supposed to mean?"

"Nothing. And that's all I'm telling you, nothing. We're not on
the same side. There are no sides. It's every man for himself. You'd
sell me out in a minute, just like Lockard."

"Why did he really send you out here?"

"Guess."

"Okay. I'll guess it was to keep an eye on John Piers Whitehead."

Faris turned in his chair. "Lemme outta here!" he yelled at the door.

"I thought a lot about Whitehead on my drive down here," I said. "I finally got around to asking myself who financed his trip and bought him the fancy clothes. He didn't have the price of bacon and eggs when I saw him in Hollywood. It could have been some soft touch from the old days, but Whitehead's surely run through all of those. I'm guessing it was Lockard.

"I think he sent Whitehead out here to keep Drury off balance— and so there would be a likely suspect on hand when the sabotage started again. Lockard was behind the attempts in Hollywood, wasn't he?"

"No," Faris said, "he wasn't. Lockard thought it was Whitehead. He did some checking around after you came to Alora to accuse us. He wanted to know what was really going on. His Hollywood friends told him about the bad blood between Drury and White-head. Lockard sent me to talk to him."

"Did Whitehead admit setting fire to the studio and tampering with the camera crane?"

"No. I never asked him about it. That wasn't why I'd been sent. I was just scouting. I told him that I represented an investor who was anxious about the future of Drury's movie. Whitehead let me know how desperate he was to be involved in it again. He mentioned that he'd begged an old friend for a job here in Indianapolis so he could be close to Drury. The friend was a college professor."

"Walter Carlisle."

"Yeah. But Whitehead didn't have the money to make the trip. When I told all that to Lockard, he sent me back with a plane ticket and cash. He considered it a cheap insurance policy."

"He hoped that Whitehead would pick up out here where he'd left off in Hollywood."

Faris nodded. "I never thought there'd be violence—not after meeting Whitehead. But there was. Now you know why I have to get away. Ralph Lockard and I could be named as accessories in Shepard's murder. Lockard is safe in California, hiding behind his lawyers, but I'm here with my neck stuck out."

"You're only an accessory if Whitehead is the murderer. And he has an alibi. He was in Indianapolis with Carlisle on the night of the shooting."

Faris waved my cigarette smoke away from his face and mumbled, "His friend could have lied for him."

He tried to make it sound like no more than another guess in the guessing game we were playing together, but he was too tired to carry it off. I was suddenly wide awake.

"You *know* Carlisle lied for Whitehead," I said.

"I don't know anything."

"Your brand of scared doesn't come from could haves or maybes. You're sure Whitehead's alibi is no good. That's why you tried to get on a plane tonight."

He addressed his friend the door again. "Hey!"

"They'll come when I call them, Faris. First I'm going to tell you the latest news from Traynorville. Whitehead did a little skipping out of his own tonight. He's disappeared. He may be halfway to Canada by now. Or he may be waiting around in the shadows to shoot somebody. The longer you cover up for him, the more years he adds to your sentence."

That bit of hard sell got me zip. I tried the high ground. "If Whitehead is the killer, it's up to you to stop him before he hurts someone else."

Faris sat for a long time without saying anything. I couldn't think of another way to get at him, so I stood up.

"Wait a minute," he said. "Sit down. I'll tell you. The night Shepard died, I drove Drury back to the farm after dinner. But I didn't hang around. As soon as I got him into his wheelchair, I left. I'd had enough of his company for one evening.

"I'd just turned out of the drive when I saw a man walking along the road toward the farm. He stepped down into the drainage ditch to hide as I passed, but I saw him clearly. It was John Piers Whitehead.

"I didn't know how he'd gotten there or what he was up to, but I was glad to see him. Drury had been cocky as hell at dinner, telling me how the Traynors were going to write him a blank check and how Lockard was going to be out in the cold if he didn't come across with more money fast. I knew it would cost me my job if I told Lockard that Drury had outsmarted him. I was looking to Whitehead to bollix up the deal somehow."

"The next day," I said, "when you heard about Shepard, you were sure Whitehead had done that and more."

"Yes."

"And you kept quiet about it."

"I had to. You can understand that. I couldn't tell what I knew without implicating myself. I was safe as long as I sat tight and kept my mouth shut. But the pressure of staying there, knowing what I knew, got to be too much. I had to get away."

"So you went to see Carson Drury, to ask for his help. And who should answer the door but John Piers Whitehead. No wonder you came in looking like the Grim Reaper was a step behind you."

"I still don't understand it," Faris said. "Why did Drury take him in?"

I couldn't remember which of Drury's five explanations I'd believed that day, so I didn't bother reciting them.

"It was all so much like a dream by then," Faris was saying. "I keep telling myself that. I keep thinking I must have dreamt it all."

This time he didn't object to my standing. I crossed to the door and rapped on it hard.

While we waited for our keeper, I asked, "What do you have against Linda Traynor? When I mentioned her name just now, you almost spit."

"Nothing, I guess," Faris said. "I can't figure her out is all. At the farmhouse on the morning the deputy drove me out, the morning after the cross burning, she really ripped into me. She finished up by offering me a drive back to my motel so I could pack up and leave town."

"I remember," I said.

"I took the ride. I didn't want to walk or go back in a sheriff's car. She didn't say a word to me the whole way there. Okay, I thought, I'm beneath her notice. Then, when we got to the motel, she leaned over and kissed me. I mean really kissed me. I jumped out of that car like a spooked rabbit, and she peeled off."

"That's the part you dreamt," I said, angry and not sure why.

"Maybe I did," Faris said.

chapter

38

THE INDY COP WHO showed me the way out was a friendly guy trying to get through a long shift. He was happy to lend me a city directory and then to tell me how to get to the address I found in it, Professor Walter Carlisle's address.

After he'd given me the directions, the cop pointed to a wall clock that was covered with greasy dust. "It's a little early to be calling."

"Tell Carlisle that if he should report a prowler," I said.

According to the directory, Carlisle lived alone on a street called Kenwood, not far from his college and his precious outdoor theater. The simple frame house looked well kept, but it was a dark night, and my eyes felt as filmed over as the police station clock. Carlisle's screen door was certainly warped. It put out a very satisfying reverberation when I beat on it.

I raised a dog down the block first. Then I got a light in a neighbor's house. Finally, I got Carlisle. That is, I got his disembodied voice. The front door opened a crack, and he asked, "John?"

"Nope," I said.

He switched on the front porch fixture. It had a yellow bulb of the type guaranteed not to attract moths. It took the professor a long time to place me. When he did, he said, "John's not here."

"So I gathered. Have you gotten a call from Sheriff Gustin tonight?"

"No," Carlisle said, looking a little ill in the yellow light. "I was at a rehearsal until very late. Why would the sheriff be calling me?"

"Let me in. You don't want the neighbors to hear the rest of this."

The dog down the street was still barking. With him on my side, I won the argument. Carlisle opened the screen door and stepped back into the darkness. A second later, the darkness was shooed into the corners of the room by a standing lamp.

It was a music room of sorts. An ancient upright piano took up most of stage left. To my right was a very modern hi-fi, its Hollywood blond top littered with records. At the center of the platters were wineglasses, two of them. Carlisle was standing near the phonograph, retying his bathrobe. The robe was the gray-brown color people used to call "mousy," back when they admitted to occasionally seeing a mouse. There was no trace of pajamas above or below the robe, but then, it was a hot night.

"What's happened to John?" Carlisle asked.

"In a minute," I said. "First tell me why you lied about last Sunday night."

Carlisle drew himself up and stuck his ball-peen chin out at me. There's a limit, though, to the dignity you can muster when you're barefoot in a bathrobe. His "How dare you?" missed the target low.

"You told Gustin that Whitehead was down here Sunday night while a pal of Drury's named Shepard was getting himself murdered up in Traynorville."

"That is correct," the professor said.

"I just came from the Indy lockup. They're holding a witness who can place Whitehead in Traynorville on Sunday night. In fact, he can place him within a few hundred yards of the barn where Shepard died."

"Then it will be his word against John's and mine. And I must say, he doesn't sound like a very reputable witness."

"He was only a mildly crooked accountant until he met Drury," I said. "And it will be his word against yours, period."

"Why? What's happened to John?"

"You live here alone, don't you, Professor?"

"Yes."

"Do you have company?" I nodded at the wineglasses.

"Not now. A colleague stopped by earlier, after the rehearsal for *Knickerbocker Holiday*. I have to direct the play myself now, since John deserted me to rejoin Drury."

"When did you get the word on that?"

"This morning. I mean yesterday morning, Tuesday morning. John was driven up to Traynorville on Monday afternoon for questioning. He never came back. On Tuesday morning he called and asked me to send up his things. He didn't apologize or offer an explanation. I didn't ask for one."

"Why not? He was hanging you out to dry."

"Because he sounded so happy. It was more than that—he sounded reborn. Please tell me what's happened to him."

"He disappeared tonight. He walked away from an important dinner in Traynorville and hasn't been seen since. He may have met with foul play, or he may be hiding somewhere. Here, for example."

"There's no one else here," Carlisle said.

"Then you won't mind if I look around."

I hadn't taken a step, but Carlisle moved to cut me off from the rest of the house. "I most certainly do mind. You're not a policeman, and you don't have a warrant."

"I can have both here faster than you can sneak Whitehead out the back." It was a thin bluff, but I was too tired for embroidery.

"You don't need a policeman," a voice behind Carlisle said. The speaker was standing at the foot of the staircase. She was dressed even more casually than the professor, in a bedsheet toga. She had red hair as artlessly arranged as her sheet, and legs that could have given Arlene Dahl's lessons in geometry. I guessed her age at eighteen, give or take a semester.

"Go back upstairs, Daphne," Carlisle said.

"We're not ashamed of anything," Daphne said in parting. She couldn't see Carlisle's face. If she'd been able to, she would have chosen a different tag line.

I now understood why Carlisle had stayed with the academic life so long and maybe why he changed colleges so often. "Relax, Prof," I said. "I'm from Hollywood. I've stumbled across auditions before."

"The point is," Carlisle said, "John Whitehead isn't here."

"I'm more interested in where he was on Sunday night."

Carlisle gave his face a good long rubbing. When he'd finished, he said, "John was in Traynorville—at the Traynor farm. He went up that evening on the Interurban. I'm not sure why. He didn't get back here until dawn. He'd walked and hitchhiked the whole way down. He was in a terrible state, exhausted and frightened to death of something he'd seen at the farm."

"Or done," I said.

"I'll never believe that. I told you before that John is incapable of violence. Nothing I've seen since he arrived here in Indiana has changed my mind about that. Do you think I would have agreed to give him an alibi if I'd had the slightest doubt about his innocence?"

"Why did you agree to it?"

"To save him from the kind of small-town justice they have in places like Traynorville. The lock-up-the-stranger style of justice. You've seen what it's like up there. Tell me I'm wrong."

I couldn't. I'd not only seen that kind of justice, I'd almost been a victim of it. "What scared Whitehead at the farm?"

"He never told me. He was too spent. He slept until noon. Then he barely had time to pull himself together before the police came to collect him for questioning in Traynorville. The next thing I heard, John had been hired by Carson Drury. I still can't make sense of that."

"No one has," I said.

...

I should have stopped by my father's apartment and borrowed a couch—or, better still, checked into a hotel under an assumed name. I was too tired to make even the short drive to Traynorville safely. But I'd left Paddy in a bad spot, so I pointed the Studebaker northeast.

I was also too tired to think, but that didn't stop me from kicking around the possibility that Whitehead was the murderer. It seemed a likely enough idea, now that I was beyond the range of Walter Carlisle's stubborn faith. He was remembering his friend as he'd been in New York in the thirties. The whole world had changed since then, and Whitehead with it. He was a broken man now, unable to get past the loss of Drury. And poor Hank Shepard was the sap who had taken Whitehead's place in Drury's affections. It had been an even worse career move than Shepard had thought.

The problem with the Whitehead solution was the weapon, the Liberator. How had Whitehead come to have it? He'd never been to the farm before the fateful night. He'd have had no reason to suspect a gun was even there. And he couldn't have searched the house even if he'd hoped to find a gun. Drury had already been there, dropped off by Faris before the unlucky accountant had spotted Whitehead. Then there was the question both Faris and Carlisle had raised: Why had Drury taken Whitehead back? Had Whitehead performed a service for Drury that night, with the job his reward? Or had Whitehead been telling Carlisle the truth when he'd said he'd seen something terrible at the farm? If so, had that something also been valuable?

I made it to the Roberts Hotel in one tired piece. The night shift desk clerk left his post and took me to the seventh floor himself. On our way up, I asked him if I'd missed any excitement.

He said, "It's been as quiet as a cemetery," and then got embarrassed about it, maybe because he'd tied me in with Shepard or maybe because I looked as if I had one foot in the grave.

Paddy answered the door to Drury's suite in his undershirt and suit pants, one suspender on his shoulder and the other hanging down like an empty scabbard. He took one look at me and postponed his lecture. "Let's hear about it," he said instead.

I gave him my report in a low voice, knowing that Drury was somewhere nearby. When I'd finished, Paddy said, "We'll chew it all over in the morning. There's a spare bed through that door over there. I'll wait up and watch for a while."

"As long as you're going to be up," I said, "how about making a call to California for me?"

"It's one A.M. in California. Your kids have been asleep for half an hour at least."

"I want you to call one of your other operatives. Lange would be best; he could intimidate Khrushchev. Tell him to visit Dr. Petry, Drury's pill pusher."

"What, yet tonight?"

"Yet tonight. Tell Lange to demand to see Drury's X rays. He can say he's a fraud investigator from RKO's insurance company. He can say anything as long as it throws a scare into the doctor."

"What's this about?"

"A boy who ran away to join the circus," I said and called it a day.

■ ■ ■

I couldn't escape Traynorville, not even in my dreams. They were a reworking of my day, with the episodes and the players jumbled. I was in the rail yard again, being menaced—ineffectually—by Whitehead. Then I was in Gilbert's office to collect the Liberator. The man behind the sleek desk, who pulled the gun from its hiding place and pointed it at my chest, was Gilbert's dead brother, Mark. Before he could shoot me, I was in Carlisle's house, pointing to the incriminating wineglasses. The professor stepped aside to reveal his latest conquest, Linda Traynor.

I awoke with Paddy shaking my shoulder. "Sorry, Scotty. I let you sleep as long as I could. We just got a call from Gustin. He's finally found John Piers Whitehead."

"Safe?"

"For good and all. They pulled him out of the local river at a spot called Victory Park. Drury and I are headed there now. Follow us when you can."

chapter

39

I WAS SURPRISED to find my bag packed and standing at the foot of my bed, next to a breakfast tray. A Traynor footman had brought the case over at dawn, Paddy told me as he left. Gilbert had wasted no time in severing his last tie to Carson Drury's hired man.

Thirty minutes after Paddy wheeled Drury out, I pulled the Studebaker into the gravel lot of Victory Park. It was a little stretch of sycamore trees and concrete picnic tables on the bank of the White River a mile out of town. A limestone marker at the gate dedicated the park to the "Men and Women of the Armed Forces, 1941 to 1945." The marker was mossy with age.

I felt a little mossy myself. I'd gotten all of four hours' sleep and five minutes in the shower, but I'd done better than Gustin. I found the sheriff by the bank of the river, looking like the before picture in an ad for nerve tonic. He and Paddy were inspecting an outcropping of land on which stood a particularly brave sycamore. The current, eating away at the little peninsula, had exposed the stone underneath the soil and the roots of the tree, creating miniature caves that collected the debris of the river. Gustin was explaining to Paddy how the snag had collected Whitehead.

"I had some men out on the river before dawn. They found the body here about nine o'clock. They'd been past this spot earlier, but they'd missed him in the darkness—if he'd made it this far by then."

Gustin lost his balance climbing back up the bank. Paddy caught him at the last second and hauled him up one-handed.

"Thanks. It'd serve me right to fall in the damn river. It would have served me right if the river had washed Mr. Whitehead up to my door. That's where his death should be laid," he said, addressing me now. "If I'd gotten myself out to Traynor House last night when you'd told me to, he'd still be alive."

"How did he die?" I asked.

"We're guessing it was a cracked skull," Paddy said. "Or drowning brought on by a cracked skull."

"He wandered out of Traynor House and into the arms of that maniac Nast," Gustin said. "That's how he died. Nast killed him— maybe just to keep him from calling out—and dumped him in the river at the edge of the property. The body drifted down this far before it caught."

"It could have been an accident," I said by way of consoling him. "The terrace behind the house is a good thirty feet above the water. Whitehead could have wandered out to be sick, fallen in, and hit his head. The river's lined with stone."

"Thanks for trying," Gustin said. "But I'm through looking the other way. It was murder and it was my fault. There were the marks of two heavy blows on his head. One on the front and one on the back. You can't fall once and bash both sides of your skull. I'd show you the marks, but I already sent the body to O'Connor's."

"Drury's there now making the formal identification," Paddy said. "He has a deputy along to push his chair, but I'd feel better if one of us was on hand."

Meaning me. Paddy elaborated as we walked to the parking lot: "Sheriff Gustin is going to pay a call on Marvella Traynor. I've offered to keep him company. Ever since you described the lady to me, I've been wanting to discuss Irish immigration with her."

"I want to be there, too," I said. "I've earned a ticket."

"You have," Paddy said. "But we're unlikely to sneak up on her if you're along."

"Don't worry," Gustin told me. "I won't be standing there with my hat in my hand. I've had enough of this job and enough of the Traynors. I'm getting the truth today if I have to take that place apart brick by brick."

■ ■ ■

I got to O'Connor's in time to help Drury's new bodyguard manhandle the director and his wheelchair down the front steps. The bodyguard was the tall, thin deputy who had been hanging around on the edge of the case since the cross burning. In a movie, a character like that might suddenly reveal a secret identity, that of FBI agent or chief inspector of the Yard. I wanted to give the deputy a chance to unburden himself, so I asked him his name.

"Rodman," he said, without adding "Texas Rangers" or "Northwest Mounted Police" or anything else.

"Rodman," Drury repeated and then paused to collect his thoughts. He was uncollected in general, sitting slumped in his chair with his dark suit in disarray and his black hair in his eyes. He'd gone from looking thin and fit to gaunt and tired overnight.

"Rodman," he said again after a moment. "I forgot to tell Mr. O'Connor something. I insist on John's being treated decently. I don't want anything of potter's field about his arrangements. I'll be responsible for the bill. Would you mind going back and telling him that?"

Rodman loped off, leaving Drury and me standing in the sun. The day was already very warm and very humid. I wheeled the antique chair into the thin shade of a honey locust tree.

"Thanks, Scotty," Drury said. "Might I have one of your cigarettes?"

I gave him a Lucky and a light. He thanked me again and added, "You ought to find somewhere else to be. My assistants have suddenly become marked men."

"I'll take my chances."

He squeezed my forearm briefly. "Poor John. Of all the indignities he's had to undergo these last few years, this might be the worst—ending up in the basement of a tank town mortuary, being examined by a horse doctor who somehow got himself appointed coroner."

"It's not bothering Whitehead any," I said.

"I know. It's bothering me. As long as I'm being honest, I should admit that what's happening here isn't really a new phenomenon. My assistants have always been marked men—not marked for murder but for frustration and mediocrity. I certainly didn't make Hank Shepard's life a song, and he fared better than John.

"What is it, do you suppose, Scotty? What makes me such a lodestone of bad luck?"

"I don't know."

"John thought it was a curse connected with *First Citizen*. I remember the night he first mentioned the idea. We'd just finished shooting the picture. It was very late, or rather very early, and the two of us were in an editing room working on the opening shot. You remember it—the tracking shot of the movie studio our D. W. Griffith character had built for himself in upstate New York when he thought he was bigger than Hollywood. The model we used was based on Griffith's own studio in Mamaroneck, on the studio as it had been after Griffith had failed and taken to the bottle, a boarded-up place, dark and haunted."

"It was a great opening," I said.

"Yes," Drury said. "It was powerful and uncompromising. John didn't like it. He called it heartless. I remember him asking me if I wasn't afraid that our unfeeling dismissal of Griffith's life wasn't an invitation to the fates to revenge Griffith by visiting the same kind of failure on us."

I felt the sweat under my shirt turn cold. Drury, who'd been watching my eyes, nodded in agreement.

"I laughed at the idea, at John. I'd already begun to think of him as a fool, a hopelessly out-of-date fool.

"But it all came true," Drury said, his voice flat for once. "It happened just that way. John became a drunkard no one would employ, and I became a has-been genius, someone everybody stole from and no one respected, someone who couldn't touch the hem of his first triumph. I became a man doomed to live on like Griffith, for decades after his welcome ran out. At least poor John has been spared another day of that."

Rodman rejoined us, ending Drury's reminiscences. We drove back to the Roberts, Drury in Rodman's cruiser and the Speedster and I trailing behind. We snuck Drury in through the loading dock, as Paddy and I had done the night before. I left the deputy and the director at the freight elevator with instructions to meet me on two. Then I made my way through the hotel's kitchen and dining room and out into the lobby to order up Drury's personal elevator.

The kid at the controls saw me coming and pointed to the desk behind me. The hotel manager was there, waving me over. Gilbert Traynor had cut off our credit, I thought, and I was going to hear the bad news. I sent the elevator up after Drury and Rodman, and crossed to the desk.

"A party is waiting to see you in the lounge," the manager said, his pencil-line moustache twitching like a wren's tail as he spoke. "A lady."

For a happy minute I let myself believe it was Ella, in a day early because the engineer had known a shortcut. The hope had flickered out by the time I reached the bar. It was almost empty, as befit a small-town bar at noon. The out-of-town reporters were all at Victory Park, I told myself, picnicking on John Piers Whitehead's sorry end.

The mystery woman was seated at a booth in the far corner. She was wearing a black dress, a flat, broad-brimmed hat, also black, and very dark glasses with harlequin frames. I recognized Linda despite the disguise, as the discreet hotel manager surely had. Any of the locals would have known her, a small part of the large price she paid for being a Traynor, so the glasses had to be for the reporters.

Linda must have been afraid I wouldn't see past the cheaters. She'd resorted to a private signal, the equivalent of a carnation in her lapel. It was a Gibson, set on the table before her and untouched. I got the bartender's attention and pointed to the drink as I sat down.

Linda removed her sunglasses before she spoke. Her almond-shaped eyes were sunken and dull. "Hello, Scotty."

I took her gloved hand. "You look all in."

"Who isn't today? I came when I heard there had been a . . . second death. I tried the courthouse first, but the sheriff wasn't there."

"You must have missed him somehow on the road. He's at Traynor House, questioning your mother-in-law."

"If he got in to see her," Linda said. "She hasn't let me inside her room, not after dinner last night or later, when you'd all gone. Gilbert managed to have an interview with his mother this morning, but he wouldn't talk to me about it. He did tell me about the Liberator from the farmhouse being the murder weapon. I should have thought of that myself. I've seen it out there."

It was natural enough for the head of the Traynor Company to know about the Liberator. And I remembered then that she'd been old man Traynor's right hand during the war when the gun had been made.

Linda was still discussing her brother-in-law. "Something about that gun seemed to terrify Gilbert. I'm worried about him. He's always useless in a crisis, but this morning he seemed to be in a daze. I think he was already drunk."

She looked down at her own drink and pushed it away. "Tell me about this new killing, Scotty."

I told her how Whitehead had probably died and where he'd been found. "Gustin thinks he met up with Nast while he was wandering your grounds last night. If the sheriff's right, Nast killed him to eliminate a witness or just because he had time on his hands. Then he dumped the body in the river."

The bartender brought my drink. When he was out of range, I said, "Is Marvella hiding Nast?"

"No," Linda said. "I don't think so. She hasn't been out of her room since Drury and Whitehead arrived for dinner last night, which was hours before Nast could have gotten there. Besides, it wouldn't be like her. She'd use a man like Nast, but she wouldn't condescend to help him."

"She would to save herself from a murder charge."

"Marvella couldn't have been involved in that, Scotty. She doesn't have the backbone. None of her kind does. They had it bred out of them."

"Marvella thinks the Pallisers were fighters."

Linda almost smiled. "Some fighters. When their world was threatened by immigrants who spoke with the wrong accents and went to the wrong churches, what did they do? They dressed up like hobgoblins and tried to scare them away. They used fear because they were so familiar with it. They were frightened by every new thing that came along. Marvella's the most frightened of the lot because she's the only one left, except maybe for Gilbert. He's having a hard time choosing a side."

"What side would Mark have chosen? His mother remembers him as a Palliser in the rough."

"She's wrong there, too. Mark really was a fighter. If anything had threatened something or someone he loved, he'd have dealt with it directly and finally. He wouldn't have wished it away like the Pallisers. Like Marvella."

"She doesn't have to have ordered the murders to be involved," I said. "Drury thinks she lost control of Nast, and the murders are the result."

Linda leaned back slowly, until her shoulders rested against the padded wall of the booth. "He may be right. I've had the feeling for a while that things were out of control, that events were directing themselves. It has frightened me as much as the twentieth century frightened the Pallisers."

She didn't sound frightened as much as dreamy and distant. "Why?" I asked.

"I've only gotten through the last ten years by keeping myself under the kind of rigid control Marvella likes to exercise over her whole world. Now I can feel all the control slipping away, mine and Marvella's. I don't like it, Scotty. I don't like the idea that forces I can't see or understand are pulling my strings. It's even scarier to think that I might have set those forces in motion myself."

"How?"

"I don't know. I know I arranged to see Hank Shepard, and he died."

"There's no connection."

"None that we can see. But I have a feeling that there are connections we can't see—like the one between my decision to withhold my evidence about the night Shepard died and this new killing. I've a feeling I've set something going that's ricocheting around in the darkness still."

I pushed her drink back into her hand. "Gustin thinks Whitehead's death was his fault because he didn't take off after Nast. Drury thinks he brought it on by making a film about D. W. Griffith. They're both just imagining things, like you are. You're all imagining too much."

"Or you're not imagining enough, Scotty."

She took a break after that and sipped her drink. It was a chance for me to introduce a subject that I didn't really want to discuss, a subject that wasn't any of my business but bothered me anyway.

"I spoke with Eric Faris last night. Remember him?"

"Yes," Linda said. She relaxed slightly and said, "All the energy of a terrier and none of the teeth."

"That's the guy. He told me you drove him to his motel after you'd warned him off Drury last Saturday."

"That's right. I did."

"He said when you got him there, you kissed him."

"What?" Linda said and laughed.

I smiled myself, from relief. "Out of the blue, you kissed him."

"Why would I do that? It's crazy. He must have made it up."

It was the answer I'd wanted to hear. Linda read the line well enough. Then she undercut her delivery by blushing and fumbling her sunglasses back into place.

"Why would he say a thing like that?" she asked. "To get back at me? I didn't treat him that rough." She laughed again, but now it was forced. "Is there something about me that says 'desperate widow' to you California men?"

Before I could answer her, I heard Paddy's name being called out, his Sunday name: Patrick J. Maguire. I turned in my seat in time to see a bellhop pass the open door of the bar.

I told Linda I'd be right back and chased after the kid. I caught him easily, since he was weighed down by a silver salver that held a single telegram. I traded him a coin for the flimsy envelope and returned to the bar.

Linda's side of the booth was empty. The bartender pointed to the street door and shrugged sympathetically.

chapter

40

I OPENED THE TELEGRAM with the sympathetic bartender looking on. There was no reason not to. He and I kept no secrets from each other.

The wire was from Los Angeles, and it read: "Drury's leg not broken. All a publicity stunt says doctor. Lange."

"Bad news?" the bartender asked.

"Yes," I said. "I've been drafted again."

I left the lounge and crossed the lobby to the elevators, thinking as I went how thoroughly Paddy's attempt to move me from center stage to the wings had backfired. I thought, too, of Linda Traynor and how near the breaking point she seemed to be. And for what? Why was she suffering, and why were Shepard and Whitehead dead? The words from the telegram—"All a publicity stunt"—danced around in my head like the latest radio jingle until I felt like shouting them out.

The elevator jockey sensed my mood. "Who ran over your collie?" he asked.

"Just drive, kid," I said, "and you won't get run over yourself."

Rodman answered the suite door, looking none too happy about his new duties. Beyond him, Drury was lighting a cigar. He'd lost his dark suit jacket. It had been covering up an open-collared shirt of white silk. The loose-fitting shirt and his wild hair gave him the look of a B-picture buccaneer.

"Scotty," he said. "There you are finally. Do you feel up to eating something?"

I was still standing next to Rodman. "I need to talk to Mr. Drury privately," I told him.

The deputy looked to Drury, who said, "It's all right. Go find yourself a sandwich."

Drury's mind was still on food after Rodman left. "Can we order up lunch, Scotty? Or has Gilbert cut off our meal allowance?"

I'd noted before that Drury tended to find the center of any room he entered. True to form, he was parked in the open middle of the sitting room. I walked over to the side of the wheelchair.

"Can we eat while we talk?" he asked.

"No," I said and tipped his chair over onto its side. It didn't take much tipping, geniuses being top-heavy by definition. My foot on the chair's arm and one good shove did the trick.

Drury ended up on his stomach, too startled or winded to call out. I pulled the chair away from him and patted him down for a gun. Then I extracted his cigar from the hole it was burning in the carpet and stepped away.

Drury had inhaled by then. "Scotty! Have you gone mad? My leg!"

"Good news from Dr. Petry," I said. "He got your X rays crossed with another patient's. You're having twins."

I left Drury lying on the floor, looking like a man poised for his first push-up, and went into the bedroom he'd been using. The maid had already straightened up the place, which was a shame. I intended to toss it, to use one of Paddy's apt terms.

I started by emptying the drawers of the dresser onto the bed. I checked the nightstand next, finding only a Gideon Bible and the replacement script for *The Imperial Albertsons,* dug out of the RKO archives after Drury's original had been stolen in California. Next I pulled the bedding onto the floor and checked beneath the mattress and under the bed itself. Then I emptied the closet of suits, shoes, and, finally, luggage. The last piece I checked was a large traveling bag of maroon leather. The bag made a thumping sound when I tilted it, but when I looked inside, it was empty.

The answer to that paradox turned out to be a false bottom held in place by hidden snaps. Inside the secret compartment was a duplicate of something I'd already found, another copy of the shooting script for *Albertsons.* This one had Drury's name embossed on its beaten-up cover and marginal notes on every page, written in every color of ink.

I carried the script back into the sitting room. While I was away, Drury had managed to roll over onto his back. He sat up as I entered. I tossed the script on his lap.

"If there's a reward out for that," I said, "I'll take cash."

"How did you know, Scotty?"

"If you're asking how I knew you'd stolen your own script, the answer is, I didn't. I was looking for something else in there and just happened across it."

"I meant, how did you know my leg wasn't broken?"

"I should have guessed that the night of the cross burning. You were supposed to be weeks away from walking on crutches, but you stood up that night like a guardsman. When you realized what you'd done, you pulled a fainting spell, and I bought it.

"You counted on my buying everything. You were so confident, you even told me how you'd survived the fall from the camera crane. That was the point of your reminiscences about the Banfi Family Circus. You wanted to tell me you were a trained tumbler. It amused you to. You were that certain I'd never figure out what was really going on."

"But you have?" Drury asked, showing me his perfect teeth.

I fought the urge to kick them down his throat. "What are the odds, right? That it should be me who tracked you down, the man you handpicked from all the has-beens and failures in Hollywood."

"You're being too hard on yourself. You came highly recommended."

"I know. By Torrance Beaumont, no less."

Drury tucked his teeth away where they'd be safe, and I chalked up one for me.

"How did you learn that?" he asked.

"Dumb luck. I happened to visit Beaumont, and he happened to mention that you'd been to see him. I know Beaumont, so I can guess what he told you about me. He'd have said I was a down-on-my-luck ex-actor with more loyalty than brains, that the thing I was most loyal to was a silly, romantic dream of Hollywood as it used to be, that I'd be a sucker for your plan to turn back the clock by resurrecting *Albertsons*. In other words, I was just the security man you were looking for, one who wouldn't get in the way of your schemes. 'A prize sap,' as Tory likes to say."

Mr. Drury was reserving comment.

"I may even have gotten a plug from Hank Shepard. He might have mentioned that he'd slept with my wife. That was another point in favor of hiring me. It made me a potential fall guy for a murder rap. Were you planning to kill Shepard as far back as that?"

"What?" Drury demanded. "Scotty, please! What are you saying?"

"You haven't asked me what I was looking for when I came across the missing script. I was after the gun you used to kill Hank Shepard. It's called a Liberator, in case you're interested. You found it in the Riverbend parlor, along with comic book instructions showing how to load it and fire it."

"I couldn't have shot Hank."

"That's what we thought yesterday when we believed your leg was broken."

Drury tried to laugh. "You found out about my leg and jumped to the conclusion that I'm a murderer?"

"It was the other way around. Thinking you might be the murderer led me to the truth about your leg. We all believed that you couldn't have shot Shepard because he died of a contact wound, and a man in a wheelchair couldn't have climbed up into the tack room to press the gun against his chest. But a witness saw you do it, so it followed that your leg couldn't really be broken."

"What witness?"

"John Piers Whitehead. Eric Faris will testify that he saw Whitehead at Riverbend on the night of the murder."

"John never told anyone he saw me kill Hank."

"Of course not. You'd paid him too well to keep quiet. He came to you here in this suite on the night after the murder, just as you told me he did. Only it was to blackmail you. You agreed to take him back. In exchange, he promised to take your secret to his grave, which is how it worked out."

"Why would I kill Hank Shepard? He was my friend."

It was a piece I hadn't had when I'd entered Drury's suite, but I thought I'd found it there. I looked down at the script in the director's lap.

"This?" Drury asked, picking up the script and shaking it at me. "This was my motive? This was a publicity stunt. Okay, I admit it. Hank and I faked all the sabotage attempts back in Hollywood. But it was just for publicity, so we'd get a big play when we took the wraps off the production. And, yes, we faked my broken leg. What was so terrible about that? Worse frauds than that are worked in Hollywood every day."

"You and Shepard slashed the car tires at the RKO lot?"

"Yes," Drury said.

"And stole your own script?"

"Yes."

"And set fire to the editing room?"

Drury missed his cue.

"I suppose Shepard burned himself to make it look good. Don't tell me his burns were faked. Max Factor himself isn't that good."

"We never intended for Hank to be hurt," Drury said. "The fire got out of hand."

"Maybe the shooting got out of hand," I said. "Maybe you only meant to hit him in the fleshy part of his heart."

Drury winged the script at me. I caught it by its title page and tucked it under my arm.

"I don't think the attempts against *Albertsons* were faked," I said. "I think they were genuine sabotage, and I think you're the saboteur. Shepard was never in on it, but he may have figured it out. That may have been why you shot him."

"Why would I hire a security company if I was behind the sabotage?"

"For window dressing. You had to do it to keep up the pretense that the sabotage attempts were real—and the bigger pretense: the idea that your comeback was real."

Drury squirmed an extra inch away from me, and I knew I had him—thanks to Tory Beaumont. I had remembered something else from my visit to the dying actor.

"Do you know why Beaumont calls me a sap? I made the mistake once of telling him that I thought it would be better if every man's life could fade to black after he'd done his best day's work, the way it does for a character in a movie. Beaumont doesn't believe that— he's got too much inside—but you do, Drury. You're hollow from the neck down."

"I have no idea what you're raving about," Drury said, more and more of his native Cleveland sneaking into his speech. He rolled over onto his stomach and began to drag his prop cast toward a table that stood in the corner farthest from me.

"I'm talking about the central problem of your life. Where do you go from up? Your answer has always been to jump from one thing to another. Tired of setting Broadway on its ear? Move to radio. Conquered radio? Move to Hollywood. Never let the critics tire of your gimmicks. Never let them see the bottom of your bag of tricks."

"There were no gimmicks or tricks in *First Citizen!*" Drury yelled, his back to me as he crawled. "It was a work of art!"

"It was," I said, "but that only made your dilemma worse. You'd made the greatest movie of all time, first shot out of the box, and you had nowhere left to jump. There were no new worlds to conquer. It's a shame television wasn't up and running. You could have been Milton Berle."

"I made a second masterpiece! *Imperial Albertsons!*" Drury grappled with the table, struggling to pull himself up and sending the table's load—his box of cigars, a bowl of fruit, a vase of flowers—crashing to the floor. "If Whitehead and the studio hadn't ruined it, I would have gone on to make a dozen more."

"You tried to make a second masterpiece—I'll give you that much. But sometime late in the going, you lost heart. You saw that *Albertsons* wouldn't top *First Citizen,* or maybe it dawned on you that another success would just double the pressure to perform. So you ran off to England for the State Department and left your unfinished movie in the hands of John Piers Whitehead, a man you knew couldn't handle the job."

"John was a fine producer."

"In the theater. In radio, he'd been adequate. In Hollywood, he was plain lost. And you knew it. You knew just what would happen the second your back was turned. You couldn't have destroyed your movie any more surely if you'd dropped it in the ocean on your way to London."

Drury had struggled to a standing position by then, supported by the table and the wall next to it. The effort had taken all his strength. His thin chest was heaving under the sweat-stained silk of his shirt.

"Your comeback must have worked the same way," I said. "It must have been genuine at the start. You wouldn't have risked Eden otherwise. You must have felt you were far enough removed from the old, scary days to try again. So you sucked in poor Hank Shepard for one more go at the brass ring. He'd watched you throw away chance after chance, and his own career with them, but he went along for one more ride.

"Sometime after you'd bought the negative and set yourself up at RKO, you lost your nerve again. You were afraid it wasn't going to come together maybe, or afraid that it was. You started looking for a way out. You decided to burn the negative after doing some minor vandalism as a warm-up. You were going to torch your last chance and Shepard's. But he stepped in and saved it.

"He was close to the truth after that. Something about the fire must have made him suspicious. So you arranged the accident with the camera crane and made sure you were the only one on the platform when it fell. You probably set the whole thing up with Dr. Petry in advance. Shepard believed, like the rest of us, that your leg really was broken. That put him off your trail for a time. When he got suspicious all over again, you killed him."

"Perhaps I killed him because he saved the negative from the fire in Culver City," Drury said. He'd recovered his wind and his swagger. He was staring me down from behind a veil of black hair that curved almost to his mouth. "That would fit in better with your psychoanalysis. I suppose I murdered John, too. How did I manage that? With a slingshot?"

"You murdered Whitehead in 1942," I said, "when you made him the patsy for *Albertsons*. You just finished him off last night. After Linda and Gilbert left you, you went with Whitehead onto the terrace. He probably pushed your chair."

"Down the stone steps and onto the grounds?"

"Whitehead never made it onto the grounds. You got him to the edge of the terrace and slugged him with a piece of the ornamental statuary. Then you tipped him into the river. That's why Gustin found the marks of two blows on Whitehead's skull: one from the murder and one from the fall."

Drury released the table long enough to brush the hair from his eyes. The face he revealed was as white as his shirt. "I ran a considerable risk."

"It wasn't as risky as letting Whitehead go to pieces in front of the Traynors. Sooner or later he would have spilled what he'd seen at the farm."

"Gilbert already knows what John saw," Drury said. He was smiling at me again, a long, thin smile that curled at the ends. He'd jumped ahead of me somehow, just when I'd had him all tied up.

"How could he?" I asked.

"Because John told him. You haven't solved the murders, Scotty, but you've cleared up a mystery for me. You see, I didn't take John back because I felt lonely or sorry for him or because it had been Hank's dying wish. I did it because Gilbert forced me to. Gilbert came to see me on Monday night, not John. He told me to take John in or lose all his financial support. He even threatened to hold the *Albertsons* negative hostage—it's still in a Traynor vault—until I complied. Unlike you, Gilbert still believes I intend to make a movie."

"Why would he intercede for Whitehead?"

"That's the mystery you've solved. I didn't know that John had been at Riverbend the night Hank died. I believe now that he saw something there and used it to blackmail Gilbert."

"You're playing for time," I said. "How could Gilbert be involved in Shepard's murder?"

"I don't know. You're the psychiatrist. Maybe Hank reminded Gilbert of his dead father or a dog that had bitten him as a child. I don't understand Gilbert at all. I thought I did once. I thought he sincerely wanted to help me as a way of rebelling against his family. But since we've arrived here in Indiana, he's been sitting back and waiting like a man who has set a match to a fuse. I don't know who he's hoping to hoist or why."

"You don't know anything," I said. "You're improvising."

"Aren't we both?" Drury asked. "What happens to your improvisation if Gilbert was the target of John's blackmail and not me?"

It and I were out of commission.

Drury knew it, too. "Would you mind handing me my cigar, Scotty?"

I was still wording my reply when a key scraped its way into the lock on the door behind me. It was Rodman, back from his break. The deputy looked from the wheelchair to Drury and then to me without blinking. On the basis of that feat, I decided it was safe to leave him in charge. I handed him Paddy's telegram and the recovered script.

"Get Gustin over here," I said. "Give him those."

"He's still at Traynor House."

"Call him there. Tell him you're holding the murderer at gunpoint."

I nodded at Drury, who obliged me by grinning sardonically. Rodman shifted the script to his left hand and put his right hand on his gun.

I patted his shoulder as I left. "If he tries to talk," I said, "shoot him."

chapter

41

I TOOK THE SCENIC ROUTE to the mansion. On the way I stopped at the Traynor plant to ask at the front gate for Gilbert. I didn't expect to find him at the factory after Linda's comment on his early morning drinking. Then again, he might have wanted to drink in peace, which would have been hard to do at home with Gustin and Paddy stomping around. The factory guard recognized my borrowed Studebaker. On the strength of that, he told me politely that Gilbert had not been to work that day.

I had another reason for taking the long way to Traynor House. I wanted to give Rodman plenty of time to reel in Gustin. Drury had tossed the deck in the air with his claim about Whitehead blackmailing Gilbert. Until I had all the cards collected again, I didn't want the sheriff's company or even Paddy's. I especially didn't want them rooting about in Traynor House, Linda's home. I'd begun to fear that she needed more help from me than an occasional comforting word.

The private guards were still on duty at the mansion's pylons, but they seemed dispirited. Gustin might have kicked the stuffing out of them on his way to storm Marvella's tower. One of them stepped forward as I turned into the drive, but when I drove past without slowing, he only shrugged.

Greta the maid had lost some starch herself. She was wiping her eyes with the tip of her apron as she opened the door. "They're gone," she said simply.

"The family?" I asked.

"No, the sheriff and the other bully. You go, too, mister. Mrs. Traynor has been through enough."

"I'm here to see Gilbert," I said as I stepped around her. "Please tell him I'm waiting on the terrace."

I made my way to the site of my own confrontation with Marvella Traynor. Her chaise lounge was there, but it was unoccupied. The table next to it had not been set for tea today. The table's big, striped umbrella was furled, like the flag of a beaten army.

I'd chosen the terrace for my interview with Gilbert because I wanted to confirm my guess that Drury could have tipped Whitehead's body over the railing and into the river. At its farthest point from the house, the semicircular terrace overlooked the river itself, with no intervening bank. Whitehead could have fallen straight down from there and found the water. Dropping from that height, he would also have found the rocky bottom. In the bright afternoon sun, I could see the floor of smoothed stones clearly, and the fat bass patrolling it.

Next I checked the statuary on the terrace balustrade to verify my guess that one of the dancing figures had been Drury's weapon of opportunity. The statues weren't anchored to the railing's stone cap, and they were small enough to heft easily. Neither of the figures on the tip of the terrace closest to the water showed any trace of damage or blood. But there was something wrong about one of the figures, a woman doing a beginner's pirouette. I remembered it being behind Marvella's lounge chair on the day I'd interviewed her.

I checked the stretch of railing behind her empty chair and found a potted fern. Someone had used the pirouetting woman to fill a gap in the line and then replaced it with a plant. Had Drury taken the time to make the switch after he'd tossed the murder weapon into the river? It didn't seem likely. But if not Drury, who?

I looked back to the house for an answer and saw Marvella Traynor staring down at me from an upstairs window. I only got a second's glimpse of her before she yanked the window's curtain closed. In that second I saw the familiar hatred and something my talk with Linda had prepared me to spot: fear.

I expected the hired muscle to appear after that, nightsticks at the ready. Gilbert came out instead. He was unarmed, and he walked with the ceremonial precision that always gives away a drunk.

"Glad to see you're still with us," I said.

"I can't say the same," Gilbert replied, his speech as stiff as his walk. "I was hoping I'd seen the last of you. And Carson Drury."

"I may be able to help you with that. I need the answer to a question. Drury told me he took Whitehead back because you forced him to. Yes or no?"

Gilbert's beady eyes grew to normal size, and his thin face flushed red.

"Damn," I said. Drury hadn't been bluffing. Whitehead hadn't blackmailed him, which meant Whitehead hadn't seen Drury kill Shepard. What had frightened the old man that night?

Gilbert was still pondering the question his face had answered. I grabbed the front of his polo shirt and shook him. "How did Whitehead force you to back him? What did he threaten to say?"

"I don't know what you mean," Gilbert said. "He never threatened me. He came to me because I was Carson's backer. He asked me to use my influence for him. He was such a sad case, I decided I would. That's all there was to it."

He put a hand on my wrist to remind me that I was still holding his shirt. I let him go. "You're lying, Gilbert. Whitehead had something to sell. You wouldn't have helped him otherwise. You've never looked out for anyone but yourself."

Gilbert was tucking his shirt back in. He paused to look offended. "You wouldn't even be out here if I didn't think about other people. If I hadn't tried to help Carson, you'd be back in California at your usual stand, peeking through some hotel keyhole."

"Stop it," I said. "You're making me homesick. You never meant to help Drury. You've been working some scheme of your own from the start."

"I've never had a scheme," Gilbert said, and his eyes filled up with tears.

"Damn," I said again. I knew he was telling me the truth. He'd been telling me the truth all along when he'd insisted, first whimsically and then fearfully, that he hadn't known what was going to happen next.

"You've never had a plan," I said, working it out as I spoke the words. "Linda thought you did. So did Drury. He started off believing that you were using him to cut your mother's apron strings. But he was selling you short."

"Was he?" Gilbert asked hopefully.

"We all did. Back in Hollywood, I took you for a small-town playboy with so many stars in your eyes you couldn't see to shave. But it was all an act. You were taking everything in—and everybody.

"Even Drury. While he was setting you up, you were researching him. You found out the essential truth about him, which is that he's a walking disaster area. Bad luck follows him wherever he goes. Did your old college buddy Tyrone McNally pass that on to you when he told you he'd sold Drury the *Albertsons* negative?"

"No," Gilbert said, shaking his sleek head. "You're making it sound too much like a plan again. Tyrone only gave me an excuse to go to Hollywood in the first place and an introduction to Drury. I just wanted a break from the monotony of my life. And I didn't research Drury. I just spent time with him. I heard what was happening to his movie, what had happened to his last dozen projects. I listened to the jokes about how unpredictable life in his circle could be. Hank Shepard liked to tell them. You heard those jokes yourself."

"Yes," I said.

"And I thought how wonderful it would be to live around a person whose life was never the same two days in a row. Who unsettled everything and everybody just by being himself. And I got an idea—not a plan, not a scheme, just an idea. I decided to bring Carson to Traynorville. To introduce him into my routine, predictable life just to see what would happen."

I was feeling the heat. I sat down on the edge of Marvella's lounge chair. Gilbert, whose brandy-soaked skull should have been cracking in the full sun, looked totally unaware of the temperature.

"Drury told me you were like a man who'd lit a fuse," I said. "He hasn't realized yet that he's the bomb."

"It was exciting at first," Gilbert said, "just the way I'd hoped it would be. I enjoyed the tension of not knowing what the next phone call or knock on the door would bring. It was a feeling I've never really known. And I enjoyed watching the rest of you react. Especially my mother."

"And Linda," I said. "Don't leave her out. Your little experiment is squeezing her hard."

He looked away. "I never meant for it to."

"You're lying again, Gilbert. You're jealous of her."

"Of course I'm jealous. Who wouldn't be? But I'm fond of her, too. I don't want to hurt her. I never wanted anyone to be hurt—not Hank or Whitehead or Linda."

"But they all have been. The first two are dead, and Linda has herself half-convinced that she's responsible. She made arrangements to meet Shepard at the farm Sunday night. She's afraid he died because she almost gave in to her loneliness."

Gilbert was still staring out at the river. "The only man who would kill to keep her faithful is dead," he said.

"Being dead doesn't hold your relatives back. Your uncle is dead, and his bedsheet goes marching on, courtesy of your mother and Nast. Did she send Nast to the farm to act for her dead son? So she could keep Linda faithful and chained to this town? Is that what Whitehead saw?"

"I can't tell you."

"You wonder how you would have done in the war. You're in a war now. The people around you are in danger, and you can help them. What are you going to do?"

"Nothing," Gilbert said. Then he started to cry again.

TEARS WERE ALL I GOT from Gilbert after that. Tears and pleas for another brandy. When I gave up hoping that he'd dry out, I went looking for a bottle on the slim chance a drink would get him talking again.

The only supply I knew of was in the living room's corner bar. The bar wasn't locked up. Either Greta was a teetotaler, or she had the run of the place. I found a bottle of Gilbert's favorite brandy, cleverly hidden among six other bottles of the same brand. As I reached for it, I felt someone's eyes caress the back of my neck.

I swung around with the brandy bottle drawn back for a forward pass. There was no one behind me, but that didn't make the feeling I was being watched go away. The only eyes I could see belonged to the portrait of Mark Traynor. I crossed to its place of honor over the mantel to verify that the eyes were really the painting's and not those of Nast, peering out at me from some secret passage. That gag was so hoary, Hollywood scriptwriters only used it in comedies, but the old traditions died hard in Traynorville.

The eyes I found in the portrait were the ones the painter had put there, blue eyes that had a hard edge. They created the impression that the boy lieutenant was looking into his own hard future. It hadn't been the noble death that soldiers think about when they let themselves think of death at all. He'd simply died, according to his widow. I'd never asked her what she'd meant by that. It couldn't have been a training accident, although those had been all too common during the war. Mark had died in Germany. He might have turned his jeep over. He might have stepped on a mine. Ella's own brother had met that end.

Or Traynor might have had an even more wasteful death. He might have been a victim of friendly fire, like Clark. The thought stopped me cold. Clark. I stared up into those hard blue eyes, my mind an empty space in which Clark's name echoed on and on. It was finally overlaid by a replay of Gilbert saying, "The only man who would kill to protect her honor is dead." Like everything else I'd been told in Traynor House, it was a lie.

I ran back out onto the terrace, but Gilbert had gotten away. I could see no sign of him down on the grounds near the river, so I reentered the house using a different door, one that led to a library. I searched the first floor without finding another soul. Then I went up the grand staircase, taking the right fork when the stairs split beneath the stained-glass homage to the Traynor Phaeton Six.

The second floor was served by a single hallway, the center of which overlooked the first-floor foyer. Opposite this balcony were three doors opening on rooms that faced the front of the house. They were bedrooms. The leftmost was Linda's comfortable, uncluttered room. Next to it and serviced by a connecting door from Linda's was the room Gilbert had told me about, Mark Traynor's room. It was preserved as he'd left it when he'd gone off to fight, complete with school pennants and model airplanes. The third door of the trio opened onto a guest room that was as impersonal as any hotel's.

I had company when I came out from checking the third bedroom. Greta was standing at the end of the hallway to my left, her arms thrown out protectively across a set of double doors—Marvella's suite.

"Go away," Greta said.

The opposite end of the hall dead-ended in an identical pair of doors: Gilbert's rooms. I crossed to the locked doors and banged on them.

"He's gone," Greta called to me. "He's gone."

Gone to warn his brother, I thought, thanks to the head start I'd spotted him.

I left the house at a run. My Studebaker hadn't been impounded by the family chauffeur. I drove it full-out to Riverbend, pushing seventy until I came to the dip in the road where Casey Atherley had hidden his car. Beyond it, at the end of the drive, a familiar deputy was on duty: the old man who had spotted Clark on the farmhouse porch the day before. He wasn't spotting anybody today. He was snoring away with his head back and his mouth wide open. The sound of my car sliding to a halt on the gravel drive next to his cruiser brought him up, swatting at bluebottles and asking, "Who the hell?"

"Elliott," I said. "Scott Elliott. Has Gilbert Traynor passed here?"

"What?"

"Call Sheriff Gustin on your radio and tell him I need help at Clark's cabin as soon as he can get there. Tell him I'll have the murderer waiting for him."

"Yes, sir," the deputy said and then, less encouragingly, "Who'd you say you are?"

I drove on, wondering whether he'd find Gustin and whether the sheriff would respond to another call from me, the guy who had just cried wolf over Carson Drury. I shook off that doubt. Paddy would march Gustin over if he had to push him with a gun.

I checked my own gun as I left the coupé. I kept the forty-five in my right hand as I made my way across the backyard to the path along the edge of the field. The automatic gave the game away, hanging there at the end of my arm, but I didn't think empty hands would fool Clark. I'd tried that approach on my last visit to the cabin, and he'd all but attacked me. I knew why now. He'd assumed when I'd shown up that I'd discovered his secret, that I'd figured out he was really Mark Traynor, alive but so disfigured that he could live unrecognized in his own hometown. I'd set his mind at ease when I'd asked about the cross burning. He'd handed me a red herring, Nast, and sent me on my merry way. He wouldn't try finessing me this time. He'd be sure I knew the truth.

Who else knew? Gilbert, of course. He'd bowed to Whitehead's blackmail in order to save his brother. Clark was the one Whitehead had seen go into the tack room that night. No wonder the old man had still been frightened hours later when he'd stumbled into Carlisle's house. But how had Whitehead connected Clark and Mark Traynor? He couldn't have expected Gilbert to pay off to protect a caretaker. And when had Whitehead even heard that Gilbert had an older brother?

I asked myself another question I couldn't answer as I reached the start of the woods. How did Linda Traynor fit in now? She had to know Mark was still alive. Even if he'd been reported by the army as killed in action, she had to know the truth. She couldn't have lived so close to him for ten long years and not known. She'd told me she had a hard time believing that Mark was really dead. Had she been hinting that he wasn't? Why hint at it? And why pretend to be uncertain about the connection between her tryst with Shepard and his murder? She could have told me everything if she'd wanted her husband punished. If she'd wanted to protect him, she could have kept quiet about her appointment with Shepard.

The answer had to be Linda's old dilemma of being held in check by opposing forces. This time the rival pressures were the need to protect her husband and the desire to prevent further violence.

I put my doubts and questions away as I neared the clearing. Gustin could work it all out at his leisure, once he had Clark behind bars. It would probably require no more than sweating Gilbert, which the sheriff could handle with his feet up.

The little forest seemed unnaturally quiet. I decided it was due to the heat of the afternoon, that the birds and the squirrels were all napping in the shade. If I was lucky, I told myself, Clark would be napping, too. I'd never felt less lucky in my life.

Even so, there was no sign of Clark in the clearing around the cabin. No sign of any living thing. I'd left the farm without the slightest thought of sneaking up on Clark. My plan had been to march in and take him, period. Somewhere along the way I'd wised up. I waited at the edge of the clearing for a long time, watching and listening and sweating.

When I finally crossed the open ground, I ran in a crouch, something I wasn't often called on to do as a civilian. The moment brought the war back so vividly, I almost reached up to hold my helmet in place.

I arrived at the timber building at the corner to the left of the front door. Between the corner and the door was a window. Because the cabin stood above the dirt floor of the clearing on stone legs, the sill of the window was at the height of my nose. I could stretch just enough to look into the structure's single room. No one looked back.

I tried the front door. It was made of three roughly sawn planks, and it was unlocked. I stepped inside—still moving on my toes—with one last look behind me for a glimpse of a red ball cap.

The floor plan was bed and fireplace to the right, cook stove and sink with hand pump to the left, and a table and chairs in the center. I couldn't see any cover in which Clark could be lying in ambush. The furniture was all unpadded wood. The two chairs were homemade, their legs and arms still covered with bark and their seats with leather straps woven loosely. The bed was a surplus cot straight from an army barracks. Clark's closet was a pole that spanned the walls of the corner nearest the bed. The few clothes hanging there wouldn't have hidden Frank Sinatra. I checked the clothes anyway, tapping the shirts and pants with the barrel of my gun.

I was looking for the Liberator. Having it accounted for would make me that much happier about confronting Clark. I checked the supplies that stood on open shelves above the stove–sugar and flour and cornmeal in canisters, everything else in cans–and the stove itself.

As I searched for the gun, I thought back on the hunger I'd seen in Clark's eyes when I'd produced Gilbert's copy of the Liberator. If that had been an act–if he'd really been a murderer and not a suicide cut off from his weapon of choice–it had been a great act. And why had Clark torn Riverbend apart looking for the gun? The murderer had to know where the gun was. Had that been another dodge?

I shut the questioning off as soon as it started. I couldn't let it distract me from what I was seeing and what I was listening for: the sound of Clark's footfall behind me. For the same reason I blocked out images of Whitehead when the smooth river stones of the fireplace brought him to mind.

That is, I tried to block them. As I pulled apart the stack of firewood on the hearth, I saw Whitehead rolling along the black bottom of the river. I even heard the tapping he made as he touched the stones with every slow revolution.

Then I realized that the faint tapping sound was real, that it was coming through the floor beneath me. I went back out through the front door and down the block steps, scanning the woods as I stepped onto the clearing floor. When I felt able to turn my back on the wall of trees, I stooped and looked under the cabin. My view of the corner where I'd heard the tapping was blocked by a stack of lumber.

I circled the building, noting for the first time that the ground fell away at the back. The stone legs supporting the rear of the structure were twice as tall as those in front. Their added height created a storage space below the cabin floor. Clark had filled it with the lumber I'd seen from in front, as well as drums of kerosene and olive drab cases that I recognized as surplus ammunition boxes.

I took all those things in peripherally. What grabbed my gaze and held it was the source of the tapping sound: a pair of human legs that ended in work boots bound together by heavy cord. The boots were kicking feebly at an outcropping of stone.

I put a hand on the bound ankles, and a low moan floated out from beneath the cabin, followed by a strangled attempt at speech. I stuck my gun in its holster and dragged the unresisting form down the slope and into the daylight.

It was Nast, bound and gagged and half-dead. His greasy hair was caked with dirt, and his eyes were black and blue. His gag was a twisted strip of dirty rag that cut into the corners of his mouth like a bit. I untied it first. Nast worked against me by struggling to speak before I had the gag clear of his parched tongue. His voice, when he could finally use it, was a croak.

"Did you kill him?" he asked. "For the love of God, tell me you killed him." Then his bruised eyes locked onto something over my shoulder, and he screamed, "No!"

I rolled away from Nast and drew my gun. Clark timed his first kick perfectly, knocking the gun from my hand. It rattled down the slope toward the trees. His second kick was off balance. I grabbed his foot and twisted it, and he went down, tumbling well clear of me. We scrambled to our feet at the same time. Clark was nearer to my fallen gun, but he didn't turn to pick it up.

"I've been waiting for you," he said. "I knew you wouldn't quit."

"It's time *you* quit," I said. "I know what's been going on."

Clark shook his head. "If you knew, you'd still be running. Now it's too late to run."

He came at me up the slope, his fists held low like another John L. Sullivan. He had no choice with his left; he couldn't raise it any higher. Knowing that, I stood my ground, jabbing with my left and throwing everything into a right cross aimed at the unprotected side of his head.

He'd been waiting for that. He showed me how a man with no left held his own in a fight, tilting his head away from the blow and letting it bounce into his ruined ear. Then his big right hand brushed by my guard and caught me square on the jaw. I staggered backward against the side of the cabin but kept my feet under me. Clark nodded his approval as he closed in for round two.

I led with the same left jab and then faked a right. Clark leaned his head away again, as I'd hoped he would. I snuck in a quick left, hitting him on what passed for his nose. He backed away, wiping at blood.

When he came for me a third time, he did it with open hands. I couldn't back up the slope fast enough to stay away from him. I tried throwing another combination, but this time *he* had the plan. Instead of shrugging off my right, he grabbed my arm and drew me into his knee. As I buckled, he chopped at my head.

Gravity saved me. I rolled into Clark's legs as I fell, taking him down with me. At first it didn't seem like much of a break. He didn't need any swinging room to land blows that hurt all the way to the bone. He rained them on me as we tumbled over and over down the slope. But when we came up against the trees, I was on top, and my left hand was on the barrel of my gun.

Clark's right arm was pinned under him. I hit the right side of his head with the gun. It was a quick, desperate blow that had as much of my hand in it as gunmetal. All the same, it stunned him.

I hit him again with nothing but gun and told myself that I'd killed him.

chapter

43

GUSTIN AND PADDY and Zimmerman, the sheriff's state police advisor, showed up soon after that. They found Nast still tied up and whimpering away in the shadow of the cabin, Clark lying where I'd left him, and me propped against a tree, covering Clark with my bloody forty-five.

I hadn't killed him after all. When I'd spotted his chest moving up and down in quick, shallow breaths, I'd pointed the gun at him and held it there. The fear that he might spring up like a jack-in-the-box and come for me again was the only thing that had kept me conscious.

"It's all right, Scotty," Paddy said as he eased the gun from my hand. "We'll take it from here."

He handed the gun to Gustin. The sheriff was nominally in charge, but as the youngest man still on his feet, it fell to him to trot back to the farmhouse to call for an ambulance. Before he left, he asked me for the short version of my story.

"Clark is Mark Traynor. He killed Shepard and Whitehead." I

didn't say why he'd killed them. I couldn't bring myself to drag in Linda. I'd have to, though, soon enough.

"What about him?" Gustin asked, gesturing to the spot where Nast was being worked on by Zimmerman.

My employer had already done that calculation. "Nast was Clark's insurance policy," Paddy said. "As long as you were looking for Nast, you wouldn't be bothering about other suspects. Clark's been holding him since the night we broke up Nast's little party in the rail yard. Clark told us that Nast had run, but all the time he'd had him tucked away somewhere safe."

Paddy interrupted his own lecture. "Mother of God, Scotty. Do you suppose Clark only agreed to help me track you down so he could put his hands on Nast before the sheriff did? And here I thought it was my winning personality."

"I thought it was your straw hat," I said, my cleverness making me dizzy.

Gustin left us after that. I had things to occupy me—spitting blood and counting my teeth—but Paddy was restless. He paced up and down the slope, burning up his latest cigar instead of smoking it. He wanted to read me the riot act now that he knew I wasn't at death's door, but he couldn't bring himself to start in. To help him let off steam, I asked him what he thought of Marvella Traynor.

"That one," he said and spat out some Indiana dust. "She's a fine example of a type that has almost died away. And thank God for it. She's tough, I'll say that for her. She admitted to hiring Nast to burn the cross and even to supplying his thugs with their pointy costumes. Admitted it and snapped her fingers under our noses at the same time. It's her family's farm, after all, she said. She'd burn the whole shebang to the ground whenever she liked and to hell with us.

"For all the bluster, though, she had the wind up over something. Not over our visit but over something."

"Her bedroom overlooks the terrace," I said, remembering her frightened face in the window. "She might have seen her son kill Whitehead last night."

"She might have at that," Paddy said. "We were just getting to the Whitehead questions when the call came in about Drury."

"Drury," I repeated. "I guess I owe him an apology."

"Save it," Paddy said. "He's admitted that he was the one trying to scuttle his picture and that he faked his broken leg to put Shepard off his trail. So, in a way, he's responsible for all this mess. But he wouldn't tell us why he did it. He told me to ask you."

I got to my feet and, with Paddy's aid, stayed there.

"Why did he do it, Scotty?"

"Because he isn't twenty-one anymore."

When Gustin came back, he was leading three men dressed in white. Two of them carried a stretcher. The third and youngest carried a doctor's bag. He looked Nast and Clark over and sent Nast out first, with the two attendants doing the lugging and Zimmerman along in case Nast made a miracle recovery. On the second trip, Clark's trip, the kid doctor and Gustin helped carry the stretcher, with Paddy and me following along behind like a pair of hired mourners.

Gustin, who was the left rear support of the stretcher, said without turning his head, "Clark and Mark Traynor. I can't believe it, Elliott. Are you thinking the whole town knew about it and kept quiet?"

Paddy was guiding me with a hand on my upper arm. He clamped down on my arm now, his private signal for "Watch what you say."

"I think the whole town was taken in, just as we were," I said.

"But I knew Traynor—not well, but I knew him. Clark's nothing like him. I'm not talking about a face. I'm talking about the man I knew before the war."

"What and who we knew before the war doesn't count these days," I said. Paddy's grip tightened again, this time to keep me upright.

A shiny new county ambulance—a gift from Marvella, probably—had been backed up to the edge of the woods. The intern supervised the process of squeezing Clark in beside Nast. Then he turned to me.

"You can ride up front," he said.

He kept a cigarette going in the corner of his mouth to make him look less like a choirboy. I moved the cigarette to the corner of my mouth—the unbruised corner.

"Thanks," I said. "I'm staying put."

"You can't stay here," Paddy said. "There's talk of a big storm coming in. Besides, the doctor will want to look you over."

"He'll want to hold me until a week from Tuesday. I'm picking Ella up at the station in twelve hours. After that, they can put me in an iron lung if they want."

We worked out a compromise. The kid sent Gustin and Zimmerman ahead with the ambulance. He and Paddy and I followed in Linda's Studebaker, the doctor enjoying himself behind the wheel. When we arrived at the county hospital—a sprawling building that bore an ominous resemblance to Traynor House—the kid shone a light in my eyes, poked my ribs, and decorated my face with antiseptic and bits of tape. But he didn't admit me. When he'd finished, Paddy and I found a quiet visitors' lounge and settled in to wait for word of Clark.

Paddy had been given instructions to keep me awake for an hour or two, so he told me stories of other visits he'd made to Indiana back when he and Peggy had been traveling the vaudeville circuit. I'd heard most of the stories before, some of them with different settings, but that didn't bother me. Paddy's strength as a composer lay in his variations, not in the tunes themselves.

As the afternoon gave way to evening, he grew restless. I knew he wanted to be working on what was left of the job, not nursing me. After a silence he said, "I couldn't help but notice that you didn't speak to motive when you were briefing the sheriff."

"Couldn't you?" I asked.

"When you get cagey, it's always one of two things. Either you're being gallant toward a lady, or you're feeling sentimental about an ex-soldier."

"How about Hollywood? Tory Beaumont thinks I'm mushy over the whole town."

"A perceptive man, Mr. Beaumont. But as we're currently in the wilds of Indiana, I think we can eliminate that possibility. Which leaves the lady and the veteran. Clark's a veteran, to his cost, but the way you two went at each other today bespeaks no partiality. So it's a lady—Linda Traynor, if I'm not mistaken, the one who was giving you the googly eyes last night."

I told him about Linda's arrangement with Shepard on the night of the first murder. While he listened, Paddy blew smoke rings, his usual perfect ones. They took on a pinkish hue as they floated past a west-facing window.

"Are you thinking Linda knows that Clark is her lost husband?" Paddy asked. "That she's known from the start?"

"How could she not know?" I said, giving words to the question I'd been asking myself since I'd left Traynor House.

A nurse came in and switched on the waiting room's overhead light. She looked at Paddy's cigar and sniffed. Then she looked at my face and stepped back.

"Expectant father," Paddy said, patting me on the shoulder. "His wife went into the delivery room swinging."

When the nurse had gone, Paddy said, "If Linda knows Clark's true identity, why did she arrange to meet Shepard at Riverbend, in her husband's domain, so to speak? Any other spot in the state would have been safer."

I had to admit I didn't have the answer. "Maybe Shepard insisted. He can't have known about Clark."

"I shudder to think of the moment he found out," Paddy said without shuddering noticeably. "So Whitehead happened by in time to see the murder?"

"I think so. Don't ask me how he connected Clark with Mark Traynor. Maybe he overheard Clark identifying himself to Shepard."

"I'm more interested in how Whitehead and Clark connected at the Traynor manse on the night Whitehead died. Any thoughts on that?"

"Clark left us at the rail yard and went to the house. I don't know why. But he'd found out that Whitehead was blackmailing his brother as a way of getting back in with Drury. Did Drury tell you that he'd been pressured by Gilbert to take Whitehead back?"

"Yes," Paddy said.

"Gilbert surely told his brother about it. So when Clark and Whitehead came together by accident outside the house, Clark eliminated a witness."

Paddy snorted. It was another of his private codes, this one expressing skepticism. "The timing was tight enough when we thought it was Nast hotfooting it over to Traynor House alone to get his orders from the DAR's own Dragon Lady. Now we have to add in the time Clark spent dealing with Nast. I don't like it."

"We know Clark got there somehow," I said. "John Whitehead is dead."

"My old logic teacher would have had something pointed to say about that construction—if I'd ever had a logic teacher."

Before Paddy could come up with something pointed of his own, Zimmerman ducked his head into the room.

"There you are," he said. "Clark's awake." Then he was gone.

Paddy was on his feet almost as quickly. When I didn't jump to mine, he said, "Don't feel up to it?"

"No," I said. This was one finish I didn't want to be in on.

Paddy understood. "What can be done for Mrs. Traynor, Sheriff Gustin will do. He's a good man. You don't mind my going, do you?" he added as he backed toward the door.

"No. There's no point in giving Zimmerman the inside track."

They could hear Paddy's laugh down in reception. "My thought exactly. A pushy, interfering sort if ever I saw one. The poor sheriff's probably desperate for a disinterested opinion."

He got as far as the doorway and stopped. "Here's something to think about if you start feeling drowsy. Why is Nast still alive?"

chapter

44

WHEN I COULD NO LONGER feel Paddy's footsteps through the worn linoleum of the waiting room floor, I got up and went in search of a drink of water. As I wandered, I chewed over my homework assignment. Why was Nast still alive? Why hadn't Clark killed him? He'd already murdered two men by the time he'd gotten Nast to his cabin. Why hadn't he made it three? If he'd murdered Nast and buried him in the woods, Gustin could have searched for him until doomsday and never found him. Nast would have been a permanent red herring, a second mask behind which Clark could have hidden until long after the town had lost interest in the deaths of two outsiders.

But Clark had kept Nast alive. Why? Was it because Nast hadn't threatened Linda, and Clark would only kill to protect her? Maybe. But that wasn't what Paddy was getting at. He was really asking: If Clark was unable to kill Nast, a man as worthless as they came, a man whose death would have covered Clark's tracks forever, was Clark capable of murdering anyone?

The answer that came to me was both fuzzy and concise: Clark hadn't killed Shepard and Whitehead; Mark Traynor had. Traynor was a personality Clark hadn't used since the war, one he might not remember all that clearly in his conscious mind. Linda had told me that Traynor would have reacted directly and decisively to counter a threat to his family. Traynor was the murderer. He'd risen up through the debris that was Clark whenever something had threatened Linda. Somehow, Nast hadn't inspired that same transformation.

An orderly directed me to a water fountain. Next to it was a lavatory. I went in and splashed water on my face, bandages and all. Then I looked up into the mirror over the sink.

The tap water was running down my face like a boiler room sweat. It made me think of the famous climax of one of Drury's lesser efforts, *The Gentleman from Macao,* the scene in the fun house where the detective looks into the mirror and sees the sweating murderer staring back.

It was a parallel to the Traynor case so tight that I must have had the movie in the back of my mind as I'd considered Paddy's question about Clark. I pictured Clark staring into a mirror at some moment of crisis and seeing his old face reassemble itself, seeing Mark Traynor appear, the man who would act decisively. The man who would kill.

The more I thought about it, the less exact the parallel to *The Gentleman from Macao* seemed. In his film, Drury had been playing with the idea of two personalities inhabiting the same mind, two different people in one body. Clark *was* Mark Traynor, however deeply he'd buried that secret. For Drury's movie to be the real key to the murders, Traynor would have had to come back as a hidden fragment of some other person—his brother Gilbert, say—someone so obsessed with Mark that he could have slipped into a mad dream of being Traynor and acted on his behalf. Acted to protect Linda. Linda.

I remembered something else then: the moment outside Gustin's office when Whitehead had been brought in for questioning. White-head hadn't spoken to me. I'd thought at the time he hadn't recognized me. Now I could see him again as he stared right through me. His eyes were fixed on Linda.

I found I was squeezing the sink hard, twisting it in its mounts as I struggled to hold myself upright. Outside, the first rumbles of Paddy's storm were arriving. They made me think of Linda, too, the woman who thanked God for thunderstorms because they helped her put Traynorville and all its pressures into perspective. Because they helped her keep a grip on her sanity.

I was questioning my own sanity as I left the hospital and went out into the cool stillness that heralded the storm. The kid doctor had returned my keys to the Studebaker. I drove it into the approaching darkness.

The wind came first, changing the fading colors of the fields I passed as it laid over every leaf of every stalk of corn. As sleek as the Speedster was, the wind pressed it down and shoved it left and right as I followed the curves of the road. Then the rain came on like a wave, fat silver drops intermixed with tiny bits of hail. The hail skittered across the black pavement before me like a million dice thrown in a desperate attempt to make an incalculable point.

It was fully dark between lightning strikes by the time I reached Traynor House. There were no guards at the brick pylons. Either the storm had chased them away, or they'd realized there was nothing left to protect, that the Traynors had been stripped bare right under their noses.

The storm soaked me through during my short run from the drive to the porch. I was shivering as I pushed the front doorbell. There was no answering chime inside the house or the faintest reflection of a light. The power had to be out. I knocked on the door, making far less noise than the wind alone. Then I tried the knob. The door was unlocked.

I stepped into the foyer and forced the door closed behind me. I called hello, and Linda's voice answered me from the dark living room: "Scotty?"

She was sitting where I'd first seen her, on the sofa beneath the portrait of her husband. A well-timed flash of lightning gave me a vivid snapshot of the scene: the vast emptiness of the room; the portrait staring down; the woman sitting with her head bowed and her hands folded in her lap, her skirt carefully smoothed across her knees.

"Where is everyone?" I asked.

"The wind blew them away," Linda said.

I sat down beside her. The lightning came and went again, and she saw my face. She started to reach out to touch it and then drew back her hand. "What happened?" she asked.

I didn't answer her. I was no longer sure what had happened, not at Clark's cabin, not anywhere in Traynorville. "I've come to ask you something, Linda."

"Yes?"

"Where were you Sunday night?"

"I told you, I didn't go to the farm."

"I know. I want to know what you did. Did you stay here?"

"Of course," she said, but she was frightened.

"Do you remember staying here? Do you remember what you did?"

"I'm not sure. I must have fallen asleep. Why are you asking me, Scotty?"

"Is there any other time you can't account for?"

She was moving away from me, pressing herself into the corner of the sofa. I found her wrist and held it.

"What about the night Whitehead disappeared? What did you do after you left the dining room?"

"I went up to check on Marvella."

"She didn't let you in, remember? What else did you do?"

"Nothing. I don't remember doing anything." She drew the wrist I was holding close to her chest. "You're hurting me."

"Did you go back to your room? Did you come back downstairs? Did you go out onto the terrace?"

She pulled her arm away from me with a force that caught me off guard. I lost my grip on her wrist, and she was gone, her running footsteps disappearing toward the foyer.

The lightning let me down then. I collided with the coffee table and then with a chair as I tried to follow her. By the time I reached the foyer, I could hear nothing but the steady drumming of the rain on the flags outside.

Then a door slammed somewhere over my head. I took the stairs two at a time, the ascent feeling like a rocket ride to my dizzy head. The door to Linda's room was closed but not locked. I pushed the door open and took its place in the doorway.

With no more lightning to dazzle them, my eyes had grown accustomed to the darkness. I took in the simple room—bed, bureau, nightstand—without spotting Linda. I did notice something I'd overlooked when I'd checked the room earlier in the day: a framed photo on the nightstand. It was another portrait of Traynor. I felt drawn to it for some reason. Instead of going off to search another room, I crossed to the side of the bed. Just as I picked up the heavy, metal frame, I heard a sound from the corner to my right.

I turned in time to see Linda step through the connecting door that led to her dead husband's room. She was pointing a gun at my chest. It looked like a toy gun, even in her small hand: the missing Liberator.

"Linda," I said.

"Don't die with that whore's name on your lips," she said, her voice flat and strange.

It was all I could do to keep from saying her name again. Instead I said something even more likely to get me shot. "You kept your appointment with Shepard."

"*I* kept it. Not her. I took him by surprise."

"You murdered him."

"Punished him. For laying hands on my wife."

I stepped backward into the nightstand. "Mark Traynor," I said.

"You all thought I was dead."

I hadn't in the end, for all the good it did me now. Linda was only a foot or two away from me—too close for me to count on her missing with the Liberator but close enough for me to knock the gun away with the photo I held. If I could find the strength to swing it.

"You all thought it was safe to move in," Linda said. "It never will be safe." She raised the gun a careful inch.

Before I could make my play, a voice behind her said, "Linda. Wait. It's Mark. I'm here now. I'm back."

The speaker was standing in the hall doorway, where he was nothing more than a shape in the darkness. Linda backed away from me but kept the gun pointed my way.

"It's okay, Linda," the shadow said. "It's okay. You can put the gun down. I'm back for good now, honey. I'm sorry I was away so long."

"It's too late," Linda said in the voice I knew. "Too damn late."

The Liberator swung from me to the doorway. The figure there had time to say one more word before the gun roared out. He said, "Linda."

I'd drawn back the heavy frame when Linda turned. I threw it as the muzzle flash lit the room. It caught Linda on the back of her head and dropped her.

I stooped over her long enough to check her pulse and collect her gun. Then I went out into the hallway.

I was expecting to find an escapee from the county hospital named Clark. The man lying flat on his back on the plush carpeting was Gilbert Traynor. He had a hole in his shoulder. It looked like a clean wound, the kind a soldier in combat would pay serious money for. A million dollars had been the going price in 1944.

Gilbert was thinking of the war himself. "Now what kind of soldier do you think I would have made?" he asked, his words as shaky as my hands.

The kind of soldier who got himself killed the first day, I thought. I said, "A good one."

"Poor Linda," Gilbert said. "Is she okay?"

I pressed my handkerchief against his shoulder. "I don't think she's badly hurt, if that's what you mean."

"She killed Hank Shepard. John Whitehead, too. Whitehead saw her go into the barn on Sunday night. He heard the shot. That's what he blackmailed me with. I had to go along. I couldn't hand Linda over. I knew it wasn't her fault."

"Save it," I said. "I'll call an ambulance."

"I have to tell you first. It was Mark. He's taken hold of her."

"I know," I said.

Gilbert didn't seem to hear me. "I don't understand it," he said, "but it's true. Mark's the real killer. He clubbed Whitehead on the terrace. Mother saw the whole thing from her bedroom. Linda had gone out for air. Whitehead followed her and confronted her. He must have told her that he'd go to the police if she didn't give back Drury's money. He didn't know what he was dealing with.

"Linda struck him with a statue and pushed him into the river. Mother's been terrified ever since. She said that Linda tried to get into her room last night after you'd gone, that she claimed to be Mark come back to kill her."

Gilbert's eyes were lolling in his head. I started to get up, but he grabbed my sleeve.

"It's my fault, too. Mine and Mark's. I was the one who did this to her. I tried to make it right. I tried to watch her as night came on. I didn't want it to happen again."

He'd gone chalky, and his teeth were chattering. His time was running out, but I still wasted some of it asking a question: "Who is Clark?"

Gilbert's hand dropped away from my sleeve. "Clark?"

"He's not some soldier you took in because he happened to answer your ad for a caretaker."

"No," Gilbert said. "He's a soldier from my brother's squad. He was wounded the day Mark died. I traced him so I could hear about that. When I saw how things were for Clark, I offered him a job."

"He's not your brother?"

"My brother? No. My brother's dead. At least he was."

chapter

45

I NEEDN'T HAVE bothered questioning Gilbert about Clark's identity. Sheriff Gustin had already solved that mystery. He'd contacted the veteran's hospital in Indianapolis where Gilbert had found Clark after the war. The Traynor caretaker was Sergeant Walter Clark of Madison, Indiana, the man who had kept Lieutenant Mark Traynor's squad in line.

That discovery did nothing to increase the warmth of Gustin's greeting when he and his advisors arrived at Traynor House in the wake of the ambulance. Nor did Paddy's "Third time's a charm," which he pronounced on the mansion steps as the still-unconscious Linda was carried down them. Even the ambulance driver and his assistant were looking at me critically. I should pull my next victims out now and save them a round trip, they seemed to be saying.

Gustin backed me one last time. He sent the ambulance off under Zimmerman's supervision and then marched up to Marvella

Traynor's suite. The old woman and Greta had been hiding there throughout my cat-and-mouse with Linda.

Marvella was close to needing her precious hospital herself by the time we found her. She broke down immediately, confirming everything Gilbert had told me about Linda's attack on Whitehead and her attempt to force her way into Marvella's room.

We left Mrs. Traynor in the care of her private physician and her faithful maid. On the front porch of the mansion, Gustin lit a cigarette and offered me his pack. I turned it down.

"Why did Clark kidnap Nast?" the sheriff asked. "Why did he get himself involved?"

"For the very reason we guessed," Paddy said, "to keep you off the track of the real murderer. We thought he was acting to protect himself, but it was really out of loyalty to his old lieutenant and the lieutenant's family."

Or because, I thought, he was in love with his old lieutenant's wife. If so, Clark would never tell us, any more than he'd ever tell us what he'd seen at the farm on Sunday night. He'd let a hint of what he'd witnessed slip just before he jumped me. He said then that if I knew the truth of what had happened, I'd still be running.

"How could Mark Traynor have taken hold of his widow like that?" Gustin asked.

Paddy deferred on that question, but not to me. "God knows," he said.

■ ■ ■

In the end, it was Carson Drury, and not God, who did the explaining. Drury was at the hospital when we got there, closeted with the doctors who were examining Linda. When the psychiatrist summoned from Indy arrived in the wee small hours, Drury talked his way into the consultation.

He was welcome to kibitz, as far as I was concerned. I stayed up until Gilbert was out of surgery and out of danger. Then I caught a couple of hours' sleep on a waiting room sofa. I'd left a wake-up call with a sympathetic nurse who had a little laugh in her voice that reminded me of Irene Dunne. She shook my shoulder at five and told me I'd better get up if I was going to meet my wife's train.

I heard Drury intoning as soon as I entered the hospital hallway. The sound led me to a consulting room where I found the director and Paddy and Gustin. Drury held center stage as usual, which is to say he was seated behind the room's only desk. Paddy and Gustin sat before him like a pair of patients steeled for bad news.

"Scotty," Drury called to me. "I was about to brief the sheriff. I've just come from a talk with the psychiatrist they hustled up from the state capital, a nice young chap named Kronenburger."

He'd slipped back into his stock tone of glib superiority. I wasn't the only one who noticed.

"Was this Kronenberger able to tell you why you're so anxious to ruin yourself?" Paddy asked.

"We didn't discuss my case," Drury said. "I never will discuss it with a doctor. I'm an artist, after all. My problems are the raw materials of my art. I have to work them out for myself. With the occasional aid of an astute private eye, perhaps," he added with a nod to me, "but in the main, by myself."

He might have been trying to sound noble or heroic. He came off sounding lonely. I almost felt sorry for the guy. "What did the doctor say about Linda?" I asked.

"As I was telling the sheriff, Dr. Kronenburger supports your diagnosis, Scotty, the one that sent you out to Traynor House last evening."

"That was no diagnosis," I said. "That was a bad feeling."

Drury nodded. "I had a similar feeling when I heard about your confrontation with Linda. Rodman, my deputy guardian, told me the details. It sounded to me then like we might be dealing with multiple personalities within the same individual."

"I don't believe in the dead taking over the living," Gustin said.

"No more do I," Drury said, "nor in reincarnation. This is nothing like those things, though I dare say our great-grandparents might have mistaken Linda's illness for a possession or a haunting."

"Just what illness are we talking about?" Paddy asked.

"Multiple personality syndrome. I encountered a description of it in a journal of abnormal psychology during the war. It fascinated me so much, I explored the idea in a film."

The Gentleman from Macao," I said.

Drury nodded again. "Interest in the subject goes back much further than the war years, of course—as far back as the nineteenth century and the work of Pierre Janet. It's been a neglected area, in my opinion, but it remains legitimate."

The director studied the desktop before him for a moment, composing his big scene. "It may interest you gentlemen to know that Linda created imaginary friends as a child."

"So does my little boy," Gustin said.

"So did I," Drury said. "As a creative solution to the odd lonely moment, there's nothing wrong with it. But if an imaginative child who's too young to have a firmly established sense of identity uses the same trick to deal with some traumatic event or unbearable situation, it may be the first step toward fragmentation."

Gustin was passing a hand back and forth across his bristly head. The hand stopped halfway through a pass and grabbed hold. "You're losing me," he said.

"Linda's mother died when Linda was very young," Drury said. "Linda saw it happen. You didn't know that, Sheriff, I'm sure. Did you, Scotty?"

"Yes," I said. "Her mother stepped in front of a truck. Gilbert told me about it."

"I heard of it from another source," Drury said, "a little girl named Annie."

"Who is she?" Paddy asked.

"Linda's childhood friend," I said.

"Yes," Drury said, "the first personality Linda created to cope with an unbearable situation. Dr. Kronenburger introduced me to Annie around three this morning. She's doing all Linda's talking at the moment. Annie has helped Linda before. Years ago she absorbed the loss of Linda's mother, so Linda wouldn't have to. That's why Linda created her. She couldn't deal with the pain, so she split part of herself off and delegated her pain to the fragment, to this other personality, this alter ego."

I found myself missing Hollywood at that moment, and the little, sordid jobs that Paddy and I often did. They were clean and simple compared with this. Gustin seemed to feel the same way about it. His stolid features were drawn like those of a man whose arm is being twisted. Drury kept talking.

"And, if it works when you're a child, chances are you'll use it again as an adult when the world hurts too much. The more pain you have, the more allies you'll summon up." The four of us sat for a moment before Paddy spoke.

"Are there others?" he asked. "Besides Traynor, I mean."

"At least one other. She hasn't a name of her own, but I suspect that one of you has met her. She's a personality Linda created to deal with the pressure of being the town's most famous war widow and with the tension that arose when a still young woman tried to suppress her very natural sexual desires because of her mother-in-law's expectations or her own loyalty to her dead husband—or both.

"This fourth personality exists to express the sexual side of Linda. I haven't met her yet, but I heard about her from Eric Faris. He and I briefly shared a cell yesterday afternoon after he was driven up from Indianapolis.

"As I said, I think Mr. Elliott has met this sexually aggressive personality, too. I won't ask him to confirm or deny it. I wouldn't want him to violate his Hollywood operative code of honor. If you did meet her, Scotty, you're lucky to be alive. I believe she was the personality who responded to Hank Shepard's overtures."

"But Linda knew about that," I said. "She knew she'd agreed to meet Shepard. How could she be taken over by this alter ego and still have a memory of what happened?"

Drury shrugged. "There are varying levels of awareness and control between the primary and secondary personalities. Linda could have been aware of the influences or actions of one of her personalities and been completely oblivious to another's. I think Kronenburger or whoever takes up the case will find that Linda knows nothing of the Mark personality but that Mark has access to her thoughts and memories. He knew all about the date with Shepard, for example. He even knew where to find that very interesting gun, because Linda had once seen it in the farmhouse. He must have collected it just before Faris brought me home, which means I narrowly missed making his acquaintance myself."

Gustin was pulling at his hair again. "Are you saying Mrs. Traynor whipped this Mark personality up just because Shepard propositioned her?"

"No. I side with the theorists who believe that these alter egos always begin as friends, that their initial functions are always positive. They can later become destructive, even self-destructive or homicidal, but they come into being to effect some good. I believe her Mark Traynor personality has been functioning for some time, perhaps only in the background, perhaps as a response to the stress of her position at the Traynor plant."

"Linda told me she was in the habit of asking Mark for advice," I said. "She made it sound like a game she played with herself."

"That may be how it seemed to her," Drury said. "In actuality, her personality was fragmenting again. When Gilbert added to the stress she was already under by using me to disrupt the delicate equilibrium of his family, the shadowy Mark Traynor personality stepped to the forefront. He took control to counter the activities of Linda's sexual personality—to counter them violently by shooting poor Hank and trying to set fire to the barn."

I'd forgotten about Traynor's—Linda's—attempt to burn the barn. I remembered her telling me about the wartime barn burnings, acts of retribution against philandering men. They'd occurred just after word had come about Mark Traynor's death, Linda had said, during the period when she'd been in shock. I wondered now if those burnings hadn't signaled Traynor's rebirth as a fragment of Linda's mind. When she'd set fire to the Riverbend barn, had she been reenacting a memory of those old crimes?

I didn't ask the question aloud. Gustin was loaded past the breaking point already. His head was bowed, and his big frame was sagging forward in his chair.

chapter
46

I'D HEARD THAT DRURY had had his cast cut off, but it still surprised
me when he stood up. The novelty of the action seemed to increase
his already impressive height. Or maybe my time in Traynorville
had worn me down. I was feeling smaller and older.

"When you looked in just now," Drury asked me, "were you on
your way to the Roberts?"

"Just to change my tie," I said. "I have a date at the train station."

"Let's walk to the hotel together. I want to exercise this leg."

We left Paddy and Gustin in the consulting room and crossed the
empty hallway to the elevator, Drury limping slightly and supporting his weight with a cane. It was an elegant cane, of course, a
long ebony stick with a silver handle. He'd probably traded his
wheelchair for it at some Traynorville antique shop. He used the
cane to press the elevator's call button and then to open our last
conversation as we rode the car down.

"This stick is not a prop, Scotty, I assure you. You wouldn't believe how stiff my ankle and knee are after my short time in that
cast. Which only serves me right, as you're probably thinking.

"I hope you're letting me off that lightly, Scotty. I hope we can part friends. I made a clean breast of things to your boss; did he tell you? I told him how you'd uncovered my sordid little plot against my own best self. It helped to say it to Maguire, the least sympathetic audience I could find, but it only helped a little. I'll never forgive myself over what befell Hank and John."

Outside, the sun was a gray possibility in the eastern sky, and the air was almost cool. Drury paused to light one of his expensive cigars. Then he struck out for the Roberts. He set a pace that was hard for me to match, but then, he only had two stiff joints to worry him, not to mention two ghosts to prod him along.

To help him with those, I said, "Shepard and Whitehead had a lot more to do with what happened than you. Shepard couldn't keep his hands off Linda, and Whitehead turned blackmailer. He must have seen Linda on the terrace when the two of you were waiting for Gilbert in the dining room. She went out there from the library or some other room, and you missed her because your back was to the doors. Whitehead went looking for trouble and found it. Any responsibility left over belongs to Gilbert."

"The unhappy little guy," Drury said. "I must say, it isn't very flattering to be considered a modern dress Jonah." Being Drury, he sounded flattered about it anyway. "Tell me, was his plan really to inject me into this town like a mystery virus just to see what symptoms would break out?"

"He didn't have a plan," I said, repeating Gilbert's own lament. "Just a sincere contempt for his life. I don't think he meant to hurt anyone, least of all Linda."

We finished our walk to the Roberts without speaking. An old man in gray overalls was using a hose to wet down the sidewalk in front of the hotel. Drury stopped to let him finish.

"Will you stay to help Linda?" I asked.

"Me? No. I doubt I'd be welcome. I'm no healer in any case. I'm an egotistical artist. I'm interested in Linda Traynor's problems only because they're grist for my mill. All night new conceptions have been storming my brain. What do you think of a production of

Hamlet in which the same actor plays the prince and the prince's dead father? Or how about a *Macbeth* in which a single person plays both Lady Macbeth and her homicidal husband? Do you think that could work?"

"Depends on how you look in drag." I thought he was trying to get one last rise out of me, and I didn't want to give him the satisfaction. "I think you hung around last night because you wanted to help," I said. "I think for once you were looking beyond yourself and your goddamn brilliant conceptions."

Drury would only grin and shrug.

"So you're going back to California?" I asked.

"No. There's nothing waiting for me there but bill collectors. My Eden belongs to Ralph Lockard now, fair and square. I'm almost relieved in a way. That estate was my last tie to my fatal success. With that link broken, perhaps I'll finally be able to move on."

"Move on where?"

"I've been offered a chance to direct a film in Europe. The financing is shaky, but I'm used to that. If it should fall through, I can always look up the Banfi Family Circus."

His laugh ended in a sigh. "I'll miss having Hank around. What do you say, Scotty? Would you like to take his place?"

"No, thanks. I'd like my nice quiet life back."

Drury laughed again. "I wish more people felt as you do. I'm afraid an increasing number of our fellow citizens are anxious to repeat Gilbert Traynor's mistake. We're far enough from the wars now, your war and Korea, for people to begin to take their peace and quiet for granted. I sense a general and growing desire to throw babies out with the bathwater, to change things for the sake of changing them or with the arrogant assumption that we can disregard the lessons of the past. Poor Gilbert's learned what a fragile thing our illusion of order is and what a persistent influence the past can be. I sense that the country, perhaps the world, is poised on the edge of the same hard lessons."

"I hope you're wrong," I said.

"I'm wrong a remarkable number of times," Drury said. "For a genius, that is."

He started to drop his cigar on the sidewalk, caught the eye of the old man winding up his hose, and flicked the butt into the gutter.

"But if I'm right, if we are on the brink of a national version of Gilbert's experiment, you'll think of me often. Every day will remind you of the time you rode shotgun on the Carson Drury roller coaster!"

chapter

47

I WENT UP TO DRURY'S suite long enough to shower and change my clothes. I shaved, too, or made a pass at it. The process was complicated by Clark's handiwork, which was healing colorfully, and by a strange reluctance I felt to look into a mirror.

I asked at the hotel desk for a cab, and the clerk directed me to the drugstore where I was almost a regular. The cabbie was at the lunch counter, ignoring his coffee. I drank it for him by way of getting his attention. He delivered me to the station just as the first rumbles of the Chicago train were sounding in the hazy distance.

I'd found my pipe while rummaging through my bags at the hotel. I filled it as I waited, packing the tobacco loosely, as my father had recommended. The pipe had dried out since my last attempt to smoke it, back on the porch of the farmhouse on the long ago Friday evening when Linda Traynor, or someone very like her, had stolen a kiss. The pipe didn't gurgle now or burn my tongue or go out on short notice. It just hurt my teeth.

I was hoping the pipe might distract Ella from my face, but there wasn't that much smoke in it. She was the first one off the train, stepping onto the platform as the steam from the obsolete engine was still swirling about. I liked the effect—and her traveling attire: a white suit that looked crisper than the shirt I'd just put on and a simple matching hat, under which she'd tucked her hair. Against all the white, her pale eyes looked bluer than normal. That is, they did until they narrowed at the sight of me.

"Scotty," she said. "Are you okay?"

"Yes," I said.

"Paddy, too?"

"Paddy always."

"The job over?"

"My part of it."

She stepped up close enough for me to take her in my arms. "To think I married you for your looks," she said.

"Serves you right," I said and kissed her.

The kiss told Ella something, bruises and sore teeth and all. "Welcome back," she said.

"Sorry for being away so long." I wasn't speaking of the time I'd spent in Indiana, and Ella knew it.

"It was only the tiniest part of our time," she said, and we kissed again.

When we'd finished, I asked, "What are the chances of shipping the kids out parcel post?"

"Are you suddenly feeling paternal?"

"Their grandfather would like to meet them."

The answer sounded better than my real reason for wanting the kids to see Indiana, which was that it might not be around to see much longer, not my Indiana, not if Carson Drury's screwy prophecy was right and the country was about to throw itself off a cliff.

It didn't seem very likely to me just then, standing on the Traynorville platform while porters unloaded newspapers and produce from the train, and the few heads visible in the passenger car waited patiently for Ella and me to kiss again.

Ella was aware of our audience, too. "Is there someplace private where we could go to get reacquainted?" she asked, nestling against me. "Unless you'd rather see a movie."

"It has been a while," I said, holding her tighter still. "I wonder what's playing."

about the author

TERENCE FAHERTY has created in *Come Back Dead,* along with the critically acclaimed first Scott Elliot mystery, *Kill Me Again,* an exciting new series that sparkles with the eccentricity and style of its postwar Hollywood setting. Faherty is the Edgar-nominated author of six other mystery novels. He lives in Indianapolis, Indiana, with his wife, Jan.